D1598708

NICK'S STORY

You CAN Get Here From There

Nicholas Bilotti

a memoir

BABYLON PUBLIC LIBRARY

Copyright © 2016 Nicholas Bilotti.

All rights reserved. No part of this book may be used or reproduced by any means, graphic, electronic, or mechanical, including photocopying, recording, taping or by any information storage retrieval system without the written permission of the author except in the case of brief quotations embodied in critical articles and reviews.

Archway Publishing books may be ordered through booksellers or by contacting:

Archway Publishing
1663 Liberty Drive
Bloomington, IN 47403
www.archwaypublishing.com
1 (888) 242-5904

Because of the dynamic nature of the Internet, any web addresses or links contained in this book may have changed since publication and may no longer be valid. The views expressed in this work are solely those of the author and do not necessarily reflect the views of the publisher, and the publisher hereby disclaims any responsibility for them.

Any people depicted in stock imagery provided by Thinkstock are models, and such images are being used for illustrative purposes only. Certain stock imagery © Thinkstock.

ISBN: 978-1-4808-3358-6 (sc)
ISBN: 978-1-4808-3359-3 (hc)
ISBN: 978-1-4808-3360-9 (e)

Library of Congress Control Number: 2016912090

Print information available on the last page.

Archway Publishing rev. date: 11/07/2016

BABYLON PUBLIC LIBRARY

To Camille, the "Girl on the Wall". For all of your patience while watching this book come together, especially for the hours spent in suggesting and revising and for keeping me on the straight path. Be with me. "It all starts with you."

Henry Harrison. The deadlines got me there, Hank.

Finally, but most of all to my children, Claudia, Nicky, Elena, and Doug, and to my twelve grandchildren, Laura, Jimmy, Grace, Isabella, Marissa, Gabrielle, Christina, Andie, Charlotte, Savannah, Michael, and Nicholas, I love you all.

CHAPTER 1

THERE REALLY WAS NO WAY OUT. I KNEW IT ALL along, but true to form, I tried not to think about it in the hope that by some miracle it would turn out all right. It was August 1953 and it was hot sitting in an economics summer school class offered to students who were either incapable or unwilling to do the work required to pass during the regular school year. The class was full of reluctant students just like me. Even at that moment, my mind was somewhere else. I wasn't listening to a word the instructor was saying. I allowed my mind to escape the imprisonment of the steamy classroom where we were all held captive. It was the silence in the room that finally brought me back to reality. The teacher had stopped his lecture. I looked up to see why he had stopped but nothing seemed unusual. The classroom windows were all opened as far as they would allow, but there wasn't even a hint of a breeze. Outside a car radio was turned up, and a voice was singing, "You saw me crying in the chapel…." We all sat listening as the music, a welcomed relief from the droning economics lecture, drifted into the room. I turned toward the teacher and I saw that he had removed his suit jacket. The perspiration stains had run down the sides of his shirt nearly to his waist. He was suddenly aware that the students were watching him, and a self-conscious smile crossed his face.

"That's a pretty song," he said. The students were too drained to agree or disagree.

He stood silently for a moment, and then as if he realized that continuing the lecture with this group and under these conditions was pointless, he mopped his brow with a handkerchief that he pulled from his back pocket and said, "Okay, final test tomorrow. Go home, try to stay cool and study."

There was the shuffling of paper and the scraping of chairs as the students collected their belongings and headed for the doors in a hurry to distance themselves from the steamy building.

As I walked home, I had already made up my mind to not even bother to come back for the final test. What would be the point? I had used the maximum number of classes that you were allowed to miss, and I had found it impossible to concentrate on the long, daily lectures even though I had promised myself each day that I would make an effort to be attentive. It was impossible. It would only take a few minutes and my mind would be off somewhere again, and now it would take a miracle for me to pass the final exam.

Besides that, I still needed one more semester of physical education, which was a requirement for graduation, and physical education was not offered in summer school, so I would have to come back in the fall anyway. I could double up on the courses that I needed in the fall, take physical education, and wrap the whole thing up in my senior year. That would allow me to graduate with my class the following June, or if not in June, then in August. There was time. It would all work out.

The fall came and went and things didn't get better, and nothing really worked out, and by January of my senior year, I knew the situation was hopeless. Even though I did well enough in my senior year, I had to make up so many courses that there just weren't enough periods in the school day for me to do it. I knew that a June graduation was not possible. August was more likely, and pretty soon I'd have to tell my family not to plan a graduation party. That would be a rough one, because I knew they were looking forward to celebrating my graduation and they were already planning a party.

There was another way out of the mess that I had created and that was to convince my father to allow me to enlist in the service as many of my friends had done. It would be a hard thing to sell to my dad, because here we were in January 1954 and I had assured him that I would graduate in June. How could I convince him to allow me to go into the service when I had led him to believe that graduation was a few short months away?

"What are you talking about? Why would I allow you to join the marines or the army in January if you're going to graduate in five months? That doesn't make sense. First get your diploma, and then you can join whatever you want to join."

My dad was counting the days for when I would graduate in June, and now I was about to let him down. I had so much contempt for myself at that moment that I came close to making a full confession about the mess I had made of my high school career. The only reason that I didn't tell him everything was because the thought of how he would receive the news, and the additional pain that I would cause him, prevented me from telling. There had to be a less painful way out of this.

"Okay, Dad, I'll wait until June." I still didn't have the courage to tell him that August was probably more likely. "But there's something else that I'd like to talk about with you."

"What's that?" He looked at me with suspicion.

"A friend of mine in school belongs to the National Guard.

I thought it might be fun to do something like joining the National Guard. It would be good just for the experience and to see if I like the service, so that I'll have a better idea about going into the service after I graduate. What do you think about me joining the National Guard?"

My dad had served in the National Guard, and I loved to listen to the stories he would tell about the good times as well as the good friends he made while he was in the National Guard, so I had the feeling that he might allow me to join, if only for me to get a taste of military life.

"Well, that might be alright," he said. "The National Guard might give you a good idea about the military, and maybe after that experience you'll want to further your education. It's not all fun and games. Let me think about it. We'll see."

A few days later, my father gave me his consent, so I joined the National Guard and was sworn in on a Wednesday in April. I was issued fatigues, boots and some equipment, most of which seemed to be used army surplus. That Friday, by coincidence, my battalion was scheduled to report for a weekend of training at Camp Smith, New York. Timing is everything.

CHAPTER 2

I WAS THE ONLY RECRUIT AS I SAT ON A BENCH IN THE back of a truck, with an M1 rifle between my knees. I had never held a real gun or rifle in my life, and having one thrust at me was absolutely intimidating, even though I knew that it was not loaded. I remember the oily smell and feel of the rifle. It appeared to be well worn with nicks and deep scratches all over the stock, and I wondered if it had ever been fired in anger. My imagination began running wild. Maybe this same rifle had killed someone. What a come down that would be, going from the hands of some forgotten battle-hardened combat veteran fighting for his country and for his survival, to a novice like me. But I was a soldier, at least for this weekend, and I had the rifle to prove it, so I tried to look the part.

When we got to Camp Smith, everyone seemed to know one another as well as the routine, but to me it seemed to be mass confusion, and except for taking us to ancient-looking barracks that looked like remnants from the Civil War, no one bothered to speak to me or to give me any directions.

We were to sleep on cots that had no sheets, blankets, or pillows. The top of the walls of the barracks were opened for about eighteen inches down from the ceiling, with screening covering the open spaces that extended throughout the ceiling area of the barracks. There were two screened doors, one in the front and one in the back. Although it was April, the day was sunny but cool, so I knew we were in for a cold night.

As if the conditions of the barracks weren't bad enough, I was totally dismayed when I saw the toilets, which I was quickly told were to be referred to as latrines. The latrines were a short distance away. When I first got a look at that set up, I knew that there would be worse problems than freezing all night on a bare cot in what amounted to a building opened to the elements.

The latrine had a row of perhaps fifteen sinks, each with a cloudy mirror over it. Opposite the sinks and toward the corner were toilet bowls, three against the wall and two to the side. All were currently occupied by guys dumping and nonchalantly chattering away as if they were sitting at a picnic table. I quickly diverted my eyes, ears, and nose away from the contented quintet on the commodes, and I put all thoughts about going to the toilet for the weekend out of my mind. I said a little prayer to the god of constipation to lend me a hand as I headed back to my barracks.

"Are you Bilotti? Where the hell were you? The first sergeant has been looking for you." It was the company clerk.

"I'm Bilotti. What does he want?"

"I don't know. I only know that he's looking for you. You better go find him."

I saw the first sergeant coming out of the barracks to which I was assigned. "Are you looking for me, sergeant?"

"Yes, I am. Have you packed a towel, Bilotti?"

"Yes, I did. They told me to pack a towel, a bar of soap, and some shaving gear."

"Good. Tie the towel on the foot of your cot where I can see it before you turn in tonight."

"What's that for?" I asked.

"You have K.P. in the morning. You report to Sergeant Scofield in the mess hall, and help him out in there. The reason that I want you to put your towel on the foot of your cot is so that I can spot it easy to wake you up."

"What time will that be?" I asked.

"Between 0400 and 0500, so get some sleep, and don't forget about the towel."

I got back to my barracks, and the sun was already down and the temperature was dropping fast. There was a chill breeze blowing through the barracks because there was nothing to keep it out. If I had known this, I would have squeezed a blanket into my bag along with my towel and other stuff, but no one had suggested it. I looked around and it didn't appear as if any of the others had a blanket.

There was no question in my mind that I would be sleeping fully clothed. I debated if I should sleep in my boots too, but I finally took them off. It was at that point that I began to wonder whether I had made the right choice in joining the Guard. I was only here a few hours and I was already longing for my old routine. You know, not much, a bathroom with some privacy, and a blanket would have been nice. The kinds of basic things that I had taken for granted.

The night was even colder than I had anticipated it would be. My nose and my ears were like ice, and my feet were freezing. I sat on the side of my cot and reached for my boots in the darkness and I put them back on, but that didn't help much. I couldn't get warm. I was tempted to wrap the towel around my head for some relief, but I kept hearing the first sergeant telling me to be sure to keep the towel at the foot of my cot, so I decided against it.

At about 4:30, I heard the screen door open. The sergeant made his way toward my cot. The towel had worked.

"Bilotti," he whispered. He shook my shoulder. "Wake up and report to the mess hall."

"I'm already up," I answered. To tell you the truth, I was

glad to go to the mess hall. Maybe I could get to a stove and sit by it. Anything would be better than freezing on that cot.

"Okay. Report to Sergeant Scofield. He's waiting for you," he whispered.

I was fully dressed so I got up immediately and I walked out of the barracks with the first sergeant a few feet in front of me. On the way to the mess hall, I thought that this might be the opportune time to use the latrine. It was hard to imagine that there would be much traffic in there at this hour, unless the five were still huddled together trying to keep warm.

Thank God, it was empty. I was as quick as I could be and got out before anyone else could come in. No sense in pushing my luck.

I made my way to the mess hall. There was a full, silvery moon and there still wasn't a hint of daybreak. The whole camp was asleep, or at least they were trying to sleep. All I knew was that trying to fall asleep hadn't worked for me.

I opened the door to the mess hall and I saw a man with khaki sergeants' stripes sewn on to a white uniform. He appeared to be alone. "Sergeant Scofield?" I asked.

"That's me. Are you Bilotti?"

"Yes, Sir."

"Don't call me Sir. I'm a sergeant not an officer. I work for a living," he said with a chuckle. I sensed that he was waiting for me to smile so I nodded my head up and down and managed to smile back.

"Well, there's just the two of us. And you got here just in time. There's not much to it, but let's get started. Do you see those cans of condensed milk over there?" He motioned with his head because his hands were busy as he moved around what appeared to be chopped meat on the griddle. I looked in the direction that he had indicated and I saw a metal table, stacked with large cans of what the labels indicated was condensed milk.

"You can start by opening all those cans. Then, as soon as I fry all of this chopped meat, I'll put the meat into that big pot. Then you pour the milk into the meat, and we'll let it simmer for a while. Then we'll toast up some of that sliced bread, put the chopped meat on the toast, and breakfast will be set."

He must have seen the revulsion in my face.

"What's wrong? There's nothing healthier. It's called creamed chipped beef."

I didn't give a damn what he called it, it looked like vomit to me. There would be no way for it to ever make it into the Bilotti kitchen. I knew right then and there that I would be passing on breakfast, which didn't bother me very much. An empty stomach had appeal to me especially when I thought about the bathroom set up.

At about 0600, the troops started arriving for breakfast. There was a menu tacked on a board at the entrance of the mess hall, listing creamed chipped beef and coffee for breakfast, and when the men read it, the griping began.

"Son of a bitch. Not S.O.S. right off the bat."

"Are you kidding me? Shit on a shingle. Why do they keep that crap on the menu if everyone hates it?"

"It shortens wars. That's why," one trooper said.

"How the hell does it shorten a war?" his friend asked.

"It makes you fight harder, because once you taste that crap you want to get out of the army as fast as you can so you don't have to ever eat it again," and he broke into laughter enjoying his own joke, while his friends rolled their eyes.

With few exceptions, the reaction was always the same. Call it creamed chipped beef, or whatever Sergeant Scofield chose to call it, there was no fooling these guys. It might have been creamed chipped beef on paper, but it was S.O.S. in their mess kits. It was my first experience with a military retreat, as I watched a good number of the men went mumbling on their way out of the mess hall and back to their barracks having decided to skip breakfast and to take their chances with lunch. Some of the more hardy men decided to risk it all, and so they did.

Having gotten through, and cleaned up after breakfast, Sergeant Scofield began preparing for lunch. Some of it would be served in the mess hall, but some of it would be brought to the field for the troops who were out there at the moment.

Once again, my job was to open can after can, but this time they were cans of tomato sauce. After I opened the cans, I was to pour the contents into a huge cauldron where the sauce would simmer for a while. Then, when directed by Sergeant Scofield, I was to add water to the tomato sauce to thin it. The tomato sauce was then to be poured onto heaps of boiled and drained macaroni, which appeared to be more like noodles to me.

After stirring the sauce and tasting it, the sergeant concluded that he had added a bit too much water to the sauce and that now it needed to be thickened.

"Bilotti. Go into the pantry, and you'll see five-pound bags of flour. Bring back a couple of bags. We'll use the flour to thicken up the sauce."

Now, I know that Italians think that they are the only ones who know how to make a proper tomato sauce, which by the way, we refer to as gravy, and to tell you the truth, having eaten in some of the homes of my non-Italian friends, I was of the same opinion. Well, anyway, Sergeant Scofield was doing very little to change my mind or my beliefs about how to prepare proper tomato sauce. I had seen my mother fry garlic and onions, add tomato sauce and tomato paste, and then throw in some basil and then pork and meatballs for flavor. She would add more seasoning, oregano and sometimes wine and let the whole thing cook for a while. In fact, the whole neighborhood was pervaded by the aroma of tomato sauce on any given Sunday morning in my part of Brooklyn. All of those ingredients were missing from Sergeant Scofield's recipe, and I could understand it. After all, cooking for a few hundred men was far more challenging than cooking for a family of ten.

I came back from the pantry with two five-pound bags of flour. The sergeant tore open one of the bags and poured it into a pan. You know, at first I thought that my eyes were playing tricks on me. After all, I really hadn't slept much since Thursday night, and here it was Saturday morning, but I thought that I had seen some movement in the flour. I got up closer to the pan and stared in, and sure enough there were tiny insects crawling around in the flour.

I shouted the alarm. "Sarge! Don't pour that flour into the sauce. Look at it. It's crawling with insects. Look at all of the bugs in there. This flour is spoiled. It must be old." Sergeant Scofield took a look at all of the activity in the flour, but he wasn't nearly as impressed as I was. In fact, this old combat veteran had seen it all and nothing appeared to rattle him. As a matter of fact, he seemed to be downright amused at my panic. It was much ado about nothing to him.

"That's nothing. Those are just flour beetles. They're harmless." Then, as I looked on in disbelief, the sergeant began to pour the contents of the pan, flour and bugs, into the cauldron of boiling tomato sauce. I had mixed emotions right there. I felt bad for what the tiny beetles that were being cooked alive in the tomato sauce were feeling at that moment, but I felt worse for the unsuspecting troops that would soon be digesting them. I must say that when I looked at the finished product, there were no survivors, and it was hard to distinguish whether you were looking at dead little beetles who had given their all, or at oregano. For me the latrine seemed even less of a problem as I passed on Sergeant Scofield's second offering, and as we shifted from lunch to dinner.

I was spared the experience of helping to prepare the final meal of the day. The first sergeant came by the mess hall because several others and I were to go to the firing range to fire our weapons. I was a bit apprehensive about firing my weapon because it had only been handed to me a few hours earlier, and I had absolutely no experience with firearms. But I saw this as an opportunity to get away from the mess hall. I had no idea how Sergeant Scofield planned to trump breakfast and lunch, and I did not want to wait around to find out, if I expected to eat at all today. I figured what I didn't know wouldn't hurt me, and at that point I really didn't want to know. My plan of attack for supper was not to look too closely and just swallow.

I had my rifle slung over my shoulder, and tried my best to keep in step with the others and not look too raw in the process. I had listened to some of the conversations of the other men about firing the M1 and I was trying to remember what they said.

"When you insert the clip into the chamber, make sure that you push the clip all the way down, but get your thumb out of the chamber quickly before the operating rod slides back and smashes your finger. Boy that hurts like hell. They call it M1 thumb. Also, be careful that the rifle doesn't kick back into your face after you fire it."

The sound of live firing grew louder as we approached the range, and off in the distance I could see a long row of targets that seemed to be about three hundred feet away from the men who were firing at them. What struck me was how quick after the report of the rifle firing, the bullet would kick up a puff of dust as it struck the berm behind the target. It was as if no time at all had elapsed between the firing and the strike.

We were nearing the end of what seemed like a long day, and I could tell that the sergeant who was walking toward me was in a hurry to get this over with and be done for the day.

"Have you fired this rifle before?"

"No."

"Okay. Let me have your weapon."

I handed him my rifle and he inserted a clip so quickly that I didn't see how he had done it, and he wasn't interested in showing me how. Well, at least I had avoided M1 thumb. He handed my rifle back to me and told me that it was locked and loaded.

"Keep that damned thing on your hip and point it straight up until I tell you to point it at the target and remove the safety."

I could see the target clearly but I had no idea of how to remove the safety.

"Where is the safety?" I asked.

"Get in the prone position and I'll show you."

I assumed the prone position was lying flat on your stomach, because people on both sides of me were already lying that way. As I dropped to my knees, he grabbed the front of my rifle and pointed it forward and toward the target. When I was finally settled, he took the same position alongside of me.

"Okay. Here is the trigger lock or safety. Push it forward and it frees the trigger. Okay. Now look at the target and aim at the bull's eye. You want to see the front sight through the hole of the rear sight, and when you think that you have it lined up, squeeze the trigger."

The target looked like a tiny speck off in the distance, and the bull's eye looked like a dot. I tried to line up the front sight with the rear sight, and when I thought that I had done that I jerked, not to be confused with squeezed, the trigger. To my surprise, the rifle didn't kick back toward my eye, but kicked up, and as soon as the bullet left the chamber, I saw a puff of dust hit over the top of the target and into the berm. I had missed the target completely.

Most everyone had finished firing by that time and they were all beginning to stand up. I sensed the sergeant's impatience when he looked at me. He was probably thinking that I was hopeless.

"I think that I would have hit it if it were the whole bull and not just the bull's eye." I thought it was funny and I looked at him for confirmation but he wasn't smiling. It was probably the breakfast, or maybe the lunch.

'"Okay. Just do what I tell you. Try again."

I tried to be a bit more relaxed now that I had some idea of what to expect, and I fired the next seven rounds in quick order. I didn't know if I had even come close to the bull's eye, but at least I didn't see puffs of dust hitting above the berm.

The sergeant took my rifle from me, opened up the chamber and made sure that there were no more rounds in it. When he was sure that it was safe, he handed the rifle back to me and told me to line up with the others, and then we were marched back to our companies.

We got back to the company area a little after everyone else. There was laughter and good-natured teasing, and just about everyone was cleaning a rifle or getting ready for dinner or for "chow", as it was referred to. I really had no idea how to break down my weapon, but I decided to ask someone for a little help even if I was somewhat reluctant to do so. I knew that most of them just wanted to finish what they were doing, have chow, get cleaned up, and get ready for the truck ride home tomorrow, but before I could ask for any help, a sergeant approached and shouted over to me. I recognized the sergeant. He was one of the guardsmen who had been in the truck with me on the way up to Camp Smith. I was told that he was the sergeant in charge of plotting fire missions for the 105 mm cannons.

"Hey Bilotti. Did you sign the Cannon Report?" he asked.

"The Cannon Report? What's the Cannon Report?"

"The Cannon Report. If you don't sign it, you won't be paid for the weekend. You can clean your rifle later. Put it inside on your cot. The clerk with the report is over that way by Charlie Company. You'll see guys signing it. Better hurry up."

After all of the crap that I had put up with this weekend, there was no way that I was not going to be paid. I hurried to my barracks, put my weapon on my cot, and I rushed out of the screened door.

When I got to Charlie Company, I looked around for the clerk with the report but there was no sign of anyone signing anything. Charlie Company area looked pretty much like my own company area with guys cleaning rifles and washing up. I ran up and down the company streets, and then I decided to ask a few guys who were sitting on the grass, having finished cleaning up, if they had seen the clerk coming through with the Cannon Report.

"Has the clerk with the Cannon Report been through here?"

"Yeah. You just missed him. He was walking over toward Dog Company."

"Which way is Dog Company?"

He pointed. "Two rows over."

Where the hell was this guy? I was tired and I was hungry not having slept or eaten much since I had gotten to this place the night before, but I needed to find him.

When I found Dog Company, things were about the same. A few guys were milling about, with last minute details. I knew that I was getting close, because everyone said that he had just left.

"He's just ahead of you. We've finished signing here, and they're probably just finishing signing over at Easy Company."

It was starting to get dark now, and the temperature was starting to fall, but Easy Company was the last company left, so I knew the clerk was just ahead of me. I figured that I had probably missed chow by now, and as hungry as I was, I thought that missing chow might not be such a bad thing anyway. When I got back to my own company, I'd clean my rifle the best that I could and go to sleep. Tomorrow I'd be glad to get home.

Easy Company was quiet. It was dark now and the company streets were empty. I could hear some conversation inside the barracks so I opened the screened door of one and I saw a room full of strangers, no more familiar to me than the men from my own company with whom I had shared quarters the night before.

"Have you guys seen the clerk with the Cannon Report?"

A couple of them looked up, and one said, "Everybody has signed that thing already. By this time the clerk must have brought it to the C.O.'s house."

He walked me outside and pointed in the direction of a big white wood-framed house. "Do you see that house over there?"

It was almost completely dark now, but I was able to make out the house that he was pointing to.

"Well, that's the C.O.s residence, and he probably has the report by now. It won't do any harm to knock at the door and just ask him if you can sign the Cannon Report. No big deal."

"Okay, thanks a lot," I said.

I made my way to the old wood frame, and when I got to the front walk, I saw a sign that read, "Lt. Col. John Stanton, Commanding".

I knocked on the door and after a minute the door opened. I had never seen Colonel Stanton but I was sure that was him.

"What can I do for you, son?"

"Excuse me, Sir. I'm sorry to bother you, but I've been chasing the clerk with the Cannon Report for a while now, and I couldn't catch up with him. They said that I wouldn't be paid for the weekend unless I signed the Cannon Report, and that by now it would probably be here."

"The Cannon Report." He stuck his head out of his door and looked up and down the road that ran outside of his quarters. "Come in, son," he said.

He closed the door behind me. I could see an elderly lady sitting on a sofa looking up from a magazine that she was reading. The colonel put his hand on my shoulder.

"Look, son," he said, "there is no Cannon Report."

"No Cannon Report? But everybody I asked said that they had signed it. They told me that I needed to sign it to be paid for the weekend."

"There is no Cannon Report, but you'll be paid for the weekend." I looked at him. Maybe they hadn't told him about the Cannon Report. Everybody else knew about it.

"They were just having fun with you. Just go back to your company and act as if nothing has happened. You'll be fine."

There was nothing else to say. He patted me on the shoulder and walked me to the door.

I heard the door close behind me, and the colonel's words

echoed in my ears. "They were just having fun with you." Anything for a laugh, I thought, and the joke was on me. I wondered if he and his wife were smiling too.

When I finally got back to my own company area, I heard the sergeant who sent me off in search of the "Cannon Report" say, "Here he comes, here he comes."

I acted as if I hadn't heard him. "Just go back and act as if nothing happened," the colonel had said.

I made my way back to my barracks. It was totally dark now, and I was grateful that almost everybody was asleep, and boy, it was cold.

CHAPTER 3

THINGS HADN'T CHANGED MUCH IN SCHOOL IN THE weeks that followed. I should have been preparing for graduation, and I should have been elated about that event, as most of my classmates were. I knew that the best I could hope for would be to graduate from summer school in August of 1954. A June graduation would be unlikely, making me a four and a half year graduate.

It had all caught up with me and soon everyone in my family would know exactly how I had been misleading them. I was embarrassed by the hole that I had dug for myself, and now I would have to face the music. What was really keeping me up at night was the knowledge that the mess I had created would not only disappoint my whole family, but it would crush my father to his core. I always had remorse but I never had the discipline that I needed to prevent me from being remorseful in the future. The thought of having to tell my father of the extent of my deceit, and then seeing his disappointment, made me sick to my stomach. For that reason, I looked and I prayed for some way out, and as it always seemed to happen with me, I thought I saw one.

My guidance counselor, Mrs. Travis, called me to her office. I sat there waiting for her to arrive, looking at the pile of books on the radiator. Near her desk was a sign with one word on it: "THINK!" She entered the room and sat at her desk, with what I imagined was my folder in her hands.

"You know, of course, Mr. Bilotti, that graduation is next month and you need two more classes to graduate." I forced a smile and nodded. She knew me well, having been my Italian teacher, as well as being my grade advisor, before I dropped out of Italian. She surveyed me carefully and she continued, "I see that you're wearing a senior pin." I realized too late that I was still wearing it, as well as a senior ring. It was all part of the charade. I had intended to remove them before entering her office because I wanted to avoid the lecture I knew I would get if she spotted them, but I had forgotten to do so, and so I braced myself for what was coming.

"Just because you're wearing a senior ring I notice, and a senior pin, doesn't mean that you're graduating." No one knew that better than I did, unless it was her, but I thought it best not to say it. The truth was that when the ring man came to the school the year before, I went to the auditorium with all the potential seniors to be measured for ring sizes. My dad wouldn't think twice about giving me the money for the ring, even though money was tight, but I had taken the money anyway as well as the money for pictures and the yearbook. It was just like stealing and I realized it. I was surely going to hell, but by wearing the ring and the pin there would be no doubt in anyone's mind that I was graduating, except for my guidance counselor, Mrs. Travis. She had all the hard evidence on me in my file, which she was thumbing through.

"Yes, and since I'm graduating in August, I took the yearbook picture too," I said. I didn't think that was the right thing to add right there but she was starting to annoy me with her graduation zingers, so I thought I'd throw in one of my own. She had an astonished look on her face.

"Bilotti, you have been going to school twelve months a year since you were a sophomore. From what I'm seeing in your transcript, you've accomplished very little during the normal school year. Sometimes you complete a course in summer school but most of the time you stop attending classes." She looked at me and shook her head in frustration. It was a look that I recognized well, having seen it so often.

"The sad part of all this, perhaps the saddest part from my point of view, is what might have been in your case. I remember you very well from Italian and I knew then with just a little application, you would have no problem passing the course, but you put no effort into it, so you failed. I was speaking to Mrs. Davis, your English teacher, and she was actually pleasantly surprised, even impressed, by the composition that you wrote on the English regent. She enjoyed it that much, and because I'm your guidance counselor, she showed it to me, but she said that she hardly ever saw you. Her comment was, 'What a waste,' and I agree. Your standardized test scores are all very good," she said as she looked at my file. What are you thinking? Don't you have anything to say?"

I really didn't have anything to say. It was desperate.

"Well, it's too late now, and why do I care? I just don't know where you go from here but I hope that somewhere you have a plan, because the world you're going into can be a dog-eat-dog place. Are you listening to me?" I was really listening to her but to tell you the truth, I already knew the truth of what she was telling me and it wasn't making things better to hear them from her.

"Well, Bilotti, since you have all the accouterments of a senior, except of course the actual credits needed to graduate, I imagine that you plan to attend the graduation exercises." Boy, she could zing with the best of them, or did I just bring out the worst in her?

"I would imagine that after all of the months your family has watched you going to school around the calendar that now they would like to see you at the graduation ceremony. I'm sure there were times that they had their doubts that you would ever make it, and by the way, I still have my doubts you will even make it this summer given your history.

"I don't agree with Mr. Abraham's decision to allow summer school students to attend June graduation exercises. There's no guarantee that they'll even attend summer school but he's the principal."

Mrs. Travis had been correct in everything she had said so far about me, but she was all wrong about me wanting to attend graduation exercises.

We both knew that the principal gave potential summer school graduates permission to attend graduation exercises in June, providing that they would register for the required classes for an August graduation.

We were also informed that diplomas would not be distributed at the graduation ceremony since the class was as large as it was, as that would extend the ceremony to an unreasonable length of time. Instead, diplomas would arrive in the mail during the course of the summer. The graduation ceremony would be all about speeches by administrators, valedictorians, clergymen, and choirs singing. I would rather have spent the afternoon in a dentist's chair having a root canal than to have to sit through one speech after the next, or to have to listen to spirituals while waiting for the next speaker to deliver words of inspiration, especially since I really had not earned the right to be there. I also knew the last thing Mrs. Travis wanted to hear from my mouth was that I found long-winded ceremonies to be inconvenient, so I allowed her to believe that I was actually looking forward to attending the graduation exercises.

Now, this is where I believed that my prayers had been answered, and this is where I saw a way out of my dilemma.

Graduation was to be held on the last Friday in June. My battalion was to leave for two weeks training at Fort Drum on the Friday before graduation and my unit wasn't due to return until the Friday after graduation. That would make it impossible for me to attend graduation exercises. Not only did I not want to sit through the graduation exercises, but even more than that, the thought of watching my classmates and their families celebrating their achievements, and my own family sitting there in their innocence thinking that they had reason to celebrate too, and perhaps having a graduation party for me, was more than even I would put them through. The timing was perfect. I would be able to miss the graduation exercises and I could start summer school after July 4th when I returned from camp.

I didn't say anything about camp to Mrs. Travis. I had no idea about what her reaction would be, but I knew that she wouldn't be patting me on the back for putting my patriotic obligation at Fort Drum before graduation.

"Oh, of course I'll be there. And don't you worry, Mrs. Travis. I'll graduate in August. I'm just too close now not to finish." I knew that was pretty much what she wanted to hear, and I really wanted to get out of there before she could discover something else that I didn't want to deal with. I left in a hurry and headed for home.

I squeezed through the opening that someone had cut through the cyclone fence that enclosed the elementary schoolyard that I had attended years ago when life was uncomplicated. I took a shortcut diagonally across the playground, and I tried to figure out how and when things had gotten so out of hand for me. The problem was that I lacked discipline. It was so much easier to avoid doing the unpleasant things that were required for success. I couldn't imagine that anyone really wanted to sit in one classroom or another, day after endless day, taking notes, doing homework, and taking tests. To me it seemed unnatural, yet I knew that many, if not most people, overcame the overwhelming urge to avoid responsibility, or to take the shortcuts or the Cliffs Notes through life, and for them it had paid off. They had seen the bigger picture. They had made the sacrifices and now they were ready for the next step. For many, that meant college or a job with a future, and eventually marriage, and a well-provided for family, but for me it meant going home and breaking the news to my parents because I couldn't put it off any longer. I would not be going to the graduation exercises because I had to be in Fort Drum. Those were the circumstances, I would say, and there was nothing that I could do about it.

"What are you talking about?" my father said. "I've never heard of such a crazy thing. We've waited all this time, and now you're telling me that you can't go to your graduation. Are you, or are you not graduating? If you're graduating, you should be attending the graduation ceremony. Why should this whole thing be so complicated? Are you graduating?"

"Well, yes I'm graduating. But probably not until August."

"August, I don't understand how that works, but if you're not going to be there in June when everyone else is there getting a diploma, how do you get your diploma, because I want to see that diploma?" I could see the look of disappointment in his expression.

"Nicky, your story keeps changing."

"No one is getting a diploma that day. All of the diplomas will be mailed. They'll be coming to everyone over the summer, so you're really not missing anything except a lot of people talking and making speeches."

I thought that he would see the perfect logic of my argument, and I thought it best not to remind him that even if the diplomas were to be handed out on the day of graduation, I would not receive one until I fulfilled graduation requirements in summer school.

"It's no big deal, Dad. All the diplomas will come in the mail."

"Maybe it's no big deal to you, although I don't know why it isn't, but it's a big deal to me, and we all want to see you in a cap and gown. By the way, I don't mind sitting there listening to speeches. I'm looking forward to it and the place is air-conditioned, but now you're telling me that's not going to happen because instead of a cap and gown, you'll be wearing a helmet somewhere four hundred miles from where you should be. That's bull."

He left the room and I sat there for a while feeling totally miserable because of all the ways in which I had disappointed him. My dad worked tirelessly for his family, and I had created a situation which was now entirely out of control. A line from the play, *Marmion*, by Walter Scott, that we had read ran through my mind. It had impressed me when I read it in one of my English classes. If only I had learned from it. It read, "Oh! What a tangled web we weave, when first we practice to deceive." I could not have imagined how much more tangled things would become.

CHAPTER 4

THIS WAS MY FIRST TRIP TO FORT DRUM AND MY BATtalion was making the trip in a jeep and truck convoy. The trips to Camp Smith, which I had taken before seemed like a jaunt around the block in comparison. It was mile after mile of rolling hills and pastures. The weather in June was perfect. It was a far cry from the cold April of my first trip to Camp Smith. I spent most of the time sitting on the bench of a truck that they referred to as a deuce and a half. The canvas cover had been removed from the back of the truck, so that approximately twenty of us sat in the sun-bathed cargo area. There was a refreshing summer breeze swirling around us, and the meadows in different shades of green rolled on for miles. There were neat farms all around with livestock grazing peacefully in a most beautiful pastoral setting. It was a memorable sight, especially for a city kid who had never experienced anything quite like it before.

The drivers would accelerate their trucks up long grades that sometimes extended for a quarter of a mile or more. When they reached the top, they would speed down an equal distance and their momentum would help their laboring vehicles up the next ascent, and that process was repeated over and over again. Some of the drivers, in order to keep awake and to break up the monotony of the long drive, would put their transmission into neutral and then turn the ignition switch off as they coasted down the hills. When the switch was turned back on, the truck would give off a loud and explosive sounding backfiring boom, and the sound or the vibrations would cause hundreds of frightened butterflies to soar into the air like a June snowstorm of fluttering wings, as they sought refuge in a safer part of the meadow. And so it went on, mile after mile, until we finally reached Fort Drum.

There were several men in the battalion who were veterans of World War II and of Korea. Some had enlisted in the Guard because of the little extra income that they received from it, but for others soldiering was addictive. I had a great deal of respect for them and I never had a single problem with any of them.

A month or two after I had joined the Guard as I was walking into the armory, a sergeant who was in charge of the radio section was walking in close behind me. He was a veteran of World War II, and he had received several commendations for repairing radios while under fire. He was respected and admired by everyone in the unit.

"Hey, Bilotti." I turned around and saw that it was Sergeant Russo. "Hi, Sergeant Russo. How are you?"

"I'm fine, Bilotti." He was a solidly built man of average height with a dark beard and complexion. "You know Bilotti, I'm looking for a guy to operate a radio as a standby, just in case the phones malfunction during a fire mission. There's not much to do most of the time, but if the phone wires are cut, or if they break down for any reason, it's important to have someone standing by on the radio as a backup. Do you think that you'd be interested?"

It didn't take me long to think about that. This was a great opportunity to get away from the 105 mm cannons, and to become a radio operator. "It sounds great to me," I said.

"Sometimes you'll take a post by the fire direction center near the plotting tent, and sometimes you'll be in the field relaying target positions from the spotter planes or from forward observers to the guys in the fire direction tent. Are you interested?"

I thought it sounded great, except for the part about standing by the fire direction tent. Most of the guys in the tent who were plotting out coordinates for fire missions to the 105 crews were the same guys that had a great laugh at my expense as I searched for the Cannon Report. I didn't like them and they didn't like me. The thought of spending significant time in their company, gave me second thoughts about accepting Sargent Russo's offer, but this was a great opportunity for me. Even if they had objections for his choosing me to operate the radio by the plotting tent, I didn't think that any of that crew would have the courage to protest my being there to Sergeant Russo.

"I don't know anything about operating a radio, Sergeant Russo, but I'll give it a try."

"There's not a whole lot to it. You've got to start somewhere and you can learn about radio procedure in no time when we get to Fort Drum. I'll arrange your switch into the radio section."

My first four days at Fort Drum were spent familiarizing me with radio systems and procedures. It was pretty much a crash course and Sergeant Russo took no shortcuts. He took me everywhere that he went so I could learn by observing, and everything was by the book.

On Thursday of the fourth day at Fort Drum, I was given my first assignment, and as you might have known, it was outside of the fire direction center, where all of my "Cannon Report" buddies were plotting out coordinates for fire missions.

As Sergeant Russo said, there wasn't much to do because the phones were working efficiently. The hardest thing for me to do was to stay awake, while the hot June sun beat down on my helmet cooking my brains. I preferred baking in the sun and sitting in the jeep next to my radio rather than to take refuge in the plotting tent where I'd be as welcome as a skunk at a picnic. The constant rattling of the cicadas calling to one another, and the aroma of the pine forest created a perfect serenity all around me, and I had all to do to keep my eyes open. Man that was the perfect place for a hammock.

I got out of the dust-covered jeep and checked my radio for what seemed like the tenth time. I had worn the grass flat from all the turns I had made walking around the vehicle. I found a rag under the seat and I started wiping the jeep down better and in more detail than I had ever wiped my own car down, if only to keep awake. I knew that my buddies in the fire direction tent would love the opportunity to chew me out for sleeping on duty, and then to report to Sergeant Russo about the poor choice he had made in choosing me for that particular job.

So I rubbed away and it wasn't long before I had that jeep looking like it had been washed and simonized from the windshield to the tires. As I was polishing away, three or four linemen, the guys who run all the communication wires, emerged from the woods carrying spools of wire which they were running through the underbrush. We had only been in the field for four days, but all of them had already contacted poison ivy and they were covered with calamine lotion, so they looked like an Indian war party as they emerged from the woods.

As they approached me, I could see the perspiration stains on their fatigue shirts and the bramble scratches on their hands and wrists, which they had received laying wire in the underbrush.

"Hey, look at the shiny jeep. Cheez, Bilotti, what the hell

are you doing? Getting that jeep ready for a parade?" one of the linemen asked as he approached the vehicle.

"Yeah, he's driving for Eisenhower," his buddy added.

Although we were in different sections, I knew these guys. They were blue-collar troops, and they had the poison ivy and the numerous scratches to prove it. They were the total opposites of the guys in the fire direction tent, who looked down their noses at anyone with dirty hands.

"Yeah," I said. "The general knew what he was doing when he picked me to be his chauffeur."

"Oh, boy, here it comes. I didn't know that you even had a driver's license, Bilotti," the first guy said.

"No, I'm serious," I said. "The general told me that if I didn't have this jeep totally G.I.'d to his liking, he'd make me a lineman, and I'm really allergic to poison ivy, even worse than you guys. It's bad enough that I already have an itchy mosquito bite."

As they walked toward the jeep, I ran to the other side. "Hey guys, don't get too close. You don't want to give that to anyone else. And try to avoid scratching that stuff. It makes it spread."

"Let's rub some of this on him," the first guy suggested.

"I would, but it's too damned hot to chase him," and they headed toward the woods.

I watched them go and I yelled in their direction, "Hey, where are you guys going? Do you have any extra calamine lotion for this bite I got?"

They smiled good-naturedly and walked through the clearing into the woods, and then, almost on cue and simultaneously, they flipped me the bird. It was the best example of military precision that I had seen so far.

I climbed into the jeep, wishing that those guys hadn't been so efficient so that the wires would malfunction and then I would have something to do. I was thinking about looking under the hood, when my radio crackled on. At last. Maybe it's a fire mission, I thought.

"Tombstone Four, this is Tombstone One. Do you read me, over?" Tombstone One was Sergeant Russo, and I was Tombstone Four.

"This is Tombstone Four, over."

"Tombstone Four, this is Tombstone One. I'm sending relief to your position. When relief arrives, you are to proceed to base camp. Do you read me, over?"

"Tombstone One, this is Tombstone Four. I read you loud and clear. Roger. Out."

Now what the hell was that about? I hadn't been out here long enough to screw up and now I was being called out of the field on my fourth day in camp.

As I drove back to the base camp, I went over my every action since I had arrived at Fort Drum, because I knew that you weren't pulled from your post except to be disciplined or praised, and I didn't think that they gave out awards for having a shiny jeep, so I must have screwed up.

When I walked into the company office, Sergeant Russo was already there. I tried to read his face to prepare myself for what was coming, but I was not able to get a read. He sat behind his desk and pointed at an empty chair for me to have a seat.

"Bilotti, why didn't you tell anyone that you were supposed to be at graduation exercises tomorrow?" Without waiting for a response, he continued. "Captain Lewis received a call from your father. Your dad asked the captain if there was anything that could be done in order for you to be back in Brooklyn for your high school graduation exercises, which are scheduled to begin tomorrow at 1200. Why the hell didn't you say something to someone about this?"

I wasn't about to go into all the reasons and all the schemes that I had perpetuated precisely to avoid graduation exercises. As a guy who never ducked and always took problems head on, Sergeant Russo would never understand or accept a truthful explanation for why I had not informed my superiors about my impending graduation. The truth in this case would be unacceptable to him.

"Well, I just assumed that my two-week obligation took precedence over a three-hour graduation ceremony. I know from having heard some of the other men talking about it that it would have to be pretty much a life or death situation for anyone to get out of summer camp, and since it was neither of those, I just didn't ask." That sounded like a pretty good explanation to me since I was thinking on my feet.

"Well, I can appreciate that, Bilotti, but we're not talking about missing two weeks here. We're talking about missing one day. You've got to get home for this. Captain Lewis and I have arranged for you to fly home to Floyd Bennett Field tomorrow with the Air National Guard. They have flights going in and out of here all the time. There is one leaving here at 0530 tomorrow. I want you on it. You'll be on the ground at Floyd Bennett no later than 0730. Your father will be there waiting for you. You'll have more time than you need to get home, and then to the Loews Oriental where I understand the exercises are to be held. Your father picked up a cap and gown so that's all ready for you. You'll be with your classmates at 1200. Then your dad will drive you back to Floyd Bennett, for an Air National Guard flight, which leaves at 1800. You should be back here at about 2000 hours, and everybody will be happy especially your family. I want you to be ready at 0400 tomorrow in your full dress uniform. I'll be here to drive you to the airfield. Any questions?"

Any questions? This guy must have helped to plan D-Day.

I had schemed for months about how to avoid the whole embarrassment of graduation. I didn't want to answer any questions. I just wanted the whole thing to fade away, and in a few hours, Sergeant Russo and my father had undone all of my plans.

I didn't sleep much that night, and at 0400 I was dressed, ready, and waiting for the jeep to take me to the airfield. Precisely at 0430, Sergeant Russo himself pulled up to my barrack. Guys on missions don't sleep.

There was a faint glimmering of daybreak in the east. I walked down the two well-worn wooden steps of the barracks and jumped into the passenger seat. I settled in and Sergeant Russo handed me a box.

"I stopped by the mess hall on the way over. I got you a B.L.T. sandwich, an apple and a container of apple juice. That should hold you until you get home." This guy had everything covered.

"You know, Sarge, I feel bad that I put you through all of this. You could have been getting some sack time instead of having to drive me to the airfield, and thanks for the food."

"That's okay. I'm not much of a sleeper, and I wanted to be sure that everything went off smoothly from this end. You will be at those graduation exercises."

From the way he emphasized the word "will", I wondered if he suspected that I had purposely tried to avoid graduation. Maybe he hadn't bought the explanation that I had given to him for why I had not brought the graduation and training camp conflict to his attention.

When we got to the airfield, daylight had pretty much taken over, and you could take the whole airfield in with one glance. It wasn't a particularly impressive sight, and I instantly knew the difference between an airfield and an airport. There was one runway, a small two-story air traffic control building, a windsock, and a few scattered hangars. At the end of the runway, there was a silver two-engine DC-3 with Air National Guard stenciled on the fuselage.

Sergeant Russo drove the jeep toward the DC-3. When we were close enough, he cut the motor and we both got out. There were two officers walking around the plane, checking every inch of it, which was encouraging to me. As we approached them, I could see that one was a first lieutenant and the other was a second lieutenant. It was a safe assumption that they were pilot and co-pilot. They returned Sergeant Russo's and my salute, and we introduced ourselves.

"This is your high school graduate, Sir. This is a big day for him and his family. We want to make sure that he gets to Brooklyn in plenty of time for him and his family to enjoy the ceremony," Sergeant Russo said looking over at me. I still hadn't figured out how much this guy knew or what he had guessed about me.

Lieutenant Ryan was the pilot. He didn't look much older than I did. "Have you ever flown before?" he asked.

"No, Sir. This is the first time."

"Well, this is a good way to begin." He reached down near the landing gear of the plane and handed me what appeared to be a parachute. At first I wasn't sure that it really was what I thought it was, or if he was really serious. Then I realized that he was serious and it was a parachute.

"Sir, do you know something that I ought to know about this flight?" I wasn't joking. I imagined that most people were a bit nervous before their first airplane flight, but now they were strapping a parachute on me. That really didn't inspire confidence.

"Don't worry," Lieutenant Ryan said. "It's just routine. It's standard operating procedure, but it doesn't make sense to have it on unless you know how to use it. I don't want to make you nervous but you never know."

It was too late for him to worry about whether he was making me nervous or not. He reached over across my chest and said, "Do you see this ring right here? Well that ring deploys the chute. If an emergency should arise, grab hold of the ring before you exit the plane. Once you exit the aircraft, count to three or four, pull hard on that ring and your chute will deploy. At least, it's supposed to. If it doesn't, you can return it for a different one." I guess he read my expression because he quickly added, "No, I'm just joking. It should work. I mean it will work fine, but that's the easy part. Finding a safe place to land is the tricky part, and has more to do with luck than anything else, but I'd rather try my luck than to stay with a plane that is quitting on you. Well, that's not the way they teach it at Fort Benning but that pretty much sums up what they do. You've had a five-minute crash course, no pun intended."

I lifted my eyebrows and I shot Sergeant Russo a glance. He gave me a wink and a thumbs up and said, "Piece of cake, Bilotti. Okay, mount up and I'll see you back here at 2000 hours." Sergeant Russo saluted the two officers, thanked them both, and then headed for the jeep.

A portable stairway was pushed to the open door on the side of the DC-3. When it was in place, Lieutenant Martin, the co-pilot, checked to see if my parachute was secure. When he was satisfied, we climbed the stairs and entered the plane. Lieutenant Martin told me to choose one of the metal bulkheads that ran from the front of the plane to the back on both sides.

"If you're not comfortable on that side, you can cross over to the other side," he said with a grin on his face. I looked at the bulkheads and they were identical.

"Excuse me, Sir. Are you and Lieutenant Ryan wearing parachutes too?" Without looking up as he was adjusting the straps on my chute, Lieutenant Martin said, "Nah. We've seen them packing these chutes. We'd rather take our chances with the plane."

Looking around this tired plane, and listening to these two guys, I figured there was still a good chance that I might not make graduation after all. I settled in on my bulkhead while my eyes adjusted to the poor lighting in the plane. There were no windows in the fuselage of the plane. The only light coming in was from the windows in the cockpit. Lieutenant Ryan was already seated in the pilot's seat flipping switches up and down.

Lieutenant Martin said, "Okay, Bilotti, make yourself comfortable. If you're not comfortable where you are, you can move to the other side of the plane," pointing to the exact bulkhead opposite the one that I was already seated on.

"We should be off in a minute or two here," he said as he turned and headed for the cockpit.

Maybe I should have joined the Air National Guard. At least these two guys had a sense of humor. I wanted to think that they weren't serious about much of what they said.

I looked around in the semi-darkness of the plane. There were several containers stored off to the rear of the plane, and as I looked up at the ceiling of the plane, I noticed holes where you could see light coming through from outside. It appeared that some rivets had come loose and had fallen out, but I tried to convince myself that the holes were part of the design of the aircraft, I felt for the ring on my parachute.

I sat there thinking of the absurdity of the situation that I had created. I had involved my family, my school, the Army National Guard, and now the Air National Guard in this hoax. If the truth about this situation ever surfaced, I had no doubt that I would have to pay back or do some hard time in Fort Leavenworth, for sure.

The whining sound of the engine as the pilot attempted to fire it up, brought me back to the moment. There was a sudden ignition, a huge puff of blue smoke, and an odor of burning oil seeping into the cabin. I looked toward the cockpit expecting to see concern on the faces of the pilot and the co-pilot, but instead Lieutenant Martin was smiling and looking in my direction, while Lieutenant Ryan began cranking the second engine. Again, there was the whining sound and the explosion into action by the second engine, followed by the cloud of blue smoke, and the additional odor of burning oil. It was reminiscent to me of the series of jalopies that my father had salvaged, which burned almost as much oil as they did gasoline.

The sound of the engines increased in intensity and soon we were bumping and racing down the runway. I felt the airplane suddenly lurch into the air, and I was aware of a feeling of exhilaration that I hadn't anticipated.

At about 0730, precisely as Sergeant Russo had said we would, Lieutenant Ryan put the plane down on Floyd Bennett Field, taxied to a stop and cut the engines. Lieutenant Martin came back to the fuselage of the plane and opened the door. I could see the traffic on the Belt Parkway, as they were positioning the portable stairway alongside of the plane so that we could disembark.

"Well, that was a pretty routine flight, Bilotti." Lieutenant Martin was already tugging on the straps of my chute in order to remove it. "We'll leave your chute right here on the bulkhead. You'll need it for the flight back. You're a veteran now, so you know the routine. In fact, Ryan and I were saying that you looked so natural in that parachute, you might want to think about Fort Benning after you graduate."

"Yes, Sir. I'll give that some thought after I graduate." I wanted to add, "If I'm not too old by then," but instead I thanked him for the flight and asked him to pass on my appreciation to Lieutenant Ryan as well.

"No problem," Lieutenant Martin said. "We'll see you back here at 1800 hours. There are some people waiting by the gate in a green Mercury. I imagine that's your family waiting to pick you up."

"Yes, Sir. That's probably my mom and dad." As I started walking down the portable stairway, Lieutenant Martin stood in the doorway and waved to my parents and they waved back. He then said to me, "See you at 1800," and he walked back into the plane.

My mom and my dad greeted me as if I were some sort of a hero, which only intensified the disdain that I was feeling for myself at that moment. The Belt Parkway was heavy with traffic, which was typical for that time of day during the week. Both of my parents had lots of questions, especially about how I had learned that they were flying me home and about my flight, since neither of them had ever been inside of a plane. I went into some detail, but I decided not to tell about the parachute. I didn't want to cause my mother, especially, any more concern than she already had about air flight. I thanked my dad for speaking to Captain Lewis about arranging for me to be at graduation exercises. I could see how happy and proud they both were that we would be at the graduation exercises. I tried to put aside the whole charade for the moment. As phony as the whole thing was, it was all real to them, and I was happy to see their joy at that moment. That made me even more determined to keep the truth about my graduation from them forever. It was that important to them and I didn't want to ever spoil it.

With my cap and my gown over my class "A" uniform,

I sat in the midst of the graduates. Somewhere between the invocations of the Catholic, Protestant, and Jewish clergymen, followed by speeches by the principal and valedictorian, both of whom believed that the future of the world was dependent on us and in our hands, the glee club sang a medley of Negro spirituals. It was all so tedious to me that I would have almost preferred jumping out of the airplane and testing my parachute, if doing so would have helped me to avoid all of this. Well, maybe nothing quite so dramatic, but perhaps sitting in a dentist's chair having two impacted wisdom teeth extracted would have worked as well.

And then it was over. For my family, even though they said there were times they doubted that I would ever graduate, it had happened. They had seen me graduate and for them seeing was believing, and they were content. For me, even though I had my doubts for a while that it would all ever end, I had survived what I had so desperately sought to avoid. I could never have imagined that I would ever be back for my graduation exercises, especially when a few hours earlier I thought that I was safely away, four hundred miles from Brooklyn, in Fort Drum. But unbelievably I was there and I had endured the speeches, the singers, and the back slappers, and now I just wanted to leave as fast as I could.

At 1800 hours, I was back in the DC-3, strapping on my parachute, sitting on the bulkhead of the plane. At about 2000 hours, Lieutenant Ryan landed the plane. Sergeant Russo was waiting to drive me back to the company. He dropped me off at my barracks, wished me the best of luck for graduating, and was on his way. I crawled into my sack and fell into a deep sleep. It had been a long and crazy day.

CHAPTER 5

IT WAS SO OBVIOUS TO ME THAT THE NATIONAL Guard that my father had been in, the one in which he had made close friends and had such raucous good times, had very little similarity to the Guard in which I was now a member. I was nineteen and tired of the whole experience. Most of the other guardsmen were married and in their twenties or thirties. They spoke about their children, and generally they had little in common with me. But soon I discovered that except for the veterans who were in because they truly enjoyed soldiering and the camaraderie that it brought, it was also the time of the draft at the tail end of the Korean War, and most of the others had joined the Guard to avoid being drafted into the regular service. I had little respect for that group, and I disliked the thought of being associated with people I considered to be little more than draft dodgers. I could spot those who had joined to avoid the draft by the disdain that they had for the military. They made no secret about their contempt for the military, and that was often manifested in the slovenly manner in which they wore their uniforms.

Attending weekly meetings was becoming an ordeal for me, as were the occasional weekends at Camp Smith. Once again we were preparing to go up to Fort Drum. The thought of spending two weeks for the second time with that group was starting to become a nightmare.

My enlistment had been for two years. Anyone who did

not reenlist when his term of enlistment expired would have his name submitted to his draft board, and he would be inducted into the regular service. The group that I was associated with would go to any extreme to avoid regular military service, so they stayed in the Guard until they were no longer eligible for the draft, and then they walked away from the military forever, secure in the knowledge that they would never have to fear hearing a shot fired in anger.

This would be my last enlistment regardless of what my draft board would do when I didn't reenlist in the National Guard. It was a hot June day at the fort. There were ten of us returning from the field. We sat in the back of a three-quarter ton truck. Once again, the canvas that covered the top of the truck was removed and the sun was beating down on us. Everyone was covered in perspiration and clouds of dust stirred up by the truck were settling down and sticking to our sweat-stained bodies.

I reached for my canteen that was hanging from my gun belt and I twisted the cap off. I took a mouthful of water, which was warm enough to brew tea. Besides being warm, the water had a medicinal taste to it, so I spit the rest of what I had gulped into my mouth over the side of the truck.

"Yuk! I've had showers with cooler water." There was a guardsman sitting alongside of me who was one of the few guys that I had a friendly relationship with. His name was Evans.

"I wouldn't want a warm shower right now but I'd really love a cool one. I just want to cool off and to get this sweat and dust off me," Evans said.

I flicked some water from my canteen at Evans and said with a grin, "Here you go. Is this too warm?"

Evans sat their grinning, the canteen water making little rivulets as it coursed down his dust covered arms. "Oh, now you've done it." He reached for his canteen, so I knew what was coming. "This is war. Water fight!" And with that Evans emptied the little bit of water he had left in his canteen on me.

"Oh, refreshing," I said as I watched the water turn the dust on my arms into little streams of mud. "Here, Evans, cool off," and I poured the rest of what was left in my canteen on his crew cut head, which he seemed to be enjoying. It was just a moment of silliness and harmless good fun between the two of us, but wouldn't you know it, "Sergeant Cannon Report," sitting opposite of us was annoyed by the unwinding antics of what he probably thought were two annoying kids.

"Why don't you two assholes just knock it off?" The smile was instantly gone from Evans' face, as I looked in the sergeant's direction. He was the chief non-commissioned officer in the plotting center and I particularly disliked the guy, because I remembered how he enjoyed seeing me run up and down various company streets in Camp Smith, looking for the Cannon Report. For whatever his reason was, I could see the contempt in his eyes as he looked at both Evans and me. I was particularly offended by his description of us. This guy never even acknowledged my presence before even though I spent hours on the radio jeep outside the plotting tent. This was not the way for him to begin a conversation with me.

"What's your problem?" I asked. "You're all the way over there and we're over here. Why does it bother you if we're unwinding and having a little fun? Oh, I know, the only time that you think something is funny if it's at someone else's expense?" He knew that I was referring to the Cannon Report incident.

"My problem is that the two of you act like juvenile delinquents. Why don't you grow up?"

I disliked this guy to such a degree at that moment that

I couldn't bring myself to even address him as sergeant. All I wanted to do was to get under his skin. I probably should have considered the fact that he was a sergeant and that I was a private before speaking, but my short fuse kicked in. I had observed the guy since I had been in the Guard and nothing military had ever seemed of importance to him before this.

"Look," I said, "I can't speak for Evans, but I'll plead guilty to acting like a juvenile delinquent if you'll plead guilty to being a draft dodger." I threw it out there and just stared at him.

It worked. You could tell instantly that I had gotten under his skin. There was a palpable silence on the truck. I was convinced that what I said was the truth about him, and about his friends as well, but rather than to set me straight about my accusation, he said, "I could say the same thing about you. You're on this truck too."

"Give me a break," I said. "I'm nineteen. I joined the Guard when I was seventeen and still in high school. What am I dodging? Figure it out." We stared at one another, neither of us hiding the contempt that we felt for each other.

During the whole exchange, his friends sat looking from me to their sergeant. I was especially enjoying seeing his face red with anger.

I knew that he could seek some sort of punishment for me for what I had said, but a few minutes earlier he had referred to Evans and me as assholes and juvenile delinquents; what was military about that? That was street talk in my part of Brooklyn. Suddenly he addressed me using military language and he also decided to pull rank on me.

"Look, private. You better wise up for your own good and learn to keep your mouth shut and keep your thoughts to yourself, or else."

I hated threats from anyone, but especially from that guy. I had to do everything I could to restrain myself and to remember that I was on a military truck and not in a schoolyard in Brooklyn.

"You know," I said, "when we're in the armory or when we're out here, we have to do it your way, but when we leave here, or when we leave the armory in civilian clothes, we can continue this discussion. In fact, I'm looking forward to it. How about you?" Except for the bumping and jostling of the truck, there was a heavy silence all the way back to the company.

That weekend, the whole battalion was to go to a dinner in Canada. The Canadian border was not very far from Fort Drum. The company dinner was a yearly tradition and it was a fun evening. We all brought our dress uniforms in anticipation of going up to Canada, and I was especially looking forward to the trip, partly because I had never been outside of New York or New Jersey.

Each company had to leave one man behind to stand guard duty and that person, usually a private, had his name drawn from a hat. There were many privates in the battalion so the odds of your name being pulled were slim. The fact that I had "won" the lottery the previous year led me to believe that lightening would not strike twice. Whatever the case, it was one lottery that you wanted to lose. Somebody had to have his name pulled, and as fate would have it, when the drawing came, I "won" the lottery again. What were the odds? I had to stand guard by the motor pool a second time. No trip to Canada for me. I was terribly disappointed, but fair was fair. The names had been pulled at random from a hat and somebody had to lose.

So there I was on Friday night, on guard duty, standing by the gate of the motor pool, watching truck after truck taking guys to the annual company dinner in Canada, when I saw a jeep approaching in a slow and deliberate way. As it got closer, I saw sergeant draft dodger sitting in the front passenger's seat surrounded by his buddies. When he got close enough and was sure that I could recognize him, he and his buddies gave me a wave and big smiles as they headed for the Canadian border. He had not forgotten our exchange on the truck and revenge was sweet.

CHAPTER 6

THEY CONTINUALLY WARNED US BEFORE OUR EN-listments in the National Guard was up that if we didn't re-enlist, it wouldn't be very long before we would go to the head of the class and be conscripted into active duty. A thought like that would have put the fear of God into most of the men in my unit and would have made them sign on the dotted line in a hurry because the reason that most of them had joined the National Guard was to avoid active duty.

I really enjoyed seeing the expressions on some of their faces when I dropped a duffle bag with my whole issue on a table in the supply room. After I checked out, I said goodbye, and walked away from what had been a mostly disappointing experience. Guys didn't usually join the Guard in order to expedite their entrance into the regular army, but I had enough, and despite my disappointment, I had learned a lot over the last two years that I knew would serve me well in the future.

It was March of 1956, almost two years since my bogus high school graduation, and in that time, I had three jobs. My first job, working in a cabinet-making shop lasted one day. My second job was working in the mailroom for Robert Hall Clothes in New York City. It was a job that I liked very much even though it paid very little. Within six months of obtaining that job, and because of petty thievery by the man who ran the mail department, I was temporarily asked to run the mailroom, and I loved it although I was still earning very little money. Soon I was made the permanent head of the mailroom but I had to quit that job because my family moved to New Jersey, and I did so reluctantly. I thought that it wouldn't make much difference because each day I expected to be hearing from my draft board anyway. My third job was as a meter reader for a northern New Jersey gas company.

Then there was my girlfriend, Ann, whose family strongly disapproved of me. With a dossier like the one that I had, and with which they were totally familiar, they were of the strong conviction that I would not be the best choice for their daughter. Who could blame them? I was a nice boy and all that, but it was not hard to understand why Ann's parents would do all that they could do to discourage her from having a long-term relationship with me. It was nothing personal, but they viewed me as a ship without a rudder. They had high expectations for their daughter's future, and mine were not the kinds of credentials that would endear me to parents whose daughter believed that I would be a permanent part of her future. It was painful but I got it and as painful as it was for me, at least I didn't live in that house. I could get away from it, but Ann had to live with it each and every day.

As I was driving into Brooklyn to see Ann, I was listening to the McGuire Sisters singing the theme from *Picnic,* while I was trying to ignore the throbbing pain in my right hand, which I had to have stitched earlier in the afternoon.

That morning my partner, Bob Garfield, and I were reading gas meters in an affluent area of north New Jersey called Mountain Lakes. It was a beautiful area of rolling hills, elaborate estates, and free roaming dogs. The homeowners hoped that the dogs would discourage thieves who preyed upon them by robbing their homes. I wasn't sure how effective the dogs were in discouraging thieves, but they certainly discouraged me. I had a few close encounters with their free roaming pets, some of which were slightly larger than White Fang. On the other hand, Bob Garfield never saw a dog that could intimidate him. He was fearless.

"Look, Nick, if you act like you're afraid of them, they can smell the fear in you and that just makes them more aggressive. That's why they come after you. Just walk toward them. Talk to them. Don't turn your back or run."

"Try to get this through your head, Bob. I'm not acting like I'm afraid of them. I am afraid of them, and if they really can smell fear, I must be giving off quite a stink. They probably can smell me the minute that we turn off the highway into this place. Maybe that's why packs of them seem to be laying in wait for me. These are watch dogs you know, and I think that what they watch is the calendar, because they seem to know when we're due to read this route."

"Look, just get the meter in that house over there," he said, pointing to a large and opulent house, which was typical of the area. "I'll get the last one in the court up there, and then we're done with this book and we can get out of here."

I looked at the address on the page of my book, which matched the house number on the mailbox. At the bottom of the page, someone had written in bold letters: **BAD DOG**!

"Damn it, Bob. Look at what someone wrote here: **BAD DOG**. I'm not going on to that property. This guy is gonna get an estimated bill. What are you, nuts?"

"Nick, I would gladly change houses with you but look at what my page says." I looked at his page and it also warned about a bad dog in the house that he was going to.

"That's what I've been trying to tell you. This whole area is full of partially domesticated wolves," I said.

"Just relax will you? Do you know who used to read this route?" He looked at me. "Well, I'll tell you. It was Leonard

Rapga. He wrote 'bad dog' on every other page. He'd write that if the people owned a fifteen-year-old toothless Chihuahua. That guy was even afraid of the squirrels. It got so bad that everybody on the route was getting an estimated bill. There were so many complaints that if he didn't quit when he did, he was going to be fired."

"He quit, huh. Maybe he knew what he was doing."

"Will you stop? We're wasting time. Look, I know these two houses. The one that I'm going to has dogs running loose on the property. I'm not sending you there. The one that you're going to has a dog, but he's upstairs. You're going in through the basement. They leave the door open when they know that we're going to read the meter."

"I can't believe that they leave the door open. What's the point of having the damned dog? Wait until the thieves get wind of that," I said, hoping to joke away my fears, but he ignored me.

"Once you're in, look straight ahead. Flash your light in front of you and you'll see a row of closets alongside of the stairway. Open the closet door nearest the stairway and you'll find the meter. Get the read and we'll be done with this book."

Bob jumped out of the truck, turned around and said, "Just don't be afraid. They can smell it a mile away."

"It's too late for that now," I shouted back. "I told you that they got a whiff of me the minute that we turned into the development."

I got out of the truck and I walked cautiously up the long driveway that led to the back of the house and the basement door. With every step I took, I peered around anxiously, fully expecting to see a hound or two come bounding after me. Bob had warned me more than once to never turn and run if a dog came at you, but instead to confront the animal and to try to make yourself appear bigger, while shouting something like, "Hey! Hey!" Oh yeah, that would stop them in their tracks I'm sure. "Help!" "Help!" That was what I planned to shout in such a confrontation.

I got to the end of the driveway and I looked around the corner. There was no sign of danger, and I could see the doors leading to the basement. There was an outer aluminum and glass storm door and then an inner door.

I pulled the storm door open and I turned the knob on the inner door to let myself in. I let go of the storm door and it slammed onto the latch. I didn't bother closing the inner door behind me because the minute that the storm door slammed behind me, there was a booming deep throated barking coming from upstairs. I purposely left the second door open. That would be one less door for me to have to open if I had to beat it out of there in a hurry.

I spotted my flashlight on the wall in front of me, and just as Bob had said, there was a staircase and a row of closets alongside of the staircase.

The dog upstairs was in a frenzy by now. Just as Bob had warned, he could smell the fear in me all the way upstairs and through the door in front of him. The fear he smelled must have been like what blood in the water is to a shark. I could hear the frantic scratching at the door. He must have been hurling himself at the door, because there was a thumping like you would hear if a man were to put his shoulder into a door that he wanted to break down, and all the time there was a whining and a barking because of his frustration at not being able to get at me.

I hurried across the room to the closets, opened the first one, and found the meter. I flashed my light and quickly jotted down the numbers, and then I hurriedly turned and headed for the doors to get out of there. As I did the barking stopped, and instead there was a guttural crying. Somehow, the dog had managed to open the upstairs door, and I could hear the sound of his claws on the linoleum covering on the stairs. He was racing down as I was scrambling toward the door. I pulled the inner door to close it in front of him before he could get to me and I reached for the handle of the storm door. Before I could close the inner door, he threw his whole body against it and slammed it shut on me. The force of the door slamming jerked my hand off the handle of the storm door and forced my hand through a pane of glass. I pulled my hand away from the shattered glass, and caught the sleeve of my leather jacket on the handle of the storm door. The handle ripped my jacket from the elbow to the shoulder. I looked down and saw blood streaming down my hand, onto the narrow walk that went back to the driveway. From inside of the house, I could hear the dog crying and scratching at the door in frustration, unhappy that he hadn't gotten to me in time.

Bob was in the truck thumbing through his book as I approached it. He looked up and instantly saw me cradling my bleeding hand and the condition of my jacket.

"Oh my God. What the hell happened?"

"I'll tell you on the way to the emergency room," I said, "but Leonard knew what the hell he was talking about."

It took seven stitches to close the wound on the palm of my hand. All the way back to the office, Bob kept telling me how freakish the whole thing was.

"Something like that would probably never happen again," he said.

"Well, one thing is for sure. It won't ever happen to me again. When we get back to the office, I'm doing a Leonard. I'm turning in my flashlight."

"A Leonard," he said.

"Yeah, a Leonard. I'm done, Bob. This is not for me. It's not like someday I'll be able to work myself up from a meter reader who was afraid of dogs, to the president of the company. Where am I going with this?"

"What will you do if you quit?"

"I need some time to tread the water and to figure things out. I've had three dead-end jobs in the last two years. I have a wonderful girlfriend whose family would probably wish that I had cut my throat, and not my hand this morning, so what I'm gonna do is say goodbye to everyone in the office, get into my car, and drive straight to my draft board office in Brooklyn. I'm gonna put my name in for the draft. I keep waiting for the National Guard to do it for me, but I haven't heard from them, and it wouldn't surprise me if those clowns forgot to submit my name. I'm gonna do it for them."

"Hey, that's a big move. Once you do that, you can't change your mind. Why don't you sleep on it before you do that? You've had a rough day. You might feel different about it in a day or two."

"You know what I discovered, Bob? If you think too hard and too long about something that you want to do, you'll just keep thinking about it and postponing it, and then you'll do nothing. Just do it, and then whether it was the right thing or the wrong thing to do, you live with your decisions and you go on from there."

I parked my car on 86th Street, and headed for the selective service office. I knew that it would be smarter to go into the service through the National Guard. If I did that I would keep my rank, which was only private first class, and I would have two years longevity for pay purposes, but why would I start doing the rational thing now? Besides, the more that I thought about it, the more I did not want to have any association with the Guard. In fact, the National Guard experience had left such a bad taste in my mouth that I didn't want anyone to know I had once been a part of it. I also knew that they might keep me hanging before they submitted my name for induction, which could have been in the dead of winter. Doing it this way would be quicker. It was spring and I preferred to take basic training in warm weather if I had a choice.

I walked up the stairs of the draft board office and I gave the girl my information. Signing on the dotted line was a bit of a struggle given the condition of my hand, but I managed.

"How long will it be before I'm drafted?" I asked the girl as I handed her back my papers.

"There's gonna be a big call up so it'll probably be about a month," she said.

When I got to Ann's house I explained about my hand, but I didn't tell her that I had just signed to be drafted. That was something that I decided to keep from her at least for a while. I hadn't made up my mind about ever telling her at all, even though she knew that there was always the chance of the National Guard calling me up. She wouldn't understand what was going on in my head, in fact, she would be hurt if I told her that I just needed to get away. One thing was for sure and it was that I would never tell my parents. I didn't know if any of them, my parents or Ann, could ever understand what I was feeling or why I needed so badly to get away.

Less than a month later, I was on my way to Whitehall Street to be sworn in.

CHAPTER 7

MOST OF THE INDUCTEES ARRIVED AT WHITEHALL Street by public transportation, but since I was now living in North New Jersey, my father, who never missed a day of work, took the day off, and both of my parents drove me to the city so that I could report in at 0700 as required. Ann thought the right thing for her to do was to not take time away from my parents as they saw me off, so although she could have taken the subway to Whitehall Street, she was not there that morning.

It's difficult for me to admit it even now, but I was embarrassed in front of the other inductees because I was accompanied by my parents. No longer a child, I wasn't going off to camp for the summer; I was going into the army, but as I look back at those days, I have come to realize that at times my lack of gratitude knew no bounds.

Most of the inductees appeared to be older than I was and, unlike me, most of them had arrived alone. I obviously didn't know any of them but it still bothered me to have them see me with my parents, so I quickly said goodbye to my mom and dad, and watched them as they reluctantly walked away, even though we were told that processing would not begin for an hour or so.

We had only been there for a few minutes but the bonding of complete strangers had already begun. Men who had not known each other until a few minutes ago were now engaging in conversations about themselves and their families, as if they were old friends at a reunion. Not knowing what to expect, and the feeling that they were all in this together, caused them to disregard the natural barrier that they would ordinarily impose between themselves and total strangers.

I looked over and noticed one inductee who was difficult to miss. He was standing away from the others. He was of medium height but he was obese to the extreme. His face had a smooth, ruddy complexion, and it appeared that he had no need of a razor to this point. He was with a middle-aged woman and a girl of perhaps fourteen or fifteen. Both the woman and the girl appeared to be holding back tears with great difficulty. It was obvious that he was as uncomfortable and as self-conscious as I had been while my parents were still there and probably for the same reasons.

I assumed the two women to be his mother and his sister, and as they held his hand, it was clear that they had great worry about his well-being. He had a self-conscious smile on his face, and his round, smooth cheeks were flushed red.

"Eddie, do you have everything?" He nodded his head in assent, the smile still on his face. "You'll be fine, Eddie," the older of the two said, although without much conviction. The little girl was too choked up to say anything, but instead fought back sobs.

The woman who I assumed was his mother had been reassuring him, but now he was reassuring her. "It's okay, Mom. I'll be fine," he said in a voice that I was just able to hear. "I'll call you the first chance I get. I'll be fine," he repeated. "Now I've gotta go, so why don't the two of you go home now? I'm gonna have to go inside now." They looked as if they weren't convinced that everything would be fine. "Don't worry. I'll call you." He kissed the two women one final time and the two of them reluctantly walked away and then turned to wave to him one last time.

I gazed at Eddie's enormous bulk and I thought that this poor guy was in for it. I had learned enough about the military at that point to know that the weeks ahead would be a challenge for us all, but they would be especially challenging for that poor guy given the fact that he appeared to be at least one hundred pounds heavier than he should have been given his height. I knew that in basic training recruits were constantly running or jogging, and looking at him, I couldn't imagine that he would be able to keep up. The bad news would come to him later because at this point Eddie couldn't even imagine what was in store for him. As we drifted into the building, I thought that Eddie's mother and sister's concerns for him were not unfounded.

The physical examinations that we received were a joke, and about as thorough as you would get if you were trying out for any high school sports team. The object was to process us as quickly as possible, in order to process the next group. There just wasn't time enough to give everyone an extensive examination. It was kind of like an honor system. If you had a real physical problem, the doctors and medics were pretty sure that you would bring it to their attention for them to follow up.

Everyone gave a urine specimen, followed by a doctor who listened to our hearts. Our blood pressure was taken, and then we were all told that we would have brain examinations. We all stood there, naked and self-conscious. Not many of the men had ever stood naked in a crowd before, so from one part of the room or another they began to make jokes that ended in a unanimous laugh when we realized that "the brain examination" consisted of all of us spreading our buttocks, as we were given visual examinations for hemorrhoids.

When the doctor had gone all the way down the line, we were told to stand up, and that now we would be checked for flat feet. I do have flat feet, but there was no way that I was going to allow my flat feet to cause me to be rejected. That would mess up my plans to get away. Having good arches was a very important part of any army physical, so knowing that, I had practiced how to conceal the fact that my feet were flat. I arched my feet slightly, giving the illusion that I really did have arches, and I breathed a sigh of relief when the doctor breezed by me.

"Okay, that's it. Everybody here looks good to go, so this is your last chance before we swear you in. If anyone has a doctor's note indicating that there is a reason for you not to be inducted, put your clothes back on and then report back to this room with the note from your doctor so that we can check it out. The rest of you get dressed and report to the room across the hall for swearing in."

There were about two hundred of us, and about a quarter of that number went off to get their doctor's notes, and I'll bet a quarter more wished that they had my flat feet. When those of us without notes finished putting our clothes back on, we reported to the room where we had been told that we would be sworn in. We raised our right hand and we swore to be faithful to the Constitution and to the Commander-in-Chief, and it was done.

After the swearing in, we had some time to kill before we would be transported to Fort Dix. A bus was supposed to pick us up at five o'clock and to get us to Fort Dix by eight o'clock. You had to wonder why we were all expected to report at seven in the morning if we had about five hours to waste, but there was a saying in the army, which I already knew and the others would soon come to know, which was, "hurry up and wait."

"Alright, you guys," a sergeant barked. "I want two files in the hallway right now!"

We all jumped to our feet and began forming two columns in the hallway, anticipating that the buses had arrived earlier than expected. When we emerged from the building, there were no buses in sight.

"Okay, you guys. We're going to walk around the whole block, and you're going to police the whole area. That means that you will pick up any litter that you see and place it in the buckets which I have here."

The sergeant had about ten buckets, which he handed to the ten men nearest him.

"You guys with the buckets make yourselves available to anyone with litter so that he can deposit the litter into the buckets. Any questions?"

One guy standing next to me said barely loud enough to get a chuckle from the guys around him, "Yeah, I have a question. What the hell am I doing here?" He eyed the litter, which was mostly cigarette butts and some candy wrappers. "I don't even smoke. Why do I have to pick this stuff up?" he said from the side of his mouth.

So there I was, part of a group walking around Whitehall Street, some of us in suits and ties, obeying our first military orders, picking up cigarette butts, used cups, and candy wrappers while the civilian population walked by and looked at us in amusement.

We made one complete circuit of the block and sure enough, there were the buses ready to go. We collected our bags, which we were told were to contain toiletries and a change of underwear and socks, and we scrambled into the buses, dirty hands and all.

I walked down the aisle and I saw Eddie, sitting by himself halfway up the bus, so I took the seat alongside of him.

"Hi. I'm Nick Bilotti," I said.

He stuck out his hand and grabbed mine, which I had extended to him. "I'm Eddie Hughes."

"How are you doing, Eddie?"

"I'm alright. Just a little nervous," he said. "You know, not knowing what to expect."

"Well, you can bet that one of the things that we can all expect is lots of intimidation. There will be lots of screaming and yelling and people getting into your face. You can count on that, but it's nothing personal. It's just the way it's done. All of us will have to put up with it but it's easier if it's not a surprise when it happens." Eddie looked at me and nodded his head.

"What's important is the way you handle it. That's what they're waiting to see. If you handle it well, then you'll get less of it. If they think that they're getting to you, they'll pile on."

I had been touched by his mother and sister when they had said goodbye to him earlier, and I was really trying to prepare him for what I knew was inevitable, especially in his case, but I didn't want him to think that I was a blowhard or a know-it-all. Although I had promised myself that I would never admit it to anyone, and so that he would not have a negative opinion of me, I said, "I was in the National Guard for two years. I'm not Combat Kelly, but I know what they do."

"You were in the National Guard? Then why are you doing this?"

"I just had to get away. It's hard for me to explain. It was as if everything was closing in on me. I had one crummy job after the other. I had lots of confusion about where I was going with my life. I needed some time to figure this all out," I said. "The army will send me here and there and plan things out for me for the next two years. In the meantime, I'm hoping that the experiences that I'll have will help me to sort things out, and that I'll have a better handle on my future than I do now. None of that was happening for me with things the way they were."

He nodded, "Yeah, I understand."

"What about you?"

"Pretty much the same," he said. "This was a big decision for me too, but maybe a little different. My dad passed away a couple of years ago, and I live with my mother and my sister. My mom works and my sister is a junior in high school." He looked at me as if he were wondering how much he should reveal to a total stranger, and then he continued.

"After I graduated from high school, I worked in the A&P for awhile, and then I worked for Goodyear Tire. You know, taking the old tires off and putting new tires on cars. I did that until I got sick of it so I quit, which I shouldn't have done, because then I couldn't find another job. I answered ads and I went on interviews, but I couldn't nail anything down."

I could tell by talking to him that he wasn't a stupid guy, but I couldn't help thinking that one of the reasons that people were reluctant to hire him was because of his obesity. I had never had problems finding jobs. The problem was finding good jobs.

He continued, "So one day, after looking at all of the unemployment ads, which were the same ones that I had been looking at over and over again, and some for which I had already had interviews, I reached a point of desperation. I was really down. I was bored, so I was constantly looking into the refrigerator, and one look at me should tell you that I should be avoiding refrigerators at all costs." Again, there was the self-conscious grin on his face as he made a joke at his own expense. "Well, I thought of my mom, who was out cleaning offices while I was sitting around feeling sorry for myself, so I made up my mind to join the army. I figured that if I did that, at least my mother and my sister would receive an allotment check every month, and I'd be less of a burden on them. And maybe I could get into better shape. I knew that I wouldn't be raiding any refrigerators in the army, and they say the food is lousy anyway. It all just made sense.

"I went to a recruiting station before my mother or my sister got home. I knew if I tried to discuss it with them, they'd try to talk me out of it, and then if they started crying, I'd never do it. I was concerned about the army rejecting me because of my size, but the recruiting sergeant was more concerned about making his quota than how big I was and so they accepted me."

"How did your mother and sister handle it when you told them that you enlisted?" I asked.

"Just as I expected they would. I mean, they weren't hysterical, just a lot of quiet tears, which hurt even more. Watching the two of them was painful."

"Yeah, I saw both of them this morning on Whitehall Street saying good-bye to you. I know it's tough on them, but do you know what, Eddie? They'll handle it. It's not like you're going to war. Can you imagine what it was like for the families of the guys during World War II or Korea?"

I was starting to regret getting to know this guy. His story was depressing me, and I didn't have the heart to tell him that the army didn't make exceptions for guys who weren't in shape, and it didn't have the patience to wait for you to get into shape. If you were able to do the physical things that were asked of you while you were getting into shape, fine, but no excuses. Either you performed up to expectations or you did not. There was nothing in between.

We had known each other for about an hour, and we had spoken openly about things that you might reveal only to someone who you had known for years. It was the kind of bonding that men inexplicably do in the service, and I imagine that men had done in armies throughout the course of history.

In the middle of our conversation there was a loud bang, and the flapping of rubber under the wheel well of the bus. We had blown a tire somewhere on the New Jersey Turnpike.

"Hey," Eddie said. "Maybe I should offer to lend the driver a hand and fix this flat and win some points. I'm an expert tire changer from my previous life."

"That would win you some points if the driver was in the army. The guys that we want to win points with are waiting for us in Fort Dix, and they don't drive buses. Let's just sit here."

By the time we received road assistance, and had the tire changed, we had spent a considerable amount of time on the New Jersey Turnpike. We arrived at the Fort Dix Reception Center a little after 11 P.M.

CHAPTER 8

THE NEXT THREE DAYS WERE TAKEN UP BY TESTING and learning about military life and expectations. We were still wearing our civilian clothing, but we all wore army overcoats and hats which had been the first items issued to us. All in all, we were a motley looking group with no military bearing at all.

After our third day, we were all marched to the barbers. I watched as man after man was sheared, much in the same way that I had seen sheep sheared. Some of the men appeared not to have had their hair cut in years and I watched as the barbers, with no particular skill, ran the electric razors from the back of the individual's head straight through to the man's forehead, until the floor was covered with hair of various colors and textures, so that individual differences were less defined. In short, we were all starting to look the same. It was the army's way of saying that we should no longer consider ourselves as individuals, but as an integral part of one unit.

When it came to my turn, I took two dollars from my pocket and, winking at the barber, I handed the money to him and I whispered, "Go easy on the top." He winked back at me, put the two dollars in his pocket, and then proceed to shear off all of my brown curly hair in the same unmerciful manner in which he had sheared the hair off everyone else's head, but it hadn't cost them two dollars. Idiot, I thought. Not the barber. Me.

After having our hair cut, we were marched to the quartermasters where we were issued every item of clothing that most of us would need for the rest of our enlistments. All of this gear was stuffed into a duffle bag that weighed nearly as much as I did.

I had seen Eddie Hughes, and I had spoken with him briefly from time to time over that three-day period, and now he was a little way behind me as we were fitted for uniforms. I pretended not to notice, but I could see how uncomfortable he was as almost nothing that he tried on fit him properly.

Quartermasters and cooks were notorious for their lack of patience in the army and that was most likely because they took lots of verbal abuse. Quartermasters were defensive because of the constant complaints about the clothing that they issued. "Look, Ace, this ain't Brooks Brothers so quit ya bitchin'. Put that stuff in your bag and move out."

I already knew that it wasn't Brooks Brothers, and not even Robert Hall Clothes for that matter, when instead of measuring us with a tape measure, the quartermaster simply asked us for our height and weight and then pulled a shirt or a jacket from a particular bin.

It was even worse with cooks because of the preparation and the quality of the food that they served. Rarely did a compliment ever come their way. If they weren't subject to verbal abuse about the food that they had prepared, the body language and facial expressions of the troops who they were feeding communicated all that cooks needed to know about how disagreeable the menu that they prepared was to the people they were feeding.

Cooks hardly ever made eye contact with the men they fed. Instead they would look down at the tray of food in front of them as the troops tried to figure out what it was that was about to be served to them. If a trooper lingered a bit too long deciding if he really wanted to put whatever that was into his mouth, the cook would say things like, "Do you want it or not?" Then with a wave of his serving spoon, he would indicate that the soldier had better get out of his sight and move to the next delicacy.

"Listen, big boy. This is not the fat man's shop. I don't have anything here that will fit you except sheets and blankets." I looked to my left and saw that that a supply sergeant was addressing Eddie.

That got a big laugh from anyone near enough to hear it, but a few of us who had gotten to know Eddie just winced and pretended not to hear.

"You're gonna have to wear your civilian clothes until I check with the warehouse and see what's available in your size. What's your name?"

"Edward Hughes."

"Edward Huge? Man, that's a perfect name for you."

"No. Not Huge. Hughes. Edward Hughes."

"Okay, Huge," the quartermaster said, ignoring Eddie's correction. "You'll hear from us early tomorrow. We should have your complete issue by then. In the meantime, we'll tell them at your training regiment why you're out of uniform when you're bussed back over there tonight." With that, the sergeant turned away from Eddie and gave his attention to the next guy in line. The rest of us picked up our packed duffel bags and headed for the next station. Eddie followed the slow-moving line, carrying two pairs of boots and two pairs of shoes, which he placed into his otherwise empty duffel bag. He saw me looking at him and said, "Hey Nick, can you imagine? They found shoes and boots that fit me," the self-conscious grin that was now familiar to me spreading across his face.

"You get the last laugh, Eddie," I said. "You get custom-fitted clothes. The rest of us have to take our chances."

"Hey, you're right. I never thought of it that way," he said, and he followed along with the rest of us carrying his almost empty duffle bag.

It was pitch black when we arrived at our training regiment, which would be our home for the next eight weeks. We sat on the bus with our duffle bags on our laps. The door of the bus opened up and a drill sergeant jumped onto the steps of the bus. We could hardly see him because of the dark moonless night and because our duffle bags were at least three feet high. Looking into the darkness we heard him utter, "Oh, my God." It was as if even in pitch-blackness he was able see the pathetic, useless collection of excuses for human beings that had been sent to him.

As we remained seated under our duffle bags in the darkness, the sergeant stood next to the driver and began swearing at us and threatening us, while reminding us the whole time about what useless maggots we were and how we had made his job impossible. He went on for a couple of minutes and I had to remind myself of the advice that I had given to Eddie on the bus when we left Whitehall Street. It was not personal, but just part of the indoctrination and the reshaping. It was the breaking down before the building up.

After a few minutes, the tirade stopped and I thought that they were going to let us get off the bus. Instead, another guy took the place of the first guy, and he had even more contempt for us than the guy before him.

I noticed that the person sitting next to me, someone who I had not seen before, was starting to become more and more agitated.

"What the hell did we do to these guys to piss them off like that?" he said to me above a whisper. Before I could whisper back my "don't take it personal" response, and in the dark anonymity of the bus, he shouted loud and clear from behind his duffle bag, "Fuck You!"

There was a stunned silence that could not have lasted for more than three or four seconds, but in that brief period, two thoughts flashed across my mind. The first was to say a prayer that they would not think that I had shouted that at them, and the second was to pray that they would not ask me if I knew who had shouted it. In their perverse way, they would probably have more respect for someone who would stand up to them, even if it was from behind a duffle bag, but they would have everlasting contempt for the person who gave him up.

At first, they were in no hurry to let us off the bus while they ripped into us, but now they couldn't wait to get us out of the bus. The two who had originally boarded the bus were now joined by several others and they were all shouting threats, while vowing to find the one who had cursed at them. They screamed us off the bus. It was shear panic as guys tried to squeeze through the door that was barely large enough to allow one person through at a time, and now two or three were trying to get through the opening while bear hugging their duffle bags, which must have weighed eighty or ninety pounds. Some guys tripped and fell right on top of their duffle bags, while others, who couldn't see that they were down, fell over them, and so it went until the last man was off.

We stood on spots that had foot prints outlined on them, our bags in front of us. I was relieved when not a single drill instructor, or cadre, as they were also called, asked who it was who had cursed back at them in the bus. Instead, there in the darkness, they shouted into our faces until we learned that we were to shout back an acceptable response to them that began with sergeant and ended with sergeant.

Then it was off to what they called the dayroom where we sat on metal folding chairs, stiff as mannequins, listening to more verbal abuse and indoctrination about what was expected of us, as well as what our schedules would be like. All the while, we were reminded about how soft and hopeless we were. Periodically, someone would shout, "Tenhut!" That command would get us all to snap up as one, screaming while jumping onto our feet. Then a command of, "At ease," would crash us back to our seats, and that was repeated over and over again.

I saw one recruit who had reached a breaking point pass out and lurch forward. His head went between the seat and the steel supporting rod of the chair in front of him. No one moved to help him and he lay there wedged under the chair making strange gurgling sounds, still unconscious, until one of the sergeants told two guys next to the unconscious recruit to pull him out. They got the man out and carried him out of the room.

After our orientation, we were marched to our sleeping quarters where we were issued sheets, blankets and pillows. We were assigned bunks, taught the proper way to make up a bunk, and how to make military corners on the sheets and the blankets. After practicing on the right way to make up our "sacks", we stood at attention alongside of the finished product as our bunks were inspected. If someone's bunk was not up to standard, it was turned upside down, and had to be redone to the drill instructor's liking. And so on it went, and none of us could go to sleep until the last man had it right.

When they were finally satisfied that everyone had learned what was expected in making a bunk and that we would never forget it, we were allowed to crawl into our sacks. Not one of us even bothered to wash his face. It had all been just as I expected. There would be physical challenges ahead, but the mental challenges would be far greater. Soon we were all asleep, totally, but mostly mentally exhausted.

CHAPTER 9

BASIC TRAINING WAS RIGOROUS, BUT FOR ME THERE had been few surprises, and it wasn't long before the rag tag bunch who had scrambled off the bus that first night were forming into a cohesive unit. We helped one another and most of all we covered for each other, until the man next to you, who you hadn't known a few short weeks ago, was as close to you as your own brother had ever been.

Some had more difficulty than others in successfully accomplishing the task before them, and their names were quickly learned by the cadre. They were always singled out for more harassment than the rest of us. They were made to repeat an activity over and over again, until the drill instructor was satisfied, and the process usually whipped them into shape.

Eddie Hughes seemed to make no progress. It wasn't because of lack of effort on his part. Eddie never quit trying and never complained, but his starting point was so far back from the rest of us, that it seemed to me that there just wasn't enough time in the eight weeks that we had for Eddie to get into the condition required to complete basic training.

It would start early for Eddie. There was a pull-up bar just outside of the mess hall, and we were required to do at least ten pull-ups before we could enter the mess hall for breakfast. Those who did the required ten pull-ups went directly into the mess hall to eat, while those who could not went to the back of the line to try again, which left them less time to eat.

That served to add to our frustration since we were already pressed for time in everything that we did. Some were able to do the required ten pull-ups on their first attempt, whereas others made it after several attempts. A tally was kept to see if each recruit finally totaled ten before he would be allowed to go into the mess hall. Some took so long completing the exercise that they had all to do to wolf down a couple of hard boiled eggs or a box of cereal before they were rousted out of their seats for formation to begin the day's training. It was a familiar sight to see Eddie on the line to empty his tray, while at the same time trying to get a little breakfast into his stomach before he had to dump the rest of the food on his tray into the trash.

That went on for three meals a day unless we were in the field, and soon everyone was able to do ten pull-ups, at least after two attempts. Yet it never appeared to me that Eddie had made much headway or that he had lost very much weight. There was nothing any of us could do for him to help out and to his credit, Eddie would go down to the pull-up bar on his own before lights out, and after we were all squared away, and struggle to pull himself up on the bar, but with very little success. We pretended not to notice when he returned to his bunk.

When we were in the field, all of those who struggled with the pull-up bar had a reprieve, but in Eddie's case, there was always another obstacle to deal with.

It was July and it was hot. We were sitting on the ground in an open field. We had just finished having lunch, most of us were trying to relax, and some of us laid back and dozed. The sun was relentless. It was high in the sky and beating down on us.

There was a system that they called, "water discipline", which meant that you were only allowed to drink from your canteen when you were given permission. Your canteen was periodically checked to be sure that you had not exceeded the amount of water allowed to you. Lack of water, and the salt pills that we were encouraged to swallow, had the backs of our fatigue shirts crusted white from dried up perspiration and salt residue.

We would have formation early in the morning with the moon and the stars overhead in the darkness. It seemed that except for us and some migratory birds, the rest of the reasonable world was asleep, and it wasn't until three hours later that same world was bathed in brilliant sunlight. The up side to being up and training so early in the dark was that for at least a few hours we were able to avoid the unrelenting sun.

Sometimes we would sit on bleachers that were located in various parts of the field. We each carried little note pads that we used to jot down information about weapons and their capabilities, which we would be tested on later. We all suffered from sleep deprivation, and sitting in the bleachers, with the intense sun on your helmet and fatigue setting in, made it almost impossible to keep your eyes open while a lecturer droned on.

Sitting in the first row was something that I always tried to avoid. The recruits who sat there and were obviously nodding off were reachable and would suddenly be awakened by a sharp blow to the top of their helmet as it was whacked, usually by the lecturer.

Those of us who were out of reach were forced to participate in a little game called "Jab". When the lecturer noticed men falling asleep all around him, he would shout, "Jab!," at which point everyone would throw their elbows furiously back and forth, partially in self-defense, hitting the person on each side until the instructor would call it off by shouting, "At ease." That would leave eyes wide opened, at least for a little while, when it would be repeated. Oh the games we played.

But at least for now we lay there enjoying a few moments of respite when suddenly the voice of a drill instructor whose name was Sergeant Delaney, but who we referred to as the "Walrus" because of his large girth, broke the tranquility of the moment.

"Huge! On your feet! Get out here, Huge." The name had stuck and now most everyone referred to Eddie Hughes as Eddie Huge, except those of us who were close to him, and he no longer bothered to correct them.

Despite the fact that he was about as overweight as Eddie, to our amazement the "Walrus" was able to perform any of the physical tasks with ease that we were asked to do. He showed no compassion for Eddie as Eddie struggled because of the burden of his weight. It was as if the Walrus was personally offended that Eddie had in some way contributed to the stereotype, which said that fat people were not up to par. It was a stereotype that the Walrus had worked hard to disprove, often at our expense. He would usually have us run from place to place with him matching us step for step. Eddie was undoing all of the Walrus' efforts. I believe the Walrus took it personally and because of that, he showed no pity to Eddie.

"Grab your weapon, Huge."

Eddie reached over, picked up his rifle, and pulled himself up.

"Hold your rifle at port arms and take a couple of laps around perimeter of the field."

We all watched as Eddie began jogging around the field with his rifle close to his chest.

"How much can that poor bastard take?"

I looked over to where Frank Nanci, another guy from Brooklyn, was resting on his side. Frank, a stem of grass in his mouth, was looking across the field to where Eddie was struggling under the gaze of the Walrus.

"I bet that guy loses his mind before he loses any weight. I'm starting to think that they've given up on him. They know damn well that he'll never be able to do this stuff, and they just want him to quit."

"Frank, how the hell do you quit? This isn't a club. You just can't quit," I said.

"Oh, you can quit," Frank said, flipping the grass stem away. "Sometimes, after you've tried everything, you just give up. Some guys sooner, some guys later. This guy has no place to go. They're trying to break him down."

"There are consequences. If you quit in the army, you go to jail, or you're marked for life with some crummy kind of a discharge," I said.

"Yeah, that's part of it, but right now I don't think that Eddie is thinking much about the future or consequences. He's wondering how the hell he's gonna get through the next few minutes. Nick, he's in over his head. Where is this going for him? How much more can he take?"

The truth of Frank's words had been apparent to me for some time, but I had put it out of my mind because I didn't want to deal with it. It's funny how when you're in a bad situation, even when people are sympathetic toward you as we were to Eddie, in the end, all of their genuine sympathy does absolutely nothing to make the problem easier. You're in it alone and you've got to deal with it on your own.

We looked across the field, and it was obvious that Eddie was having difficulty continuing. He was having trouble lifting his feet but the Walrus kept prodding him to reach down for a second wind and to keep going. It was clear that

Eddie had no more reserves to the point that he probably didn't even have the energy to pitch forward but instead he was more likely to sag to the ground in exhaustion.

It was painful to watch and at that moment, I pictured Eddie, his mother, and his sister saying goodbye at Whitehall Street. It all seemed to have happened a long time ago, and it was a good thing that they were unaware of what was happening to Eddie. That they weren't aware of Eddie's predicament was the only good coming out of the ordeal that Eddie was going through at that moment.

As recruits, none of us was allowed off base for the two months of basic training. We were allowed visitors on weekends, but one day the army made an exception for me and about twelve others.

We had come in from the field from what was a typical basic training type day of running, crawling, jumping, and general insanity. We had chow and now we were cleaning our weapons before showering and crawling exhausted into our bunks. I was talking with Frank Nanci and Eddie Hughes when the first sergeant walked in.

"Bilotti, come outside a minute. I want to talk to you," he said.

I felt my heart leap in my chest as I tried to think of what I had done or how I had screwed up. Maybe something was wrong at home, I thought. I looked at Eddie and Frank and both of them looked at me, and I could tell that they were as confused as I was.

"Okay, Sergeant," I said, and I followed him out, my heart thumping.

When we got outside he said, "Bilotti, we got a call from the Philadelphia Police Department. One of their officers has a three-year-old son who has to have heart surgery. They called us because the boy is going to need several blood transfusions and he needs B-negative blood, and they were wondering if we could find about twelve guys on post with that blood type who would be willing to donate some blood for the boy. You have B-negative blood. Now you don't have to do it, but it would be nice if you would donate some blood for the boy. What do you think?"

At that point, I was so relieved that the first sergeant wasn't looking for me to give me some bad news that without even thinking about the situation I said, "Of course. Of course I will."

"Well, that's great, Bilotti," he said, and it works out fine because tomorrow is Thursday. After chow tomorrow night, you and a bunch of other guys will go to Philly on a deuce and a half to donate the blood. When you guys get back, you will all get three-day passes to recuperate. Friday, Saturday, and Sunday are all yours, but it's rise and shine on Monday."

"A three-day pass? Can I leave the post?"

"Where do you live, Bilotti?"

"I live in New Jersey."

"If you can have someone pick you up Friday morning and get you back here Sunday night before 2200, then do it. That's it, Bilotti. I'll see you tomorrow after chow. Good job," and he walked away.

I walked back into the barrack and I told Eddie and Frank about my conversation with the first sergeant.

"Oh, my God," Eddie said. "They only want a pint of B-negative? I'd give them a gallon of O-positive for three days away from this place, but they probably figure that once I leave here, I might never come back, and they're not done with me yet."

Thursday after chow, the truck was waiting to take the twelve of us to Philadelphia. After we donated our blood and just before we were about to climb back into the deuce and a half that would take us back to Fort Dix, a tall black Philadelphia police officer walked quickly over to the truck.

"Before you guys go back, I just want to say, and I know that you have heard it before, but my family and I will never forget as long as we live what you have done for us. And my son, Chris, will always be reminded about your generosity, because I know that he's gonna make it." The tears welled up in his eyes. He brushed them from his face and turned away awkwardly. Almost in unison, the guys shouted, "Good luck, sir," and we left. I've thought about it often over the years but I never found out if the little boy made it.

Chapter 10

THE CHATTERING OF .50 CALIBER MACHINE GUNS fired several feet over our heads filled the night air. We crawled on our chests or switched to our backs to get under barbed wire and around obstacles. We had been repeatedly warned that live ammo would be fired over our heads. Any doubts that we might have had about the sincerity or the sanity of using live ammo on a training course was soon removed when we saw the occasional tracer shell hit the berm at the end of the course and ricochet straight up into the darkness of the night. Cans were filled with stones and hung from the top strands of the barbed wire and rattled loudly as a trooper inadvertently sprung the wire. The rattling gave away his position, but also served as a reminder to the rest of us to stay low or risk being hit by a machine gun round.

Now and then, a flare was launched and as it slowly parachuted down to earth, the whole field was illuminated as if it were mid-afternoon. The bright light caused us all to stop our movement until the flare burned itself out and we were invisible once again. The explosion of a hand grenade, loud enough to drown out the sound of the machine guns, shook the ground. The cacophony of sounds and sights as well as the smell of cordite, which would be part of a firefight, was an attempt to simulate the desperation and confusion of war as close as possible, and was enough to make most of us hope to never have to experience it.

It had been a long and physical week of training, which had us walking through the woods at night with a compass, and walking or running while shooting at silhouettes that would suddenly appear. One of the highlights had been the experience of the gas chamber. Although the use of gas was prohibited by the Geneva Convention, it was thought best to familiarize us with both chlorine and tear gas, and how to use gas masks in the eventuality that someone broke the rules, although it seemed silly to me to have rules about the way that you slaughtered people in a war.

We spent a good amount of time on what they called dry runs, learning about the gas mask before we were allowed to enter the gas chamber that looked more like a large shed. We were to experience two types of gas, tear gas and chlorine gas. I would soon discover that although chlorine gas is lethal and tear gas is not, the exercise with chlorine gas was the easier of the two.

We entered the chlorine chamber, with our gas masks already on. I was aware of the strong odor of chlorine even through my gas mask. It was not unlike the odor from my high school's pool. We remained in the chamber long enough to see that our gas masks were effective in a lethal chlorine environment.

The tear gas chamber, although not lethal, was the more difficult of the two, because we walked into that chamber without our masks on as the tear gas was piped in. We stood holding our breath for what seemed like an eternity but it was probably no more than a few seconds. Finally, we were instructed to put on our masks and to clear them as we were taught to do and we stood in the gas-filled room. After several minutes, the gas was turned off, the chamber door opened, and we rushed out, with our skin burning, our noses running, coughing and spitting, and trying to fill our lungs with fresh air, while tears streamed down our faces. Although the gas masks had worked once they were on, the few brief seconds in which we had stood without them on was enough to cause all sorts of discomforts.

The tear gas had completely saturated our fatigues and for the rest of the day, the vapors rising off our clothes kept our noses running, and our eyes tearing, as if we were contracting the flu or as if we had been peeling onions all day. That kind of irritation continued throughout the day until we were able to change into fresh fatigues.

The week in the field would end with a ten-mile speed march, with full gear, back to our training regiment. I knew that would be a challenge for me, because at five feet five inches and one hundred and twenty-five pounds, and with seventy pounds on my back, I was at a distinct disadvantage. I guessed that most of the other recruits averaged around five feet nine inches, and weighed around one hundred and seventy pounds, and were also carrying the same seventy pounds of gear that I was carrying.

To make matters worse, we seemed to be always marching in sand, and if you've ever tried walking on a beach while carrying heavy items, you know how exhausting that can be. I realized that this ten-mile march would be a challenge for all of us but I would have loved to have been four or five inches taller and forty or so pounds heavier. They did a more equitable job handicapping horses.

The drill instructor's main concern was to be sure that as many of us finished the march as possible and that we finished in the same order that we started in. The company who had the most men finishing the march, and finishing in the order that they had started the march, would receive a trophy that would be displayed in the mess hall until the next group of recruits made the same march. When one of the recruits brought up the inequity given the size and weight of each man and the burden that he carried, the drill instructor responded that was not his concern, but that the recruit should take it up with his parents and not him. "All we want to do is to keep that damned trophy in our mess hall." I wasn't sensing much empathy there.

We broke camp the next morning, and Nanci and I saw Eddie Hughes.

"Hi, Eddie. How's it going?" I said.

"Hi, Nick. How's it going?" he asked Frank, who was rolling up his shelter half.

Frank looked up at Eddie. "Did you have as much fun on the obstacle course as we did last night?" Frank jokingly asked of Eddie.

"The whole thing was insane," Eddie said, shaking his head. "The best thing about the whole week was the gas chamber."

"The gas chamber? I hated it," I said.

"Not me," Eddie said, "no running or crawling." He had the same self-conscious grin on his face that I had first seen on Whitehall Street.

"The infiltration course was brutal," he continued. "I rattled every can on every wire that I tried to haul my ass under," he chuckled. "Talk about not wanting to draw attention to yourself. What a joke. When I tried going under on my stomach, my back got snagged on the barbed wire, and I couldn't reach around to unhook myself. I tore up my back pretty good. Blood was all over my fatigue shirt. What a comedy. I tried going under on my back, and I ripped my shirt and every button off my shirt. There were guys passing by on both sides of me. Thank God that it was too damned dark for the cadre to see me, but they must have had a pretty good idea about where I was with all those cans rattling. I was afraid they'd spot me when those flares went off but everyone froze when that happened anyway. They were sure as hell waiting for me at the finish line. I was so damned late that they must have thought that I was A.W.O.L." He began laughing at his own expense.

"What did they say to you?" I asked.

"You know, Nick, they wanted me to run the course again. I would have had to except that the course officer wouldn't allow it. What a nightmare."

He sat on the ground, looking first at Frank and then at me. Neither of us had a suggestion for him, because there really wasn't much we could say. After a few seconds I said, "Well, it's over. That's one less thing to have to worry about."

"You know, Nick, when I was in the middle of that course and making no progress, and only getting torn up, all of this bullshit came crashing down on me. I just didn't give a damn anymore. I had all to do to keep from standing up."

"Standing up? And taking one of those .50 caliber shells?" I asked.

"Exactly," Eddie replied.

Nanci looked over at Eddie. "Maybe you think that might have solved your problem, and I guess it would have for you, but it probably would have caused problems for a few others."

Eddie looked at Frank. "At that moment, all I could think of was that there were worse things than dying. I've screwed up so much around here that if I had done that everyone, including you two guys, would think that this time I really screwed up, but that now I had paid the price. It would be an accident, and if I got killed in a training accident, my mother and my sister would get ten thousand dollars insurance money. It's ten thousand isn't it? Anyway, I'd be worth more to them dead than alive."

He paused for a moment. "You know, the more I thought about it, the harder it was to stay down, because I really can't see much upside for me." He paused again. "Then I thought about them. How would my mom and my sister handle it, especially my mom? Maybe I'm putting too much value on my life. My dad died, and as terrible as it was, we moved on. I don't know. The thought of hurting them more than helping them, kept me hanging on that damned barbed wire."

"Eddie, I only saw your mother and your sister briefly on Whitehall Street, and from what I saw, I don't think that they would ever recover if you had done that. Look, that part is over and now we move on."

"That's over, but it's not all over," Eddie said. "Tomorrow we have that ten-mile speed march back to the regiment. It's gonna be hot. We'll all be walking through that beach sand and you know that a lot of guys will be falling out. Lucky for them, Eddie Huge will be there to take the heat off them. The cadre will be so focused on me that they won't even notice that half of them will have to be hauled away in jeeps. It's Eddie to the rescue. I wish it wouldn't be like that, but that's just how I expect it to be." Eddie remained quiet for a while and then started again. "At least the infiltration course was at night, and except for the welcoming party at the end of the course, I wasn't harassed, but tomorrow, on the speed march, they'll kick my ass every step of the way."

I had some guilt looking at the guy. As tough as it was for all of us to do the required training, there was some comfort in the knowledge that we were all part of the group, and we all blended in. For Eddie, there was the additional pressure of constantly being singled out. It was a pressure I am sure none of us could imagine, and none of us wanted to think about.

After a minute or two, Eddie picked himself up and said, "Well, guys, I'm out of here. I'm gonna try to get some rest and see if I can be ready for tomorrow," and he walked off into the darkness.

When he had gone, I said to Nanci, "Do you really think that guy is capable of killing himself?"

"Nah. I don't think so. You know why? Guys who kill themselves never think about the effect it will have on anyone else. They only think about themselves and the desperation of their situations. They think that death is their only way out, so they jump off a bridge or hang themselves or something. As bad as his situation is, and it's pretty bad, Hughes was thinking of his mother and his sister before himself. He probably figured out that as bad as his situation is for him, theirs would be worse if he killed himself. He was more concerned about their problem than he was about his own. That's why I think he didn't stand up, or else I think he might have. He didn't hurt himself because of his family, but if they keep pushing him, he might hurt someone else. I know I would."

"I guess you're right," I said. "How long are we here now? A month? That's not a real long time, but a month of misery must seem like forever."

Frank nodded and began to unlace his boots. "Maybe it'll work out. I know it sounds selfish but I've got my own problems and I've gotta get some sack time." He crawled into his shelter half and was soon fast asleep.

It was a pitch-black moonless night, which accentuated a sky full of glittering stars. The stars were so numerous and close together that they appeared to be one huge cloud rather than individual bodies. Nightfall had done little to relieve the oppressive heat of the day. It remained hot and humid, and tomorrow promised to be a scorcher. Except for finding a way to finish the sandy ten-mile speed march on my feet, I had no problems.

CHAPTER 11

THE SUN HAD COME UP OVER A HAZY SKY LIKE A BIG orange ball still low in the east, but at that early hour it was already casting enough heat on us so that it was plain to all that if we hoped to reach the finish line we would have to earn it. Each of us carried what was called a horseshoe roll. It was comprised of your half of the shelter half, which was half of a pup tent and which would be buttoned on to your buddy's half with just enough room for the two of you to sleep and store your gear. There was also a backpack, which contained eating utensils, tent pins, rain gear and toiletries. We also carried our weapons and a canteen full of water.

We marched at a steady pace in order to finish within an acceptable time limit. At about three or four miles into the march, I began to understand why the army rejected guys with flat feet. My shins were aching from my ankles to my knees. They were so sore that when I reached down to rub them, the pain intensified and I was certain that my flat feet were the cause. Guys all around were complaining about having to breathe the dust being kicked up because of the dry sand or about the intense heat, but I seemed to be the only one with shin splints.

We marched in two files, one on each side of the road, and occasionally you could hear the familiar distinctive whine of a jeep as it split the files and came up from the rear. There were usually two guys, sprawled in the back of the jeep, unceremoniously dumped back there because they were too exhausted to continue. To me those were guys who allowed their bodies, which might have continued, to surrender to their minds that screamed out at them to quit and that had prevented them from continuing. I really believed that your mind would give up on most things before your body did. If you believed that you couldn't, then you were defeated before you started. It was a matter of will. There was no way I would allow that to happen to me.

My parents and Ann usually came up on Sundays when we were free, and we usually ate and talked about what we had done the previous week. I knew that one of the topics of this week's conversation would certainly be about the speed march, and the humiliation of having to admit in front of them that I had finished the march loaded into the rear of a jeep, motivated me to keep on going.

I hooked one thumb around the strap of my rifle and the other thumb around the strap of my horseshoe roll, and I leaned forward at the waist to such a degree, that my field of vision only allowed me to see my legs and the ground in front of me. I went on that way, but the pain in my shins was becoming so unbearable that I knew it would only be a matter of time before I would no longer be able to continue, but then only if my legs would go out from under me.

I continued that way hoping that the next step would not be my last. My eyes remained focused on my legs, and I felt almost outside of myself as I watched one leg and then the other move forward until eventually they seemed to move as if of their own accord, and without my willing them to move.

Mile ran into mile and suddenly I realized that I could no longer feel the pain in my shins. It all seemed so effortless now. It was as if I had broken through some sort of barrier, and now I had gotten into a rhythm and I really believed that I could walk twenty miles at the same pace if need be.

Suddenly, there was a commotion and a struggle, perhaps two hundred feet in front of me. I lifted my head to see what all the ruckus was about, and I saw two or three of the cadre trying to subdue someone. It was Eddie Hughes. The drill instructors struggled furiously as they circled Eddie and tried to figure out a way to grab hold of him in order to subdue him, but Eddie had broken loose and they were unable to get near him. I could see that Eddie was holding his rifle by the barrel and swinging it like a club at anyone who approached him. The line kept moving and as I got nearer to him, I could see that Eddie's face was flushed and red. There was saliva running down the side of his mouth and he was shouting something at them, which I could not make out. Suddenly, Eddie flung his rifle end over end at one of the cadre and ran off into the woods, with all of them in hot pursuit.

None of us stopped or even slowed our pace, and soon we had walked beyond the point where we could see or hear anything more of the skirmish.

The sun was traveling its course toward the west as we approached the finish line of our march into the regimental area. Probably in an attempt to embarrass them, those who had fallen out and had been brought back by jeep, were made to stand and wait for us to march into our regimental areas at the finish line. Most of them avoided eye contact, but all of us were too exhausted to care whether they were there or not. I did look for Eddie as I walked by, hoping that he would be one of those watching us come in, but I didn't see any sign of him although he would have been easy to spot.

We arrived in our company area, and like everyone else, I released the buckle on my pack, which released my horseshoe roll and I allowed my pack to drop behind me. I had been walking hunched over to alleviate the stress on my back and to keep the straps on my pack from cutting off the circulation to my arms. With the sudden release of the weight from my pack, my shoulders arched back. It felt as if I was being pushed backward toward the ground while my legs continued to move to the same steady pace and to the same cadence to which they had grown accustomed over the last ten miles and the last few hours, even though I was no longer moving forward. Now, with no weight to pull forward, I began to back pedal, totally unable to stop myself, until I tripped and fell on my back with my rifle under me and my legs still churning involuntarily.

The soldiers all around me were exhausted and lying on the ground. They had been watching my actions as I tried to keep from falling while I backpedaled furiously and then finally fell to the ground while my legs continued marching on their own.

Most of them were not in a laughing mood at that moment. They were exhausted and they had no patience for what they believed was clowning on my part.

"For crying out loud, Bilotti, knock it off," I heard someone say, but I imagine that the expression on my face, and the sight of me clutching at one leg and then the other in an attempt to stop them from churning, convinced them that it was not an act. They watched as I held my legs.

"I can't stop them," I said, and now they did begin to laugh convinced that I was not clowning.

After about a minute, my hands were able to communicate to my legs what my brain seemed unable to do, which was that it was over now, and most of us had made it. It was time to relax.

Several weeks had gone by, and basic training was nearly completed. No one had heard a word about Eddie Hughes and the drill instructors never brought his name up. One rumor said that he had been recycled to start once again from scratch and that Eddie had been put into a class with all new recruits. With the constant demands of training, we all stopped thinking about him, and we looked forward to graduation.

One day, as we were returning from the field, we reached a crossroad just outside of the company area. We were made to halt and to stand in the at ease position. Stopping for no apparent reason like that was unusual. We had never stopped before reaching our company area. We were impatient because for us the day was over. We were tired and we wanted to get back to our barracks to clean our equipment, to eat and shower, but still we waited with no explanation.

After a while, one of the cadre shouted, "Attenhut!" We all snapped to attention, and the next command was "Parade Rest." Parade Rest differed from At Ease. While at ease, you had to hold the position but you could talk and move keeping one foot planted. Parade Rest meant that you must hold the position without talking or moving.

We were standing silently in our places when we saw two figures approaching, at about twenty-five feet to our front. One was a soldier carrying a shotgun, with the butt resting on his hip, and there was no mistaking the other. It was Eddie Hughes. He was wearing an orange jump suit and he was carrying a duffle bag on his shoulder.

"Hey, that's Hughes," someone whispered behind me.

Nanci was standing on the side of me. "Holy crap, they're taking him to the stockade," he whispered. "They made us wait here. They wanted us to see this crap to teach us a lesson. Look at that poor guy."

"To teach us what lesson?" I whispered. "He never deserved this crap. It wasn't that he stopped trying. They just wouldn't let up. He had to do more than the rest of us. Now look at him. He said that this was gonna happen. Do you remember, Frank?"

"Yeah, they broke him, and then he tried to whack them with his rifle before he threw it at them and ran off into the woods. Not a good idea. He should have gone down and hitched a ride in the jeep like the other guys did," Frank said.

"They should have given him some points for not getting into the jeep and for not quitting anything they put in his way," I whispered back.

Eddie was in front of me now. He saw me and gave me that self-conscious smile of his and a little wave. I mustered a half-hearted smile back, as he walked by me. As he passed, I could see the back of his orange jump suit and in black letters was stenciled: "PRISONER."

The letters were bold and black, but in my mind, there was no more unlikely guy to be a prisoner or a threat. I could only wonder how much his mother and his sister knew.

It was probably four, maybe six weeks later. We had completed our basic infantry training, and most of the men with whom I had started had been sent to other forts or bases around the country for different kinds of advanced training. I was fortunate enough to continue my training at Fort Dix, where I was now able to go home every weekend, unless I was earmarked for a particular detail.

On one such weekend, I was detailed for what they referred to as "prison chaser". As a prison chaser, I was sent to the fort stockade, where my assignment was to watch over certain prisoners who were not considered dangerous. Because they weren't considered dangerous, they were assigned menial tasks such as grass cutting details, or painting details, or jobs of that nature. When I reported to the guardhouse with several others, we were given instructions regarding what was expected of us.

"Any questions?" the sergeant of the guard asked, and as there was none, the sergeant handed out shotguns.

"Each of these shotguns has two loads. Use the same precautions that you would if you were on the range. Any questions?" There were still no questions. The men were led to their various details and I was led to mine.

"Okay, Bilotti," the sergeant said. "You have six guys to police on your detail. Do you see that pile of railroad ties?" he said, pointing at a huge pile of ties. "Well, the six prisoners assigned to you are to load those ties onto that truck until they're all out of there, then the ties will be trucked away."

"I understand," I said.

"The shotgun has two charges in it. I don't think that you'll have any problem with these guys. They're all short timers, but if one of them gets stupid and decides to take off, don't hesitate to use the shotgun. The first shot is to hit the runner and to scare the hell out of the other five in case they think that they're part of a relay team. If you miss and he doesn't stop running, you might want to use the next shot on yourself."

"Thanks for the advice, Sarge, but I think that I'd rather use the last charge for a second try at the prisoner."

"I'm just joking," he said.

"Well, thanks for clearing that up for me, Sarge."

"We haven't had a problem in a while now, and I don't think that you will either, but you have two live ones just in case. Don't miss," and he left.

The six prisoners had already begun to load the railroad ties on the truck as I approached. Four of them were carrying ties to the truck and two were on the truck stacking them neatly. As I approached the truck, there was no mistaking that one of the prisoners was Eddie Hughes.

"Eddie!" I shouted.

He looked up and recognizing me, I saw the familiar grin spread over his face. "Nick. What are you doing here?" Then, eyeing my shotgun, he said, "What did they do, send you here to shoot me?" and he began to laugh, as the other prisoners put down their railroad ties and used them as seats.

"Don't be nervous guys. This is my buddy. We were on the range together. He's a lousy shot."

I can't tell you how bad and self-conscious I felt standing next to Eddie with a rifle. This was Eddie, who went all the way back to Whitehall Street with his mother and sister. Eddie who had poured his heart out to me on the bus ride to Fort Dix, the guy that we had all rooted for during basic training, and now I was standing there with a rifle. The absurdity of it all was crushing.

He must have seen how uncomfortable I was. "Aw, Nick, don't worry about it. These guys aren't going anywhere. All of us will be out of the army soon with Bad Conduct Discharges. It's like getting a "D" on your report card in school. They tell us that if we stay out of trouble and get jobs, we can apply to have our Bad Conduct Discharges changed to General Discharges. And even if I were doing a life sentence," he stopped again, "Nick, you've seen me run."

"I know Eddie, but geez," he wouldn't allow me to finish, but he tried to lighten up the moment.

"Do you know what just came into my mind, Nick? The time for me to run was when we were talking on the bus to Fort Dix. You were trying to warn me about what was in store for me. I should have listened. I had my chance to run or hitch a ride the hell out of there when the bus broke down. And you didn't have a rifle then," he added.

"Eddie, stop it," I said.

"I'm just kidding."

We stood in an uncomfortable silence.

"Well," Eddie said, "these railroad ties aren't gonna jump on the truck by themselves. Hey, Nick," then hiding his mouth behind his hands, he said, "I'm in charge of these guys. That's how bad things are around here. Watch this. Okay, you guys, break is over." As he shouted to them, they got up as one and started loading the ties on the truck. "Pretty good, right, Nick? If you see the Walrus around, tell him about the progress I've made. He'll be proud for all fat guys."

"I never want to see that guy again," I said.

"Don't be angry, Nick. It's all good, and I don't give a damn. What else can I do?" And he walked away to help loading with the other guys.

I watched Eddie and his crew loading railroad ties all day, and true to form, Eddie worked step for step with the others. At the end of the day, when my detail was over, I went over to Eddie to say goodbye. We shook hands and he gave me a bear hug, and I never saw him again.

CHAPTER 12

I DON'T KNOW FOR SURE, BUT IT SEEMED AS IF TWO or three thousand of us boarded a World War II Victory ship, the *George S. Randall,* which was docked at the Brooklyn Army Terminal, and would transport us to Germany, where some of us would then be transported by train to France or Italy.

The fact that the Yankees would win the 1956 World Series that day by beating the Brooklyn Dodgers, yet again, made it easier for diehard Brooklyn fans like me and some of my Brooklyn buddies to leave the country. When we returned to the United States two years later, the Dodgers would have broken our hearts one final time by relocating to Los Angeles.

For some, it was the first time that they would see the ocean, but for me it was all so familiar. The army band played *Vaya Con Dios,* as the families of some of the men who lived near enough came to see us off. The guys who were from other parts of the country looked on wistfully as the parents, wives, or girlfriends of those of us who lived in the area appeared at the dock to bid us farewell. They thought that we were very fortunate to have our families there, and at first, I did too. Then we were told that our families would not be allowed to cross the barriers that separated us, so as we stood in formation I tried to locate my parents and Ann, and I did. We weren't able to hear one another over the playing of the band from that distance, so we mouthed I love you and goodbye and tried smiling to hold back the tears.

My father managed to slip through one of the barriers, and when I threw my duffle bag over my shoulder to step onto the gangplank, I felt some one grab my arm. I looked up surprised to see that it was my father. His eyes were watery and he quickly hugged me. "Be careful, Boy. I love you," he said. An M.P. came up quickly and ushered him back behind the barrier. "That's my son," I heard him say. "I just wanted to say goodbye."

"I understand, sir, but they're about to board and you'll have to watch from behind the barrier."

The soldiers around me looked on with smiles on their faces. I was experiencing the same feeling of embarrassment that I had felt when my parents had said goodbye to me on Whitehall Street. It had amused my buddies who were all around me when they heard my dad call me "Boy," when I was doing everything I could to be a man. My dad had always addressed me as Boy as far back as I could remember, but now I was in uniform and it made me wince. The day would come when I would realize that no matter what my age, I would always be his "Boy" and now all these long years later, I so miss hearing it. But on that day I stepped onto the ship, I turned and waved to my parents and Ann, and then I moved on.

A tugboat pulled us out of the slip and then nudged the bow of the ship and pointed us east up the Narrows toward the Atlantic.

I could see the flow of traffic on the Belt Parkway heading east toward Long Island and west toward New York City. My friends and I had walked the path along the parkway past Fort Hamilton numerous times on beautiful summer days. We had watched the fireworks from Coney Island, and we sprawled on the grass, watching ships, many of them troop ships or hospital ships returning from or going back to Europe, and now I had come full circle and I was on the troop ship.

We sailed past the 69th Street Ferry slips, and past the Fort Hamilton Veterans' Hospital. I could make out the familiar Bay 8th Street exit, our exit on the Parkway. Then I was sure that it was my family that I saw as tiny specks in the distance, as they waved their jackets as they stood close to the overpass that spanned the Bay Parkway crossing, as they promised that they would. Fifteen hundred soldiers, a sea of green stood on the deck, but my family swore that they saw me.

Life aboard the ship was a conglomeration of sounds, odors, and motion. There were the sounds of the ship's bells, whistles, and horns, which were sounded and tested throughout the crossing, as well as the raucous laughter and shouting of thousands of young men on this adventure. They were young boys barely out of high school. Their average age was about nineteen.

There was the constant motion of the ship as it plunged headlong now in the open sea, down one swell, and then churned upward on to the next, and all the time the ship rolled from left to right all day and all night. Sometimes late at night, I'd walk up to the deck and look up at the super structure of the ship as it rocked back and forth and as it was outlined against the night sky. The ship that had seemed so large when it was dockside in Brooklyn now seemed inadequate and small against the vast night sky and the deep ocean. I thought that it was insanity to challenge the sea by attempting to cross it in something as puny as the boat that we were in.

If we were to be swallowed up, it would be as if we had never existed. We would never be located and the boat and all of us would only exist in the minds of those who loved us. The ocean seemed to toy with this insignificant speck on the sea. Just a collection of half-inch plates and rivets all put together hurriedly during World War II, and which was all that kept us from the depth of the sea and eternity. At times, it seemed impossible to believe that everything would hold together in face of the unrelenting buffeting of the sea against the ship.

There was the odor of the combination of diesel fuel and ocean air on deck. Below deck, there was the aroma of food from the galley, along with the smell of exhausted and over used urinals and toilets clogged with paper and cigarette butts. The urinals appeared to be nothing more than bathtubs. Using them was an adventure because they seemed to be always clogged. The constant rolling and pitching of the ship caused the clogged and fouled water to rush down from one end and up to the other and then to splash up and slush down, making it dangerous to use the urinals except if you had an amazing sense of timing and terrific bladder control as well.

The commodes were even greater adventures for the troops. Some of the more creative pranksters on the ship with too much time on their hands, had devised a way to break up the monotony of the crossing by making a floating raft of toilet paper which they would then set on fire. The raft of flame was then floated down a five inch pipe on its slow and steady journey past each commode and out to sea. Anyone unfortunate enough to be sitting on the commode when the pyromaniacs were in action would be launched off the commode as the flames floated by, while everyone screamed with laughter. It gave new meaning to the expression, "taking a hot one." It got to the point where you wouldn't attempt to use the commode unless you had a friend who you could trust to play fireman, who would stand watch and alert you at the first sign of someone rolling up toilet paper with a lighter in his hand, and you would do the same for him.

All of that, along with the ubiquitous stench of vomit from the hundreds of seasick soldiers blended with the body odor of the troops, on a ship not provided with showers except for the Navy crew, quickly overwhelmed the ship's inadequate ventilation system, and made the trip memorable.

The stairways were almost straight up and down, and were better described as narrow ladders rather than stairways. They were challenging to use not only because of the design but because of the constant pitching and rolling of the ship.

On our first day out, and shortly after losing sight of the coast, someone did topple off the top of the stairway onto the steel plates below, and had to be evacuated by helicopter to Newfoundland for medical treatment. We had to turn back toward the coast so we lost a day or two while the ship's carpenters constructed a platform on the fantail of the ship. A helicopter landed on the newly constructed platform and took the injured soldier away for treatment.

Once we got under way again, it was pointed out that the S.S. United States was a few miles off on our starboard side heading east as we were. Fortunately, it wasn't a race, because seven days later we saw the S.S. United States again. This time she was on our port side heading west after delivering her passengers and cargo to her European destination and now after taking on new passengers and different cargo, she was making her way back to New York. And we, like the little engine that could, just plowed on, until we entered the English Channel on the final leg of our journey. I was fascinated by the sight of the white cliffs rising abruptly out of the channel. It was obvious to see how the cliffs had served as a natural fortress of protection from invading armies over the centuries. They were a natural deterrent and protection for the English on their island nation.

I couldn't help remembering the line from the World War II song that said, "There'll be bluebirds over the white cliffs of Dover tomorrow when the world is free." Now we waited for an English pilot to board our ship to guide us through an area of the channel still littered with the wreckage of ships from that recent war. Some of their super structures were clearly visible where they still protruded above the surface of the water, although the human carnage beneath the waves was left to your imagination. The price of freedom had not come cheaply. The pilot steered us clear of the danger posed by that graveyard of ships, and twelve days after we left Brooklyn, we docked in Bremerhaven, Germany.

I stood on deck with Frank Nanci, who had been seasick from the moment that the ship began to move away from the pier in Brooklyn until the moment that we docked in Bremerhaven. Frank had remained in his bunk for the whole twelve days of the crossing and he had subsisted exclusively on premium crackers that I would bring him from the galley. He would curse me out on the occasions when I had forgotten to bring them to him, and he looked emaciated as we stood on the deck with all of our gear waiting for the gangplanks to be lowered.

"Achtung, achtung," a voice said over a loudspeaker and continued on in German. "We're here," I said to Frank.

"We're here?" They're gonna bury me here if they don't lower that gangplank soon so I can get something to eat."

Suddenly a fleet of black taxicabs pulled up to the dock. The doors of the cabs opened and dozens of women emerged from the cabs, waving at crewmembers who waved back from the deck and shouted to the women with whom they seemed to be familiar.

I looked down in disbelief. I had heard some of the older guys talking about prostitutes while growing up in Brooklyn, but I had dismissed their stories when I realized that most of their talk was bragging. But the scene on the dock was intimidating.

"What the hell is that?" I asked Frank.

"Looks to me like they're all prostitutes," Frank said.

"Do you think all of them are?" I asked.

"All these sailors seem to know them and I don't think they sent their wives here," Frank answered. "When the hell are they gonna lower that gangplank?"

On the way across, a grizzled old sergeant had warned us not to engage with hookers at the dock or by a train station. "When we land, they'll come out of the woodwork. Those are always the oldest and the ugliest ones. They take and they give. They'll take your money and they'll give you a dose. Wait until you get settled in. Then you'll find younger frauleins, and you'll be less likely to take away something more than memories. You guys might have missed the war, but there's a lot of other ways to get even with Hitler. Wait, you'll see."

The gangplank was finally lowered, and the sailors rushed down and got into the cabs with the women, and disappeared while the rest of us picked up our gear and made our way down. All of the guys who had boarded the ship with me were replacements and so most of us were going to different places.

Frank and I had become close friends over the last five months, but now we made our goodbyes. He was going to France and I was going to Kaiserslautern as a clerk in a medical unit.

"Well this is it, Frank," I said as we shook hands.

"No it's not," he said, "everyone wants to see Paris, so we'll see it together. We'll take a leave and do it."

"It's a date," I said. "We'll get settled down and we will pick a time to do it."

We exchanged addresses, hugged one another and promised to take leave and meet again in Paris, but we both knew that a meeting in Paris was probably unlikely, and this was most likely a farewell.

The army had given each of us a box lunch, which consisted of a bacon, lettuce and tomato sandwich, an apple, and an orange drink. It was the same lunch that Sergeant Russo had provided me when I flew home from Camp Drum, so although there was a vast difference between the army and the National Guard, they seemed to have the same caterer.

A few of the men had eaten very little over the last week or two because of being seasick. They wolfed their sandwiches down, and gladly accepted a half-eaten sandwich or apple if it were offered to them. It was amazing to see how quickly they recovered from being seasick the moment that they stepped off the ship.

Everyone going to Kaiserslautern boarded the train and I knew most of them because we had gone through our second eight weeks of training at Fort Dix. I stared out of the train's window as we made our way through German towns and villages. It was suppertime, and as the train moved along, I was able to peek into the dimly lit homes of German families, almost expecting that life in those homes would be very different from life in my part of the world. My provincial upbringing had convinced me that even other Americans, not from New York and not Italian, were different, so I didn't really know what to expect in a foreign country with a foreign language, and from a people so recently removed from a disastrous war. Despite all of my curiosity, I was soon asleep, waking only when the bouncing of the train caused my hand supporting my head to slip off the windowsill.

CHAPTER 13

IT WAS SUNDAY MORNING WHEN WE ARRIVED AT the Bahnhof in Kaiserslautern. Bahnhof I learned was the German name for railroad station. Most of the guys who were on the train with me were met by a soldier who would drive them to their new assignment. They were all going to a Headquarters Company in Kaiserslautern. I was the only one going to a medical unit and the person who was to pick me up had not arrived yet. We said our goodbyes and my friends all boarded the truck and I was left waiting for my ride.

For five months, I had lived among thousands of uniformed men, and there were times when I felt alone in that crowd, but I truly never felt as alone as I felt at that moment. I stood in the terminal with my duffle bag waiting for someone in my new unit to come soon to pick me up. I was the only one in uniform, an alien in a foreign country, and in a place where a few years earlier there had been life and death struggles. I realized quickly that many of the wounds were still open, and sometimes they were still festering.

As I stood and waited, I saw a little boy who was perhaps one year old. He was wearing a blue knitted sweater with matching knitted pants. The little boy was running with both his fists clenched alongside of his shoulders as toddlers do on shaky legs. A man, whom I assumed to be his father, was chasing after the child. The little boy ran toward me, and before he could crash into my duffle bag, I put my hand out to help him avoid my bag. Just before the child reached my bag, his father snatched him off the ground. I looked up smiling because of the child's antics, and I found myself staring into his father's eyes. I looked at the man's face and the smile on my face froze. I spoke no German but I fully understood his father's language as he lifted his son away from me. The depth of the animosity in the man's eyes chilled me to my core. In that moment I saw all the pent up hatred and frustration of a defeated nation epitomized in the man's eyes. I was the hated antagonist and the interloper, and if he could have taken my heart, I believed at that moment that he would have. He picked up the child and walked away, but he continued to look at me over his shoulder.

"Are you Bilotti?" I turned to my left, and to my relief I saw an American soldier with private first class stripes on his arms. His appearance broke the palpable tension of the moment.

"Yeah, I'm Bilotti."

"I'm George Schneider," he said, extending his hand. "I'm company clerk with the 7779th Medical Group. Sorry if I kept you waiting."

I grasped his hand and said, "Man, you didn't get here a minute too soon."

"Why. What's going on?"

"Geez," I said, "I was just looking at that little kid," indicating with my head in the direction that the boy and his father were walking, which was a short distance off by this time.

"So what happened?"

"I smiled at the kid, and his old man looked at me like he wanted to cut my throat."

"You smiled. He's not smiling. We won and it's not easy to be a good loser. Hey, you might not be smiling either if it were reversed. Some of these people lost their families, forget about friends and property. It's understandable. You'll get a lot more of those looks, so get used to it. You're gonna be here for a while. But screw them. We didn't start the damned war, and we didn't start the first one either. You'd think that they would have learned, and what's more is that the ungrateful bastard should be happy that he's not in the Russian zone. Screw him. Here, let me have your duffle bag."

Before I could stop him, he grabbed my bag and threw it on his shoulder.

"No, no," I said. "Let me take it."

"That's okay," Schneider said, "I've got it now." I followed him out of the terminal to a jeep that was parked right outside.

We drove along roads and past fields that once had contained neat German neighborhoods, but now contained the scattered remnants and broken fragments of buildings that were all that remained. Sometimes we went past concrete walls still heavily pock marked by what appeared to be machine gun bullets.

"They've pretty much reconstructed the center of town," Schneider said. "By the time that you and I are ready to rotate, they'll probably have this end cleaned up too. You see them all the time salvaging bricks and stones. They don't waste a minute."

Ten minutes later we turned past the guardhouse and into Panzer Kaserne. Kaserne was the German term used to describe any military post where troops were stationed. This would be my home for the next nineteen months. At first glance, the place looked more like a college campus than it did a military post. It was neat and well kept and quite a contrast from the carnage that I had just witnessed.

"Check out these buildings," Schneider said. They were truly imposing buildings constructed of a rusty colored stone. "They call this Panzer Kaserne," Schneider said. "The krauts built it as a training center for tank commanders. They built them to last for a hundred years, and these buildings will probably last longer than that, but thank God, they were only in them for ten years. They're home for us now. Look up there."

He pointed up, and I looked over the massive doors located on each side of the building, which looked to be about two hundred feet long. Each building was two stories high with a short third story that might have been an attic. At the roof line above each of the doors was the bust of a German soldier, wearing the distinctive helmet that the German troops had worn in both world wars. The soldier's eyes were focused straight ahead staring into the distance. The expression he wore was one of arrogance and of a grim determination to achieve what they had accepted as the destiny of their nation. There could be nothing less than world conquest. It was inevitable and for a brief period, it looked as if they would succeed, but the dreams of victory and conquests had literally turned into ashes and ruination, and I had witnessed the final results outside the gate of Panzer Kaserne and in the expression on the face of the man in the Bahnhof.

"They didn't chisel out the busts over the buildings for some reason, but they did chisel out that swastika over the mess hall doors."

I looked toward the direction that Schneider was pointing. There was a building almost identical to the first two, except that it had only one entrance, which was located directly in the middle of the building. At the very top of the building, over the massive door, was an engraved eagle with its wings extended wide. The eagle was perched on a wreath of oak leaves. In the middle of the wreath were clearly discernable scars, where someone had chiseled out the swastika that had been in the center of the wreath. I remembered seeing that same emblem on the uniforms of German soldiers in the many World War II movies that I had seen.

"I think that the krauts used that building as an administrative building, but now it's our mess hall. That building in the front of us houses Headquarters Company, the army band, and us, the 7779th Medical Group. We call it the Triple Seven Nine." Schneider turned and pointed to the building opposite the headquarters building and across a wide beautifully manicured campus that would have made any Ivy League school proud.

"That building on the other side of the campus from us houses WACs, but before you get any ideas, the ones who aren't lesbians were whacked with the ugly stick. Most of them are clerical, but the real hard core drive trucks or work in the motor pool." He raised his eyebrows, "Like I said, try your luck in town."

"What's the 105 mm cannon doing in the middle of this beautiful setting?" I asked Schneider. I recognized the workhorse cannon immediately from my early days in the National Guard field artillery.

"They fire it on Memorial Day, the Fourth of July, and special occasions. It's also visible from the road. You know, just a reminder."

I followed Schneider as he jumped out of the jeep and lifted my bag to his shoulder. He waved me off as I tried to take the bag myself. He made his way to the building and used his other shoulder to shove open the massive door. We walked up a flight of wide stairs and through two inner doors located at the top of the stairwell. We turned right down the hallway and went about ten feet from the main stairway, to a door, which Schneider pushed open. He walked in and dropped my bag on the bedspring of a rack with a folded up mattress. There was a pillow and pillowcase, sheets, and two blankets on top of the doubled up mattress. There was a wall locker separating two racks, one of which I thought was probably mine. There was a footlocker at the foot of each bed.

Opposite the empty bed that I assumed to be mine, was another bed. Sitting on the bed, knees drawn up toward his chest to support a book that he was reading, was a frail-looking, lanky and bespectacled individual. It appeared to me that the three of us were the only ones in the building, and perhaps in the whole kaserne. It was that quiet. I imagined that everyone had left the area as you might expect that they would on a Sunday afternoon. I knew why Schneider and I were there. I had just arrived, and Schneider had picked me up at the Bahnhof, but this guy had chosen to remain behind with his book, while everyone else was out having a good time.

"Bilotti, this is Richard Avery. Avery, this is Nick Bilotti."

Avery looked at me, pushed his glasses up on his nose, and gave me a grunt and a nod.

"Well, I'm out of here," Schneider said. "I'll leave you two guys to get acquainted. Rich will fill you in on your other roommates. Have fun." And he was gone.

I looked over at Avery and thumbed my hand at the door from which Schneider had just exited.

"Nice guy," I said. "He wouldn't even let me carry my own duffle bag."

"Hmmm," Avery said, still not changing his position, knees up, his book resting on his legs. "That's probably the last time that he'll ever talk to you. That's what he does. He carries everyone's duffle bag the first time that he meets them. I got here three months ago and he carried mine. I don't think that we've exchanged five words since. He might not even remember you the next time that he sees you."

"Are you kidding?" I said. "He gave me the whole guided tour of the town and the kaserne, and he never stopped talking. I thought that he was a friendly guy."

"He drinks too much. There's scientific evidence that every time you consume alcohol you kill some brain cells. If that's true, there must be a graveyard on top of Schneider's brain because he's constantly drunk. You'll see. There's no such thing as moderation with a lot of these people."

"That's too bad," I said. Avery turned back to his book. I tried to make conversation. "Are you reading something interesting?" I asked.

"It's a book about anatomy," he said.

I walked over and looked down at the book, and there was a figure of a human being with plastic overlays. Since I had been in the army I had met lots of guys who were interested in the human anatomy, but all of them had studied it in *Playboy* magazine. He must have seen the confusion on my face and he started to explain.

"It's a long story. Let me give it to you before someone else does. I graduated from Stanford University and I was accepted into UCLA medical school. Before I could begin medical school, I received a draft notification from the army." He had a pained look on his face, and adjusted his glasses.

"I had no problem with that, but I appealed to my draft board to allow me to finish medical school first. I presented letters from my college professors, who implored my draft board to allow me to complete my studies, and that after I completed my medical training to then induct me into the army. I could certainly be more useful as a doctor in the army than what I'm doing now. It all made perfect sense to me, but nothing that I could say would change their minds, so I was drafted and now my whole life is on hold for two years. If they had listened to reason, there would have been no wasted time, which is pretty much what I feel that I'm doing now. I would be halfway through medical school by now, and in two years they could have inducted me and then I could have provided health care for the troops. So instead, I'm in the veterinary corps, doing sanitary inspections."

He stopped and looked at me but I didn't know him long enough to know if he was wasting his time. I didn't even know what his job was.

"I'm sorry for that long explanation but the whole thing was so unreasonable and such a waste of time. I can't get past my frustration."

"I don't know," I said. He was so down and I was trying not to make the situation worse but I was afraid that I would. "You never know whose life you're touching. You're probably doing a lot more good around here than you can imagine, even though you may think that you're just standing around wasting time. I read somewhere 'They also serve who only stand and wait.'"

His head shot up. "That's John Milton." With new enthusiasm, he asked, "Do you read?"

"Not as much as I'd like to." I didn't want to get his expectations too high.

"Have you gone to college?"

"No. Just high school," I lied. Well, it wasn't a total lie. I had gone to high school. I just didn't graduate.

He seemed a bit disappointed. He sagged back down. "I guess it's important to make sure that cooks and bakers wash their hands, and that they have clean fingernails, but you don't have to go to medical school for that line of work. So until this nightmare is over, I read books like this in an attempt to keep my edge. It's been a miserable experience, and all the more so because of lowlifes like Chance Lastings."

"Chance Lastings? Who's that?" I asked. Avery pushed

his glasses up on his nose and turned to me with a pained expression.

"Oh, unfortunately you'll know him soon enough. In fact, you'll hear him five minutes before you'll see him. He'll be howling, 'You ain't nothing but a hound dog', or some other ridiculous song. It'll be loud enough to be heard all the way from the main gate."

"So, he's in our medical group?" I asked.

"Not only is he in our medical group, but he's also in our room. He's in our lives. That's his rack over there." He pointed at a disheveled rack separated from mine by the wall locker between us. There were shoes, boots and socks scattered alongside as well as under the bed. There was a small step stool with a cylinder of Alka-Seltzer tablets and a glass, coated with a residue and dried froth inside of it. A pair of underwear dangled from the handle of an opened locker, and a pair of fatigues was piled in a heap in front of the locker, and the inside of the locker was in shambles.

It was a Sunday, and there are no requirements for good housekeeping on Sunday, as long as everything is ready for inspection on Monday, but it was difficult to imagine how rundown this guy's area had become in a few short hours, or how he would get everything squared away by Monday.

I looked up at Avery, who was looking at the expression of disbelief on my face.

"Is he always like this?" I asked, nodding my head toward the disaster area.

"Hmmm. Oh no. Maybe he knew that you were coming and he wanted to make a good first impression, because, as rule, it's usually a lot worse than this."

"It's hard to imagine that it could be a lot worse than this," I said.

"Lastings gets away with murder around here, because

Captain Davis is always bailing him out of trouble. Captain Davis is C.O. of Triple Seven Nine," Avery said.

"Does Captain Davis do that for everyone? Is that just the way he is?" I asked.

"No. Not really, but none of us require that kind of attention. You know, the squeakiest wheel gets the most grease. Most of the guys in the unit do their jobs in a conscientious way. Lastings keeps medical statistics, and Captain Davis keeps Lastings on a short leash. He's hardly ever out of Captain Davis' sight, but the weekends are another story."

"Why all of this special interest in one guy?" I asked.

Avery stared over at Lastings' area and began. "Lastings was caught stealing cars in East St. Louis. That's where he's from. It wasn't the first time that he had broken the law, and usually he got away with a slap on the wrist because he was a minor. The last time that he got into trouble he was no longer a minor, and he was about to be sent away for four years. Some bleeding heart judge decided to give him a choice. He could go to prison for four years or he could see if one of the branches of the military would accept him. The only one that would was the army, so the prisoners in some penitentiary somewhere were spared, while we have to deal with him every day in our unit and in our room no less."

"How do you know this personal stuff? I mean why would anyone talk about it? It's not something that you would want people to know I would think."

Avery pushed his glasses back and shook his head. "He is absolutely shameless. He speaks about all of these crimes in his life openly, as if they're a part of some great adventure that he wants to share with everyone for the laughs he gets. He has no remorse. It's all one big joke. He's just a lowlife.

"Once Lastings got here, he became Captain Davis' reclamation project. Captain Davis actually believes that there is hope for him. Davis is always joking with Lastings, and pep talking him. It's enough to make you sick. He calls him Last Chance, instead of Chance Lastings. The name is really appropriate. I think that Davis realizes how accurate he is even if Lastings doesn't, because the army is Lastings last chance. Captain Davis doesn't want Lastings to forget it. For all of the decency that Davis shows to Lastings, I know that somewhere along the line Lastings will let Captain Davis down. He doesn't miss an opportunity to make jokes about Captain Davis behind his back, of course. Captain Davis is black and no one is more prejudiced than Lastings. The man treats Lastings like a son and Lastings doesn't appreciate it. But why would that be a surprise to anyone? From what he says, Lastings has repeatedly let his biological parents down. Captain Davis means less to him than they did, so what do you expect?"

With that, Avery turned his attention back to his book, and I let down my rolled up mattress and began making up my bed. I emptied the contents of my duffle bag, and began hanging my uniforms up, and I put various items of clothing into my footlocker.

When I was satisfied that everything was squared away, as outlined in the army field manual, I lay back on my sack. Before I could doze off, I heard Avery close his book. I looked over at him.

"Were you sent to Fort Sam Houston for medical training?" he asked.

"No. I came here right from Fort Dix," I said.

"Was there medical training at Fort Dix?" And then, before waiting for me to answer, he said, "I wasn't aware that they had medical training facilities at Fort Dix."

"I didn't receive any medical training. I went to clerk/

typist school after basic training, and then I was shipped here. I was told that my job would be to work on medical records."

"Hmmm," Avery said. He pushed his glasses up on his nose. "Well, you're correct. There are medical records and statistics to be kept, but we also run a dispensary here, and it's pretty much like any major hospital's emergency room. We see every kind of illness, accident, or emergency that there is. We give immediate care and send them home. What we can't handle we send on to Landstuhl Army Hospital. To that extent, I have learned a lot here because you see all kinds of medical emergencies. Even the guys who keep the records have had some medical training. The problem for someone like you, without any prior medical training, is that once a month you'll be expected to pull emergency room duty in the dispensary. That usually begins on Friday morning, and runs through Monday morning. You get the rest of Monday off, and go to your regular job on Tuesday. And you do the whole routine over again in a month, but if they're short in the dispensary, you can spend lots of time there and not in an office."

That was the first time that I had heard that I would be expected to work in an emergency room in a dispensary, and I was starting to become a little anxious about the idea. I knew that once you became permanent party and no longer in training, you would be expected to pull what was called "C.Q.", which meant that you were in charge of quarters. That was like being a watchman in the building, answering phones and such, when everyone was away, but C.Q. in a critical care unit was something that I was unprepared for.

"What exactly will be expected of me when I pull C.Q?" I asked.

"What we typically see are bumps, breaks or bruises and

various health-related complaints. We go to scenes of accidents and assist there. We give inoculations and draw blood. Some of us stitch minor wounds. As I said, it's primary care. It's the same sort of things that you would see in any emergency room."

That job description only made things worse for me, although I could tell that it was probably the only thing about his military experience that Avery enjoyed, even if he probably would not admit to it.

"I've never done anything like that. I wouldn't know what the hell to do. Will the doctors know that I'm really a medical records person? Not a trained medic?"

Again, Avery looked me, and without the slightest sign of sympathy said, "When you show up for duty on that Friday morning, you'll be wearing whites, not combat fatigues. Everyone, including the doctors will think that you know what to do when they see you in that uniform. You don't want to tell the doctor that you're the great impostor. Friday is a busy day as a rule, especially if it falls on a payday, when most of the troops can't wait to be turned loose with all that money to burn. There should be all kinds of action in the dispensary, which will keep the doctors busy. If the doctor gives you an order, the last thing that he's going to want to hear from you is that you're a clerk/typist, and not really a medic."

"Oh my God," I said, "this could really get ugly."

"Well, it figures. They send a guy to clerk/typist school and then they expect him to perform as a medic in an emergency room. It would have been too reasonable to send you to a place without a hospital or a dispensary where all you were expected to do were medical records, or to give you a crash course in medical technology before sending you here. Even some on-the-job training would have helped. At least you would have learned how to give a proper inoculation, or how to draw blood, but that would have made too much sense, so we'll do it the army way. What a joke."

"Does everyone else have some medical training?" I asked.

"I've been here three months, and as far as I know, you're the only one that has none," Avery said.

I was just beginning to wonder where this was all going to take me, when the door burst open, and I knew instantly that this was Chance Lastings.

"Sheeit, Ovary! Y'all ain't moved an inch since I left this morning. Man, I thought that I'd come in here and find the room empty. Y'all ain't never gonna find a better time to go searching in the latrines and showers for Dial soap chips. Tell you the truth, Ovary, I was gonna leave y'all a chip myself, but I figured I could wash my butt a couple a more times before I left it. You know I switched to Dial soap just for y'all, and y'all tell everybody I ain't done nothing for y'all."

Avery avoided eye contact, determined to totally ignore his tormentor, and looked intently at his book.

Lastings looked to be about my age, and average height. He sauntered into the room. He was wearing civilian clothes and both of his hands were in his pockets. He had blue eyes and light brown hair, and a ruddy complexion. He reminded me of the actor, James Dean, or at least of how James Dean would have looked if he were playing a rascal.

"Hey, man. Y'all the new guy?" He stuck his hand out for me to shake, and introduced himself.

"I'm Chance Lastings, and don't believe a God damned thing ole Dick Ovary tells you. That boy is never serious. Always joking around. He keeps all the guys in stitches in this room. He's a funny guy. Ain'tcha Ovary?" he shook his head and laughed in feigned amusement.

"I'm Nick Bilotti," I said, as we shook hands.

"Hey, Nick," he said, as if he had known me all of his life, "do y'all believe that ole Ovary over there ain't never been to town unless he's on the job? No women, no fun. Come on Nick. That ain't even natural. Tell the truth."

I looked over at Avery. He glanced up, shook his head, and returned to his book.

"You know, Nick, I even asked ole Ovary if he wanted me to ask my schotz to set him up with one of her friends. Even one who liked books. Do y'all believe that he wouldn't answer me? I guess he couldn't tear himself away from the chapter on large intestines or something. Ain't that right, Ovary?" He laughed again.

"How 'bout you Nick? Let me give ya'll a tour of K-town."

"Thanks a lot, Chance. It's been a long day and I'm wiped. Some other time maybe," I said.

He seemed genuinely disappointed. "Okay, but I'm gonna hold y'all to it." He reached into his locker, pulled out two packs of cigarettes, and stuffed them into his jacket pocket.

"Hey Nick, one more thing. If y'all head down to the showers, make sure that you lock your things up. Ole yellow stain over there ain't sent nothing to the laundry since he's been here. I'm telling y'all, he ain't done it yet but things must be getting critical for him. I expect that pretty soon he'll be taken someone's drawers, and their shoe polish too, to paint the back of his heels to cover up the holes in his socks, and I seen him do it that tricky rascal. He ain't never gonna buy no new socks or underwear either, so watch your own.

"Okay, I'm off. Me and my schotz are gonna check out some new watering holes. Ovary keeps putting the best ones off limits, don't cha Ovary? Hey, Ovary! Are you listening to me? Turn to the next chapter. The one on bladders. Even I couldn't stop reading that one." He laughed again. "Hey, Nick. Welcome aboard. I'll catch y'all later. Oh, one more thing, Ovary. Don't bother cleaning up my area. I'll do it before I sack in, heh, heh, heh."

He turned toward the door, and was gone as suddenly as he had appeared.

It was silent for a while, and I had completely forgotten my apprehension about pulling C.Q. in the dispensary because of my whirlwind introduction to Chance Lastings.

I looked over toward Avery. It was an awkward moment. He had been the target of all of Lastings' barbs. I shuffled some of my gear around and decided to break the awkward silence.

"Well, you weren't exaggerating when you described Lastings to me."

"I have never had difficulty with words," Avery said, "but sometimes I'm speechless when I try to put into words what a contemptible a human being he is."

"What was all that talk about shoe polish and underwear and soap chips? He kept rambling on. I couldn't make sense out of all of that, and the other part about you putting his favorite watering holes off limits?"

Avery looked up, straightened his glasses and said, "I'm in the veterinarian section of the medical group. Part of my job is to be sure that all of the facilities used by the troops conform to the sanitary standards set by the army. We check everything from food quality and all sanitary conditions, right down to fingernail and skin checks on post, as well as off. If we determine that there are unsanitary conditions on or off post, we make sure that the situation is corrected. If the problem exists on post, it is to be corrected immediately. If the condition exists in an establishment off post, the place is put off limits immediately, and they are given one month to correct the problem. After a month, we return. If we are satisfied that the problem no longer exists, we return the establishment to acceptable status. If we aren't satisfied, the place is permanently off limits, and any serviceman caught using the facility is subject to company punishment and possible loss of rank. There is a listing of places that are off limits on the bulletin boards in every company. The whole point is to keep guys from getting infectious diseases and spreading it around to everyone, and it works.

"I know that you only met Lastings for a few minutes, but having met him, what kind of dives would you imagine that he would be comfortable in? If you accept his invitation to have him show you around, you'll get to know firsthand. I have no personal knowledge about the places where he hangs out but I seem to run into them by simply checking out every sleazy dump on the wrong side of town. So, when I gig them, and put them off limits, he comes roaring at me as if I were doing something personal to make his life miserable.

"I told him not to flatter himself into thinking that he is ever on my mind, even when I have no alternative but to be in the same room with him. I try to never give him a thought, and I don't, but I do my job and that brings us into more conflict. He's just obnoxious. Hmmm."

My question had given Avery an opportunity to vent all of the pent-up frustration that he had held back when Lastings had made him the brunt of his attack. We sat in silence for a while and I asked, "What did Lastings mean when he said that he expected to find you picking up Dial soap chips in the latrine?"

The anger and frustration that Avery had worn on his face seemed to be replaced by self-consciousness. He fidgeted with his book and pushed his glasses up on his nose.

"It's a long story. I'm not sure that you really want to hear it."

He saw that I continued to look at him, and after a pause

he said, "Well, I told you how angry and disappointed I was because of the army disrupting my life and preventing me from going to medical school after I had been accepted for medical training. When that happened, I vowed to treat these two years as two dead years in my life. I would fulfill my obligation to the best of my ability, but I would not bring a damned thing to it. I would not bring a single item of clothing of my own, but I would wear only what was provided to me. I would not spend a penny replacing anything, unless it was absolutely impossible to avoid doing so. I've had to buy toothpaste, shaving cream and blades, but guys leave soap chips in the latrine, and I have yet to buy soap in the year that I have been in the army.

"I use the laundry sparingly and wash most things by hand. I don't want a laundry bill if I can avoid it.

"And then there's the underwear remark and old yellow stain comment. They were passing *The Caine Mutiny* around here some time ago, and I would never have imagined that Lastings would ever read a book, but Lastings was on company punishment for some sort of infraction and confined to quarters. Can you believe that caveman actually read the novel? That remark that he made, calling me 'old yellow stain,' was a reference to when Captain Queeg threw a yellow dye marker into the water and ran, rather than stay and chance being hit by artillery fire."

"Oh yes," I said. "I read the book. So is he calling you a coward?"

"No. He's just a wise guy. He's referring to my underwear. I told you that I don't use the laundry much. Well, he knows that I wash anything that I can wash myself by hand, so he calls me old yellow stain among other things."

"Oh, I see," I said, as if all of this was perfectly normal

behavior, but I was beginning to feel as though I was a crew-member on the *Caine*.

I was trying to make sense out of all of this, and I took a minute for it all to sink in. I lay back on my bunk and decided to ask one final question.

"Hey, Richard. Why did Lastings tell me to guard my shoe polish?"

Avery slid his back down and adjusted his glasses again. He shook his head slowly back and forth, and then I guess he decided to explain in the hope that I would understand.

"I've worn holes in the back of my black dress socks, and rather than buy new socks, I put black shoe polish on the backs of my feet so that you can't see the holes. That's all there is to it."

"Oh, is that all there is?" I said, acting as if everybody blacked the backs of their feet when they had worn holes in their socks.

"Yeah. And Lastings makes a big deal of it. He tells it to everybody."

The sun was starting to set, and I lay on my bunk trying to process all that I had seen and heard, not only since I had checked into my room, but since I had landed in Bremerhaven.

I asked Avery for directions to the shower room. I left my locker open, and I must admit that I was a little apprehensive in doing so, but I wanted to show Avery that I didn't put any credence in Lastings' accusations about him, but I believe that I would have locked it if Lastings was the only one in the room.

The shower room was located downstairs on the main floor of the building. As I was about to go down the stairs and through the huge inner doors, the same ones which George Schneider earlier had led me to show me my new quarters, I heard loud talking and raucous laughter coming from the room, which was separated from my room by the doors. I walked past the doors and stood outside of the room from where the noise was coming. The voices and the laughter sounded familiar. Could it be? I opened the door and looked in. It was Gene, it was Al, and it was Roger. It was all of the guys who I had gone to school with in Fort Dix. It was the same guys who had sailed to Germany with me, and then said goodbye to me as we had parted ways on the Bahnhof early that morning.

Al looked up when I entered the room, "Nick! What the hell are you doing here?" and then they all jumped off their racks and came toward me greeting me and smacking me on the back.

"The hell with this," I said. "I told them over there that there was no way that I was gonna spend the next year and a half in Germany without my buddies. We've been through so much and together too long, so I walked out of the building, found a jeep and tracked you guys down."

They looked at me and they were skeptical, and then Al said, "Get the hell out of here. What are you doing here?"

"You're not buying my story?"

"We're waiting," Al said.

"Okay, but I hate when I have to tell the truth," so I explained. "We're in the same kaserne, only I'm in the Triple Seven Nine and you guys are Headquarters Company. I heard your voices. Man, I couldn't believe it. We're together." Their room was an open bay about twice the size of mine and contained eight bunks.

"Where are you?" Gene asked.

"How many guys are in there?" Al asked.

"My room is right on the other side of the doors. There are four of us. I met two of my roommates already. A couple of weirdos," I said.

"Maybe we can squeeze another rack in here and you can be with us," Roger said.

"Let's wait awhile and see what happens first," I said, "but that would be nice."

We spent the rest of the time catching up on what had happened since we parted that morning and talking about our first impressions of Germany, Then a few of us headed for the showers and then back to our rooms to turn in.

When I returned from the shower, Avery was in a deep sleep. His book still propped up on his lap. I was convinced that Lastings was nuts, but I was also convinced that Avery was at least eccentric.

It had been a long and strange first day, and I was happy that my friends were on the other side of the hall. If this was the way that it began for me in Germany, I wondered what else was in store for me. I made the sign of the cross, said a Hail Mary, and fell asleep before I could start another.

CHAPTER 14

I SETTLED INTO MY NEW SURROUNDINGS PRETTY quickly, and except for Lastings constantly baiting Avery, things were relatively quiet. Four of us shared the room. Besides Avery, Lastings, and me, there was Bob Duncan. Bob had been a graduate student pursuing a doctorate in mathematics before he was drafted. Both men had found their continuing education interrupted. Their situations were similar, but they could not have been more different from each other if not for that. Avery was serving under duress whereas Bob saw his stint in the army as a minor bump in the road.

Bob's father had been a B-17 pilot during World War II, and ironically had flown multiple bombing missions over the Frankfurt/Kaiserslautern area of western Germany. Bob would teasingly thank his father for having a bad enough aim so that the bombs he dropped had missed Panzer Kaserne, assuring Bob of a beautiful place to stay while he was in Germany.

"Yes" Avery added, "and his poor aim also spared the dives where Lastings hangs out. I'm certain that they were there at the time of the bombings and probably long before. No decent German will ever forgive your father for that oversight. Put that in your letter the next time that you write to him," Avery added.

The four of us were a strange, improbable group of characters thrown together by chance. Two were on their way to doctorates, one in medicine and the other in mathematics. Another was a candidate for reform school or even worse, and I was a high school dropout who had made such a mess of my early life. Instead of trying to figure out how to turn things around, I had run away from everyone and everything while taking refuge in the army. I was too embarrassed to ever admit the truth to my roommates so I continued to live the lie, and except for the fact that I was not a thief, I felt that I had more in common with Lastings than I did with Avery or Duncan.

Avery, Duncan, and I passed the time away in the evenings speaking about home, family and the events of the day, while Lastings was usually out somewhere in town celebrating. He was usually sober enough to drag himself back to the kaserne before lights out at 10 P.M., and then he would strip naked in the dark and throw himself onto his bunk. There were times when Lastings would come back to the room so drunk that he would stumble around in the darkness, speaking and cursing to himself. During bad episodes of heavy drinking, he would vomit on the floor near his area, forcing one of us to open all the windows allowing the cold winter air into the room as we lay shivering under our blankets.

The following day, Lastings would be apologetic and humble even toward Avery as he cleaned up his mess, but that behavior only widened the gap between Lastings and the three of us.

"I'm telling you, Bob and you too, Nick," Avery said, "we can't keep putting up with Lastings' behavior. He's contrite for a few hours after he vomits all over the room. He thinks that he's back in our good graces and after a few days when he thinks that we forgot about how we had to freeze to death before he cleaned up his mess, he starts his bad behavior all over again."

"You're right," Bob said, "but what can we do? Are you gonna try to appeal to that guy or to reason with him? It won't work. He's not gonna change because we'd like him to. People don't change for others. If they change at all, they change because they want to change for themselves, and Lastings doesn't want to. He's enjoying himself, except for the hangovers that is."

"I have a good idea," I said. "The next time that he comes in and starts puking all over the place, I'll get up to open the windows, but this time I'll pick him up and throw him out. He'll be so drunk that even if he survives the fall, he'll never know what happened to him."

Bob looked at me and laughed, "You're right. That would solve the problem."

"The two of you have to get serious," Avery said, "and I don't know if it will work or not, and I really don't care, but it can't be business as usual for Lastings when he goes on his binges. What I'm suggesting that we do, and it won't work unless we all do it, is this. The next time that Lastings comes in here drunk and disruptive, we freeze him out worse than the way he freezes us out when he causes us to turn this room into an igloo. And we don't freeze him out for a day or two. No one acknowledges his presence until and unless there's a change in his behavior."

"So we're gonna wage our own cold war," I said.

"We have to," Avery said. "Are you both in agreement?"

Bob looked from me to Avery, raised his arm and said, "All for one, and one for all."

We didn't have to wait very long before Lastings returned to the room totally soused and we put our plan into operation. The next morning Lastings tried to make small talk as he usually did after one of his drunken bouts. He was contrite and polite to the three of us but he noticed quickly that none of us responded or even looked in his direction. To us, he was a ghost.

"Hey, Nick man, what's going on?" he asked me. Not responding was one of the most difficult things that I had ever done. I had to make a concerted effort not to answer, but we had made a pact, and even though it was killing me to keep my end up, I did.

That went on for quite some time and before long Lastings attempted to break the ice by speaking to either Bob or me, individually, but never to Avery. One day he tried to interject an idea into our three-way conversation and the three of us continued as if he wasn't there. At that point, Lastings stormed out of the room.

"Guys," I said, "I don't know about either of you and I don't know exactly what effect it's having on Lastings, but this intentional rudeness is killing me."

"Nick, don't quit on us now," Avery said. "Bob is right. We'll never get him to change completely but maybe we can get him to modify his behavior. Not only will it make things better for us in this room, but we'll be doing Lastings a favor too."

After that, Lastings spent less and less time in the room except to sleep. Not seeing Lastings until the lights were out could not have made Avery any happier. At least for a while Avery wasn't subject to Lastings' barbs, although I must admit that even though Lastings brought it upon himself, I felt sorry for him.

Eventually Lastings' behavior did seem to modify a bit. He would still come in to the room a bit tipsy now and then, but he seemed to stop drinking to the point of being blind drunk and vomiting all over the room, so Bob and I suggested that we let up on the freeze a little.

"We said that we wanted Lastings to modify his behavior,

and I believe he has," Bob said. "Let's open things up a little for him. What do you think, Nick?"

"I agree," I said, "and it's not like we can't go back to the cold war if he backslides and we need to, but I think that we're all ready for a thaw." I looked over at Avery.

"Well, it looks as if I'm outvoted, so I'll go along with both of you, but if he turns this room into a vomitory again, I'm warning you both, a freeze out might not work after this, and then we'll have to take more drastic measures, so reluctantly, okay."

I tried to imagine what drastic measures we could take if freezing Lastings out would be ineffective in the future, and then just before Christmas of 1956, I found out. Avery, Lastings, and I were in the room. Lastings began telling me about how good a wrestler he was in junior high and high school. Avery ignored the conversation and continued reading his medical books.

"Let me show ya'll this hold, Nick. Nobody can get out of it. They always usta give up when I put it on them. I wrapped them up so tight, they couldn't move their eyeballs."

He walked over to my bunk and I allowed him to clamp his arm around my waist and to twist my arm behind me, and it hurt. I managed to squeeze out, but he pursued me, and we wrestled but it was all in good fun, with Avery seeming to ignore the goings on and still absorbed in his book. Then I lifted Lastings off the ground and carried him to the windows, which could be opened wide left and right.

"Okay buddy boy, out the window you go," I said, as I carried the struggling Lastings toward the windows.

Suddenly, Avery jumped off his rack and rushed to the windows, opening them as wide as they could go. "Throw him out Bilotti, throw him out!"

Lastings and I had been laughing the whole time, but

now when we looked at Avery, who stood by the opened windows, our laughing stopped. There was a serious expression on his face and in his eyes that was not part of the game that Lastings and I were playing. I realized that Avery really wanted me to throw Lastings out of the windows and Lastings saw it too.

"Nick, Nick, put me down!" he pleaded and I did.

Lastings moved away from the windows toward his rack, and I pulled both the windows closed.

"Nick, what the hell is wrong with that boy?" Then looking at Avery, he asked, "What the hell is wrong with ya'll, Ovary?"

Avery didn't answer, but went back to his bunk and his book. After a few minutes, Lastings left the room, and as I lay on my rack, I thought about what had just taken place. Two things were apparent to me. I didn't realize the depth of Avery's hatred for Lastings, and that Avery wasn't kidding. He wanted me to pitch Lastings out of the window.

CHAPTER 15

AT THE END OF EACH WORKDAY DURING THE WEEK, many of the men would leave the kaserne and go out for some sort of revelry. Others were homebodies and remained in their rooms and on their bunks, mostly out of loyalty to their wives or girlfriends. Avery was in another category and had absolutely no desire to see anymore of Germany than what his job caused him to see in the course of his workday. Occasionally Avery would go to see a movie on post or he would take a trip to the main P.X., but otherwise he never left Panzer Kaserne.

"I'll come back to Europe on my own someday with my wife and my family. I'll go to places and see things of my choosing and in my time without the army looking over my shoulder. Until then, I'm happy reading my books and checking the days off on my calendar until I can leave here and start my medical training," he would say, and although we didn't always understand that line of thinking, Avery was so firm in it that neither Duncan nor I ever questioned it.

Bob Duncan received a letter from home and wrote a letter to his girlfriend every day, and Bob was too much of a "straight arrow", as we referred to guys like him, to go to town to party.

Although I didn't write a letter every day, I received one from Ann each day, and she and the promises that we made were too fresh in my mind for me to go off to town for fun, so the three of us were often in the room together.

Avery and Duncan would have long soul searching, often philosophical discussions, and at such times, I was mostly a listener absorbing much of what they had to say. On one such occasion, the conversation turned to the subject of life and afterlife. Avery declared himself as being born a Christian but now he was an agnostic. Duncan was a practicing Catholic.

"To me, life is little more than a cruel joke," Avery said.

"In what way?" Duncan asked.

"How can you understand the meaning of life with all the unspeakable misery and suffering there is in the world? Add to that the contemplation of your own death and the death of those whom you love. Their deaths concern me more than my own. Then there's the finality of death for eternity, as if you and they had never even existed. It's an absurd joke and it's hard to make sense of any of it. It would almost have been better not to have been born."

Avery stared out the window. It was obvious that for a person who believed that he had the answers for most things that he was having great difficulty finding answers for the questions that he posed. He adjusted his glasses and looked from Duncan to me. He appeared to be reluctant to continue, but finally he began.

"It seems to me that tragedy is the rule of life. Tragedy dominates our lives. It is the most vivid of all of our memories. It leaves the greatest impression. Yes, tragedy dominates and it is interrupted by brief periods of happiness." He paused again.

"I didn't come to these conclusions haphazardly," Avery said. "I had a younger brother. I was two years older than he." He smiled at the thought of the little boy. "He was a cute kid."

"My mother took the both of us shopping one day. As we

passed by a store window, I saw a plastic gun that shot out rubber-tipped darts. You know the kind with rubber tips that stick onto flat surfaces.

"I begged my mom to buy it for me, and she said no at first, mostly because she didn't like guns whether they were toys or not. She asked me to choose something else but my mind was set on the gun. I just had to have it, so finally she gave in." Avery pushed his glasses back and nodded his head in remembrance.

"I loved that damned gun. I loved the sound that the spring made when you forced the plastic shaft back into the barrel so that it could launch the rubber-tipped missile. It sounded real to me. I loved it when I was able to get the rubber suction cups to stick onto the refrigerator or the glass doors in the family room.

"Then, one day, while my brother and I were playing in the family room, and I can see it happening so clearly in my mind, I heard funny sounding gurgling and wheezing sounds coming from behind me. I turned to look and there was my little brother lying rigid on his back. He was gagging and turning blue. I ran to him but I didn't know what to do. All I could do was to shake his arm and call his name." After a pause he continued.

"I screamed for my mother and she came running in. She too, began screaming at what she saw, only now my brother was unresponsive; no more sounds coming from him just frothing from the mouth. My mother picked my brother up and began shaking him. She tried to open his mouth to breathe into it, and to look into it. She was frantic, and all I could do was stand there and watch them both, with my hands covering my ears.

"By the time help arrived, it was too late. That was it. He was gone that fast. My brother had put one of the rubber tips into his mouth and it had lodged in his throat. It was my gun." He looked over at Bob and me.

"My mother was never the same after that. Never once did she blame me, but she never stopped blaming herself for making the decision to allow the gun into the house."

Avery paused awhile. He continued to look into the darkness of the open window as he relived every detail of his painful past. Neither Duncan nor I said anything. We understood the inadequacies of words at such a time.

Avery turned toward us and continued. "They say that time is a great healer, but the years became more and more difficult for my mother. She continued to pay attention to me and to my father, and my father did all he could do to help her through her bouts of depression. We sought professional help. We took vacations. But nothing seemed to work for long. One day I overheard my mom telling my dad that try as she might to accept what had happened and to move on with her life, and even though she loved the both of us, what she missed the most was the one that she didn't have any longer. It was a constant yearning for my brother.

"When I was fifteen, I came home from school one day to see police cars in front of our home. A policeman met me by the front door. I rushed in and I saw several officers in the living room questioning my dad. I was helpless once again and I looked around in disbelief one more time, and I slowly comprehended that my mom had taken an overdose of her prescription medicine, and despite all that the paramedics could do, she had died in the ambulance. She died in the ambulance," he repeated, nodding his head faintly as if it were all still sinking in.

"My dad had a hard time accepting my mother's death as a suicide, and he continued to say that it had to have been an accidental overdose, since there was no note.

"Mom would never leave us that way," he would say.

"I told you that neither of my parents ever blamed me for my brother's death. They continued to be as affectionate to me as they had ever been, but I have never been able to put that damned plastic gun that I just had to have out of my mind. It's difficult to comprehend how something that seemed so innocent, so insignificant at the time, like a toy plastic gun, could change all of our lives so dramatically and so painfully forever. It's just unreasonable. It's a joke. It doesn't make sense." Avery looked away from us and I could see that time had done very little to heal him.

I looked over at Bob Duncan, who was rarely at a loss for words, but he remained silent after Avery finished his story. I knew that Bob was a man of strong religious convictions having heard him express them from time to time during some of his discussions with Avery. I thought that this might be the time that he would say something about turning to faith, as many do in times of crisis, but that would be difficult to do with Avery who claimed to be an agnostic. So Bob remained quiet.

I had always felt out of my league when I listened to the conversations between Bob and Avery but I had, like everyone, given some thought to the scary prospect of death because it was inevitable. I preferred not to think too much about it because there was only so much that any of us could do to avoid it. Much of it was out of our control. I'd rather think of things about which I had more control.

But before I took the time, as I usually did, to think about whether I should say something rather than to risk sounding silly to the two of them, I said, "Do you know, Rich, you're right. It does sometimes seem as if life is absolutely meaningless, especially if you search for meaning in light of the tragedy that you have just told to Bob and me. It does seem as if you're dropped into the world, and then you're told to handle impossible situations that can tear you apart. So many things are beyond our control. Crap happens to you through no fault of your own, and if you find yourself in situations like that often enough, it can only take one such impossible situation for you to become cynical and walk away from it all. I think that your mom was probably at that point where she couldn't handle it anymore, so she just walked away. That's why I believe that it makes no sense to look for the meaning of life. You're not gonna find it. Where have you ever read or heard someone give you a satisfactory explanation for the meaning of life? You guys read all the time. Show me where anyone has ever answered the question satisfactorily about what the meaning of life is, or where his definition has given you peace of mind."

I looked from Avery to Duncan and expected to see polite but perhaps dismissive expressions as they listened to what I was saying, but they seemed to be paying attention, so I continued.

"How can there be any meaning for what happened to your brother and your mother? I don't want to speak for Bob, but I think that Bob's message might be to keep the faith, and that in times of crisis only faith can get us through. They say that there is something better for all of us somewhere or someplace else. Well, I hope that there is. Maybe words like 'keep the faith' or 'he is in a better place' have meaning for people of strong faith, but I'm not sure about how much comfort words like that would be to you right now, Rich." I stopped because I needed to get what I was saying together.

"So let's accept that life is often or even mostly meaningless. We didn't ask for it, but we're here and now we to have to deal with it. As miserable as we might be, most of us put up with the misery, because let's face it, we prefer it to death.

Death is so damned final and I guess there are some, but very few of us, who are absolutely certain that there's something more after we die, and most of us are hesitant to find out. It scares the hell out of most of us.

"To me the question we should ask is do I have purpose in my life, rather than searching for the meaning of life? Meaning before purpose is backward. Do you understand what I'm trying to say?" I asked, but neither of them answered so I continued to try to explain.

"Purpose gives meaning to life. It has to be purpose first and then meaning comes. Purpose is up to you. You have to find your own purpose. Nobody decides that for you. It isn't there automatically, and if you choose the purpose of your own life, that puts meaning in your life, but not in anyone else's life. Everyone has to give his own life meaning by finding purpose, which is what most of us are looking for all the time."

What a mess I'm making of this, I thought. I was embarrassed listening to myself. How many times had I repeated the words "meaning" and "purpose?"

"I'm screwing this all up. I'm not good at this and I'm repeating myself."

"No. Go ahead," Duncan said.

"Look, Rich, I don't mean to offend, and I can't even begin to imagine the horror that you and your family went through and are probably still dealing with, but human beings have had tragedies even worse than yours since we crawled into and then out of caves. Some dealt with their problems by killing themselves, which is perhaps what your mother did, but most did not. Instead, most confronted their obstacles and their grief, and moved on and tried to figure out where they would go from there. They were trying to find new purpose.

"They needed purpose even if their purpose was simply

to get themselves to the next day. In your mother's case, purpose could have been continuing for you and your dad, as your dad seems to have done, but your mom probably wasn't thinking clearly at that point. Your father had a different reaction from what you have said. Your father's purpose after the tragedy of your brother seems to have been to carry on for you and for your mother. Maybe if your mom had been thinking clearly, she could have been a comfort to you and your dad or even some comfort to others who were in situations similar to hers. There are lots of people in similar situations who need comfort from others who have gone through what your family went through. We'll never know for sure, but you seem to believe that her death was not an accident and your father liked to believe that it was an accident. If your mom did take her own life that would have just added more pain to you and your father, but probably in her state of mind she didn't see that. She was probably so overwhelmed with grief that no one was able to get through to her." I was searching for the words.

"Think of all the guys who came here who were just like us, young and looking toward the future, and now are under crosses. Every member of their families had to deal with their loss, and most of them did. Some must have taken their own lives when they got the news, but the vast majority went on with a new purpose.

"Do you remember the guy that I told you about at the Bahnhof? The guy that I said looked as if he wanted to cut my heart out? Can you imagine the misery that he has experienced in his life, especially after such a short time after the war? It was obvious to me that he was still miserable and full of hate. Well, he had purpose. It appeared to me to be a negative purpose, especially because I believed that it was directed toward me, but it kept him going. Hopefully, he'll get over it and find a more positive purpose, but some people never do. There are cases when negative purposes can do just the opposite and take meaning away from life rather than to put meaning into your life. It's like a drunk who gets up every day and then his purpose is to get drunk again. That's a purpose but it's a negative one. Only positive purposes make life worth living so we have to find them." I was done and I was quietly drained.

Duncan looked at Avery and said, "Hopefully we can find our positive purpose and we can make the most of the time that we are granted. I know, Rich, that you have positive purpose, as Nick put it, and someday you will achieve wonderful things as a doctor. I'm a Catholic and you're agnostic, but I also believe that someday that you will receive the same reward that I expect if we live the positive life. I believe that God knows what we feel at our worst because I believe that we have a loving God who experienced firsthand some of the pain and misery, and the feeling of being alone and abandoned that we all feel at times. We just have to stay focused and positive. The bonus, I believe, is that He promised us something better than this life. There has to be a reward for fighting the good fight. It separates human beings from all others."

Why didn't I just say that? I thought.

"Hey, Nick," Avery said, "what's your purpose?"

"Right now it's to do the best that I can while I'm in this uniform. I'm not sure about the distant future. I'm still figuring that out. I'm trying to keep things simple like being a good American, a good son, maybe someday being a good husband and father. My goals are modest goals and are not as ambitious as yours or Bob's. They're kind of confused and I don't know how I will achieve them."

"My God," Duncan said. "There's nothing modest about

being a good husband and a good father. That's probably the most difficult and most important purpose that anyone could ever have."

"Nick, continue your education. That will give your life meaning," Avery said.

"Well, I'd love to find a cure for cancer," I said, "but I'll leave the hard ones up to you, Rich. Between that and trying to reform Lastings, Rich will have his work cut out," I said to Bob.

Even Avery chuckled. "I'm not laughing so much at the thought of finding a cure for cancer, but more for the idea of anyone being able to reform Lastings.

"I hope that one of your purposes is to go to college, Nick," Avery continued. "There's plenty of good that will come from that if you do it, but don't let them change you into their image. College can sometimes be like an assembly line and can take away the things that make you unique. That would ruin you."

"Well, that's it for me guys," I said. "I'm turning in. Trying to educate the two of you has exhausted me." I ducked a pillow that Duncan playfully tossed at me and crawled carefully between the blankets, trying not to disturb the makeup of the bed so I would have less to do in the morning.

I thought about what Avery had said and I wasn't sure how college could ever ruin anyone. After all of the talk that night, I fell asleep thinking about what a wonderful thing it would have been if I had worked harder in high school so that I could make going to college one of my purposes.

CHAPTER 16

ALTHOUGH MILITARY LIFE COULD BE LONELY, ESPECIALLY if you had never been away from your family for an extended time before, it was also relatively enjoyable for anyone who was fortunate enough to be a part of the Triple Seven Nine Medical Group. Because of the huge dimensions of the building that we were in, there were two other units in the building besides us. There was an army band housed in a part of the third floor. Headquarters Company, the largest unit, occupied most of the second and third floors, with a smaller area set aside for the Triple Seven Nine.

The band members were constantly moving and performing in various places. None of us knew where they were from day to day.

I learned that medics received preferential treatment because they were always on call for all emergencies, and because they were not viewed as a separate unit by all the other units but rather as an extension of them all. The health and safety of all of the troops, regardless of their designations, was their primary mission. As a result, medics received a certain kind of respect, which was not accorded to many others.

By no stretch of the imagination did I consider myself to be a legitimate medic. However, I received the benefit of the respect that all of the others had earned, many of them in the heat of combat. My clerical duties afforded me access to the files of all army personnel in Panzer Kaserne. I had read and I was fascinated by the extraordinary acts of valor that such ordinary-looking men had performed in World War II and in Korea, and with whom I was now privileged to be serving. The insignias that I wore on my uniform, as well as the maroon and white braid on my cap, indicated that I was a medic and one of them. The first time that someone called me "doc", as they did to all of the other medics, I looked over my shoulder until I realized that the person was addressing me. It just added to the charade that was such a part of my life. A quirk of fate had put me into the medical group but it was not of my own making.

Since band members never knew where they would be from one day to the next, they were never detailed to anything more than to keep their rooms fit in a military manner.

Medics were not expected to perform the mundane tasks that were necessary to keep the building looking the same as it did when Rommel cut the ribbon allowing the first members of his Panzer Corps to occupy it in the 1930s.

Because the band and the medics were exempt from cleaning up the building, or "G.I.-ing" it as was the army term, we were only obligated to keep our rooms clean. All of the responsibility for cleaning the halls, latrines, showers, as well as their own living quarters fell exclusively on the men of Headquarters Company. As a result, there was a great deal of resentment on their part toward the rest of us who used the same facilities. The men of Headquarters Company saw no reason why they had to clean up the mess by themselves when all of us had contributed to the mess. The earned respect for medics was mostly forgotten about by Headquarters troops, as they routinely washed and scrubbed the massive facility on their knees. Our lack of participation in their chores was a daily source of irritation to them. Referring to us as parasites was one of the kinder terms some of them used to describe us.

To make matter worse, at least for me, all of my friends who were now part of Headquarters Company were out there in the hallways and in the latrines scrubbing away. I, along with my new friends from the Triple Seven Nine, unless they were already in the dispensary, lay low in our rooms speaking in whispers. Those were my guys out there. We had lived and died for each other while we were in basic training. Now I hid and waited with the other medics while my old friends finished their details. If I had dared to volunteer to pitch in, my new friends would never have forgiven me. I didn't know what the right thing for me to do would be.

Captain Davis, who lived off post with his family, had warned us not to antagonize Headquarters troops by leaving our rooms as they were cleaning the building.

"Stepping over or around these guys as they tend to their details each morning is not gonna make you new friends. Don't attempt to use the latrines while they're being cleaned. They don't want to see you shaving or combing your hair while they are shining sinks and mirrors. Stay hunkered down in your rooms until they are out of the building. When you do use the facilities, make sure that you leave them the way that you found them, which is ready for inspection. If you don't, I can guarantee you that this arrangement that you all enjoy will come to a screeching halt and that all of you will be scrubbing floors on your hands and knees unless you're in the dispensary."

We did as we were told. We sat quietly in our rooms, speaking in whispers, while we listened to N.C.O.s barking orders as their subordinates scrubbed on the other side of our doors. I knew that I was conspicuous by my absence to my Headquarters Company friends as they G.I.'d the building each morning, but they never complained to me. I think that they just accepted it as my good fortune that I was part of the medical group. They did rib me good naturedly about being a medic.

"Don't expect any of us to call you 'doc', you fraud, and if any of us need medical assistance you better be in another building," they said, but never a word about not helping them with their details.

The fact that they were all so gracious just made me feel more guilt. I actually considered helping out, but I knew that if I had attempted to lend my guys a hand, the mental and physical wounds that the other medics would have inflicted on me would have been too extensive to be treated in the dispensary. So I stayed out of sight with the others.

And so, life was pretty good if you were part of the 7779th.

Then, one day, just as Avery said it would, it happened. I came back to the room after chow and on my sack, all folded and starched, was a set of medic whites. Here came that feeling of panic that I had felt when Avery first told me that I would be expected to pull C.Q. once a month in the dispensary emergency room. I sat on the side of my sack staring at the neatly stacked whites. I attempted to control the feeling of panic, and I was able to do that. The panic was gone, but now it was replaced by desperation. Maybe I could trade those whites for a mop and a bucket and transfer into Headquarters Company. Unlike being a medic, no special training was needed to be part of a bucket brigade. Maybe I could just place the whites on Lastings' sack. He was usually so hung over that he might never realize that it wasn't his turn for C.Q. I sat considering what to do next, but I wasn't coming up with any answers. How would I ever be able to perform the tasks that would be expected of me since I had absolutely no training? The only thing that I knew about emergency rooms was what I had learned as a ten-year-old when I was in one having my leg stitched. There was no doubt in my mind that I might actually hurt someone in an emergency situation.

"Hey, Nick." Avery walked into the room. "Did you read the bulletin board? Your name is on it. You've got C.Q. starting Friday morning until whenever you finish up on Monday."

"Yeah. They left those whites for me on my sack," I said, pointing in their direction. "My God, Rich, how am I gonna do this? I don't know what I'm gonna do. I'm just gonna go and tell them the truth."

"Look," Avery said, "somehow you just got mixed up in the shuffle. I can't say that I'm surprised given how screwed up the army is, but you can do this. Don't make it a monster in your mind. The good thing is that they expect it to be busy this weekend because Friday is payday."

"Oh good! I was so afraid that I would have nothing to do and I'd be bored."

"No. What I mean is that because they know that it will probably be crazy this weekend, there will be four or five of you in the dispensary. That should help. You'll be able to let someone else handle major cases. Look at what I brought to help you out." He reached into a plastic bag that he was carrying, and pulled out an orange, a needle, and a syringe.

"I took the orange from the mess hall, and I borrowed the needle and the syringe from Snead, the lab tech guy." He pushed his glasses back and began to consider. "Today is Monday. Let's see, that gives us four days."

He seemed to be talking as much to himself as he was to me, and then, as if he were suddenly aware of my presence he said, "I strongly doubt that they'll ask you to stitch anyone even if the situation arises. If they should, and if you can't get one of the others with experience to do it, you'll have to tell them the truth, which is that the army never gave you any medical training, except in medical records. If you survive that revelation, all they'll trust you to do after that is to empty bed pans."

"I think that's the best idea," I said. "Why don't I just go in and level with them in the first place? At this point, bedpans and their contents would be a happy sight. I'll take my chances with that any time."

He shook his head. "Nick, Nick, you're better than that. You'll cross that bridge if you come to it, and I don't think that you will. There is an extreme likelihood that you will be asked to give someone an inoculation, such as an antibiotic if someone has the sniffles, and that's where this orange comes in. The skin of an orange is close in consistency to the skin of a human being. You're gonna learn to give a proper inoculation by practicing on this orange. We used to practice on oranges all the time in training. You'll inject the orange and infuse the water that is in the syringe into it, as if you were giving a patient an antibiotic. We have until Thursday night to get it right. We can always get more oranges."

"Oh, what was I thinking about? There go all of my problems. It's payday, it's gonna be so crazy that they've recruited three or four other guys to help. The doctors think I know what the hell I'm doing because I'm wearing whites. If you're wearing whites, it's obvious to everyone that you know what you're doing, because wearing whites is all that you need to show that you've had all of the required training. In reality I don't know a hypodermic needle from a darning needle, but hold on, I'm gonna spend the next four days injecting water into an orange. What was I thinking about? I have no problems, but I do have another idea. If you don't think confessing to the doctor in charge that I have no medical training so that I can become a member of the bedpan brigade is a good idea, how about this one? I take a sack full of oranges to the dispensary. Then, whenever I'm asked to give someone an antibiotic shot, I just inject the orange and tell the guy to suck on it. Everything that you need is in that orange already."

"Are you crazy? Why can't you be serious?" Avery asked.

"Rich. I wish that I could convince you about how serious I am. I'm libel to maim someone this weekend, and exchange the whites for whatever color they wear in the stockade. It would be no different if I put a stethoscope around my neck and said that I was a doctor. At least then I could tell someone else to give the guy an injection or to stitch him up."

"Look. If that idiot Lastings can learn to do this, then you can too."

"Let me ask you a question, Rich. Would you rather receive an injection from me or from Lastings?"

"Right this minute, and if I don't think too much about it, I'd prefer Lastings, and even then only as a last resort. But by Friday, with my training, it would be you."

The door opened again and this time it was Duncan. "Hey Nick, did you read the bulletin board? You've got C.Q. starting on Friday morning."

"Yeah, Bob. Isn't that great? You can't imagine how much I've been looking forward to this. And do you know what Bob? I'm so happy that I skipped all of that silly medical training and preparation. I was so worried about not having any of that. How could I have known that all I needed was an orange and a syringe? Silly me."

Duncan looked confused. "How did you know that I brought an orange and a syringe?"

"He didn't," Avery said. "Obviously you and I had the same thing in mind."

"You know guys," I said, "this must be my lucky day. Can you imagine what trouble I would have been in if we had bananas for dessert this week, and not oranges? I shudder to even think of it."

"Okay, enough talk. Let's get down to business," Avery said as he walked across the room, the orange in one hand, and the syringe in the other.

"Look here," he said. "Pretend that the orange is the patient's arm. As a matter of fact, it's easier to inject an arm than it is an orange, because the surface of the arm is flat rather than rounded like an orange. If you do this correctly, you'll have fewer problems with an arm than you would with an orange."

Avery was now in his professional mode. "First you take an alcohol swab and rub it over the area to be injected. We don't have an alcohol swab but you know how that's done." Avery held the orange in his left hand, and with his right hand, he deliberately inserted the needle into the skin of the orange and injected the fluid.

"You see. There's nothing to it at all," he said.

"Hey, you're right," I said. "That damned orange never flinched or said 'ouch'. Pass that orange and that syringe to me and give me some room."

Avery filled the syringe up with water again and handed it to me along with the orange.

"Now, how deep do I go in with this needle?" I asked.

"Just be sure that the tip of the needle is all the way under the skin," he said.

"Some people kind of throw it in like a dart," Duncan said. But you don't release it like you would with a dart. It's just kind of a short, quick thrust into the flesh rather than a push in. Look. Let me show you." Duncan took the syringe and with a quick motion, he poked the needle into the skin of the orange and plunged. "See. It's in and out before the patient knows it. It's just a little flick."

"Okay," I said. "First let me try Rich's method."

I held the orange firmly with my left hand, deliberately inserted the needle as Rich had done, and then I injected the water. "Hey. No problem. That was a lot easier than peeling the damned thing. Now, let me try Bob's dart technique." I held the orange firmly, bent my hand back then flicked it forward, hammering the needle into the flesh of the orange.

"Was it my imagination or did I just feel that orange flinch?" I asked.

I grinned in their direction, but neither of them wanted to encourage my silliness at a time when they thought that I should be serious. There would be even less humor for them if they were on the business end of a needle that I was wielding I thought.

"Okay. Practice that using both methods that Bob and I have shown to you, and see which one you are most comfortable with," Avery said. "Then we'll get to the shoelace."

"The shoelace? What the hell is the shoelace?" I asked.

"Whew. Will you relax?" Duncan asked. "One thing at a time. Just practice on the oranges. We're progressing toward Friday."

I practiced for the next hour or so, with both Avery and Duncan looking over my shoulder and offering suggestions. By the time that I was done, I had rendered both oranges into soggy, pocked marked, inedible sponge balls.

"I believe this orange has expired and this other one has surrendered," I said as I held both of them up. It was sad to see them. In a strange way, I felt sorry for them. They had looked pretty fresh when Avery and Duncan had brought them into the room.

"You know," I said, "when a tree is cut down it has a chance to become many different things. For instance, it could have a bright future even after it's not a part of the forest. It could become a piece of furniture or a famous document. With some luck, it might be preserved forever in a museum somewhere and go on for posterity. With no luck at all, it could become a roll of toilet paper and have a crappy ending for posterior. It's like life. It's all about chance."

Bob Duncan was laughing at my attempt at humor. "Now that was funny, Nick."

Avery wasn't smiling. "Don't encourage him, Bob. He's gotta get ready for Friday."

"No, wait a minute, Rich. I'm serious. Now, take these two oranges. I know that oranges and trees don't have expectations, but nature did create oranges for a purpose, and that is to be eaten. How unlucky are these two that of all the oranges on that tree, they wind up as pincushions and not a source of vitamin C. It is vitamin C, isn't it, Rich?"

"Yes, it is vitamin C, and you're almost as crazy as Lastings," Avery said.

"One thing is for sure," I said, "these two sad sacks had the worst luck of all the other oranges on that tree. See that, it's just random misfortune. Whether you're an orange, or a tree, or a person, most things are beyond your control and you can only hope that your luck never runs out."

"At the risk of sounding as crazy as you," Duncan said, "it's all in how you look at it. These two oranges might have served a better purpose than all of their little friends on that tree, most of whom I suppose, have been digested by now. On the other hand, our two little oranges are serving a greater purpose. They're helping you to become a real medic with a chance to help people. There are times when toilet paper is more useful than a famous document. You know what I mean if you've ever sat in a toilet with the realization that you are staring at an empty dispenser. Why do I allow you to lure me into these conversations? Is it just me," Duncan asked, "or have our discussions become more bizarre since Nick arrived?"

"I'm sorry to bring both of you back to earth, Nick," Avery said, "but it's time for the shoelace."

He picked up one of the battered oranges and carefully began tying the shoelace, which he had removed from his shoe, around the circumference of the orange. Then he tied it in a bow.

"Can you guess what this is?" Avery asked, as he pushed his glasses back on his nose.

"If you're trying to stem the bleeding, you'd be much better off using your gun belt. A shoelace will stop the oozing about as well as dental floss would at this point," I said, as I watched the water and what was left of the orange's juice ooze out of the numerous puncture holes.

Either he didn't hear me or he chose to ignore me. Avery continued, "This shoelace is as close as I can get to duplicate a human vein, unless you don't mind if I demonstrate one time on you."

I looked up to see if he was serious. He looked back at me with unwavering eyes. This guy meant it. I don't know why I was still doubting the seriousness of his intent, whether he wanted me to volunteer my vein or to throw Lastings out the window.

"Well. Let me think about that a minute. First of all, I'd probably faint a second or two into your lesson. No. I'll stick with the shoelace, no pun intended. But maybe you or Bob will volunteer your veins while I observe, all for the sake of my career in the field of medicine. I could first practice on the shoelace, and then on one of you. I've got to start some place."

"Not me," Duncan said.

"No? I'll bet Lastings would let me if he were here. In fact,

I bet that I wouldn't need those oranges if he were here. He's my pal. He's gonna show me around town."

Avery looked at me. "If Lastings were here, he'd be squeezing what's left of those oranges into vodka that he probably has hidden away somewhere. Now Nick, focus. Again, it's highly unlikely that you'll be asked to stitch or draw blood on this weekend. But over the next nineteen months you probably will have to. Bob and I don't want you to go into that with absolutely no idea about what to do. That's the reason we decided on this exercise."

Duncan said, "Everything starts with the alcohol rub on the area from where the blood will be drawn. As a rule, men have surface veins. Women's veins are usually deeper and harder to find. In any case, use the rubber tourniquet to bring up the vein. Puncture the vein just enough for the blood to flow into the vial. Show him with the shoelace, Rich."

By that time, all this talk about blood and veins was starting to make me a bit woozy. I had always done my best to avoid looking at blood. If they didn't stop talking about it, the next lesson might be about the best technique for reviving me. I knew that they were trying to help to prepare me, but the idea that in four days I might actually have to stick needles into someone's arm or veins, and not into oranges and shoelaces, was increasing my misery, despite my trying to make jokes about it. It wasn't helping that we seemed to be racing toward Friday.

"Enough for tonight," Avery said. "We have the rest of this week to practice."

"Rich, I get light-headed when I cut myself while I'm shaving. Oranges and shoelaces are one thing. Real people are something else. I don't know if I'll be able to do this."

"You'll be fine," Duncan said. "There is no better feeling than the one you get by helping others. You said that you're embarrassed when people think that you're a medic. Well, you won't have to feel that way anymore. You're getting practical on-the-job experience, and that's the only thing left since returning you to Fort Sam Houston for training is not an option."

"Did you know that up until the turn of this century most doctors had no formal medical education? They learned their profession just the way that you're learning. They followed a qualified professional around and observed and learned," Avery said.

I heard Avery say that and his words instantly caused me to think back to a tragic time in my family's history.

"I know that you're right and that they used to train medical students who were learning about the profession by allowing them to practice on people, especially poor people who had no choice, but I never understood that expression."

"What expression?" Avery asked.

"The expression that says that a doctor practices on people seems crazy to me. You practice on a piano or on a baseball field to improve, but by the time that you become a doctor, you should know what you're doing. Practice time should be over. We're talking about people here."

"Nick," Duncan said, "after a doctor gets his degree, he then practices what he has learned. That's all that means."

"I know," I said, "but it still doesn't ring right for me. They should find another word. I would rather hear that a doctor administers. He administers his skills or something like that. I'd feel a lot more confident. Most people would feel a lot better being administered to than being practiced on.

"I haven't told this story to you guys, and I never expected to, but all this talking about practicing medicine and medical techniques kind of hits home for me. My grandmother was a victim of some guy doing his medical on-the-job training.

This guy was truly practicing in every sense of the word, because he had no skills. That was obvious by what he did to my grandmother. His father was a doctor and he trailed his father around, and I guess the old man let his son take over whenever he had a person too poor or too sick to complain.

"It was August of 1914. My grandmother was twenty-four years old. She had two daughters. One was four years old and the other was two years old. She also had my dad who was five months old. The story goes that soon after the birth of her son, my father, my grandmother who was having a difficult recovery after his birth, had scrubbed the floors in her apartment. After washing the floors, and perhaps taking on more than she was ready to do at that point, she sat in a brisk breeze on the window sill to cool off. A few days later she developed a stiff back, along with a severe cough and perhaps pneumonia, which might have evolved into pleurisy. Her condition worsened and they sent for a doctor. He arrived, along with his son, and the doctor decided fluid needed to be extracted from my grandmother's lungs and that he had to draw the fluid out with a needle. He also decided to let his son do the procedure.

"Well, apparently the doctor's son inserted the needle incorrectly, because my grandmother was in excruciating pain. According to her sister-in-law, who was present at the time, my grandmother said to the doctor's son, 'You just made my children orphans.'"

"Oh, my God," Avery said.

"She died a few days later. She was only twenty-four. There's no way of knowing, but they suspect that the doctor's son pierced my grandmother's liver with the needle. But whatever it was, it wasn't an easy death."

"That's a sad story," Duncan said.

"It was a long time ago. Thank God that there are better

requirements now. And as for me, I'll give it my best. You guys have helped a lot and I have until Thursday night to practice. I'll find out this weekend what it means to be a medic. If things work the way you two expect them to, I just might be so comfortable with this that I might even be in the operating room. Hopefully, I won't be the guy on the gurney."

CHAPTER 17

THREE OTHER MEDICS AND I REPORTED TO THE DISpensary at 0600 as instructed. I recognized the others because I had seen them before, but only from a distance, when I had occasion to be in the dispensary. Two of them were career soldiers up in rank. The third was a P.F.C. who couldn't have been in the army much longer than I had been. At first glance, I fit in perfectly with the others. We were all in white, except for our black low quarter shoes and our olive drab overseas caps.

At 0600, things were quiet because it was still too early for the sick call patients who would be arriving shortly. We were told that the mayhem emergencies wouldn't be arriving in force until about 1900 hours, or seven P.M. At that point, the troops would be off duty and free to party.

Captain Randal Baker was the physician on duty when we arrived. As medical clerk, I had processed his records so I knew that he was from Pennsylvania, and that he had entered the army soon after completing medical school. It was not unusual for young doctors to come into the army that way. They came in as captains, and the lucky ones were sent to Europe. They served three years and lived the good life. They got to tour Europe while driving high-end German cars. They lived in Bachelor Officers Quarters, known as B.O.Q., if they were not married. One of the most important benefits was that they gained valuable experience for their future, because they would see everything from gunshot wounds to athlete's foot. The same was true for the young dentists who practiced on the second floor of the dispensary. The only difference was that they entered the army as first lieutenants, and not as captains.

From time to time, Avery would say that if the army had not been so unreasonable in his case, and had waited for him to complete medical school, he would have been in the same situation as Captain Baker. He would have been a captain, gaining lots of experience, and living the high life like the others.

"But most important is that I'd be living in B.O.Q., and not sharing living space with the likes of Lastings. Can you imagine? I wouldn't even know that such a creature even existed."

"But then you wouldn't know that Bilotti and I existed either. Life would be much less meaningful for you for not having Nick and me as part of it," Duncan teased.

"You're correct," Avery said, as he adjusted his glasses, "and at the risk of hurting your feelings, it's a trade off that I'd make in a second."

"Your disloyalty pains me to my core. Did you hear what he just said, Nick?"

"Oh, you can't take it personal, Bob. Look at him," I said, "can't you see that he feels bad for hurting our feelings? It's just that Lastings always brings out the worst in him."

I wondered if Avery would still be putting shoe polish on the back of his heels, or still collecting Dial soap chips in the latrines if the army had taken him after he had finished medical school, but I decided against asking him.

"Hi. I'm Paul Bennett." I was brought back to the present by the young P.F.C. standing in front of me, who was one of the other medics on C.Q. with me.

He had his hand extended, and I grasped his hand and I said, "I'm Nick Bilotti." Paul appeared to be about my age and had a good-natured smile.

"Welcome, Nick. I haven't seen you around here before, but are you ready for the insanity?"

"You haven't seen me before because I'm only in the dispensary occasionally, and this is the first time that I've pulled C.Q. I guess I'll find out if I'm ready for the insanity."

I thought that he might ask me about my training and I considered whether or not I should be truthful with a guy that I had only known for two minutes, but thankfully, he didn't ask me. The assumption on everyone's part was that if you were there, all dressed and looking ready to go, then you were one of them.

"Captain Baker asked me to walk over to the mess hall and pick up a few bacon and egg sandwiches and some coffee for us while it's calm and we still have the chance. Want to come along and give me a hand?"

"Sure thing," I said.

We walked past three rooms, each of which was a treatment and examination room. The three rooms were well ordered with the usual kinds of medical equipment required for handling medical emergencies, which I had been assured would be coming soon enough.

Paul and I walked out of the dispensary. The dispensary, which was constructed of blocks and stucco by the Americans, was nowhere near the pain-staking permanence of the buildings in which we were housed. I guess the Americans didn't expect to be here for one hundred years.

It was a short walk from the dispensary to the mess hall. Paul and I walked into the kitchen where five or six cooks were busy cleaning up or preparing for the next meal.

"What the hell are the two of you doing back here?"

someone shouted at us from across the kitchen. We could see that he was placing chicken parts on a very long hot plate.

"Oh, oh," Paul whispered, "he's one of those cooks with attitude. I hate dealing with these guys. What do we want? He's seen this before. We're in whites coming from the dispensary to the mess hall. Duh!"

"Maybe you should tell him that we want to make dinner reservations for tonight," I whispered back. As we got nearer, his name tag identified him as Sergeant First Class Collins.

Paul got right to the point. "Captain Baker sent us over to get a half dozen bacon and egg sandwiches, and some coffee, sugar and milk, to bring back to the dispensary." Paul whispered, "We might as well mention Captain Baker's name right off to cut this guy off at the pass." No response from Sergeant Collins, so Paul added, "It's probably gonna be a busy night." The sergeant didn't move. "That's why we're here."

Collins looked at us and made no attempt to hide the irritation in his expression, but he wasn't about to take on Captain Baker, who had disrupted his routine.

"Hey, Sam," he shouted, "put down what you're doing and take care of these two." Then, turning his back on us, he continued moving chicken parts on the hot plate.

We made our way over to Sam, and watched as he filled our order and placed the sandwiches and the coffee into a cardboard box. "Whew," I whispered to Paul, "you'd think that these guys were paying for this food?"

"Now you know why I hate coming up here. It's usually like this. It doesn't matter if it's Collins or not. Most of them are the same way," Paul whispered back.

"Do you know, Sam? Does he like us? I'll watch out to be sure that he doesn't throw some poison into our sandwiches. I thought that we were all in the same army?"

Paul shook his head. "They're not all like that, but a lot of them are, and I think that's because they're tired of hearing the troops groaning day after day that the crap that they throw together is usually inedible."

"Did you ever notice how good the menu looks on the board before you enter the mess hall? What the hell happens to it from the time that you walk away from the board until they slap it onto your tray?" I asked.

"The funny part about it is that on Thanksgiving or Christmas they serve up special meals as good as you get at home. They serve turkey and stuffing, mashed potatoes, sweet potatoes, cranberry sauce, and all kinds of pies. I mean you wouldn't think that it's the same guys preparing it. I don't expect that effort all the time, but at least they could come close once in a while.

"I'll tell you one thing," Paul said, "I swear when we come in here again and he starts in with that attitude, Sergeant Collins' shot records are gonna turn up missing. Maybe he'll be a little more patient when he winds up as a patient and he's told that he'll have to get his series from A to Z updated with dull needles, and I hope that I'm the guy to do it. Another guy who would do it is Rich Avery. He checks mess halls and local area bars and restaurants for proper sanitation. Do you know Avery?" Paul asked.

"Hey, sure," I said. "He's my roommate."

"Oh, so then you know him. Well, if we don't get a better attitude from Sergeant Collins this weekend, tell Avery to come in here and give him a fingernail check. I don't think that there's anything that can send a career soldier off the brink quicker than being told what to do by a guy who he has time and grade over, and he's got to do it. We'll double team this guy. I'll lose his shot records and Avery will give him a fingernail check in the same week. Maybe he'll get the message. Don't pull the kind of crap that you do with everyone else with medics."

"Have you ever done that," I asked, "lose a guy's shot record?"

"I haven't," Paul said, "but there's a few M.P.'s who have crossed paths with a couple of our guys who have had attitude changes for the better when their shot records were misplaced, especially when it happened only to guys with bad ass reputations in the same unit."

"Remind me not to get on the wrong side of you guys," I said.

"I'm not talking about you. You're one of us."

Oh, oh, I thought. Thank God, I'm one of them.

When we got back, the dispensary was buzzing with activity. Patients were being attended to so the bacon and egg sandwiches were put on hold. Paul immediately involved himself by assisting where experience told him he would be most useful. I walked up and down the long corridor, which opened into all of the examination and treatment rooms. I looked into each as if I had a purpose.

"Medic." I saw Captain Baker looking in my direction. I looked behind me. There was no one there, and I realized that he was talking to me.

"Yes, Sir?"

"Take Sergeant Hahn to a treatment room." Captain Baker handed me a prescription. "We're trying to clear up an ear infection with antibiotics." Captain Baker read my name on my name tag. "Private Bilotti will give you that shot. Then take this prescription to the pharmacy, and you should start to feel much better in a day or two." With that, Captain Baker turned into the next examination room, leaving me in the corridor with Sergeant Hahn.

Master Sergeant Hahn was a bull of a man, who looked to

be well over six feet tall. He had a barrel for a chest, and his neck was wider than his ears. He wore the Combat Infantry Badge on his jacket, as well as the Airborne Infantry Ranger Badge. It didn't seem possible that such a specimen might be taken down by a needle wielded by me. At least that's what I was thinking as we made our way down the corridor looking for a vacant treatment room.

I had known all along that this moment was inevitable, but I had hoped that when the time came for me to switch from oranges and shoelaces to human arms, that the arm would be attached to a puny private like me. In that case, if I botched up the procedure and the guy complained, I would simply tell him, "Suck it up. Quit your whining. You're in the army now. Stop bitching and be on your way. There are other patients waiting for me."

Instead I had drawn a guy who looked like he could be on an army recruiting poster, and who had probably ducked bullets and grenades, but he couldn't duck me.

We entered a treatment room, and I pointed to an examination table and said, "Sit down, sergeant. I'll be right with you," as if this was something that I did all the time.

I looked down at Captain Baker's prescription order, which was written in a clear hand to my relief. I knew that the antibiotics were kept in the refrigerator. I looked in and found a small bottle with the same name as the one written on the prescription and I placed it on the counter alongside of trays of sterilized needles and syringes. Although my heart was racing, I tried to maintain a look of complete composure.

I remembered Avery's admonishment, "Nick, everything starts by sterilizing the area with an alcohol rub." So I picked up a jar of alcohol, which was next to a silver-capped jar of cotton balls, and placed them both by the trays of needles. Now all I needed to do was to select a needle from the tray and I would have my baptism of fire. Sergeant Hahn's ample bicep would be my target. You couldn't miss it.

There were several trays of needles. I opened one but the needles inside of it appeared to me to be far too large for my purposes. Avery and Duncan hadn't discussed needle sizes with me during my crash course in inoculations. I looked into one sterilizer after the other, but the needles appeared to be either too large or too small.

I felt my ears growing hot, and I felt beads of perspiration running down the small of my back, then disappearing somewhere between my buttocks. I tried to remember the size of the needles that had been used to inject me, and now I regretted having always looked away as I was being injected. I finally opened a tray that seemed to contain needles about the size of the ones that I used when I practiced on the oranges.

I washed and dried my hands, selected a needle and placed it onto the syringe. I drew out the proper amount of serum that was indicated on the prescription.

The whole time Sergeant Hahn had been very quiet. I turned around and before I could ask him to roll up his sleeve, I saw that that was no longer an option, and that Sergeant Hahn preferred to be injected in the butt, and not in his arm. He had his back to me and he was holding his pants and his shorts by his knees. If I had known that the patient had the choice to decide between a needle in the arm or in the butt, I would have asked Avery or Duncan to bring a watermelon or at least a grapefruit back to the room.

Oh my God, I thought. Do I have to touch this guy's butt to do this? I was repulsed by the thought, so I made a quick decision to use Duncan's quick-flick technique. You didn't have to hold the dartboard to throw the dart.

All locked and loaded, I approached Sergeant Hahn. The

last thing that I wanted to do was to squat down behind a semi-nude man's butt. For a moment, I considered applying the needle fist forward from a standing position, more like a shiv than a dart. I thought that if I did that I'd have less control of the angle of the needle, so I reluctantly squatted down and winced at the target. With my left hand resting on my thigh, I gave the needle a quick-flick into Sergeant Hahn's butt.

The man had a butt of granite. It was lucky for me that I was able to catch the needle and syringe in mid-air. I was able to pull it onto my chest without shoving the needle into my throat as it bounced off Sergeant Hahn's buttock, which I now knew was as hard as a Mack truck tire.

To his credit, Sergeant Hahn never even let out an "ouch" at my first unsuccessful attempt, although he did crank his head around and gazed down at me with what I took to be a menacing glare.

I looked up and I gave him a feeble smile, but the sergeant seemed not to have a sense of humor. It was probably the ear infection. I knew that my next attempt had better be successful or it might be the last of many things for me. All bets were off. I forgot about the repulsion that I had felt about touching the bare skin on another man's rear end. Instead, I placed the thumb of my left hand on the split of Sergeant Hahn's butt while my other four fingers grabbed and squeezed the flesh so tightly that the skin in the target area popped up. Then I plunged the needle into his flesh up to its hilt and injected the antibiotics.

When I let go of Sergeant Hahn's buttock, I could see a blue welt forming in the area of my first attempt, but hey, this guy was wearing the Combat Infantry Badge.

Mission accomplished. Before I could echo Captain Baker's, "Well, you should start to feel better in a day or two," which all health care personnel usually said, Sergeant Hahn had pulled up his shorts and his pants and was headed for the door without so much as a thank you. I didn't doubt that he already had one, but I was going to recommend the guy for a Purple Heart, but he left too soon.

I grabbed a handful of paper towels and wiped the perspiration off my forehead and my neck. I had done it, and I was relieved that it was over. I believed that I would be better the next time for having had the experience.

I began putting things away and then I saw on the counter, the alcohol and the cotton ball, still unused just as I had left them. I had been taken so off guard by the specter of Sergeant Hahn's rear end that I had totally forgotten to sterilize the area with alcohol.

"Oh my God!" I said out loud. "What did I do?" Could this guy get some sort of an infection and die because I was the one who had injected him without first cleaning the area?" I had to be in the dispensary for four more days. I'd have all that time to sweat it out.

I wanted to ask Paul if he thought that omitting to clean the area to be injected with an alcohol rub would be a problem for Sergeant Hahn down the road. I would have but I decided that to ask a question like that involving such a basic procedure would reveal how little I knew about health care.

I hated being on duty in the dispensary, and I believed that if the truth were known about my lack of qualifications, I would be relieved of duty on the spot. My name would be placed on the dull needle list along with M.P.s and cooks.

I positioned myself so that I could see anyone coming into the dispensary, fully expecting to see Sergeant Hahn either walking in or more likely being carried in for treatment.

From where I was sitting, I could see that there was some commotion outside. I saw a woman carrying a little boy about three years old. She was holding a blood-soaked washcloth filled with ice on the boy's forehead.

There was no special medical training necessary to know when you needed to assist someone in distress. In fact, not having to consider the situation as I had to do in Sergeant Hahn's case, spurred me into action.

"Come this way quickly," I said to the woman whom I assumed to be the little boy's mother. The boy was screaming and the woman was trying not to panic as she followed me into a treatment room. The boy's crying had also alerted Captain Baker and Paul, both of whom came over immediately and began to examine the child. Over the din of the boy's screaming, his mother explained that he had tripped and hit his head on the corner of a coffee table. We looked to see an open wound that appeared to be about an inch long running through his eyebrow and bleeding profusely.

"Medic, shave off the eyebrow hair around the wound as well as you can," Captain Baker said to me. "You secure his arms," he said to Paul, as he handed me a razor while the boy's mother attempted to hold her son's legs still.

I was about to tell Paul that I would hold the boy's arms and that he could shave his eyebrow but before I could, Paul said, "Okay, Nick. I've got his arms. Go ahead."

The boy began shaking his head from side to side when he saw me coming toward his face with the razor. I held his chin as securely as I could as I began trying to remove the hair from his eyebrow. Not only was the boy not cooperating but the bleeding from the wound was making matters worse. It was hard to see where the wound started and where the eyebrow ended. That "oh my God, what the hell am I doing here" feeling came over me again. And now I was also concerned about the possibility of hurting the boy or of causing another wound with the razor.

When I was finally done, I moved away while Captain Baker cleansed the wound, applied Novocain, and began to close it up. The boy continued to shriek the whole time. I took a few seconds to wash my hands and then I returned to help hold the boy down and keep him from flailing.

When we were done, the boy left the dispensary with a neat bandage over his eye. He was still sobbing when his mother put him into her car.

"Nice job," Captain Baker said to Paul and me. "I'm not a plastic surgeon, and that kid didn't make it easy, but he'll be fine. He'll have a scar in his eyebrow but it'll make him appear a little more rugged for the ladies when he learns to appreciate them." He laughed and moved away.

"Have you ever seen one of those before?" Paul asked. "We see a lot of them because of all of the military families that are stationed here. Little kids and coffee tables are not a good combination."

"No. That's the first one," I said. The last time that I had seen so much blood was the time that I had cut my hand trying to escape from the dog while I was reading gas meters in New Jersey. That bloody incident was the last straw and caused me to make up my mind to join the army, and now blood again. The most worrisome part was that they kept telling me that what I was seeing now was child's play.

"Wait until the celebrations begin tonight," Paul said. "Then it will really hit the fan."

Chapter 18

"THEY FORCED US INTO AN EARTHEN STORAGE BARN which had been dug into the side of a hill. They slammed the oak doors behind us and locked us in." Dr. Karl Jauss was one of several German doctors retained by the army to assist American military doctors in the dispensary. I estimated that Dr. Jauss was about the same age as Captain Baker, but for such a young man, he had experiences that could fill a lifetime. By now, Paul and I were a team, and during a break, we had been telling Dr. Jauss about some of the crazy things that we did as kids before we entered the army. We all laughed as Paul and then I would relate one mischievous story after the other. When we were done, Dr. Jauss sat silently, still smiling at the silly stories from Paul and me.

"I missed most of that in my youth," he said. "It's a pity to not have such memories. All kids should have memories like that to look back on. You were both fortunate for being where you were. Life is chance and that makes all the difference. For me at your age, there were different experiences. I wish that they weren't so clear in my mind, but there's no getting them out of my mind," he said with a slight German accent.

Paul and I sat looking at Dr. Jauss, without saying anything, hoping that he would continue, but neither of us asked him to.

"It's not a happy memory like yours," he said, and when we both remained silent, he began.

"My father had been killed in France a few days after the D-Day invasion in 1944. The situation was bad all over Germany. The Russians were unstoppable in the East. The Allies were advancing in the West. The Americans dropped bombs on us during the day and the British dropped bombs at night."

I was surprised to hear Dr. Jauss talk about his experiences during the war. In the time that I had been in Germany, no one ever even made mention of what they had gone through, even though I had gotten to know many Germans who were employed by the army. It was almost as if the war had never happened, and yet there were constant reminders of the turmoil that occurred. If you looked around at the scarred buildings and walls, and in some areas where rubble and ruined structures still stood, there was no denying the devastation. There was sometimes a reminder in the frozen stares that some Germans would give to you on occasion. I believed that the Germans, who worked in the shops and smiled at us, and even those who worked with us, were actually hiding their true feelings behind their smiles.

Dr. Jauss must have believed that what was on his mind that day needed to be told because he continued. "I turned seventeen in January of 1945. In the little village where I lived with my grandparents, my mother, and my two sisters, we knew that for us the war was over. The last hope that we had was that the Americans would reach us before the Russians did.

"Not only in my village, but in all of the surrounding villages, there were only women, old men, and children. We knew that we had to plan on what we would do when the advancing enemy armies would arrive. There was no longer any way to stop them. Our best young men were gone. They were sacrificed by the dreams of desperate people who followed an eloquent mad man.

"There was special concern for our women. We knew well what conquering armies do to women. Isn't that part of the spoils of victory?" he asked.

Dr. Jauss looked from Paul to me, but we remained silent. He stared at the tiled wall in the examination room for a few seconds. I thought that he might be finished, but he began again.

"The men from the various villages met together and came up with a desperate plan which they hoped would spare as many of the women as possible. I say it was a desperate plan, but there were really very few options.

"In the time that was left, it was decided that we should dig hidden shelters in the woods. We searched for concealed places for what we hoped would be a brief period of time before sanity was restored. When we were satisfied that the shelters were concealed as best that we were able to hide them, we stocked our shelters with blankets, clothing and medical supplies, and food that would not quickly spoil such as potatoes, beets, apples, carrots, cheese and whatever else that we could gather, although any kind of food was scarce. Finally, we stored containers of water. Some of the more optimistic ones buried household articles in the ground with the hopes of retrieving them eventually.

"The second part of the plan concerned the men. When the news came that armies were approaching from the east and the west, it was decided that all men twelve years or older would take up arms and take up positions as far as possible from the woods which were concealing our women. The hope was that if the Allies arrived first, we could put down our arms and put ourselves at their mercy. If the Russians arrived first, we hoped that they would just pass through.

We hoped they would believe that they were looking at a series of abandoned villages, and that we could remain hidden. The worst scenario would be for us to be forced to offer some resistance as a distraction, in order to lead them in a direction away from our children, our wives, mothers, and sisters if they were in danger of being discovered. Everyone was aware that such a resistance would be suicide, but the alternative was to either carry out what we planned, or be slaughtered in our own homes, while having to watch our women being violated. Whatever the outcome, the hope was that the women could hold out in their hideouts for a month or so while the fighting passed by."

I had to strain to hear Dr. Jauss' voice now, as he spoke barely above a whisper.

"Then, one day in January of 1945, we awakened to hear the sounds of big guns from the east. We knew that the Russians were approaching and would be there before the Allies. That was our worst nightmare coming true. Everyone knew what to do. The remaining livestock were quartered on the ground floor of each home. By quartering our animals under our living quarters, we benefitted by the heat that the animals would give off in the winter, and we avoided the necessity of having to build separate barns when land was scarce.

"In better times, farmers would herd their animals out of their homes to a designated plot of land for the animals to graze, and they would be brought back home in the evening. On that day, they were herded out into the fields with all of the hay and fodder that we had left, and abandoned to fend for themselves, although we had little hope for their survival. If they didn't starve to death, they would certainly be eaten. Man and beast were all in the same situation.

"There really was nothing else to do. We said goodbye

to our wives and mothers and to all of the women, knowing full well that for many of us, and perhaps for all of us, this would be a final farewell."

Dr. Jauss looked from Paul to me and said, "I know that you're probably thinking that we brought this catastrophe upon ourselves, and that others had suffered even greater pain than we had, and you're right. But when you're seventeen, it's not what caused the situation that you're in that is on your mind. Your only thoughts are about your survival and the survival of those you love, and what is going to happen and how to deal with it. You don't think about the past, and there's not much hope about the future.

"It was well below freezing in January. My grandfather was sixty-five years old and a veteran of World War I. He and I made our way back to our home one final time. We trudged through the snow to pick up some cheese and bread that we had left behind, as well as an old shotgun and a small rifle that had been given to me as a boy for shooting quail.

"We arrived at our abandoned home with its empty stalls where the livestock had been quartered. My grandfather collected several burlap grain sacks and showed me how to tie them around my legs and my feet, as well as my body, for insulation.

"'Karl,'" he said, "'I have done this before when I was a little older than you, and when it was over I prayed that none of us would ever be in such a situation again. There was no glory in it when I was young. It was a slaughter in those days, and old men and boys are no match for the enemy.

"'Now your father is dead. I never thought that I would live longer than my son. I prayed that none of us would ever know war again. I could never have imagined that I would see it for the second time at sixty-five years of age. It is unthinkable to be fighting alongside of my grandson this time. It's insane. Nothing is ever gained from war but more war, but if you are to live this life, you must deal with its absurdities. You and your sisters are all that I have, Karl, and at a time that I should be giving you much advice about situations like this one, I find myself with little to say. But please, Karl, you are not to be overly concerned about me. I have lived my life. Take care of yourself, and if possible, avoid any confrontation with the enemy, but if it does come to that, be brave.'" We took one final look around and then we made our way to where the others would be, and we waited.

"It wasn't very long before we heard the Russian advanced guard coming up the road in trucks and on motorcycles. They were moving rapidly because they knew that the countryside was abandoned and undefended.

"I believe to this day that the Russians were in such a hurry to get to Berlin before the Allies that they would have never bothered to look for us. But some fool among us, I don't know if it was a young fool or an old fool, fired a shot at one of the soldiers on a motorcycle. It revealed our positions to the enemy and erupted into a rapid response and a fierce one-sided firefight. It wasn't very long before the whole section from where the shot had come was obliterated. The rest of us were quickly rounded up and disarmed. The Russians were more contemptuous of us than they were angry when they discovered that we were a band of old men and boys.

"They took what meager food we had on us and after some discussion they decided against shooting the rest of us. Instead, they marched us past the bodies of the men and boys who lay bleeding and dead in the snow. They took us to a nearby barn that had been used to store potatoes and grain, and then they barricaded us behind the huge oak doors. We could hear them from inside as they continued their race to Berlin.

"We stayed in the numbing cold and dark of the barn for four days with no food or water. We tried, but it was impossible for us to break through the oak doors, so we decided to try to tunnel out of the front of the barn, because the other three sides were covered by earth half way to the roof. The dirt floor was hardened by frost so we took turns using whatever we could find including the buckles on our belts to flake away the soil a few grains at a time.

"In the darkness, we were able to gather up and to eat barley or oat seeds still in their husks. Food that was meant for the livestock but we were glad to chew on them. We had no access to water. Our thirst was worse than our hunger.

"We huddled together for body heat but by the second day some began freezing to death. When someone was found dead, we carried the body to one corner of the barn. Those who were able, continued to dig.

"Sometime between the third day and the fourth day, I found my grandfather cold and unresponsive, and in the dark I realized that he had passed away. Even though he hadn't complained and he took his turn at digging, I knew that the constant cold, hunger and thirst were taking a toll on him. It was even more stressful on the elderly than it was on the younger ones. Some of the others helped me to carry my grandfather to the corner of the barn where those who had died had been placed. Then, like a robot, I went back to our spot and I waited for my turn to dig.

"Finally, on the fourth day, we managed to break through the frozen crust on the other side of the wall, and one by one we crawled out into the snow. I remember the welcomed sight of the light of a full moon made even brighter by the snow covered ground. The few of us who remained walked stiffly, like men close to death. We walked past the frozen bodies of those who were killed on the first day and who still lay where they had fallen. All of it seemed as if it had happened a long time ago, and not just four days ago. Some avoided looking at the dead, but I was curious and so I did. None of them was recognizable but I will never forget the scene or the bodies frozen in rigid positions. Except for the crunching sound that our feet made on the snow, there was absolute silence as we made our way past the slaughter and to where we knew the women would be."

Now he was done, and I looked at Dr. Jauss. I could see the muscles flexing in his jaw as he bit down and then released pressure.

Dr. Jauss looked up and saw Paul and me looking at him. He forced a smile and said, "That's it. No happy ending." He stood up and asked, "Do you believe that story?" He asked the question almost as if he couldn't believe that he had actually experienced what he had described to us.

"Well, it's true, and there's nothing to be done about the past. I have been here long enough, and there's much to be done about the present," he said motioning with his head in the direction of the waiting room, and then he left.

"Geez," I said to Paul, "I have enough depression. I didn't need that. What did he do, mistake us for chaplains? How did we get on that subject anyway?"

"I can't remember, but you know, it wasn't that long ago. It's still fresh in his mind," Paul said. "Did you notice that sometimes it was as if he was thinking out loud? It was almost as if we weren't here."

"Do you think that this guy hates Americans?" I asked.

"Hates Americans? We had nothing to do with it. It was the Russians."

"That's true," I said. "In fact, he said a few times that they were hoping that the Americans would come to the rescue. Hey, I'd be scared too if I were a German, especially after what the Germans did to the Russians. That was payback time. When you get down to it, the whole thing is Adolph's fault. In fact, it's Adolph's fault that I'm even in this damned dispensary. He's the guy that no one should forgive."

"Yeah, I don't forgive him. Did they ever find his body? I wouldn't be surprised if that piece of crap is hiding in South America somewhere," Paul said. "He's the one who deserves to get his ass kicked."

We left the room laughing but the smile froze on my face when I saw a group of drunken soldiers, some of them bleeding, being dragged into the dispensary by M.P.s.

CHAPTER 19

THE M.P.S WERE RIGHT BEHIND THE FOUR G.I.S, HERDing them into the dispensary amidst their continued shouts and threats, and general confusion. This was an "All hands on deck," call, and both Captain Baker and Dr. Jauss, followed by all available medics, rushed to the entrance of the dispensary.

"Listen. You better cut the crap, and if you put your hand on me one more time, I'm gonna level you with this club, and you're in the right place for me to do it." An M.P. sergeant, his hand holding the front of the guy's shirt, waved his club in the face of the soldier who was bleeding profusely, but who seemed to be more out of control than the others.

Turning to Captain Baker, the M.P. said, "I'm sorry that I had to bring these four knuckleheads here, Sir, and not right to the stockade. If you patch them up, I'll get them out of here and bring them some place where they won't embarrass the rest of us."

All four guys needed treatment, and I held my breath when I saw Paul walking over to the rowdiest and bloodiest one in the group. For a second I considered hitching up with another medical team but before I could Paul, without looking over his shoulder said, "Let's go, Nick."

"Man, don't shove me," the rowdy one yelled. "I aughta know my way around here. Sheeit, I been working here part time," he said with a grin, and then when he heard Paul mention my name, he looked up.

"Hey, Nick! That you man?" The voice and the drawl sounded familiar, but because his face was covered with blood, I didn't immediately recognize Chance Lastings.

"Chance?" I asked. He wiped some of the blood away with the back of his hand, and sure enough, it was him. "What the heck happened?" I asked. Perhaps it was the sight of a familiar face, but Chance seemed to calm down a bit. It was obvious that he had too much to drink.

"Yeah, Nick. Ya'll ever see anything like this, Nick? All's I did was leave my schotz for one minute to go to the latrine, and when I get back I seen that boy over there snuggling up to my girl." He nodded in the direction of one of the guys who was holding his hand on his swollen cheek and jaw.

"All's I said was 'excuse me,' and before I could even tell him to back off, one of his buddies cracked a bottle crost my head when my back was turned. That ain't right man. Like to broke my head open. Looka here," he said, showing me a long split in his scalp that was still oozing blood. "That's when I hit the boy. It was self-defense."

"That's bull crap," the guy with the swollen jaw said between clenched teeth. "You blindsided me. I went down and that's when my buddy cracked the bottle over your head." He could barely get the words out.

"Look. Stop wasting everyone's time here," the M.P. sergeant said. "I don't know who instigated this whole thing, but there are plenty of witnesses who saw what went on there, so we'll get to the bottom of it. One thing that I know for sure, you're all guilty of bustin' up that gasthaus, and the four of you are gonna answer for that."

When he saw that all of the finger pointing wasn't going anywhere, Dr. Jauss walked over to me. "Take your friend to a treatment room. Clean up his wound and shave the hair around it. I'll be down there as soon as I see if Captain Baker needs a hand. Your friend looks bad, but I think that guy with the swollen jaw is worse."

I really didn't want Dr. Jauss to think that I was a good friend of Lastings. Call me a snob but I really didn't want him to judge me by him. "Dr. Jauss, Lastings and I are in the same company, we're in the same room, but he's really not my friend." Dr. Jauss had a funny expression on his face at hearing me say that and as soon as the words were out of my mouth, I regretted having said them. This was the army and through thick and through thin; you didn't abandon guys. Better to just have said nothing. As crazy as he was, I didn't believe that Lastings would ever have cut me loose, or would even have cut Avery loose, as I had just done to him. Still, I believed that when I told this story to Avery, he'd see it as another example of the kind of behavior that was typical of Lastings, and of which we never would have been guilty. Avery would give me absolution. "Dr. Jauss doesn't have to live with that guy," he would say.

An M.P. walked us down to the treatment room and waited outside while Lastings, Paul and I went in. It was obvious that Lastings was familiar with the treatment room and its procedures. He slid a stainless steel mobile chair under a goose necked lamp and positioned the light to where he knew his head wound would best be seen.

"Hey, Nick, ya'll find a basin in that cabinet over there. Wanna fetch that for me? That damned cognac got me into this fix, and now it's fixin to get out of me and leave me all alone to my troubles. Heh, heh, heh."

I didn't get there a moment too soon when Lastings began heaving into the basin. I nearly knocked Paul over trying to distance myself from Lastings. At that moment, it happened once again. That "What the hell am I doing here?" feeling came over me.

I alternated between emptying the basin when I thought that Lastings was through and returning it clean, only to have him hand it back to me to empty again. Paul was unfazed by the whole thing and gathered what was needed to clean and close the extensive wound in Lastings' scalp.

"Here you go, Nick." Paul handed me a razor similar to the one that I had used a little while ago to shave off the little boy's eyebrow.

"Again?" I said to Paul. "This is the second time today. I might leave a lot to be desired as a medic, but I'm becoming a damned good barber, and the army never sent me to barber school either." I looked at Paul, but the reference went right over his head.

"You know, all of this is Ovary's fault, Nick. If he had put that damned gasthaus off limits like he should have, those boys would never have been there tonight. Instead, he puts the good ones off limits and leaves the bad ones alone. How do y'all put up with that boy, Nick? He like ta drive anybody outta that room. Well, I tell ya what. No more mister nice guy for me as far as Ovary's concerned. When I get outta this fix, it's no more Dial soap for me. From now on, I'm usin' Lux soap and ole Ovary will have to find his Dial chips someplace else. You should do the same, Nick. We'll hit that summa bitch in his pocketbook. That'll learn him, right Nick? Heh, heh, heh."

"So you two guys are roommates with Rich Avery?" Paul asked.

"Yeah," I said. "Me, Avery, Chance here, and Bob Duncan."

"I know Bob Duncan," Paul said. "That's quite a room."

"Ya'll got that right," Lastings said, "and of the four of us, Nick and me is the onliest ones that is normal." Then he added, "Don't worry about hurting me when you shave that hair off, Nick. And you know what? I want ya'll to numb it and stitch it up by your own self. I got confidence in ya'll. You don't need to practice on no orange with ole Chance. When his roomy is concerned, ole Chance will take a chance. Now you know who your friends are. Heh, heh, heh."

Paul looked over at me, raised his eyebrows and shook his head in amusement.

Lastings never complained as I cleaned up the area on his scalp. It didn't take an expert to know that it would take an extensive amount of stitching to close up the wound.

Paul carried a tray of instruments that Dr. Jauss would need to stitch Lastings' scalp and placed it on a table next to Lastings. "Hey, Nick," Paul whispered, "what did he mean about practicing on oranges?"

"He's drunk," I whispered back.

"Is everything ready?" Dr. Jauss asked.

Lastings looked up at Dr. Jauss. "Hey Doc," he said, "wanna take a look at my hand before ya'll start?"

Dr. Jauss examined the hand that Lastings had extended toward him. "I can't tell for sure without an x-ray, but it looks like you might have a dislocated knuckle. You might have dislocated it on that other guy's jaw. We had to send him to Landstuhl to have his jaw wired."

"Ain't no way I did that, Doc. All's I know is that I got cracked over the head with a bottle, and when I went down one of those boys started in kicking on me, while another one of them stomped on my hand. The one with the broken jaw was down there right alongside me. We wuz both on the floor. He musta had got kicked too. You're my witness, Nick."

"How am I your witness? I wasn't there."

"Well, they're gonna write this all up, and whenever they do, ya'll tell em what I tole ya while it's fresh in ya mind."

Dr. Jauss had heard enough. "Okay, hold still. I'm going to numb the area."

"Wha choo mean, Doc? People bin telling me forever that that area always bin numb. Heh, heh, heh."

Dr. Jauss failed to see the humor, but instead he shook his head and handed me the basin that Lastings had been holding. I carried it over to the sink and cleaned it, hopefully for the last time.

As soon as Dr. Jauss had finished sewing up Lastings' scalp, an x-ray was taken of his hand, and it confirmed Dr. Jauss' suspicion that Lastings had a dislocated knuckle. A cast was applied, and when it was done, two M.P.s, who were never far off, escorted Lastings out of the dispensary.

"Hey, Sarge," Lastings said to one of the M.P.s, "can I get in touch with my company commander, Captain Davis? I wanna explain to him what happened."

"We'll take care of that," the sergeant said as they hustled Lastings out of the dispensary.

"Hey, Nick, I ain't sensing the love from these two boys, so in case ya'll never hear from me again, tell Captain Davis and my momma, what I tole ya'll bout what happened to-night. An, oh yeah, Nick, give my love to Ovary. Tell him he's not to worry one bit about me. I'll be back soon. Heh, heh, heh." And he was gone. The M.P.s hustled him out of the dispensary.

"Whew, what a character," Paul said. "Have you seen him soused like that before?"

"Yeah, pretty often," I said, "but not with all the bumps and bruises."

"Well, I think that you'll have an empty sack in the room until they straighten that whole mess out. What does that leave you with, three guys?"

"Yeah, I'll have to break the news slowly to Avery and Duncan. It'll be upsetting for them."

"Yeah. From what I've seen here in the last half hour I'll bet they'll be heartbroken," Paul said, and we finished cleaning up the room.

The rest of Friday was pretty much the way that I was told it would be. We saw lots of broken bones and bruises, in between trips to the mess hall for coffee and sandwiches. When things slowed down, we managed to get a little sleep in an empty examination room. I gave a routine antibiotic shot now and then but always in the arm. I considered myself more of an orderly than a medic, but not just a medical records clerk anymore for which I had been trained, but something in between.

"No rest for the weary, guys." Captain Baker walked into the examination room where Paul and I were relaxing and having a sandwich.

"We got a call from Kleber Kaserne. The C.Q. over there says that he has two guys in the basement of his building that are 'out of it,' as he puts it. He said that one guy appears to be unconscious, and the other guy is unapproachable."

"What does that mean?" I asked.

"I'm not sure," Captain Baker said. "I think that he means that you can't get near one of them. He wants us to send someone over to get the one guy away from the other guy who isn't moving."

"Oh, thank you for clearing that up, Sir. I was a little confused before your explanation," Paul said smiling at me.

"That's all that I can tell you," Captain Baker said. "I don't know much else."

"So, the C.Q. wants us to send a cracker box over to wake the one guy up and then to cart these guys off?" I asked.

Because of its box-like shape, the ambulances that we used were called cracker boxes.

"I think it's a little more than that," Captain Baker said.

"Geez, I've had that same waking up problem my whole life," Paul said, "and nobody ever sent an ambulance to wake me up and get me out of bed. My mom usually flung a shoe at me and that worked pretty good."

Captain Baker had a smile on his face. "No, the C.Q. told me that the two guys inhaled something. So yes, this looks like a hospital run to me. You'll have to make that decision when you get there."

Captain Baker paused briefly. "Look, you two guys finish your break. There are some other guys sitting around out there. I'll get them to do it."

"No, Sir, we'll go. Come on, Nick. Let's get out of this building for a while."

"That's a good idea," I said. "Hey, Paul, let's take a shoe just in case. It worked for your mother."

The C.Q. was waiting for Paul, me, and Dave Farley, the ambulance driver, when we pulled up to the building in Kleber Kaserne. The building was another remnant of the Hitler era, built to last for a thousand years. The C.Q. explained the situation to us as he led us down to the basement.

"These two guys were assigned company punishment for breaking the curfew. So they went down here to this dungeon to clean Cosmoline off rifles. They were using carbon tetrachloride to take the grease off. The problem was that with no windows down there, there was no ventilation. They were inhaling all of those fumes. When I came down here to check on them, one guy was on the floor making funny noises and the other guy was sitting alongside of his buddy. I tried to have a look at the guy who was down, and whenever I put my hands on him to roll him over, the other guy tried to take my head off. I mean I barely got out of there. The only reason that I can figure out that he didn't come after me was that he wanted to stand guard over his buddy. I want to tell you, the wrong guy went to sleep, because this boy is a heavyweight. That's when I decided to call you guys, and it looks to me like it's gonna take the four of us."

"Oh, good," I said, "Paul and I were only sitting around having a sandwich and Paul thought it would be a good idea to break the monotony and get away from the building for a while to help you out. Isn't that true, Paul?" But Paul ignored me.

The C.Q. slowly opened the door revealing a room that did truly look like a medieval dungeon. One bare light bulb hardly illuminated the room. The C.Q. stuck his head in, and then he pulled the door closed abruptly, as what appeared to be a bucket crashed against it.

"Okay," Dave Farley said. "Let's have a huddle here. If we're gonna help these two guys we can't waste much more time. Any suggestions?"

Paul said, "First we'll go back to the cracker box and get a straight jacket."

Before Paul could finish, the C.Q. said, "The big guy ain't never gonna hold still long enough for us to put him in a straight jacket."

"We'll calm him down first," Paul said.

"Oh, why didn't I think of that?" I said. "We'll calm him down. We'll sing him a lullaby. We'll try to reason with him, and if that doesn't calm him down and he still won't let us near his buddy, we can always use the shoe."

"What shoe?" the C.Q. asked.

"What I meant was that the four of us will hold him down, and then we'll inject him with a light dose of phenobarbital. Just enough to calm him down. Then we'll put the jacket on him in case he wakes up and goes ballistic on us in the cracker box."

"It sounds like a good plan to me," I said, "except the part about the phenobarbital."

"Well we've got to give him the phenobarbital," Paul said.

"I know. It's the light dose part that bothers me."

It took a minute or two to get what we needed from the cracker box, and armed with the straight jacket and a syringe with a light dose of phenobarbital, the four of us stood behind the door.

"Okay," Dave Farley said, "on the count of three we bust in, grab his arms and his legs and hold him still while Paul injects him."

"This guy does have two arms and two legs?" I asked.

"Yeah, so?" Farley asked.

"Well that means if two of us grab one arm each, and by the way make sure it's not the same arm, that leaves one of us to deal with two legs, because Paul will be busy trying to inject this guy. Hey Paul, did you bring the alcohol rub?"

"I can handle his legs," the C.Q. said. "I used to wrestle steers on the circuit in Oklahoma."

The guy was serious, so not to hurt his feelings, and so that he wouldn't know that I was from Brooklyn, I gave him a "yee haw, ride him cowboy." Dave counted to three and we rushed in.

I didn't realize how appropriate the reference to Brooklyn was, but I was reminded of the many times that we had gone to Coney Island. We had gone on one crazy ride after the other, which had spun us in dizzying circles and heights. I held onto one arm and Dave held onto the other, and it was like Coney Island all over again.

Then, just like now, we had been flung around in circles. At Coney Island, all I was aware of was flashes of color, but

I was always secure in the knowledge that I was strapped into a seat. Now Dave and I were hanging on to this guy for dear life or run the risk of being catapulted into one of the three-foot thick walls that Adolph had built.

"Grab his legs, Cowboy! Hold him still so that I can get his pants down!" Paul shouted.

"Get his pants down?" I shouted back. "Paul, stick that needle in his ass through his pants before one of us gets killed here!"

I thought what the hell was he doing? We were hanging on for life or limb and Paul was concerned about pulling this guy's pants down or maybe sanitizing the area with an alcohol rub. Not at that moment, while this guy was trying his best to launch all four of us into a wall.

"Paul," I shouted, "unless you're afraid to make a hole in his pants, you're taking this whole medic thing a little too seriously. Now shove that needle in, dammit!"

"Okay," Paul said. "I did it." And throwing the needle to the side, he grabbed a leg from Cowboy.

After another minute or two of struggling, I sensed less intensity on the part of the patient, but we continued to hold on until he relaxed completely, and then so did we.

I looked down to where Paul was holding on to the guy's leg, which was extended all the way to the right. Cowboy held onto the other leg, which was extended all the way to the left. Dave and I let go of his arms, and we both stood up. I looked over at Paul and Cowboy who seemed reluctant to take the chance to let go of the guy's legs that they both held, spread eagle.

"I think he's okay now," I said. "You both can let go unless you want to make a wish."

"I tell you what," Cowboy said, "back on the circuit the

steer quit once you got it down, but there ain't no surrender in that boy. Lordee!"

"Let's not waste anymore time," Dave said. "Get a couple of stretchers out of the cracker box. Check their vitals and let's get oxygen on the one who's been sleeping. Let's get King Kong here into the jacket as soon as we can. The phenobarbital might wear off and I don't feel like having a rematch with him in the cracker box driving to the hospital. It's also not a good idea to keep pumping him with that stuff."

A few minutes later, we had both soldiers secured and we were on our way to Landstuhl Army Hospital. When we arrived, an emergency team was already waiting for us and took them both off our hands.

CHAPTER 20

"YOU'RE A USELESS OVERWEIGHT SACK. THAT'S ALL that I said. We've argued before and worse things than that were said. They're just words, but to carry on like this?"

"Are you related to her?" Paul asked, gesturing to the lady who was lying sobbing on a sofa and whose eyes were only half opened. She appeared to me to be totally oblivious to her surroundings. Another woman was sitting on the edge of the same sofa holding the hand of the woman in distress.

"I'm her husband. Sergeant Larry Foster."

"That's not all you said, Larry," the other woman said.

Paul, Dave, and I looked at the woman who lay sobbing softly on the couch. Her eyes were half-shut and staring straight ahead. On an end table alongside of the couch was a picture of two children. The girl appeared to be about five years old and the boy was perhaps three.

"Come on, Louise," her husband said, as he shook the sobbing woman by her shoulder. "Come on. What's wrong with you?"

Dave, who had been checking the woman's blood pressure and listening to her heart and lungs, looked up at the husband and said, "I don't believe that she hears you, Sergeant." The woman continued her soft sobbing and barely audible mumbling.

"Go through this again. Tell me exactly what happened, Sergeant Foster," Paul said.

"It was no big deal," Foster said. "The four of us were sitting at the table over there playing cards."

I looked over to a kitchen table cluttered with empty beer bottles and ashtrays full of crushed cigarette butts. There were cards scattered on top of the table.

"Well, what happened?" Paul asked again.

"Wayne Gregg, his wife, Ginny, Louise and I were playing poker." He gestured toward the other woman who was still sitting on the edge of the sofa where Sergeant Foster's wife lay.

Ginny Gregg had a look of concern on her face, and occasionally dabbed her own eyes with a tissue.

"Before you continue, Sergeant Foster, where is Mr. Gregg now," Paul asked.

As he started to answer, Mrs. Gregg said, "Sergeant Gregg went back to our apartment down the hall to relieve the babysitter. I wanted to stay with Louise until you got here."

"Okay, go ahead, Sergeant," Paul said to Sergeant Foster, "tell me what happened."

"Well, like I said. We were playing cards, and as usual, Louise made one of her typical dumb moves. She does it all the time. All I said was that only she could play a dumb hand like that. I guess she didn't like hearing that so we began arguing. I can't remember exactly what we said, but we were arguing."

Ginny Gregg dabbed at her eyes and looked directly at Sergeant Foster. "I remember Louise saying, 'Can't you ever talk nice?' That's when you called her a useless, overweight sack of, well I don't want to say the rest, Larry. It was disgusting. Louise asked you not to talk to her that way. I don't know why she needed to explain it to you but she said that she was heavy because she's seven months pregnant, and that she was the mother of your children."

Sergeant Foster glared at Mrs. Gregg, who looked directly back at him.

"That's not exactly how it happened," Sergeant Foster said.

"That's exactly the way that I remember it," Ginny Gregg responded.

"Well, how did she get to this state? Was there any physical contact?" Dave asked.

"No. I never put a hand on her," Sergeant Foster said.

"Sometimes words hurt as much as blows and even leave deeper scars. Anyway, what you're seeing here with Louise just seemed to happen," Ginny Gregg said. "Louise put her head into her hands. She was crying, and then she started slipping off the chair. We caught her and carried her over to the couch. When we saw that we were unable to wake her up, we called you."

"Listen," Sergeant Foster said, "husbands and wives argue now and then, but not everyone has an overreaction like that."

Ginny Gregg shot Sergeant Foster a look and was about to say something, but before she could, the same little girl from the picture on the end table, walked into the room. Seeing her mother on the couch, the little girl began walking in her direction.

"Mommy, can I have a drink of water?" the girl asked.

Before the child could get any closer to her mother, Ginny Gregg picked her up. "Mommy has a headache right now, Kathy. Aunt Ginny will get you some water," and she carried the child out of the room.

"Nick, you and Paul go down to the cracker box," Dave said. Bring back a stretcher and a couple of blankets. First, call Landstuhl. Tell them about the situation here and to be ready for us."

After we had secured Louise Foster on the stretcher, Dave Farley said to Sergeant Foster, "You can ride in the ambulance with us and we will drive you back here, or you can follow us to the hospital in your own car. Whatever you'd prefer."

"Maybe it would be better if I stay with the kids and make some sort of an arrangement for them. In the morning, I can pick her up when the hospital releases her," Sergeant Foster said.

"I'd be very surprised if they released her in the morning," Dave said.

"I'd be glad to watch the kids," Ginny Gregg said. When Sergeant Foster didn't answer, she said, "If you guys will take me back here after the hospital, I'll go with you in the ambulance." Ginny Gregg was sitting by Louise Foster again, holding her hand.

"We'll be glad to do that," Dave said, "but we probably won't get back before 1 A.M. or so, if that's okay with you."

"That'll be fine," Ginny Gregg answered. "I just don't want to leave her alone, and I want to be there if she wakes up."

Dave looked down on the still sobbing Louise Foster, and then looked up at Ginny Gregg. He shook his head from side to side trying to tell her that he didn't believe that Louise Foster would be waking up any time soon.

Dave and I sat in the back of the cracker box with Louise Foster and Ginny Gregg, as Paul drove us to Landstuhl. Ginny Gregg was alongside of Louise Foster, holding her hand and occasionally brushing a wisp of hair from her friend's face.

"She's lucky to have a good friend like you," I said.

"We knew each other from the States," Ginny explained. "Our families shipped to Germany together. We have kids about the same age and we've gotten real close. If you knew her, you'd see what a sweet person she is. Why she hooked up with that guy I'll never understand, as different as they are. She's so sweet and he's so insensitive. They were high school sweethearts. I understand all of that, but she could have done better than him. She deserved better. It's just another case of a woman thinking that a man will change for her. No one changes for anybody. They change for themselves if they change at all. The ones who need the most change never see their own faults, and Larry thinks that he's perfect."

Dave and I had to remain outside of it, so we listened to Ginny Gregg and nodded our heads in acknowledgment. She looked from one or the other of us.

"Why isn't he in this ambulance? That speaks volumes about him. He uses the kids as an excuse not to be in the ambulance." She continued, "Wayne and I could have worked something out for the kids. He knew that. He just didn't want to go with her. He just doesn't give a damn. She doesn't deserve this."

"People don't always get what they deserve," I said. "Some people seem to get away with murder or do bad things and they never seem to get what they deserve, while good people like you have described in your friend Ginny here, well they're victims. There's no answer. That's life. It isn't always fair."

"It's really none of my business," Dave said, "but if Sergeant Foster is as bad as you say he is, why do you bother with him?"

"It's not about him. It's about Louise. My husband and I knew early on what he was like, and that's the reason why we stayed close. It was for Louise and the kids. I kept telling Wayne that this would end up bad, but I couldn't imagine this."

We sat silently for a while, listening to the steady sobbing from Louise, her eyes closed tightly and still unresponsive.

Ginny Gregg turned to Dave and asked, "Is this a break down?"

"I don't know," Dave said. "The doctors in Landstuhl will tell you that. There is one thing that I'm pretty sure of. You can't abuse the human mind anymore than you can abuse the human body for a prolonged period of time. At some point, the body or the mind will break down. In some ways, the mind is more fragile than the body. It's easier to repair a fractured bone than it is to repair a fractured mind. Sometimes if a person finds that he can't cope with reality, he creates a more acceptable world in his mind and lives there. That helps him to get through his life. We say that they live in a dream world. In a world of their own. They're out of touch with reality. Sometimes to escape the real world, they turn to alcohol or they take drugs to help them cope. In extreme cases, I've seen it where people retreat totally into themselves without the assistance of drugs or alcohol. They just shut down and they're uncommunicative. You just can't get through to them. We'll have to leave it to the doctors at Landstuhl to figure it out."

We arrived at the hospital and filled the doctors in on what had been told to us. We left Louise Foster in the same state as she was in when we arrived at her apartment earlier that evening, and we started for home.

We dropped Ginny Gregg off at her apartment, and got back to the dispensary a little after 1 A.M.

It was early Sunday morning, and I was starting to do a countdown. I had survived Friday and Saturday. I had walked into the dispensary looking for all intents and purposes like a qualified medic, when I actually believed that I had less medical knowledge than most people. I was grateful that the medical people with whom I was detailed did not suspect how completely unqualified I was. The fear of embarrassment if I were found out caused me to carry on. So the charade continued.

I could hear Paul's heavy breathing as he lay in a deep sleep on the examination table, which was a few feet away from the one that I was resting on. Both of us were exhausted, mentally and physically, but I was still awake thinking of the activities of the last two days.

It seemed like weeks and not hours ago that Paul and I had become acquainted. We had to deal with Sergeant Collins in the mess hall. In between that first meeting with Collins and dealing with Chance, as well as the other emergencies, and the call to Sergeant Foster's apartment on Saturday evening, it had been like life in a combat zone. It was becoming more obvious as the weekend progressed, why medics or corpsmen, or however they were designated, were held in such high regard.

My object now was to get through the homestretch unscathed, finish up on Sunday, and to get back to Panzer Kaserne knowing that I had helped a little. I had gained valuable experience in the process without embarrassing myself.

There wasn't much activity in the dispensary, probably due to the fact that most of the celebrating was over. Even the party animals, having gotten most of it out of their systems, were all recuperating before getting back to their duties the next day. I continued to review the events of the last few hours and I was soon fast asleep.

It was still dark in the examination room so I wasn't able to read the time on my wristwatch. I looked to where Paul had been sleeping, and saw that he was sitting on the examination table, his legs dangling over the side.

"Can you see the time?" I asked Paul.

"0600, rise and shine," Paul answered.

"No. I'm waiting for the bugler," I said.

"Oh, the bugler. I forgot to tell you about that. Do you remember that guy that your buddy belted in the jaw? Wouldn't you know that he is the regimental bugler? They had to wire his jaw shut, so we won't be hearing from him anytime soon."

"Very funny," I said. I forced myself to sit up. I looked over at Paul.

"Hey, Paul, do you think that we should call over to Landstuhl to find out how Louise Foster is doing?"

Paul didn't hesitate. "No. I don't."

"Why not?"

"Look, Nick. I understand your concern. I felt awful about that situation. You know. The situation was pathetic. There are kids involved and all, and by the way, I don't think that the prognosis for Louise is very good. If what Ginny Gregg told us is true, now those kids are stuck with Sergeant Foster. You can't do this job very well without some compassion, especially in a situation like Louise Foster is in. You can't get emotionally involved with the people that you treat either. If you did, they'd be strapping you into a funny suit. There's a sad story behind everyone who comes into this dispensary. Anyway, do you want to get involved with Sergeant Foster? If you get involved with Mrs. Foster, that nut job that she married becomes part of the package. There are red lights all over that situation."

"You're right," I said. "Maybe I'll just send her a get well card."

Paul looked at me, shook his head and walked out of the room.

"Anonymously!" I shouted. Paul kept walking.

The rest of Sunday was uneventful. My initial anxiety about giving injections seemed silly to me now. I did that as well as performing routine procedures such as cleaning or dressing wounds or changing bandages. I did it but it was not the sort of work that I would ever want to do if I were given the choice. My greatest worry now was that I might catch something from someone, so I spent lots of time washing my hands, and keeping my hands away from my face.

"I can't wait to get back to my room, to get out of these whites, take a shower, and then to sleep Monday away," I said to Paul and Dave Farley.

It was 2200, or 10 P.M., and I was relaxing with my two close friends, both of whom I had known for all of three days. The army had a way of doing that. Paul and Dave were not attached to my medical group. They were recruited from other medical groups in the area because it was anticipated that this would be a busy payday weekend. I couldn't recall ever having seen them, but they were my buddies already.

"It's been fun working with you guys especially since this was my first shot at C.Q. in this dispensary. You made it easy for me even though it wasn't always lots of laughs, but soon we'll all go off in different directions."

"You never know," Dave said. "We could all find ourselves on C.Q. together in here somewhere down the line and that'll be okay with me. We worked well together."

"I thought so too," Paul said, "until Nick asked me to go with him to visit Louise Foster up at Landstuhl. He wants to send her a get well card." Paul smiled over at Dave.

Dave looked horrified. "What?" he said.

"I didn't say that we should visit her," but before I could finish my thought, Dr. Jauss came into the room.

"We just received a call from the military police. A vehicle skidded off the road into the woods on the autobahn. Two people are trapped in the car and they are requesting a cracker box. They identified the victims as a male and a female. They said that the male appears to be an American, and they aren't sure but they think that the woman passenger might be a German national. Remember the protocol if she is German. Here are the directions. Hurry."

As we rushed out of the room, I said to Paul, "What's the protocol if the woman is German?"

"We're only allowed to give them on-the-spot treatment. Once they're stabilized, we have to take the person who is not an American to the nearest German hospital. If a German medical team should get to the scene of an accident first, it goes the same way for them. They treat Americans on the spot, but they drop Americans off at the nearest American medical facility. It just seems like they never get to the scenes of these accidents before we do, especially if they suspect that an American is involved, whether or not there are Germans involved too."

It had begun to snow, and the snow was rapidly accumulating on the ground making driving hazardous.

When we arrived at the scene, there was an M.P. vehicle, its red lights flashing on the roof of the car. The M.P. had pointed his headlights at a car with U.S.A. plates off the road and down in a ditch. The car had skidded off the slippery road, hit some trees, and settled into the ditch. There wasn't a German emergency vehicle in sight.

An M.P. hurried to the ambulance. "We've got two people in the car. The driver seems to be an American male and the passenger seems to be a female German national. I haven't been able to get either door open."

Dave, Paul, and I jumped out of the cracker box and made our way to where the road dipped, and then we slid down the snowy embankment to where the car lay in the ditch.

The M.P. flashed his light in and we peered into the wrecked car. The M.P. said, "He's been moaning and moving his head, but as far as I can tell, she hasn't moved at all."

We tried to open both doors, but they were jammed so

badly that we couldn't get them to budge. The windows on the vehicle were cracked and twisted, but somehow they managed to stay in one piece.

I said to the M.P., "Get your tire iron. Maybe we can break the glass on this door and pull them out through the door window if I can crawl in and turn their shoulders and legs around. How does that sound?"

"It's worth a try," Paul said.

The M.P. was back quickly with his tire iron, and he broke the window next to where the driver sat. Then he broke the rear passenger window and I crawled into the car and made my way toward the injured man and woman. It was one of the few times in my life when being the smallest guy was an advantage.

By the light cast by the headlights on the military police vehicle, I could see that both victims were bleeding profusely, and there was glass scattered all over.

"Okay, Nick. As soon as you can rotate his back to the door, I'll grab him under his arms and I'll try to pull him out. Can you swivel his back toward the door?" Paul asked.

I slid head first between the man and the woman, and grabbed both his legs to try to swing them around, but I instantly let them go when he shrieked in pain.

"Nick. Do you have his legs?" Paul asked.

"I'm not so sure that we can do it this way," I said. "Did you hear how he screamed and I hardly even touched him? I don't know how I'm gonna do this."

"Nick. Now listen to me. We don't have a lot of time and we don't have a choice, and he doesn't either," Paul said. "It's gonna hurt but we might have to hurt him if we're gonna help him. Now take his legs as carefully as you can and rotate his back to this door. I'll grab his arms and Dave and I will slide him out. Let's do it right the first time."

I slid my left arm over the car seat and planted my left hand on the seat alongside of the man. Then I placed my right hand around his calves, braced my knees on the back of the front seat, and began to rotate his hips. As soon as I did, he began to scream in pain.

"Nick. How are you doing?" Paul asked.

"I'm trying to free his knees from under the dashboard and the steering wheel," I answered.

I finally managed to get the man's knees out from under the steering wheel and then I was able to rotate his hips so that Paul was able to get a grip under his arms. Paul and Dave were able to pull him through the window and out of the wreck. The man moaned in pain the whole time as they placed him on a stretcher and made their way up the snow covered hill to the ambulance.

I crawled onto the front seat, which was littered with broken glass and covered with blood to have a look at the woman. The M.P. flashed his light through the broken window.

"How is she doing, Doc?" he asked.

I looked at the woman who still had not moved the whole time that I had been attempting to free the man. I supposed that the correct thing to do was to feel for a pulse, so I lifted her hand, which was as cold as ice and searched her wrist for a pulse.

I thought that I felt the flickering of a pulse beat. "I think that she's alive," I shouted.

Paul had returned with the stretcher. "Okay, Nick. Let's do it the same way. See if you can turn her around and slide her back toward me."

I pulled the woman toward the steering wheel. She didn't cry out in pain as the man had done, which was a good thing for me, but at the same time I realized that it could be a bad thing for her. When I had gone as far as I could go, I got out of the way and tumbled back to the rear seat and Paul pulled the woman toward him as I lifted her legs. Paul and the M.P. were already carrying the stretcher up the snowy embankment when I crawled out of the wreck.

I opened the door of the cracker box to a blast of warm air. Dave had already started an I.V. on the man who we identified as a warrant officer, helicopter pilot.

I looked over at Paul who had a troubled look on his face as he switched his stethoscope to various areas on the woman's chest.

"Dave," Paul said, "she has a very faint heartbeat. I can hardly find it. Dave, we're losing her."

Paul took the stethoscope out of his ears and began to make quick short pushes on the woman's chest. Dave left the warrant officer and rushed to assist Paul.

"Nick. Get that oxygen mask on her. Hurry!"

I put the mask on the woman's face and turned the valve up while Dave injected her. Paul continued to push on the woman's chest, while Dave, listening for a heartbeat, moved the stethoscope from place to place. After a minute or two, Dave sat back and folded the stethoscope. Waiting a few seconds, Dave put the stethoscope back on and searched once again for a heartbeat, some sign of life.

"We lost her," Dave said, as he removed the oxygen mask from the woman's face. His face was grim as he stood up and turned his attention to the warrant officer.

"No, not yet," Paul said, as he continued to press the palms of his hands on the woman's chest for another minute.

Dave stood up and lifted Paul's hands. "Paul, she's gone."

Dave removed a sheet from the cabinet and covered the woman with it while I looked on in disbelief.

"She's dead?" I asked stupidly. Both of them looked at me without answering. This wasn't supposed to happen I thought. It was one thing coming upon the scene of an accident and finding someone dead. There was nothing that you could do in that case. But she was alive. After all of that effort, we had gotten her out. Where was the happily ever after? It wasn't supposed to end this way.

The M.P. opened the ambulance doors. "I found her purse in the wreck," he said, and handed it to me. Then he looked over to where the woman lay covered with the sheet, and turned to Paul.

Before he could say anything, Paul said, "We lost her."

"She's dead?" the M.P. asked. "Geez." He shook his head and then asked, "How's he doing?"

"Better than her," Paul said. "We'll take him to Landstuhl. Check her purse for I.D., Nick. I'm sure that she's a German national."

I looked through the woman's purse, and although everything was written in German, I found an identification card with the woman's picture and name on it. It identified her as Ursula Bauer.

I said to Paul, "Ursula Bauer."

Paul took the I.D. from me. "She's a German national, Dave. Let's take her to the nearest German hospital and then we'll take the warrant officer to Landstuhl."

The M.P. who had been standing outside of the cracker box said, "Well, thanks a lot guys. I'll fill out my report while I wait for the wrecker to pull the vehicle out of the ditch. Thanks for the help. Good job."

"It could have been better," I said.

"Not your fault," he said, and closed the doors.

The snow continued to fall heavily as we drove up to the rear emergency entrance to the German hospital. Dave went in and a few minutes later, he came out with two German hospital workers. One of them was carrying a stretcher.

"I gave them a copy of my report," Paul said. "They didn't have much to say to me."

Paul walked to the back of the ambulance. We opened the ambulance doors and the two German hospital workers took the woman's body out of the cracker box and placed it on their stretcher. By that time, I could see blood soaking through the sheet that Paul had placed over the woman's body. Paul saw that the Germans had removed the sheet from the dead woman's body and were about to hand the sheet back to him. They didn't have a replacement.

"No. Put the sheet back on her," Paul said. "You can keep it."

They put the sheet back on the body and placed the stretcher on the cement walk along the side of the building. Then they walked back into the building.

We sat in the cracker box for a minute or two after they walked into the hospital but they didn't come back out. "Where did they go?" I asked. "Aren't they going to bring her inside? Are they just going to leave her out there?"

I looked at the stretcher containing Ursula Bauer's body where they had placed it off to the side of the emergency room door. The snow was falling rapidly and was quickly covering up the blood stained sheet.

"Do you believe this?" Dave said. "People die easily, but other things die hard. It's their way of showing their contempt for her for fraternizing with the enemy." He shifted the cracker box into gear and headed for Landstuhl.

I looked back to see the stretcher with Ursula Bauer's body disappearing in the distance being covered by snow.

CHAPTER 21

THE HUGE FERRY PLOWED ITS WAY THROUGH THE choppy waters of the North Sea on its way to Copenhagen in Denmark. I had grown up by the port of New York, and I had seen some of the world's largest ocean liners cruising back and forth up the Narrows where today stands the Verrazano Bridge. Some were luxury liners, some were troop ships or commercial ships, coming to or leaving the United States. I don't believe that even the largest of those ships could accommodate the volume of automobiles or railroad cars that these ferries did. The train that we had taken from Kaiserslautern to Hamburg rolled right onto the ferry, and was joined by other trains that had come from other places in Germany. All of them were heading across the North Sea.

It was January of 1958. I had been in Germany since October of 1956. I was in the final four months of my deployment. Rich Avery and Bob Duncan had gotten to Germany a few months before I did, and so they had both rotated home before me. Though the privilege of rooming with them was gone, the honor would remain with me forever.

Just as military life caused complete strangers to form the closest of bonds in days or sometimes even in hours, it was amazing to me how quickly those bonds could be broken and just as quickly forgotten. It seemed to happen as soon as the men were separated from each other. Once they left Panzer Kaserne, I never heard from either Rich Avery or Bob Duncan again. I was positive that Rich had pursued his goal of earning a doctorate in medicine, and that Bob would achieve his goal of having a doctorate in math.

It was difficult for me to see Bob and Rich leave, but it was even more difficult when the army reorganized and the Triple Seven Nine was absorbed into the 540th General Dispensary. I said farewell to Panzer Kaserne.

The college atmosphere and beautiful campus of Panzer Kaserne and the private rooms that we had enjoyed were gone. They were replaced by the post-World War II barracks that had been constructed by the army, and were located in Vogelweh, which was located on the opposite side of Kaiserslautern. Now we all slept in what was called an open bay and along with my new quarters came new friends. The elitism was gone.

Tony Pace was a twenty-six year old Korean War veteran, and was now a dental technician for the 464th Dental Group, which was located on the second floor of the dispensary. The fact that Tony, like me, was from New York, made it easier for the both of us to form a close bond. In addition, we were both Italian. We were two Italian-Americans from New York. There needed to be no explaining. There was just a comfort zone. There was a sub-culture of food, tradition and religion that guys from other parts of the country could never quite understand.

"This place better be all that they say it is," Tony said. "If not, we'll make the most of it. We have three-day passes and you have your fancy camera. If worse comes to worst, we can take lots of pictures," he laughed. "I've been in Tokyo and that place was wild. The party never ended."

I listened to what Tony was saying with mixed emotions. At twenty-six, I considered that Tony was an old hand. Tony was a man of the world in my opinion. He had been raised in foster homes and had an unhappy childhood. Tony had quit high school at seventeen and joined the army. When he was just twenty years old, he was in combat in Korea where he had been wounded. After recovering from his wounds, the army retrained him as a dental technician. Tony never had a real family and the army was his family and his life.

I was a twenty-one year old kid from Brooklyn, away from home for the first time, and I was trying to make a good impression on this veteran. I wanted to give the impression that I had been there and done that. Whereas Tony was concerned that Copenhagen would not live up to Tokyo, my concern was how I would handle situations if all of the stories that guys had returned with were not the usual exaggerations. The last thing that I didn't want to appear to be was a kid in front of guys like Tony.

I had spent lots of time during our off hours, listening to the many stories told by soldiers in various accents and drawls. On occasions where I would chip in, I would often stretch the truth or make up an incident that really hadn't happened. I believed it would help me to fit in. I must have been convincing, because veterans like Tony had accepted me. I believed that I would have to behave in a way that would live up to their expectations. No matter how unnatural that behavior really was to me, I found myself in two worlds. There was the world of Avery and Duncan, and the world of soldiers like Tony. Either way, the charade was continuing.

Our train rolled off the ferry and into a train depot in Copenhagen. Tony and I carried our bags into the sunny and cold Danish streets. The contrast between Denmark and Germany was instantly apparent to me. There was none of the melancholia or self-awareness of a defeated nation that was so palpable in Germany. Here, there was a hustle and bustle of people without the guilt or shame of defeat. It was contagious and invigorating, not unlike the streets of New York City.

We walked several blocks from the depot with no idea about which direction to go, but hoping that the one we took would lead us to a hotel, which it did. There were several to choose from, and we finally picked a hotel that looked clean but not as pricey as some of the others that we had walked by.

"Good afternoon," the clerk at the desk said, with hardly a trace of an accent. "May I help you?"

"Yes," Tony said. "We'd like a couple of rooms."

"That's fine," the clerk replied. "I can give you each a separate room, or a double room if that would be better, and you can pay by the day. How long will you be staying?"

"No. Separate rooms would be better." Tony winked at me and whispered, "I like you a lot, Babe, but there are certain times when I don't like an audience." Then addressing the clerk, he said, "We'll be checking out on Sunday."

"Separate rooms, you've got that right," I said, even though I was just about to ask the clerk if it would be cheaper to go with separate rooms or a double room.

So separate rooms it was. We brought our bags up to our rooms, which were modest affairs with bathrooms and showers down the hall. Everything appeared to be general inspection clean. We settled in and a few minutes later, I knocked on Tony's door. We made our way out of the hotel and stepped out in to the cold crisp air looking for a place to eat.

We turned into a restaurant on what seemed to be the main drag. We were shown to a small table by a big plate glass window from which we could look out onto the busy street.

"You are Americans," she smiled. An attractive waitress stood close by, ready to take our order.

"How did you know?" I asked.

"A little birdie told her," Tony said. He was already in his flirtatious mode and showing interest.

"It's easy to tell," she said with a smile.

"Well, we speak English. Was that your first clue?" I asked.

"So do the British and the Canadians. They always come in here too. You can still tell the difference even before you hear them speak," she said.

"That's amazing," Tony said, "and they say that Americans can be rude, but we haven't even been here long enough to be rude," and we all smiled.

"Look," she said. "You have admirers." She pointed to the plate glass window. I looked to my right, and staring down at us was what had to be two of the prettiest girls that I had seen since arriving in Europe.

"See," the waitress said, "they know that you're Americans too even from the other side of the window."

One of the girls stood back a bit, but the other gave us a little smile.

Tony looked from the girls to me. "Do you believe this?" he asked. "They're making me blush."

"If you didn't see this in Tokyo, then we're off to a good start," I said, "but then again, you weren't with me when you were in Tokyo."

"Oh, that's true. I forgot about that, Nick."

As silly as it was, we sat smiling at them, and they stood on the other side of the window smiling back.

"It must be my black hair," Tony said. "These girls are not used to that."

"Oh yeah, I forgot," I said, "they probably think that you're Cary Grant." Tony's hero was Cary Grant. He never missed the opportunity to tell us how he was often mistaken for the actor and we fueled his ego by referring to him as Cary.

"Cary Grant's hair and mine are the same color. Look at my hair," he would say, "it's so black that it's nearly purple."

"Yeah, okay Cary," we would say with no subtlety, and there was no subtlety about the flirting going on between the girls outside and the two of us. I was taken by how pretty the girls were. There were pretty girls in Germany, but this kind of friendliness was bordering on boldness. For that matter, any display of warmth by Germans of any gender was unheard of. Without a doubt, fraternization especially for young girls from good families, was frowned upon. It was discouraged because of the reputations of soldiers. There were always the other kind of girls, but for a guy like me who wanted none of that, life could be lonely.

I wasn't sure that we would see two such pretty girls again, and I knew that I would have regrets all the way back to Germany if I allowed this opportunity, which I thought might be our last, to slip away. I would be thinking about all of the "what ifs" if I hadn't acted. Besides, doing something bold right now would impress Tony, and win me some positive conversation time when we got back to Germany.

"Where are you going?" Tony asked, as I slid my chair away from the table.

"I'm going outside to talk to them," I said.

Tony looked at me, smiled and shook his head. "I give you credit, but don't bring them in here if they're hookers."

"Hookers?" I had seen hookers from the first time that we had docked in Bremerhaven and they were there all the time in Kaiserslautern. Most of them seemed repulsive, even old and scary to me. These two girls were the farthest thing from that. They were young and had a fresh look, like two pretty girls from the neighborhood.

When I got outside, I gave a quick glance through the window where Tony sat with an amused look on his face. I better not blow this I thought. If these girls walk away, I'd be the main topic of conversation for a good laugh when we got back to Volgeweh. Now I was thinking about what I would do if these girls didn't speak English. Tony was observing.

"Don't you know that it's not polite to stare at a person when he's eating?" I furrowed my brow and smiled.

"Oh, we're sorry," the one who had been closest to the window said. "We thought that you had finished." Her English was almost flawless. Her friend stood back and smiled too. Each of them carried several, of what appeared to be, textbooks.

It was very cold and windy out there, so I said, "Well, my friend and I were just about to order dinner, and then we looked up and there you were. We just got off the train and we were having something to eat before we went to see the Little Mermaid. We have no idea where to find the Little Mermaid. Do you think that you'd like to show us where it is, but you'd better hurry up before I freeze to death?" They hesitated and I shivered in the cool winter wind.

"If I die from the cold, it will be on your conscience."

They laughed and got the joke. I liked it.

"Why don't you come in, order something, and I'll introduce you to my friend," I said pointing at Tony, who was watching it all, still looking amused, as he gave us a little wave.

"Do you know who Cary Grant is?" I asked.

"We do," they said. "He's an actor."

"That's right," I said, "well, my friend would never tell you, he's too modest to tell you, but he used to be a stand-in for Cary Grant. He can tell you lots of stories about the dangerous stunts he did for Cary Grant. Doesn't he look just like him? But hurry. I'm freezing."

"Are you both American soldiers?"

"Yes we are," I said, "and soon we'll both be going back to America, and this will be our last chance to see the Little Mermaid."

She turned to her friend and said something in Danish. Her friend nodded and turned to me and said, "Okay, we'll take you to see the Little Mermaid."

The three of us walked back into the restaurant, and as I walked by the waitress, she whispered to me, "See, everyone can tell that you are Americans."

When we approached the table, Tony gave me a quick nod of approval.

The first girl looked at Tony and said, "Please excuse us. We only came in because we didn't want to see your friend freeze to death."

"That's okay. I was just about to bring his jacket out to him," Tony said as he slid a couple of chairs from an empty table over to ours for the girls to sit on. "My name is Tony, and his name is Lucky."

"Lucky?" the quiet one said. "Is that a name?"

"No, no. Don't listen to him. My name is Nick. He means that we're lucky that I picked this restaurant and that the both of you were standing outside."

"Oh, I see," she said, but I wasn't sure that she really did see.

"My name is Marian," the quiet one said.

"And I'm Kirstin," the other girl said.

The waitress brought us our food and Tony said, "Please order something to eat."

"No, thank you," Kirstin said, and then she said something to the waitress in Danish. They seemed to be joking back and forth.

"What are they saying?" I asked Marian.

"She's telling the waitress that the two of us aren't hungry because we went to dinner after we finished working. We were waiting at the bus stop to go to night school but we came in here instead."

"Is there anything else that I can get for you?" the waitress asked.

"We're fine," Tony said, "unless you girls have changed your minds."

"No, we're sure," Kirstin said, and the waitress walked away.

"Night school," Tony said. "That's why the two of you are carrying all of those books."

"Yes," Marian said. "In June we will both graduate from high school, and perhaps we can go to the university so that we won't have to work in a factory anymore."

"What kind of a factory do you work in?" I asked.

"It's not a good job," Kirstin said. "They make all sorts of cardboard boxes. That's what we do."

"Is it a problem if you miss school?" I asked.

"No, we never miss, and one time won't matter," Marian said.

"Is that where you learned to speak English?" Tony asked.

"We have English in high school, but in Denmark children learn to speak English in what you call elementary school," Kirstin said.

I sat there taking it all in. It was like being home again. Two pretty and, now I knew, intelligent girls, who didn't appear to be scarred by war. It made me realize how lonely I had been away from home in a regimented mans' world. I knew Tony was enjoying the moment too, as he looked from one girl to the other.

"Hey Tony, I was just telling the girls about how you used to do stunts for Cary Grant before you went into the army."

"Oh yeah, but that was long time ago," Tony said, feigning modesty. "I had to get away from it. It was too dangerous."

Marian looked impressed. "Dangerous," she asked, "but isn't the army dangerous?"

"Oh, well yes it is, especially what Nick and I do, but at least we have guns, and somebody has to do it," Tony said, as he assumed his best commando face. Then changing the subject he said, "Hey, Nick, look at those glassy blue eyes on these girls. Did you ever see anything like it? I thought that you had to die to go to heaven."

Both girls laughed at Tony's not so subtle remark, but at that moment, I felt precisely the same way at our good fortune.

We finished eating and paid our bill. The girls gathered up their books and we headed out of the restaurant. When we got outside, Tony said, "Since we're new in town can you girls give us a tour of Copenhagen?"

"Yeah, Tony, they're going to take us to see the Little Mermaid. Here, let me carry those books," I said to Kirstin.

She said something to Marian in Danish, and before I could ask, Kirstin said, "I was just saying that I wish I could drop my books off at my house and change my clothes and my shoes for something more comfortable. I think it would be better. I live a little way out in the country. It's about ten minutes from here."

"Kirstin," Marian said, "if you're going to bring your books back to your house, would you take mine too?" She turned to Tony and me, "Kirstin lives closer than I do. Is that all right? Then we can all meet in front of Tivoli Gardens in about two hours."

"What's the Tivoli Gardens?" I asked.

"The Tivoli Gardens is an amusement park," Kirstin explained. "It's closed in the winter, but it's in the middle of Copenhagen. It's a central landmark. We can meet them there."

Tony winked at me, "Take your time, Babe."

"We'll see you in a couple of hours," I said.

Kirstin and I hailed a cab, and we drove past areas of pine forests, out to a modest house somewhere in the suburbs.

"I live here with my parents and my sister. Both of my parents are working and my sister is in school."

"I'll wait in the cab," I said.

"No, no. Come in," she said. "You can't wait in the cab. It's too expensive. We'll call for another one. I'll take a few minutes, and I need you to help me to carry my books and Marian's books."

We sent the cab away and we entered the house. It was small and neat with a central room with beamed ceilings and seemed to be heated by a wood-burning stove. I stood in what I assumed to be the family room, my arms full of Marian and Kirstin's books. The heat from the stove felt good after the cold from outside, and the aroma of the burning wood, made the place feel like a cozy hunting lodge.

"My room is right down the hall," Kirstin said. "We'll put these books on my desk. I'll change and we'll be off."

I followed her into a room that could be described as "girlsy", with dolls and pictures and the frilly things that girls love. Kirstin pointed at her desk, "Put the books over there."

I put the books down and looked at some of the pictures. Kirstin explained that they had been taken on class trips, and some fun times with her family and friends.

"Look, here is Marian and me when we were in what you call elementary school."

There was no mistaking the two little girls in the picture. "Have you always been friends?" I asked.

"As long as I can remember," Kirstin said.

We looked and laughed at the pictures and I was so comfortable that I had to remind myself that I had only known this girl for a couple of hours.

I looked at Kirstin and I didn't want to mistake her warm manner for something else. She was mature, but she told me that she had just turned seventeen. The last thing that I wanted to do was to scare her by acting like a jerk. I mean, I had just met her. I shook off where my mind was going and I said, "We better hurry. Tony and Marian will be waiting for us," and we walked back to the family room.

I sat on a couch, close to the stove going over the last few hours in my mind. I thought of the ferry ride, checking into the hotel, the restaurant, and of the two girls in the window. I could never have imagined this, I thought. It's a good thing that Tony was with me because no one would believe this story when I got back. I stared at the snow outside and when I looked up Kirstin was in front of me. She was dressed in different clothing, looking refreshed and pretty.

"I'm ready," she said, "and I called for a cab. He should be outside."

"Let's go," I answered.

We got into the cab, and headed back to Tivoli Gardens.

"Where the heck are Tony and Marian?" I said.

We walked around the Tivoli Gardens area, but we weren't able to find them.

"We were only gone for a little more than an hour," I said. "Maybe they got tired of standing around in the cold. Who knows?" Kirstin looked at me and shrugged her shoulders. "Well, we can't worry about it. It's starting to look like it's just you and me, Kirstin."

"That's fine with me," she smiled.

"Let the tour begin," I said.

"First we'll go to see the Little Mermaid," she said. She had the enthusiasm of a little girl.

"You've seen the Mermaid before," I said.

"Yes, but I've never seen it with you," and without taking a breath, she said, "then I know a wonderful little coffee shop that has wonderful Danish pastry. We'll stop in there and warm up. Then we'll tour the palace where the Danish kings and queens live. Then there's the statue of Hans Christian Andersen. Then…."

She really was a kid, "Hold on," I said, "let's save something for tomorrow."

"Tomorrow? The only thing for sure about tomorrow is that I must go to work. That's the only thing for sure. Let's do as much as we can today," Kirstin said.

"Well, then let's get started right now," I said. She clutched my arm, and we headed for the Little Mermaid.

It had nothing to do with being in the army, or of bawdy barracks talk and of conquests, real or imagined. It had everything to do with feeling comfortable every minute, even though it was with someone that I had known for just a few hours. Kirstin knew nothing about me, and I knew very little about her. There was none of the thoughts and pressures about the future that overwhelmed me and most young people. We were expected to have everything worked out. We were supposed to have our futures charted like a road map by the time we were eighteen. It was just the enjoyment and the serenity of the moment.

I put out of my mind the flashes of guilt that I had about Ann back home. The exchange of letters had been less frequent over the last few months. Our letters were more strained and less romantic than the earlier ones.

My time in the army was growing shorter. The thought of returning home and resuming my relationship with Ann and her family exactly as it had been when I left, was something I did not want to face. Simply picking up again, from what I had run away from was beyond depressing. What would have been accomplished?

Nothing about my situation had really changed. I still lacked an education, the hope for a good job, and a bright future. But instead of being in that situation at nineteen, I would soon be in it again at twenty-two. If Ann's parents were happy to see me leave because of all of the uncertainty and what they viewed as the futility of their daughter's life with me, they would be miserable at seeing me return. They hoped that I would be out of their daughter's life forever. I knew that they wished that both of us would have met someone else while I was gone and that we had both moved on. As far as I knew, Ann hadn't met anyone and neither had I. I believed that Ann was willing to take up where we had left off but I was not. The last thing that I wanted to do was to hurt Ann, as I knew that I would, but I just didn't want to do that all over again. Being away from one another would be a test. We both knew that. At least I did. It was not made easier by her parents' relief at my leaving and their desire for her to move on.

Our last weekend together, before my induction into the army, had been difficult. We had walked along a country road in New Jersey.

"Do you think that you will feel the same way about us when you are away?" Ann asked.

"Don't ask silly questions," I said, "of course I will."

"It'll be close to two years. A month or two seems like a long time. Two years seems like forever. I can't find anything to be happy about when I know that soon we'll be away from one another for all those months. I'm just afraid that things will not be the same two years from now."

I would never admit it to Ann, but I was afraid that things would be the same in two years. Not about Ann or me necessarily, but about my situation.

I didn't answer, but I broke a sprig of spring lilac off a bush that we saw on the side of the road and handed her a piece. "Here, half of this lilac is for you and half for me."

She held the lilac to her nose, "It smells so pretty. I'll keep mine," Ann said. "Will you keep yours?"

"I'm gonna keep it right in my wallet," I said, and I placed the lilac into my wallet and folded it shut.

The weeks of training were over and now I was assigned to Germany. There would be no more weekends together. Instead, Ann and I would have a prolonged separation. I had the choice of remaining in the United States, but I purposely selected Germany. Ann or my family would never have understood why I made that choice or why I secretly looked forward to going away. They were so sad about my leaving, so I kept my feelings to myself. I didn't want to hurt the ones that I loved.

A few days before I was to leave, I drove Ann back to her house. I was preparing to say goodbye to her family. As I turned down her block, almost as if it had been planned, a popular song of the day came over the car radio. We listened to *You Belong to Me* by Jo Stafford. I turned the motor off as we sat in front of her house and we continued to listen to the lyrics. "I'll be so alone without you, maybe you'll be lonesome too and blue." Then the final line, "Just remember when a dream appears you belong to me." At that moment, we both had the full realization that nothing was certain about tomorrow, let alone nineteen months from now, and she clung to my arm.

Here I was, far removed from that time and that place, and the lyrics from one song seemed to have been replaced by lyrics from another, "When I'm not near the girl that I love, I love the girl that I'm near." There were no expectations for tomorrow, and that made all the difference.

"This whole day was crazy and so much fun," I said to Kirstin, "and we saw everything on your list. We really didn't leave anything for tomorrow." We stood in front of the Tivoli Gardens, not far from the restaurant where Tony and I had first met Marian and Kirstin. I looked at my watch. "Oh, my God. It's after midnight, and you have to go to work tomorrow. Or should I say today?"

"I could miss work," Kirstin said.

"See what a bad influence I am," I said. "First I cause you to miss school and now I cause you to miss work. Would they pay you?"

"No. They wouldn't pay me."

"The heck with that," I said. "What time do you get off from work tomorrow?"

"Five o'clock," she said.

"And then you have to go to school?"

"No, I have no school tomorrow. It's Saturday."

"Look, I'll tell you what," I said. "I'll take you home, and then we'll meet tomorrow at six o'clock in front of Tivoli Gardens. We'll get something to eat, and we'll do something after that. Is that okay?"

"Yes, I'd like that," Kirstin said.

"Let's find a cab and take you home."

"No, no," she said. "You'll only have to come back here again. You don't have to take me home. It's silly for you to go all the way to my house, and then back here. I can go home by myself."

"But I want to take you home," I said, and with that I hailed a cab. There were lights on when we pulled up to her house. "Your parents must be waiting up for you. It's after 1 A.M."

"No," Kirstin said. "My father works late and my mother waits up for him. Why don't you come in?"

"No, no. It's late. I don't think that they'd appreciate seeing me coming through the door at this hour, and I don't even have books for an excuse. I don't want parents hating me all over the world."

She placed a finger over her lips, and with a mischievous smile she said, "Be quiet like a mouse, and I won't even tell them that you're here." We both laughed. I took her hand, leaned forward and kissed her briefly on the lips.

"I can't wait for tomorrow," I said. "It was a fun day."

"It was for me too." She looked at me for a second. "Good night, Nick." She opened the cab door, and hurried up the walk. She turned around once more, waved to me, and disappeared into the house.

CHAPTER 22

IT WAS CLOSE TO 2 A.M. WHEN I GOT BACK TO THE hotel. I went by Tony's door, and stood behind it listening for a few seconds. It was quiet. I thought about knocking, but I didn't think that he'd appreciate it if I woke him up. I wanted to tell him what a good time I had with Kirstin and to find out if things had gone as well for him and Marian, but it could wait until tomorrow. I got to my room, washed my face, brushed my teeth, fell on my bed, and I was sleeping in a minute.

I woke up at about 10 A.M. I walked down to the shower room, freshened up, changed my clothes, and then I decided to see if Tony was up. I knocked on his door a few times, but there was still no answer. I went down to the main desk and I recognized the same clerk who had checked us in the day before.

"Hi, I've been knocking at my friend's door but there's no answer. Could you tell me," but before I could finish my thought, the clerk interrupted.

"Oh, yes, Mr. Bilotti. Your friend left this note for you."

He handed me the note, and I read, "Nick, I checked out of that place last night. It's a loser. I checked into the Leif Erikson Hotel. It's just down the block from the restaurant that we ate in yesterday. By now, you know why. Check out, grab your stuff and meet me here. Tony."

I had no idea why Tony had checked out of the hotel or

what made it a loser all of a sudden. All I could think of was rats or roaches, even though it looked to me like the place could have passed inspection. I put my things into my suitcase, paid my bill and made my way to the Lief Ericksen.

The clerk at the desk in the Lief Ericksen confirmed that Tony had checked in, so I did too. He gave me a room across from Tony's room. I put my stuff in my new room and tapped on Tony's door.

"Tony. It's me."

The door opened and Tony let me in.

"I was just dozing," Tony said.

"What the hell's going on? Why did you change hotels?"

"The guy wouldn't let Marian up to my room. No female visitors. He said that was the hotel policy, so we left."

I stared back blankly. It was Tony who had the confused expression on his face now.

"Why? Did he let the two of you go up, or did you stay here?" Tony asked.

"No," I said.

"So, where did the two of you stay last night?" He waited for an answer. "Did you go to her place?"

"No. I took her home, and then I went back to the hotel. I'm gonna meet her tonight."

"What the hell did you do that for? Did she ask you to take her home?"

"No, she didn't. I just took her home."

"I don't get it," Tony said. "You mean that you didn't stay with her?"

"She's not like that, Tony. She's just seventeen."

"What the hell are you talking about?" Tony said. "You know her eight hours and you tell me she's not like that. She's only seventeen? She and Marian are best friends. They hang out together. They do the same things together."

I looked at him. "You mean you and Marian? Well I don't know about you and Marian, but I think you're wrong about Kirstin. We spent the whole day together. There was no pressure. I loved it and there was none of that."

"She's not like that?" He repeated my words. "What does it change if she is like that? You told me that you had a great day. These are different people. This is a different world, Nick. Look, in a day and a half, we'll be out of here and we'll never see those girls again. Are you kidding me? We came up here for some fun, and that's what they want too. They know the deal."

I stared back at him and I didn't say it out loud, but I wanted to tell him that he was wrong about this girl. It was just fun. There had been nothing else for either of us.

"Look, Nick. You're not in your Brooklyn neighborhood now walking your girl home from confraternity. The three date rule doesn't apply here."

"What's the three date rule?"

"It's the one that says that you're only allowed to kiss a girl after three dates and not before. Then if you do kiss her, you have to go to confession."

Even as he was saying it, I didn't want to believe that he was right, but I was beginning to wonder if Kirstin did expect that we would stay together last night. I didn't think so at that time, and when we got to her house last night, her parents were home when she invited me in. I did not want to impose on her parents at that hour but she had said, "If you are quiet like a mouse, I won't even tell them that you are here." She wouldn't even tell them that I was there, she had said. It was all beyond any experience that I ever had before, especially with a girl that I had met a few hours earlier. Regardless of what Tony said, there were actually rules. You had to know a girl like Kirstin for more than a few hours.

"Okay, okay," I said. "Maybe you're right."

"I am right," Tony said.

"Well, I like to think that she is different, and I like the three date rule by the way. I had a great time just holding her hand and enjoying the day."

"You're talking like a confraternity kid," and he continued to look at me.

"I'm meeting Kirstin tonight at six in front of Tivoli Gardens. After she leaves work."

"What happens from now until six?" Tony asked.

"You and I will see the town," I said.

"Let's go," Tony said. "We're running out of time."

"What about Marian?" I asked.

"She went to work from here, and we're supposed to meet tonight too."

"Are you going to meet her?" I asked.

"We'll see."

CHAPTER 23

IT'S COMMON KNOWLEDGE THAT IF YOU WANT TO know where the action is in any town with which you are unfamiliar, all that you need to do is to ask a cab driver. From the moment that Tony and I left the Lief Erickson, cab drivers had directed us from one lounge after the other that they knew catered to American servicemen. Some actually were lounges. Others were less fancy, better described as clubs. There were pretty Danish girls hooked on American G.I.s and the culture that they brought with them in every establishment. There were American soldiers who couldn't believe their good fortune, in hot pursuit, in all of them.

Tony and I sat in a booth by ourselves. A few couples were dancing to Nat King Cole singing *Night Lights*. Off in a corner sitting in a booth by themselves were two attractive girls in a town where there seemed to be no shortage of pretty girls.

"I've been watching those two," Tony said. "They've been sitting there a while. I think that they're alone. If the next song is a slow one, let's ask them to dance, but only if it's a slow one."

The music faded into a new song with a slow tempo. I saw the expression on Tony's face change into the debonair look that he tried to effect when he was moving in for the kill.

"Are you with me, Babe?" he said, and before I could answer, he headed for the booth where the girls sat.

I could hear Tony over the soft music. "Hello ladies. My

name is Tony and that's my friend, Lucky, over there," he said pointing in my direction. "We couldn't help noticing that the two prettiest girls in this lounge are sitting here all by themselves. That doesn't make sense." Both girls smiled. They seemed amused even if they weren't buying Tony's line.

"No, don't laugh. It's the truth. Isn't that what we were saying, Lucky? I mean two pretty girls like this sitting by themselves and no one asking them to dance." Tony shook his head in disbelief. "We will be leaving soon and maybe you will dance with us."

I had heard it all before, but I went along with the routine. "Yeah, it was a mystery to us."

"Do you mind if I sit down?" And before they could respond, Tony said, "Come on over here, Lucky." I crossed over the small dance floor to their booth. "I'm Tony and this is Lucky, and what are your names?"

"I'm Inga," one of them said, "and I'm Kiss," the other said.

"What pretty names," Tony said.

"Well, we're glad that we stopped in here today," Tony said, "because our leaves are almost over and pretty soon we'll have to go back to patrolling the border and making sure that the Russians stay on their side. We were hoping that we'd have one more good memory of this beautiful town. We hate to leave. You can't imagine how lonely and cold it is where we're going. It is awful back on that border isn't it, Lucky?" Tony said, mustering up a most pathetic expression that would have made Cary Grant proud.

I managed not to laugh out loud, and instead I nodded my head and tried to look heroic too.

Both girls looked impressed and said something to each other in Danish. One of them said, "Yes, we would like to dance." We stepped onto the dance floor, where they were playing *Stardust,* and Tony immediately went into his Cary Grant routine.

"It sounds like it's very dangerous where you are stationed," the girl said to Tony. "Where is it that you are stationed?"

The four of us were close enough on the little dance floor for Tony to look in my direction and ask, "I don't think that we'll get into any trouble if I tell her where we're stationed. Do you?"

"No, I don't think so," I said.

"Berlin. We're surrounded by Russians."

"Oh, that must be awful," she said.

"It wouldn't be so bad," Tony said, "except that we're so outnumbered."

The music stopped, and *Stardust* was replaced by Jerry Lee Lewis singing *Whole Lot of Shaking Going On.* Tony, believing that he was a convincing Cary Grant, but not a convincing Fred Astaire, led his new friend back to the booth. We made small talk for a while until the girls excused themselves to go to the ladies' room.

As soon as the girls were out of hearing distance, Tony said, "So many women so little time." He had a rakish smile on his face.

"Better than Tokyo?" I asked.

"Tokyo," he said, "where's that?"

"Let's dump most of the names on our list and just keep the two best ones for our last night. What a waste. Dumping that list will be a lot harder to do that than it sounds. The ones we drop will be disappointed, but as I said, so little time."

Tony had made a list of the names of girls that we had met in different places where we had gone. He had promised to meet each of them in one lounge or another.

I looked at Tony, and I could have laughed if he had meant it as a joke, but he was serious.

"Okay, Cary Grant," I said, "calm down. We'd have to be in several places at the same time to meet all of the girls that you have on that list."

"Nick, Cary Grant never had it so good. What the hell did they say that their names were?" Tony asked. He scribbled some names on a napkin. "These two are in the running."

"I don't know, I think they said their names were Ingrid and Kris, or something like that. Look, Tony, it's five-thirty. In fifteen minutes I'm out of here. I'm gonna meet Kirstin at six in front of Tivoli Gardens, and you're supposed to meet Marian. Let's not get involved with these two."

"Nick, I'm not meeting Marian."

"You told her that you were going to meet her."

"Yeah, but that was before I knew about any of this. Since then I told a lot of girls that I would meet them. There's a lot happening around here and the clock is ticking. Do you know what I mean?"

"So you're gonna stand Marian up?"

"Nick, this is a crazy town. From what I've seen so far, there are probably a lot of people being stood up around here. Suppose I leave here and she stands me up? Look, Babe, I gave her a promise, not a ring."

"Well, you do what you want, Tony. At a quarter to six, I'm walking over to Tivoli Gardens. See if you can handle the two of them."

Before he could say anything, both girls returned to the booth looking pretty.

"So, Ingrid, do you come here a lot? This is one of the nicer places that we have been to, right, Nick?"

"Who is Nick? Isn't your name Lucky?" the one sitting next to me asked.

"My last name is Lucky," I said. "My first name is Nick."

"Oh, I see. Well, she is Inga, not Ingrid," she corrected, "and I am Kiss. We come here a lot. We like it here because it's not too big and it's not noisy."

"Oh, I'm sorry that I got your name confused," Tony said. "Nick, she won't believe this, but I'm gonna tell her anyway, Nick. Are you ready?" he said looking from girl to girl to be sure if they were ready. "Ingrid is my mother's name. That's why I was confused."

"Is that right?" Inga asked. "Ingrid is a popular name in Denmark. Is it a popular name in America too?"

It was twenty minutes after five, and the whole conversation was becoming more ridiculous by the minute. At that point, I could not have told you who was Inga or who was Ingrid, but instead I added to the absurdity.

"Oh, yes," I said. "It's true. Tony's mother's name is Ingrid. It's a very popular name in Brooklyn."

"That is the truth," Tony said, "but I must admit even though I would never tell it to my mother, I think that Inga is a much prettier name than Ingrid."

"They're both beautiful," I said. I was just about to find an excuse to get out of there in order to keep my appointment with Kirstin, but as I was about to do so, a guy walked toward our booth. I had seen him earlier with two of his friends, and there was no mistaking them as Americans.

I thought that he was going to ask us for a match or to bum a cigarette, but instead he looked right past Tony and me and he went straight to one of the girls.

"Hey, Kiss, do you want to dance?" Bobby Helms' *Special Angel* was playing in the background. He didn't introduce himself. He didn't nod in our direction. He totally ignored Tony and me.

Tony had a look of disbelief on his face. "Is this guy

kidding?" he asked me. It took a lot of nerve, and showed complete disrespect for a stranger to walk over to your table, to look past you and to ask the girl that you were with to dance.

"No, thank you," Kiss said, and she turned away from him.

This guy wasn't taking no for an answer. "Oh come on," he said. "Just one dance won't hurt."

"Hey, what are you doing? We're talking." I said. "You're interrupting." He still wasn't listening. "Do you know this guy?" I asked. I figured that she did because he had called her by name.

"Yes," she said nervously. "I danced one time with him last night, and he wouldn't leave me alone after that. Inga and I left."

I knew in the back of my mind that I was getting involved in something that was no business of mine. I wanted no part of it, but I didn't know how to avoid it.

"Listen, pal. She just said that she didn't want to dance with you. She's with me, and you're not showing her or me or any of us any respect. In fact, you're acting like I'm not even here. Now why don't you be nice and go away?"

For the first time, he seemed to acknowledge our presence. He looked from her to me. "Screw you," he said dismissively.

I stood up between the table and the seat behind me, and I could see that Tony was also having a difficult time trying to stand and get around Ingrid or Inga, or whatever the hell her name was. Before I could get out of the booth, an explosion went off in my head, and I realized that he had sucker punched me squarely in my mouth. The force of the punch sent me back, and I felt Kiss reaching up to keep me from falling on her.

I knew from having been in fights before and from observing similar situations that this was not the time to check for damage or to cover up my face. I could not allow him to land another shot like the first one. His mistake was in stepping back to admire his handiwork. I managed to squeeze out from between the bench and the table, and in my fury and outrage at being sucker punched in the face, I pounced on him. I punched him as fast and as often and as hard as I could, looking for any opening that I could find. He was making it difficult by shielding himself in a fetal position to avoid any more punishment.

I did that for a while until a bouncer pulled me off him. I saw Tony doing his best James Cagney, glaring at the guy's two friends who were staring back at him.

"I didn't break it up, Babe, because you were doing pretty good until that friggin' bouncer came." Tony never took his eyes off the guy's two friends.

Now was the time for damage inspection. My teeth all seemed to be anchored in place for which I was grateful. My parents spent thousands of dollars on me for braces that they could hardly afford so that I wouldn't have to spend the rest of my life looking like a rodent. There was a trickle of blood coming out of my nose and my lips felt as big as catchers' mitts. Now both of my hands were beginning to throb from punching the jerk on his thick skull, but as they say, "you should have seen the other guy."

You could tell that his face had been tattooed pretty good. His left eye was closing fast and his right eye had a purple mouse underneath it. I hoped that he had remembered to bring his sunglasses with him.

"I don't care who started it," the bouncer said. "First you're going to pay for the damages, and then I want all of you out of here or I'll call the police. I want the three of them out of here, and when I'm sure that they're gone, you can leave. I don't want this to continue outside."

I looked around, and except for a couple of broken glasses, there didn't seem to be much damage. I looked over to the two girls, and the one called Kiss was holding her wrist with a pained look on her face.

"Are you okay?" I asked.

"I'm fine. I just twisted my wrist when you fell back on me," she said, trying to put on a brave face.

"Let me have a look," I said, while squeezing my nostrils together to stop the bleeding. This is where my extensive medical training came in handy. If I had known, I would have taken this leave with Paul or Dave, and not Tony. I still might need the assistance of a dental technician given the way my mouth and teeth felt at the moment. Maybe Tony was the right guy after all.

I took Kiss' wrist, and she winced if I put any pressure on it or if I tried to flex it at all. "I really think that you have a sprain, but the only way to know for sure is if you have it x-rayed. I'm really sorry about all of this."

"Oh, it's not your fault. There was nothing that you could do after he hit you like that. I got you into this. I didn't like him, and that's why Inga and I left last night. I didn't know that he'd come back here tonight."

I looked at my watch. It was a little after six and Tivoli Gardens was a fifteen minute walk from here. If I could catch a cab maybe I could be there in five minutes, but I'd have to leave now.

"Hey, Tony. I've got to get out of here. It's after six," I said. I looked over to the bouncer. "What are the damages?" I asked.

"Twenty-five dollars," he answered.

"Twenty-five dollars," Tony said. We broke two glasses. Just two. What do you want us to do, pay for a new set?"

"Twenty-five dollars," the bouncer repeated.

I took twelve dollars from my wallet and handed it to

him. "Get the other thirteen dollars from them. They started the thing. I just want to get out of here."

Inga or Ingrid was consoling her friend, whose eyes were focused on me.

"She can't take her eyes off you, Babe. These two go to the top of the list," Tony said. I looked over at Kiss who was cradling her wrist.

"How are you doing?" I asked.

"I'll be alright," she said, but I could see by her expression that she was in some discomfort.

"Do they have hospital emergency rooms around here?" Tony asked. "We'll get a cab and take you for an x-ray."

"No, I'll be fine," she said, and then turning to me, "It was so…I don't know the word in English, for you to fight for me."

"Gallant?" Tony said.

"Unnecessary," I wanted to suggest.

"Yes. Gallant. You were like a tiger."

"Oh, man, is this your lucky day," Tony whispered to me.

I didn't want to shatter her image of me by telling her that the reason that I was trying to remove that guy's head from his torso, was because I was outraged by his cheap shot to my mouth. Not because I was her champion. At the time, she was the farthest thing from my mind.

"Yeah. You're right," Tony said. "He was like Thor, wasn't he?"

"Oh will you stop. Yeah," I said. "Thor. My nose is thor, my mouth is thor, my hands are thor, and I've got to get the hell out of here." It was already a quarter after six.

The other guys had paid the balance of the damage, and the bouncer was escorting them out of the building. I looked outside and I saw them ministering to my sparring partner by pressing hands full of snow on his damaged eyes. They were in no real hurry to leave.

"Will you tell those guys to hurry up," I said to the bouncer. "I'm already late for an appointment."

He looked at me as if to say that he wasn't my messenger boy.

I paced back and forth, looking out onto the street and then back to the booth. Tony handed me six dollars.

"That's my half of the damage that the thief shook us down for."

"Keep it," I said.

Tony looked up at the bouncer. "Hey. Now that the bad guys are almost gone and the bill is paid, could we have another round and then we'll leave." The bouncer stood there trying to make his mind up.

"It's a quarter to seven, Babe," Tony whispered. "I don't think that Kirstin is going to be there. If you're really leaving and you don't come back, I'll know that I was wrong."

The bouncer thought about Tony's request for a few seconds and then sent the waitress to take our order.

"Those guys are gone if you want to leave," the bouncer said.

I reached for my jacket and Kiss asked, "Where are you going?"

"Is he leaving?" Inga asked Tony.

"He'll be right back," Tony said. "He forgot something in the hotel."

"Well, why don't we all go back to the hotel?" she asked.

"I just ordered another round of drinks, and he'll be right back. How's your wrist?" Tony asked Kiss.

"It's sore, but it's not really that bad now."

"Ask your buddy the bouncer if he can give her a little ice for her wrist," I said to Tony.

Tony signaled for the waitress. "Do you think that we can have a little bag of ice for the lady's wrist?"

The waitress nodded and walked off.

I put my jacket on and walked toward the door.

"Hey, Thor, hurry back. We'll be waiting." Tony smiled and waved.

I walked around Tivoli Gardens several times, but Kirstin had either given up waiting for me, or perhaps she hadn't kept our appointment in the first place. I turned back to where I knew that Tony and the girls would be waiting. What Kirstin had said to me the day before kept running through my mind.

"There's nothing certain about tomorrow." I walked away from Tivoli Gardens. It was snowing like hell.

CHAPTER 24

WHEN I FIRST KNEW THAT I WAS GOING TO GERMANY, I tried not to think too much about being overseas for twenty months. The idea of leaving the people whom I loved for that extent of time, and being away from the only life that I was familiar with, was best handled by not thinking about it very much. I had discovered that not giving much consideration to long-range problems in the belief, or perhaps the hope, that everything would work out for the best somehow worked for me. Immediate problems were trouble enough. It was a survival technique. The days overseas did seem to drag by, but the weeks and months had flown by. Virtually all of the people who were in Panzer Kaserne when I arrived twenty months earlier had rotated back to the United States. Once again, I was a stranger surrounded by unfamiliar faces, no longer as a rookie, but now as a veteran.

The familiar buildings and grounds of Panzer Kaserne, which had become home for me all these months, were now inhabited by memories and ghosts of people with whom I had formed close bonds. Now they had left and I had no desire to form new friendships with any of the new arrivals. The final blow came when the Triple Seven Nine was transferred out of Panzer Kaserne. It was time to go home.

Marie Bella was a small town girl from Altoona, Pennsylvania. She had joined the army to get away from small town life. Marie had a desire, she said, "to see what was on the other side of the mountain." Marie worked in transportation, and was billeted in the building housing a detachment of WACs. The building was located across the campus from the building where I lived in Panzer Kaserne.

Marie had arrived in Kaiserslautern shortly after I did. We had met in the mess hall, and we had instantly felt relaxed with each other. She wasn't a guy and she wasn't from New York, but she was Italian, even if she was from Pennsylvania. That was close enough. I considered Marie to be more like a younger sister, or at least a cousin. When things got lonely and we were fighting the overwhelming depression that homesickness can cause, we would often seek each other out.

There weren't as many options for WACs as there were for their male counterparts. The rules were different for women than they were for men. As unfair as that might sound, that was the way it was. Life could be very lonely for WACs from small towns, who up until then had led sheltered lives. None of them dated German nationals, as we did all the time. They didn't take leaves to go to places that had the reputation of being hot spots like we did. Instead, they booked American Express tours and saw the sites of Europe.

Marie would tell me about one WAC or another from her company who I would no longer see, and who had been discreetly rotated home because she was pregnant.

"I had no idea that she was even seeing anyone," Marie would say. When I would ask if she knew who the father was, Marie, wide-eyed, would say, "I don't know."

The small town girl was rapidly getting an education. Not everything on the other side of the mountain was what Marie had hoped it would be. For a small town Catholic schoolgirl like Marie, who took her Catholic values seriously, being in the army wasn't very different from living in a convent. You did your day's work and then went back to your room. One day Marie learned about other life style options, which she had never bargained for.

I was in the snack bar one night. The army menu was usually never enticing. On this day, it was particularly revolting, so I exited the mess hall and headed straight for the snack bar. I always ordered a burger because there weren't many ways to mess up a burger. I carried my burger, French fries, and a soda to an empty table. I settled down only to look up and see Marie looking flustered and hurrying toward me.

"Oh, my God, Nick."

"What's up?" I asked.

She shook her head and laughed nervously. "You'll never believe it." She looked around to be sure that no one could hear us.

"You know that I bought a record player in the P.X. to play my Elvis stuff." I nodded my head. "Well, I lent it to Rosie Cally about a week ago and she never returned it. I just bought a new Elvis album so I walked down to Rosie's room to get my record player. I knocked on her door but there was no answer, so I stuck my head into the room and then, oh my God, there was Rosie." She moved closer across the table and put her hand alongside of her mouth. "Nick. Rosie was in bed with Flo Marrin!

"I didn't want to jump to conclusions but our racks are barely wide enough for one person so why would two people squeeze into a single rack? That was the question that I was asking myself. I couldn't imagine why."

I asked a silly question, "Were they just in bed?"

"No, not just in bed, they were…, you know."

"Oh my God," I said shaking my head. "Are you sure?"

"Of course, I'm sure. There they were in the same bed together, and they were real close."

"Did you say anything?"

"I just said, 'Oh, excuse me.' I was so surprised that I couldn't think of anything else to say. I wanted to run out of the room, but I kept telling myself to be casual as if this happens all the time. I tried to act as if I had seen it before. I was just going to turn around and leave but before I could, Rosie asked me what I wanted. I told her that I wanted my record player. She pointed at the floor over by the window where I could see it, but I wasn't about to walk across the room. I told her that I'd get it later and I left. Oh my God. I have to work with these people. I don't know how I'll ever be able to look either one of them in the face after this."

"Well, you didn't do anything."

"It's not that," Marie said. "It's just so embarrassing and awkward."

"I guess it would be for anyone," I said, "but I bet that I can tell you what they're going to do the next time that you see them. They're going to act as if nothing ever happened. What are they gonna do, leave town? And you have to act the same way."

"Oh my God," Marie said. "I thought that by leaving Altoona, I would be expanding my world, but every time something like this happens my world gets smaller. I spend more and more time in my room, the one that I share with strangers, and my room becomes my world."

I pushed my fries and my soda toward her. "Thanks," she said. She nibbled on a fry. Her eyes were watering. "And now, you rat, you're going home," she said, forcing a smile, "and I have six more months to go here. Who am I gonna talk to when you're gone?"

I felt bad for her but I had no answer for her question. "I know that six months seems like forever," I said, "but it really does fly by. It did for me."

"I'm just not going to think about it. If I start counting

days, it'll just make the time seem longer. You know, Nick, when I saw the menu today, I knew that I would find you in here. I wanted to surprise you."

"Some surprise," I said. "Rosie and Flo."

"No. Not those two." Marie looked at me. A happy smile covered her face. "I got you a flight home."

I looked at her fully expecting a following punch line that we could both laugh at. Marie must have seen the "okay, what's the next line" expression on my face, so she repeated, "I told you that I would try to get you a flight home, and I got it."

Only officers flew home and not even all of them were fortunate enough to be able to avoid a nine or ten day crossing on an overcrowded troop ship. I was still in disbelief. I stood up and lifted her off her chair in a bear hug.

"Oh, Marie, thank you." I said, as I continued to hug her. I planted a big kiss on her cheek.

A bunch of soldiers a few tables away began applauding.

"Don't make any promises until he gives you a ring," a sergeant said.

"Hey, I've been here a long time and you never even gave me a glance," a soldier at the table said. "What do you see in him?" he teased.

Marie blushed at their good-natured teasing, and she turned back to me. "You're flying out of Frankfurt with stops in Shannon, Ireland, Gander, Newfoundland, and a final destination of Idlewild in New York. It'll take about thirty hours."

"Marie, this is more than I could ever have hoped for. I still can't believe it. What a gift. How can I thank you?"

"I was happy that I was able to do it. I'll be even happier when I do it for myself." She took another fry. "I have mixed emotions seeing you go, but if you want to thank me, Elvis just released a new L.P. Buy it for me and write something sweet on the jacket. I'll see if I can sneak into Rosie's room and get my record player. And I'm expecting a Christmas card when you get home." She looked down and I took her hand. I could see her eyes welling up again.

Several weeks later, our plane touched down in Idlewild Airport in New York, where a bus was waiting to take us to Fort Hamilton in Brooklyn. As a child, my family had lived a short distance from Fort Hamilton. On hot summer nights, before the advent of air conditioning and when we didn't even own an electric fan, I would lie on the top sheet of my bed, the windows opened wide, and I could hear the sound of taps coming from the fort off in the distance. Now I was to live there for a day or two.

My family had moved to New Jersey but my mother had a younger brother who lived close to the fort. Although everyone knew that I would be coming home soon, I purposely did not tell them the exact day of my arrival. I wanted it to be a surprise.

Immediately after getting squared away at the fort, I decided to take a chance and see if I could get through the gate, even though I didn't have a pass. If I could, I'd walk over to my uncle's house and surprise everyone. I could see the M.P. in the booth as I approached the gate leading out of the fort. One look at my shoulder patch, and the M.P. knew that I was recently stationed in Europe.

"Where ya'll headin' corporal?" he drawled in what sounded like Georgia.

"I just rotated out of Germany, and I wanted to surprise my family. I have an uncle who lives right down the block," I said in my best Brooklyn.

"Ya'll wouldn't happen to have a pass?" he asked.

"No, I don't," I said. "I haven't been here long enough to find out who issues them or where to get one."

"How long were ya'll in Germany?" he asked.

"I haven't seen my family in about nineteen months," I said.

He stared at me for a few seconds, and then he turned his back and looked at his logbook and said over his shoulder, "Ya'll be back here by 2200."

I thanked him and hurried out of the gate.

I knocked at the door of my uncle's house, which was located on Fort Hamilton Parkway. A woman's voice, which I recognized as his wife's voice asked, "Who is it?"

My Uncle Ben was my favorite uncle. He was a forever young, fun-loving man, but you never knew what sort of a greeting you would get from his wife. Tess was sometimes friendly, but she was mostly distant and aloof and quick to take offense. I had gone to say goodbye to my uncle before I had left for the service. His wife opened the door just wide enough to tell me that my uncle wasn't home. She said goodbye and then closed the door leaving me, my cousin Jerry and Ann standing in the hall. Her unpredictable nature was tolerated by the rest of the family. Everyone looked away for the sake of my uncle and his daughters. I hoped that my uncle would be home this time so that I wouldn't have a replay of what had happened two years ago.

"It's Nicky," I said.

"Nicky who?" she asked. Before I could further identify myself, I heard the heavy steps of my uncle rushing to the door then the sound of the lock disengaging as my uncle swung the door wide. He stood for a second, and then in a wave of emotion typical of Italians, he embraced me. When my uncle finally released me, he stepped back and with tears misty in his eyes he looked at me and said, "The army did you good. Come in, Nicky, come in. Do your parents know that you're home?" Without waiting for an answer, he said, "Tess, get him something to eat."

I gave a tentative glance to where my aunt was standing, and to my relief she was smiling at our reunion, her three daughters at her side. Thank God, that I had caught her on a good day.

"Have you spoken with your parents?" my aunt asked.

"They don't know that I'm home," I said. "I wanted it to be a surprise."

"Then I'll call them right now," she said, and she started dialing the number.

My uncle grasped my hand and held my shoulder with his other hand, while we waited for someone to pick up. My aunt handed me the phone.

"Hello." I recognized my father's voice.

"Hello, Dad."

"Nicky?"

"Yes. How are you?"

He ignored my question. "Where are you?" I could hear the anticipation in his voice.

"I'm in Uncle Benny's house."

"You're in Brooklyn? Helen, it's Nicky!"

I heard my mother asking, "Where is he?"

"We haven't heard from you. We thought that you'd be on a ship somewhere," my father said.

"I was lucky enough to get a flight, and I'm laying over in Fort Hamilton, before I go to Fort Dix for separation."

"Okay. We'll be right there," he said. "It's six o'clock. We should be there by eight."

"Great, but don't speed," I said.

"Don't worry," he said. "Wait till I tell your sister and

your brother. Let's not waste any time. We'll see you in a little while. I love you, Boy."

"I love you, Dad," and he hung up.

I spent the next two hours answering questions about Germany, in between being served one Italian specialty after the other. I truly believed that my uncle and his wife were certain that I hadn't had a proper meal since I left home. They were doing their best to make up for lost time.

I was searching for a response after the youngest of my uncle's three daughters asked me if I had ever shot anyone. Before I could answer, I heard a car door slam and the two older girls shouted, "They're here!"

I hurried out of the house and down the three front steps. I had many emotional farewells up to that time, but that little reunion was, and still remains today, one of the most joyful memories of my life.

It's funny how displays of emotion by women are accepted and even expected, but similar displays of emotion by men cause observers to feel uncomfortable. They are even viewed as unmanly by tradition, so most men avoid showing their emotions. That may be true but we didn't care. I embraced both my parents and for the moment all that the three of us wanted to do was to bury our faces on the other's shoulder. We held on to each other with the joy of knowing that we were together. With that came the overwhelming realization of how much we had missed one another. Life is strange. Two years earlier, I had made every excuse to get away and to distance myself from the people who loved me the most. Now I held them so close. I wanted to absorb them.

I looked up to see my uncle and his family standing off a bit as they watched the scene before them. My uncle, who was trying to contain himself at our joy, kept repeating to my father, "Let's go inside, Sammy. Let's go inside."

I had always dismissed the purported overemotional displays by Italians as just another silly stereotype. Now I knew that it was the truth and I was glad for it. It's still a treasured moment.

The M.P. at the gate had been good to me by allowing me off the post without a pass. I didn't want to take advantage of him, and I thought that I might need him one more time, if I were fortunate to run into him again.

At 9:30, I said goodbye to my family. This time it wasn't painful because we knew that in a day or two, our goodbyes would be casual, and not like all of the most recent ones.

The same M.P. was in the booth when I walked onto the post well before 2200 hours as I promised I would.

"How'd ya'll do?" he asked. "Did ya'll get to see the kinfolk?"

"Kinfolk? Oh, yeah, kinfolk. I saw a lot of them," I said.

"Ya'll see your girlfriend?" he asked.

Now this guy wanted to have a conversation. I looked at him for a second, "Well, I don't know if I have a girlfriend anymore. I used to. I'll know more about that this time tomorrow. Things change."

"Ain't that the truth? Same thing happened to me. My girlfriend upt and married the undertaker in my town whiles I was gone. Might as well, he's the richest guy in town," he said. A car pulled up to the booth. The M.P. looked inside and said something to the driver. Then he stepped back and saluted and he waved the car into the fort.

I took the opportunity to walk away, but I turned and waved, and he returned my wave. The sound of taps that I had heard on those hot summer nights in my room as a child came over the speakers in the fort. I was home again.

CHAPTER 25

MY RELATIONSHIP WITH ANN HAD ENDED WITH A whimper. There had never been a harsh word. Our breakup was largely because of me. If being away, as Ann had tried to tell me in our last days together would be a test for our relationship, then I had failed the test. The longer that I was away, the less I seemed to have to say in the letters that I wrote to her. There were things that I had done that I would never have told her. The routine of my job, as well as the places and people that I had met, I felt had made me a different person from the one that she knew. I often thought about our relationship while I was away and I had no desire to pick it up exactly the way that it had been. If I were to do that what would have been the point of my flight? What would I have accomplished in two years? Nothing really. I would be coming back to exactly what I had left before. Things would be the same as when I left.

I had gained some worldly knowledge by the people that I had met and the experiences that I had. I was distressed by the lack of progress that I had made in establishing something that I could build a future on. A future that seemed bleak.

I thought once again about the constant pressure that Ann's parents would be putting on her because of me. I would do anything to avoid her sharing her misery with me even though I contributed to it. I knew that Ann would be forced to defend me to her parents day and night for all of the negative things that they would say to her about me. She had done this in the past. Those were the battles that I had run from two years earlier and I did not want any part of that again. We were both young. Ann would find someone else more acceptable. When she did, she would wonder why she had put herself through all of the foolishness of the last four years. Ann had a future. I believed that for her. I had many doubts about my own future. I did my usual thing. I put it all out of my mind, but my mind was settled on one thing. I had to end our relationship.

It also bothered and surprised me that Ann seemed to accept the drifting away of our relationship. When the letters became less frequent, she never asked me what was wrong or even if I still cared for her. I didn't expect that and my ego was hurt. She seemed not to care as much as I thought that she would. It was an ego thing. I thought that she might have found someone else over the last twenty months. There was someone that her parents approved of and now she had peace with them. That made it easier for me to walk away. That was fine with me. Perhaps we had both grown up.

Even with all that, I had too much regard for Ann because of what we had been to each other for two years to not at least call her to say that I was home. I wanted to see if she had changed and to be honest, my male ego kicked in again. I wanted to prove to myself that even if I didn't care anymore, she still did.

I walked over to the telephone center and dialed her number hoping that she and not one of her parents would pick up the phone. I knew that if either of her parents would answer the phone that the discomfort that I had always felt around them and their disdain for me would return. It would be the same as if there had been a twenty minute separation and not a twenty month separation. I held my breath as the phone continued to ring.

"Hello?"

"Hello, Mrs. Terri, this is Nicky." There was a momentary pause as I held the phone to my ear. Was that a sigh or a sob, I thought?

"Oh. How are you? Are you home?"

"I'm fine. Yes, I'm home. I got home yesterday and I'm in Fort Hamilton. How are you, and Mr. Terri and the kids?"

"We're all fine, thank you." In the background, I could hear the familiar sound of Ann's voice.

"Who is it, Mom? Is it Nicky?"

"Yes, it is. Here's Ann. Take care of yourself," and she was gone.

"Hi," Ann said. "Where are you?"

"I'm in Fort Hamilton, but I'll be leaving for Fort Dix tomorrow to be discharged."

How often we had spoken and planned about the day when I would return when there would be no more goodbyes. Now that day was here and I could sense already that both of us knew that this hello was probably a final goodbye. It had started once again with the chilled greeting that I had received from Ann's mother. I had expected it and I even understood it. I had done absolutely nothing to make myself more acceptable to Ann's family. Ann was unaware that I had never earned a high school diploma. I couldn't imagine myself breaking that news to her and then Ann telling her parents. That would probably be the final shock. At that point, even Ann probably would have concern. It probably wouldn't take long for reality to set in and Ann would realize what her family, and even I, understood. Unless I did something soon, I was looking at a difficult future.

Like an ostrich, I had buried my head in the sand for two

years in the hope that something would miraculously fall into my lap and would change my life for the better. It hadn't.

"Look," I said, "if it's alright, I can catch a cab or if I can't find one, I can walk over to your house and be there in fifteen or twenty minutes. Is that okay?"

"I'd like that," she answered. We said goodbye and we hung up.

It was amazing how little we had to say to each other after such an extended separation.

There were lots of guys coming and going and the M.P. in the booth was not my guy. I could see that the M.P. on duty was looking closely at passes and even when guys tried to talk their way out of the gate, he was having none of it. He was sending them back.

Well, that's not gonna work and I have to get out of here, I thought. I walked back toward the barracks where I was billeted. Behind the barracks was a chain link fence that appeared to be about ten feet high. On the other side of the fence was a grassy section of the fort, which led to a tree-lined street where I could see private homes. When I was sure that no one was around, I scaled the fence and climbed over to the other side and dropped to the ground before anyone could see me. I made my way to Fort Hamilton Parkway but there were no cabs. By the time that I spotted one, I had walked half the distance to Ann's house so I didn't bother.

Ann was waiting for me at the top of her stoop. She walked down the steps when she saw me approaching. It was awkward. We didn't embrace like lovers, but instead we grasped each other's hands, like old friends.

"How are you?" I asked. She looked the same as she had when I had left.

"I'm fine. It's so good to see you," Ann said.

I couldn't resist a little dig. "Aren't you going to invite me in to say hi to your folks?" I knew that remark was totally unnecessary and that I was punishing the wrong person, but I said it anyway.

She rolled her eyes and shook her head in frustration at me and probably at them too. She was in the middle. She exhaled and said, "Could we just walk up to the avenue?"

"Let's go," I said.

We walked up to the avenue side-by-side. It had to have been as obvious to Ann as it was to me that neither of us had made an attempt to hold the other's hand. We turned into a small restaurant that made pizza and burgers. I ordered a burger with a soda. Ann had only a soda.

"Those two little boys are peeking at you." She nodded in the direction of two kids who were having ice cream sundaes with their families.

"It must be the uniform," she teased.

I smiled and gave the kids a little wave and they ducked down in the booth.

"They're hiding now," she said

"Yeah, they are. Little kids love to hide. Not a problem in the world for them." We sat in an awkward silence. Ann swirled her soda with her straw, neither of us saying much. It was not going well and it was not the kind of meeting that we had anticipated we would be having when I returned.

I looked over at the kids who continued to play their hide and seek. "They're hiding again. Do you know what Ann, I've been playing that game too."

"What does that mean?" she said without looking up. "What are you hiding from?"

"I've been hiding from life, I've been hiding from the future, and I've been hiding from reality in this uniform for two years. Tomorrow it comes off and it's time for some soul searching, and for the both of us to face reality," I said.

"To face reality," she repeated. "From what I'm sensing about this meeting, this might be our last opportunity for some honest soul searching. You've always held back. You never let me completely into your thoughts. Please, don't hold back now." Her eyes were welling up and she forced a smile.

"Where do I begin? Look, Ann, I have nothing more than when I left, in fact, I have less. I have no education and no job." She listened, waiting for me to continue. "Maybe my father can find a place for me in his shop. If not, I'll probably have the kind of dead-end jobs that I had before. The army is no longer an option. It gave me a place to hide but now I've got to stop dreaming and face reality. There's no place else for me to go or to hide. That's all over.

"Then there's the situation with your parents. Who can blame them for not welcoming me today? Since you met me, your relationship with them has been a misery. I don't know how the hell you did it. Do you really want to fight that battle again?" She sat silently stirring her soda with her straw.

"Are you speaking for me? You haven't asked me what I'm ready to do, but I'm sensing what you're unwilling to do." I didn't answer. "It's really not up to me," Ann said. "I've always believed in you and I know good things will happen for you in your life." I sat not knowing what to say.

"You're right. It hasn't been easy living with my parents but it was okay as long as you and I were always all right with each other. I put up with my parents because I believed they would change their minds about you. Now I feel as though you've changed your mind about me." She looked directly at me, but my mind was made up. We sat silently for a while and although her eyes looked misty, she kept herself from tears.

"There's really nothing to do or to say, is there?" She waited, but I really had said everything that I wanted to say.

She broke the silence again. "I guess I was the unrealistic one. I was always the dreamer. I am not a dreamer now." She laughed. "My motto was always, 'Everything will be alright,' and I really believed that it was your motto too. I thought we both felt the same way. I guess you didn't feel that way then and it seems that you surely don't feel that way now."

She waited for me to respond. I believed that anything else that I might say short of "Okay, we'll give it a try, and I will call you this weekend," would be insincere. I really didn't want to say that I'd be willing to try again because I didn't. If I told the truth, which was that I just didn't want to do it all over again, I would wound her even more. We sat quietly and she said, "Could we go now?" And we left.

We walked quietly back to Ann's house. I knew that if things had gone better at this meeting, there would have been so much to say and so much to explain. Nearly two years had separated us, but neither of us could go beyond what we had already said. To me, our conversation was final.

We got to the front of Ann's house and she stopped before going into her house. She turned and looked down.

"Nicky, do you still have your half of the lilacs from that day?" she asked. I didn't respond.

"I still have mine," she said, and then she walked into her house.

CHAPTER 26

WHEN HE WAS FIVE MONTHS OLD, MY FATHER'S twenty-four year old mother, Erminia, died because of medical malpractice. Besides leaving my dad, his mother left behind two little girls. One was five years old, and the other was three. After the death of their mother both little girls were taken in by their maternal grandmother, but my father was not. Instead, he was sent to the Angel Guardian Home in Brooklyn. His maternal grandmother, Anna, refused to accept the child. Anna believed that her daughter had never recovered from a difficult pregnancy and birth, and that my father was the cause of her only daughter's death. She refused to take the child, Sabino, although she took his sisters, Connie and Anna. My grandfather had to go to work to support his three children. Because he was rejected by his grandmother, my dad spent the first three years of his life in Angel Guardian Home in Brooklyn being tended to by nuns.

In 1917, my grandfather, Nicholas, who by nature was a cold and aloof man remarried. It had been three years since the death of his first wife. During that time, my grandfather had fought several efforts by the agency to have my father taken from him and given over for adoption. My grandfather even went so far as locating and appealing to prospective adoptive parents not to take the child as he was preparing to marry again.

One of the first things that my grandfather's new wife,

Rose, did after she and my grandfather were married was to take my father out of the home to live with her and her new husband. Rose told how the child had captured her heart when my grandfather took his soon-to-be bride to see the boy in the home. Rose gave the boy the love and affection that had not been a part of his life until then.

If not for my dad's new mother, and new grandmother, he might never have known the security that love brings to a child. His own father was incapable of any affection toward his son. Communication between father and son was limited to scolding or criticizing by the father to his son.

My father's two older sisters were never taken in by Rose, who loved the boy as if he had been her biological child. Instead, the girls remained with their maternal grandmother into adulthood. The reason why the two girls remained with their maternal grandmother while their brother went to a new home has always been unclear depending on the person who was trying to give the explanation.

As soon as my father was old enough to do so, my grandfather, who owned his own barbershop, required his son to help sweep up, wash the floors and keep the shop neat and ready for the next day's business.

The routine for my father was pretty much the same each day. He would go to school and then go to work in his father's shop. There was one particular day that was different from all the others. I always remember listening attentively as my father told us his story.

"I was nine years old. It had snowed heavily on the night before so I had taken my sled to the shop. I had to walk in the street because the sidewalks were covered with snow. I walked along pulling my sled, and I remember that I was singing a popular song of the day, *Charlie My Boy*. That's the last thing that I remember. I was hit by a Sheffield Milk

Farms truck and the next thing that I remember was waking up in the hospital.

"I recovered in the hospital and eventually there was a financial settlement with the milk company. My father took the money and bought a fully furnished house on Dean Street in Brooklyn. The house had belonged to a judge. We lived there until we moved to Bay 11th Street in Brooklyn, and that was a good thing because that's where I met your mother."

Almost ninety years later, I have a floral oil painting, a bookcase, and an antique clock. That is all that's left from my father's near fatal collision with the Sheffield Milk Company truck and from the house on Dean Street.

In the summer of 1930, my dad, who was now sixteen, met and fell in love with a fourteen-year old girl who lived on the same block. The two were inseparable. Two years later, when my dad was an eighteen-year old senior at Brooklyn Technical High School, and my mother, Helen Natoli, was a sixteen-year old part-time student and worker, they were married in a Roman Catholic ceremony. The only witnesses besides the priest who married them, was my mother's favorite brother, Dan, and his wife, Rose. There were no wedding pictures.

After the wedding ceremony, the bride and groom each went back to their separate homes, while they tried to figure out how to break the news to their parents. They did, and their marriage was tested over the years, but they remained married and devoted to one another until my dad died in 1968.

Both of my parents worked hard together to support my older sister, my younger brother and me, as long as I could remember. My dad worked six days a week, mostly as a machinist, and my mother worked various jobs, but mostly in the ladies garment industry. It was always my father's dream to be in business for himself. He tried to start his own auto repair shop in an old garage that he had rented but he always returned to being a machinist.

In 1955, just by chance, an event occurred that would change the course of life for my immediate family, as well as for my extended family, forever. My dad was looking through the newspaper in the business opportunity section as well as in the want ads. He was always searching for a better position than the one that he had as a machinist. That day he put the paper down and looked at my mother.

"Helen, I'm looking here and I see that there's a guy in Franklin, New Jersey, wherever that is, who says that he has presses, lathes, milling machines and other types of machines that he wants to sell. There's a number listed here. I wonder if it's worth calling to find out if there's anything to it."

My mother was always the risk taker, while my father was always more cautious by nature.

"What harm would a call do?" my mother asked.

"Eddie and I were just saying that if we could buy a press for a reasonable price, even if it needed some work, maybe we could rent a place and set it up. Maybe we could do something for ourselves instead of always working for somebody else."

Eddie was a machinist like my dad, and they both worked in a metal stamping and forming shop in Westbury, Long Island.

"Are you going to call?" my mother asked.

"Well, I don't know." And after thinking about it awhile, he said, "Okay, what the heck," and he made his way to the phone.

My dad spoke with someone on the other end for a few minutes and then returned to our kitchen. "I don't know if this guy's a nut and if he knows what he's talking about, but he says that he has about fifty of the machines that he has listed in the paper, and they're all shut down but in working order. He says he has them all in what used to be a dairy barn and he has just had heat installed in the barn to prevent them from rusting. How crazy does that sound?" He looked at my mother.

"What are they doing in a barn?" my mother asked.

"He and some other guy tried to start a business that went under. The other guy owed some money so he took off and this guy, whose name is Andy, was left with these machines. The only thing that he knows about them is that one looks different from the other. He wants to sell them all to get some of his money back." He looked at my mother.

"I made an appointment to drive up there on Saturday. I think that this guy might be nuts and I think that I'm nuts for getting involved in this."

"No you're not. It's worth a look."

"I'm gonna talk to Eddie. Maybe he'll take a ride with me on Saturday. I don't want to get my hopes up, but if it's everything that this guy says it is and the price is right, maybe Eddie and I can buy a machine and haul it back here. Who knows?" He looked at my mother. I could see the dream in his eyes.

My father, Eddie and I arrived in Franklin, New Jersey about noontime that Saturday and introduced ourselves to Andy Sayer, the man who had placed the ad in the newspaper. Andy was a middle-aged, heavyset man. He drove us through the rolling hills and farmlands of north New Jersey to a dairy barn that no longer housed livestock. Once inside the barn, my father and Eddie could only stare in disbelief at the inventory of machines in front of them, all lying idle. Eddie and my father spent the rest of the afternoon walking back and forth examining each machine carefully. They were followed by Andy, who admittedly knew very little about the machines that he possessed.

"Well, Andy," my father said, "we'd like to buy one of your machines and set it up back home."

"Why buy one machine?" Andy said. "They're already here. Maybe we can work out a deal and set them all up here. Maybe you guys can get them all up and running again."

Eddie and my father looked at one another. Neither of them had been prepared for this.

"Well, I'll tell you what," Andy said, "if you're serious, go home and give it some thought and then get back to me. Nobody is knocking my door down to buy these machines anyway. It's only costing me money to heat the barn. I'll hold off for a week until I hear from you."

The men shook hands and we made our way back to New York.

As we drove back home that night, my father and Eddie could only speak of the tremendous opportunity that had fallen into their laps. If only the money could be raised to buy what Andy Sayer had shown them? Neither Eddie nor my father could believe the strange scenario. My dad had stumbled on a fortune in machines that were stored away in a dairy barn in Franklin, New Jersey.

I had never seen my father so excited. After describing the unlikely events of the day to my mother, my dad made two calls. The first was to his brother-in-law, Mike. Mike was my mother's youngest sister, Alice's husband. Mike would be a key member of the team if this giddy dream that Eddie and my father shared were to succeed. It was Mike who would design the tools and the dyes for the jobs that were contracted. Eddie and my father would make the tools and dyes that Mike designed and keep the machines running.

The second call was to Bob Maguire. Bob would also be a crucial member of the team. He was a salesman with many contacts who would secure the contracts needed to begin the work. Between the four, Mike, Eddie, Bob, and my father, Sam, the dream was taking shape.

Over the next few weeks, there was much negotiating and legal work to do. The final agreement called for each of the new partners to buy into the business by paying twenty-five thousand dollars each for equal shares in the business. Twenty-five thousand dollars was an immense amount of money in 1955. Andy Sayer did not have to make a financial investment because he was already the owner of the machinery and the building.

In order to raise the twenty-five thousand dollars, my mom and dad remortgaged our home in Brooklyn, and took loans to raise the rest of the money. After all of the legal papers were signed, my mother was the first one to voice some skepticism. When my father informed her about the salaries that each of the new partners had agreed to, my mother instantly saw an inequity.

"You mean that you are all drawing different salaries?" my mother asked.

"Yes, we are. Mike was earning three hundred dollars a week, so he'll keep that. It's not fair to ask him to take a cut. Bob will earn one hundred and seventy-five dollars a week because he will no longer receive a commission as a salesman. Andy will earn one hundred and seventy-five dollars a week too."

"How much will you be paid?" my mother asked.

"Eddie and I were earning one hundred and fifty dollars a week, so Eddie and I will be paid that amount." My father looked at her expression and saw that my mother was skeptical about that arrangement. Before she could say anything else, my dad added, "As soon as the business gets off the ground, we'll all earn the same amount of money."

Still not satisfied, my mother said, "This is a bad way to start things off. Everyone put in the same amount of money, twenty-five thousand dollars each, right? Then everyone should be receiving the same salary. It's only fair. You all took the same risk. That's what an equal partnership is. I'm not asking Mike or Bob to take a cut in pay, but everyone should be earning the same amount of money, which is either three hundred dollars a week for all of you, or one hundred and fifty dollars a week for everyone. If not that then it should be something in the middle for all of you, like two hundred dollars a week. It should be equal. Five equal partners," she said. "Those are perfectly logical options."

"Please, Helen. Don't make waves. Give the business a chance to get started, and then we'll all make the same salary."

My mother remained silent, but she was not happy.

So, we packed things up and moved into the small bungalow where we spent our summers. It was a wonderful summer bungalow but it was never designed for year-round living. The five of us moved from six rooms into four, but it didn't matter. For my dad, at age forty-one, a dream beyond any expectation that he had ever imagined for himself and his family was now within in his grasp. He could not have known that in a few short years that his unlikely dream would turn out to be the worst nightmare of his life.

CHAPTER 27

I BEGAN WORKING FOR MY FATHER A WEEK OR TWO after leaving the army. It wasn't long before I realized that I lacked the mechanical ability needed to advance into the technical areas of the business. I would never be able to do the work that my father and Eddie did, such as setting up machines for different jobs or trouble shooting machines that were down and that weren't producing.

Perhaps I could contribute to the company as a salesman, and bring in business for the shop that way. I realized that before I could advance to that point I had to "pay my dues." I began by sitting in front of a huge press and watched as it incessantly pounded out thousands of rifle shells, or pen caps, or lipstick cases, hour after hour in order to satisfy various contracts. Each of the hundreds of times that the machine would stamp down two or three droplets of oil would sprinkle on you. At the end of the day, your work clothes were soaked in oil.

The greatest challenge was in trying to find a way not to allow the machine to beguile you into falling asleep. Even an insomniac, I believed, would have difficulty keeping his eyes open. I sat watching the monotonous motion, and listening to the steady cadence of the machine, while it spit out fifty thousand shells or casings on a shift. It was a cat and mouse game between the machine and the operator. Lose your focus for a few seconds and doze off and the machine, almost as if it had a mind of its own and sensed that you were no longer alert, would malfunction. It would take the opportunity to wreak havoc by breaking up pieces in the track, and chewing up the punches and the dyes as well. In that case, a machine would be down for repairs, and a downed machine meant loss of money and a failure to meet deadlines. Eddie or my father worked to get the machine back on line as quickly as they could. Several operators were let go for repeatedly falling asleep on the job while I was there.

Besides realizing my limitations in the shop, I also realized that although the five partners were equal by virtue of their financial investment, if not in their salaries, there had developed a hierarchy or a pecking order, established by force of personalities. It was painful for me to accept it then, and it still bothers me, but to a lesser degree today. Because of my father's benign nature, he was at the very bottom of the hierarchy. My uncle, Mike, was the alpha partner.

On several occasions, when a machine was down and not back on line soon enough, the berating of my father and to a far lesser extent to Eddie, would begin. It was almost always by Andy Sayer, who knew as much about machines as I did. Andy was in charge of shipping. He formed the opinion that he alone was responsible for meeting deadlines. In order to spare my dad any embarrassment, I pretended not to hear the insults aimed at him by Andy over the din of the machines. As time went on the verbal attacks, and my father's seeming willingness to allow them, were taking a toll on my patience.

I reached my breaking point one day during a particularly profanity-laced tirade by Sayer against my father. My dad was attempting to explain the cause of the delay while a machine was down. Sayer, his face beet red, continued to berate my father. There was no pretending not to hear the tirade this time because Sayer and my father were a few feet away from my machine.

I turned to my right and smacked the emergency cut off on the machine. The sound of the machine shutting down caused my father and Sayer to turn in my direction as I walked toward them.

"Is something wrong, Nicky?" my father asked.

I walked up to Sayer and came close to pressing against him and he took a step back. I could tell by his expression that he was aware of the contempt that I had for him by the look on my face.

"Yeah. There's something wrong," I said. My face was a few inches from Sayer. "Look you fat bastard. I'm warning you right now. If I ever hear you talking to my father that way again, I'm gonna stop whatever I'm doing, and I'm gonna wrap a friggin bar around your neck, and that goes from now on. Get it?"

Several machines operators who were close enough to see that something was not right, shut down their machines, either to help avoid a fight or to watch one.

Sayer, his jaw trembling in anger, slowly and deliberately said to me, "Who the hell do you think that you're talking to?"

"And that's the same question that I have for you," I said. "Who the hell do you think that you're talking to?"

"Nicky, Nicky, no," my father said, stepping between us. "That's just the way he talks. He doesn't mean anything by it."

"Well, he better stop," I said, "because I promise you, Sayer, you won't finish your next nasty sentence if I'm around."

By that time, Eddie and my Uncle Mike, who had come out of his office, were on the scene and came between us.

"Nicky. Come into my office," Mike said.

"Let's go. Everybody back to work," Eddie shouted.

"I want him out of here!" Sayer shouted and pointed a finger at me.

"I'll handle this, Andy," Mike said. Then, looking at my father, who was obviously upset, he said, "It'll be alright, Sammy. I'll talk to you later."

We went into his office and my uncle handed me a soda from the machine. "Are you cooling off?" he asked.

"Look, Uncle Mike. I've been listening to that guy talking down to my father and worse. All the time I've pretended not to hear. Today I just couldn't take it anymore, and I'm not going to listen to it anymore. I'm not."

"Nicky. Andy talks that way to everyone. You should hear the things that he says to his brother, Joe, who works in the back."

"Let me ask you a question, Uncle Mike."

"What's that?"

"Does he talk that way to you?" I asked.

"No. He doesn't," he answered.

I stared at him for a few seconds. Neither of us said a word, but he understood my point exactly. He broke the silence.

"Look, Nicky. I'm going to send you to the Ogdensburg plant for a week or two. It'll give you and Andy a chance to cool off, and it'll be good for you to learn the operation over there. Okay?"

"Um, hmm," I said, nodding my head slowly. The conversation was over.

CHAPTER 28

THE PLANT IN OGDENSBURG WAS PURCHASED shortly after my dad and his partners bought into the original business in Franklin. Before the Ogdensburg plant was formed, anything manufactured in Franklin had to be sent out for washing, finishing, or plating before it could be shipped out. Now with the new plant in operation, the whole process from beginning to end was done internally, with no middleman. The dream that had started at our kitchen table in Brooklyn two years earlier had become larger and successful beyond expectations.

What was supposed to be a week or two temporary cooling off period to Ogdensburg was now going on a month. I was just a face in the crowd in that plant. Very few of the employees knew that I was the son of one of the partners. Given the work that I was doing, such as cleaning product that ranged from pen caps to gun shells in vats of chemicals, to working on production lines, the fact that they didn't know who I was, was fine with me. I never received a call to return to the Franklin plant. I didn't want to believe it, but it was becoming obvious to me that the plan was to wait until my frustration level got to a breaking point and hope that the futility of my situation would cause me to walk away from the job in disgust. That would solve the problem for the powers-that-be. No longer would they have to wonder what to do with me. In this case, the mastermind of the scheme was certainly Uncle Mike. Without his approval, none of this could have happened I believed. It was Mike who called all the shots, but there was always the chance that I was dead wrong about the whole conspiracy thing, so I plowed on.

One day I was on a coffee break with a fellow worker named Rudy, who I worked with on the finishing line. Rudy learned somehow that my dad was one of the five partners who had started the business that employed so many people in the Franklin area. When someone did learn that I was the son of a partner, the usual question was to ask me if I was a spy. Why else would I agree to be down and dirty with everyone else?

"Just learning the operation from bottom to top," was my usual answer.

"You've been here about a month," Rudy said. "Ain't that much to learn around here unless you're a slow learner," he laughed.

What Rudy said was like throwing a bucket of cold water on an unconscious man. "I guess I am a slow learner," I said. "I guess I am."

The truth of Rudy's observation stuck in my mind. I was a slow learner. I believe now that I was probably unwilling to accept the fact that there was no future for me in my father's business. I had learned the Ogdensburg operation well enough in the month that I had been there, not necessarily to run the place, but to at least be given more responsibility. That had not happened. It had taken Rudy's offhand remark to make me see what I hadn't been willing to come to grips with. It was all crystal clear to me at that moment. My uncle, and probably some of the other partners as well, wanted me out. They just didn't want me out of Franklin. They wanted me out of the business. It had nothing to do with friendships, or even family. It was all about business. There was plenty for everyone involved, but greed has no limits. There would be more if fewer were involved. The elimination process had already started.

The incident with Andy, although unplanned, had just made it easier for them to isolate me from my dad. They had not wasted it but instead they had taken advantage of the event. It had become a chess game for power, and Mike was always thinking two or three moves ahead of all of the others.

Each night when I got home, my father would ask me how my day had gone and I would ask him the same sort of things. I knew that each of us would lie to one another in order for one not to embarrass the other. That was the routine and the game that we both played where each of us wanted to spare the other. What had happened to the euphoria of the dream come true?

I always avoided asking my dad if I'd be coming back to Franklin soon. In reality, it was out of his hands and forcing the issue would only have caused him more pressure. He had enough of that already, but tonight it would be different.

"How did it go today, Boy?" he asked.

"Good, Dad," I said. I waited awhile and then I began. "Do you know what? I've been thinking. You know how you've always joked that the most basic tool placed in my hands suddenly becomes a dangerous weapon. Well, in the last two months I've discovered that that's not a joke. I know now that I'm just not cut out for tools and machines. I gave it my best shot. It just didn't work." I wanted him to believe that I was leaving because I disliked that line of work, and not because I could see that there was no future for me.

He sat listening to me. "So? What?" he asked.

"That's it," I said. "Today was my last day. They can just put someone else in my spot. They won't miss a beat."

I thought that there was a sense of relief in his voice and in his face.

"You know, Boy, I never even imagined that you would be working in the same kinds of shops that I have worked in all my life. I didn't want that. I never believed that you were cut out for this line of work. One of the reasons that I worked so hard was just because I wanted to give you the opportunities that I never had, so that you wouldn't have to do what I had to do. I wanted better for you. When I saw you in there with all of those machines, it made me miserable. I knew that it wasn't your thing, but I was proud that you tried so hard and never complained."

"Well, I wouldn't have known unless I tried it," I said.

"I'm glad that you tried it and now you know that it's not for you. I don't want you to work the way I do. Look at these hands." He held out his hands revealing cuts and bruises that he always seemed to have and to live with as long as I could remember.

"Nothing would make me happier than to see you going to work wearing a shirt and a tie. Not like me. So in the end, this experience was a good thing. It served a purpose for you."

"There's something else that I've been giving thought to," I said. "I've only been out of the army for sixty days. If you reenlist before you're out ninety days, you can go back in and keep you rank. So I've been thinking...."

My mother who had been listening silently until that point looked up sharply.

"Are you talking about the army again? Is that what you're thinking?" she said. "You've done that. Please, Nicky. Not again. We just finished with that. Daddy's right. You've tried working at Accurate, and it was a good experience for you. Put it to good use, but not the army again. Don't make me miserable with always having to say goodbye."

"It's just something that I've been thinking about. Another option," I said.

"But you do have other options," she said. "I would be so happy if you would go to college. Why not? One of the happiest memories that we have is of the day that you flew in from Fort Drum when you graduated from high school. College would be wonderful for you and for your future. Why not? And it would make us so proud."

There was the unreachable goal suggested again. College had been suggested to me by my roommates, Rich Avery and Bob Duncan, in Panzer Kaserne, when it seemed that only Lastings and I had not gone to college. Avery had lost all patience with me. He took my refusal to even consider enrolling in college as a total lack of ambition on my part when I had rejected his suggestion that I enroll in college after the army. Avery even suggested that I enroll in USAFI (United Stated Armed Forces Institute) courses while I was in the army.

"Do you want to be in the same category with people like Chance Lastings? What's wrong with you?" Then, with a wry expression on his face, he would adjust his glasses, turn away from me, and turn back to his book. Avery never knew the truth, which was that I hadn't graduated from high school. I was too embarrassed to tell the truth to him, or anyone else for that matter. My elaborate hoax was coming back to haunt me again. It hurts me even now to recall my mother saying how proud she was to see me graduate from high school. The deception continued to haunt me.

"Look, Mom. Even if I wanted to go to college, we don't have the money to pay for college tuition and all of the other expenses that go with it and I can't freeload. I have to work. You and Dad are paying back the money that you put into the business when you had to take loans and remortgage the house in Brooklyn. You're paying the mortgage on this house as well."

It was all true. My family was living on a tight budget until the business would realize a substantial profit and things would start to turn around. I hoped that the financial challenge that college would present would end any further discussion about attending college.

"Nicky. Wait here a second," my mother said, a smile covering her face. "I have a surprise for you." She went into her bedroom and came out with what appeared to be a bankbook in her hand. She stood alongside of the chair that I was sitting on and handed me the bankbook.

"I have a surprise for you. I was waiting for the right time to give this to you, and this is the perfect time. Open it up."

I looked into the bankbook, which was in my name. It had a balance of two thousand dollars.

"What is this?" I asked.

"Are you surprised?" she asked. "See, there's two thousand dollars in it. It's your money. It's a start, and don't worry. We'll figure out what to do after that. Leave it to Daddy and me. I was going to give it back to you to use however you wanted to, but it comes at a perfect time. You can use it to pay for you first year or two of college."

"That should take care of at least your first year, and after that the business will get off the ground and things will be okay. We'll take care of the rest," my father added.

I held the bankbook in my hand. "I don't have any money in the bank. Where did you get this money?" I asked.

"It's your money. It's your allotment checks," my mother said. "Every time that I got one, I deposited it in the bank for you."

"But I sent them to you to help you out. It's not my money. I gave it to you. I can't take this."

"It's not my money," my mother said, "and if you say that it is my money and you gave it to me, it gives me pleasure to give it back to you for a wonderful purpose."

I was overwhelmed by their generosity. I had never needed much when I was in the army where everything was provided for me. I wasn't a drinker or a smoker, and I never gambled. I only needed a little pocket money now and then, which I always had. It had given me pleasure to help my parents out in a time when they needed every penny that they could get, yet they resisted the urge to spend it. I was sure that there were times when they could have used it. Both of them had sacrificed so much for my sister, my brother and me. They had saved it for me hoping to surprise me with it and now they were giving all the money back to me.

"Mom, you're killing me," I said to her.

She dropped to her knees next to my chair. "Nicky, don't say anything right now. Just promise us that you'll give it some thought."

Her eyes were growing watery. I took her by the hands and gently pulled her up to her feet.

"Okay, Mom, okay. I'll give it some thought."

CHAPTER 29

I TOOK A FEW DAYS OFF MOSTLY TRYING TO FIGURE out what to do next. One thing for sure was that I couldn't remain unemployed for very long. Neither of my parents brought up the college topic during that time. I was glad about that and I kept searching the want ads hoping to find a decent job. If I could, that would allow me to support myself and, hopefully, it would end any further discussion about me attending college.

We had a neighbor down the road who would have been perfectly at home living in the Ozarks even though he had been born and raised in northern New Jersey. He didn't look like the comic strip character, *Li'l Abner,* who lived in a community called Dog Patch, but he and his wife had created a sort of Dog Patch of their own on their end of the road in the little bungalow in which they lived. His name was Charlie, but everyone called him Hound Dog. There was nothing that Hound Dog loved more than following his beagle hounds as they chased rabbits through the New Jersey woods. I had struck up conversations with Hound Dog, and I had a standing invitation from him to watch what he loved to do, which was to put his beagles through their paces. As a kid from Brooklyn, I found it all fascinating stuff.

"Ya hear the baying, Nick? They're on to a scent."

There was no denying, even to an untrained ear, the

frenzied almost hysterical sound of the hounds in pursuit of a rabbit.

"Now don't move, Nick. We'll stand right here and watch that rabbit make a complete circle and run right back into us."

"How do you know that it'll do that?" I asked.

"I know because rabbits are predictable. That's what they always do and that's why they get caught," Hound Dog explained. "They run a circle from wherever the dogs first flushed them out. They'll run that circle right back to the hole where they live hoping to dive back in for safety."

Hound Dog listened intently. "Sounds like Buster and Daisy are right on his tail. Now if this was in season I'd have my rifle ready and I'd get him as soon as he hit that clearing. One thing for sure, we'd be eating rabbit tonight."

"I never ate a rabbit," I said. "What does it taste like?"

"You know the answer to that," he said. "It tastes like chicken only better. Rabbits are vegetarians. Chickens eat anything. They even eat other chickens." Then nodding his head up and down, he said, "Tell me this ain't fun, Nick."

We listened, as the baying of the dogs got closer. "One time one of my best hounds was so close to grabbing that rabbit that when I shot I missed the rabbit and hit the dog. That broke my heart. I loved that dog."

I mustered a grim expression for his sad story, and then with a sly look he said, "Yeah, old Blue, he tasted like chicken too."

"Tell me you're just kidding me," I said.

"Yeah, yeah, I was just jokin with ya. They tell me that them Chinamen eat dogs all the time, and cats too, so how bad can they taste, especially if you're hungry? I hate cats. They kill a lot of rabbits and birds. I hope them Chinamen eat every last one of them cats, and a dog only once in a while," and he smiled at me.

I wasn't sure that Hound Dog really was joking, but so much for lunch over at Hound Dog's house.

"Here they come now," Hound Dog said. The rabbit scurried out of the woods and into the clearing, changing direction from left to right and running for his life. Both dogs were in hot pursuit right behind him. Hound Dog raised an imaginary rifle and pointed it at the fleeing rabbit. "Bam!" he said, and nodded his head up and down. "Move him, Buster! Move him, Daisy!" Hound Dog shouted. The rabbit dashed across the clearing and disappeared into the woods on the other side, with both beagles screaming and nipping at his heels.

"He'll disappear in the underbrush," Hound Dog said. "Let's go get those two dogs before they exhaust themselves."

We followed the sound of the hounds to a thorny thicket where the rabbit had taken refuge. The beagles circled, whining and howling in frustration. Hound Dog clipped leashes on the two of them. "We'll get even with him this fall," he said to his dogs and led the disappointed dogs away.

"So, Nick. Have you found a job, or are you still looking?" Hound Dog asked, as we made our way back to his little Dog Patch.

"No, I'm still looking. I better find something soon," I said.

"Nick, why don't you come on down to Austinel? That's where I work. Fill out an application. I know that they're hiring. They'll fit you in some place. Hell, you could ride to work with me if they put you on the night shift."

Austinel was a factory in Dover, New Jersey that did a lot of work for the Department of Defense. I had no idea exactly what they produced, but I knew that they had a steel foundry and that Hound Dog worked in the smelting and pouring section. We walked along and I listened as Hound

Dog chatted away about rabbits and hounds. The question was did I really want to work in another factory so soon after leaving the last factory job that I had? I thought about it for a few minutes and then I decided that I was in no position to be choosy.

"You know, Hound Dog, maybe that's a good idea. At least I'll give it a try. I'll drive over to Dover tomorrow and I'll fill out an application."

"Hey, you know what? See if you can get the four-to-twelve shift. We can ride together. It's a quiet shift and the good thing about it is that you have plenty of time in the morning to do what you want. I'm out in the woods with my dogs chasing the rabbits, and you're welcome to join us. That is unless you'd rather go to the lake and chase chicks instead of rabbits." Then, with a sly smile on his face, he continued, "Now those are the kinds of choices that I'd like to struggle with. Wake up in the morning and say to yourself, 'Self, what would you like to do this morning before you go to work? Chase rabbits, or chase chicks?' Those are hard choices to make, but nobody said that it would be easy. Lawdy," he said, shaking his head and laughing.

I started working at Austinel two days later as a sand blaster. It took me five minutes to learn the procedure. A box of steel elbows, the kind used to join two pipes together, was brought to me. Molten steel poured into molds from the ovens behind me formed the metal elbows. After the elbows were cracked out of their molds, boxes of elbows were placed at my feet. My job was to sand blast any remnants of the mold off the newly formed elbows so that they were pristine.

I was given heavy-duty rubber gloves. Then I placed my hands through two holes and into a machine that looked very much like an infant's incubator. Inside of the machine was a nozzle, which forced out a stream of sand under pressure. I slowly rotated the elbow round and round until I was satisfied that none of the mold material remained on the elbow. I placed the elbow in a clean box, picked up another elbow and repeated the procedure for eight hours.

As mindless as the job was, there was none of the pressure of the last factory job at Accurate. There I found myself starting to believe that the machines were actually playing a cat and mouse game. It seemed as if the machines were conspiring to catch an operator napping, to see if he was alert enough to shut it down before it wreaked havoc on a job.

There was no chance of ruining a steel elbow by sand blasting it, and less chance of falling asleep as I soon found out. I was sand blasting an elbow when I suddenly received an electric shock that erased any cobwebs that might have been in my brain. It was as if I had touched an ungrounded appliance. I dropped the elbow into the machine and I pulled my hands out. I looked up and down, left and right, fully expecting to see a live wire dangling near the machine.

A guy working the sand blaster next to me saw me looking around in circles.

"What's going on?" he asked.

"Man. I just got whacked by an electric shock. I thought my fillings were gonna melt."

"Oh, that's nothing. It ain't gonna kill ya," he laughed. "It's a surprise if you don't know that it's coming, but it won't hurt ya unless you have a weak heart."

"Why does that happen?" I asked.

"It's a buildup of static electricity from the pressurized sand in a confined area," he explained. "You'll get used to it. You might also have a pinhole in one of your rubber gloves. That'll do it too."

"I thought that the rubber gloves were to keep me from sand blasting my hands," I said.

"And they are," he said, "but they also help to reduce the electric shocks. Get a new pair. You'll get used to it." He went back to work.

Behind me, Hound Dog and his crew were working at smelting steel rods into what looked like molten lava. They poured the liquefied steel into everything from elbow molds, to molds for automobile parts. At times, the heat thrown off by the huge ovens became so intense that I imagined that it was not unlike standing by a burning building.

I worked at sand blasting through the rest of June and into August. In that time I never fell asleep and I never got used to the electric shocks.

CHAPTER 30

ALTHOUGH NEITHER OF MY PARENTS HAD BROUGHT up the subject of college to me again, apparently it had been a topic of discussion between my mother, her sister, Claire, and Aunt Claire's son, Jerry. Jerry was my cousin, and he was three years older than I was. We were raised like brothers, and I loved his mother, Claire, who was my mother's older and favorite sister. Aunt Claire treated me as much as a son as she treated Jerry.

In those days, when none of us had very much, nothing made me happier than seeing my Aunt Claire coming into our house, her arms full of clothing that Jerry, had outgrown. I was thrilled to receive the castoffs. I didn't look at the clothing as hand me downs, even though that was exactly what they were. They were as good as if they were new to me.

I even loved the familiar scent of the clothing, which reminded me of Aunt Claire's house. I had many cousins and friends, but there was no one that I admired as much as Jerry. He was smart and had a great sense of humor. Jerry had graduated from Oswego College, in upstate New York, and now he had a job as a teacher. To me, Jerry was the person that I would most like to emulate.

Aunt Claire was truly a second mother to me. She could say things to me, and go into particular areas in my life, where even my mother would not go.

On this particular weekend in early July of 1958, Aunt

Claire, her husband, Stan, and Jerry, had driven up to New Jersey for a visit. This time it was not with an arm full of hand me downs, but with a handful of college applications.

"Jerry picked these forms up and I brought them for you to fill out," Aunt Claire said. "Now get busy and stop procrastinating. What the heck is wrong with you? Do you want to spend the rest of your life working at stupid jobs with no future? Fill these applications out and put them in the mail by Monday. There's nothing else for you to do but to fill them out. The self-addressed envelopes are already stamped. Time is running out so get going."

I could feel the resentment and the anger flushing the back of my neck. It was not only for the manner in which my aunt had spoken to me, but also because she had revived a subject that I had hoped had been put to rest.

I took a deep breath and held my tongue, because even in my anger I knew that my aunt had my best interest in mind. She had spoken to me exactly as she would have spoken to her own son if he needed it.

Nothing else needed to be said about the subject or about what my aunt expected me to do. The college application forms remained in a conspicuous place on top of the kitchen table after my mother and her sister went out shopping.

Jerry and I sat outside in the warm summer sun.

"Are you annoyed?" Jerry asked.

"No, I'm not," I said, "but there's more to this college thing than meets the eye. You don't know, Jerry, but if you only knew what my problem is then you'd understand."

Jerry looked at me, "If I only knew what? What's your problem? What don't I know?"

I decided right then and there to unburden myself and to tell the truth about my deception over the last four years. I would tell about my not having a high school diploma, no matter how shocking that revelation would be to Jerry or how embarrassing it would be to me to have to admit to it now. If I told the truth, maybe he would understand. Maybe we could get off the subject once and for all. It was something that I had never believed that there would ever be any reason to have to admit to anyone, but the subject of college never seemed to go away. I began to tell it all now, from the mess I had made in high school, up to when the Air National Guard had flown me home to attend a graduation exercise when I had not graduated.

After I finished my confession, I looked at Jerry fully expecting that he would always think of me as a jerk from that point on. I expected to find a look of scorn on his face.

"Is that it?" Jerry asked. "You don't have a high school diploma. So what's the big deal?"

"What's the big deal? Weren't you listening to me? I can't go to college because I don't have a high school diploma. You need one of those to go to college. End of story."

"Listen," Jerry said. "When I went to Oswego, I graduated with a guy who also didn't have a high school diploma. He went to Oswego after he got an equivalency diploma. Today he's an elementary school principal in upstate New York. You'll do the same thing."

I couldn't believe it. What I saw as an insurmountable problem had a simple solution and was no problem at all from Jerry's point of view. I hadn't expected this sort of a reaction. I knew that you could get some sort of a general education diploma in the service. I hadn't even taken the time to look into what was necessary for me to do to earn a general education diploma while I was in the army. Other guys had done it. That was just another blown opportunity in my mind. I had never heard of an equivalency diploma so I thought that now it was too late. I looked at Jerry, shaking my head and smiling because of his can-do attitude. I also had a sense of relief. I had unburdened myself of a secret that I had kept for four years.

"I don't know what the hell you're smiling at," Jerry said. "This is what we're going to do. I'll find out when and where the equivalency test is being offered in the city. Then you'll take the exam and you'll receive your diploma in the mail. We'll be cutting it close, but we should be able to get you into a college for September. If not, we'll look into the spring semester. It doesn't matter which college. You'll go to the first one that accepts you. Let's just get our foot in the door. We can even say that you're a late applicant because you just got out of the army and that you were getting things squared away. I think that you'll get extra consideration for being in the army."

"Jerry, even if I take the test that you're talking about and I pass it, I'm not sure that I'm college material."

"Nicky, once you pass the test that means that you are qualified to go to college and you're not stupid."

"I haven't been in a classroom for four years," I said, "and if you count the times that I was cutting school, six years is probably more accurate."

"We'll see. There's nothing further to discuss until we find out where to take the equivalency examination, and we'll take it from there." Jerry had it all worked out.

"Do you think that I should tell my parents and your mother about all of this?" I asked.

"Ah, I don't think it's necessary. Why bother? It's all in the past. Let's just spare them all of the explanation and move forward. When you take the equivalency exam, we'll just tell them that you need to take the exam as a college entrance requirement, which is partially true."

Jerry made it all sound so ridiculously easy that he had

me wondering why I hadn't confided in him long before this. I also knew that my experiences over the last four years, as well as the recent futilities that I had trying to find a meaningful job, had been necessary for me to advance to this point.

True to his word, Jerry found out that the equivalency examination was being administered at Julia Richmond High School in Manhattan. In mid-July, I took a battery of tests over a two-day period, and two weeks later at the end of July, my diploma arrived in the mail. It was just the beginning.

CHAPTER 31

I WAS SOON DISPELLED OF ANY NOTION THAT I MIGHT have had about an equivalency diploma being a panacea for all of my high school indiscretions. It wasn't as easy as just submitting my name to the college of my choice for acceptance. Besides a valid diploma, all of the colleges required a high school transcript. The transcript recorded every class as well as the grade that you had received in each class throughout your high school career. The equivalency diploma, which took me two days to acquire, would not conceal my pathetic four years of high school.

"I might as well not have even bothered taking the equivalency exam," I said to Jerry. "It's bad enough that I'm showing up with a short cut diploma, which is a red light to start off with, but wait until they get a load of my high school transcript. Maybe we can tell them that my high school transcript was burned in a fire."

"One step at a time," Jerry said. "If they make an issue out of it, we'll deal with it. Let's see what happens. For now, let's call New Utrecht High School and ask for a copy of your transcript. Then we will go and pick it up."

Two days later, and four years after my last appearance there, I walked into my old high school building and through the familiar halls that had changed very little since I was there last.

As I made my way toward the main office where I was

told that my transcript would be waiting, I experienced the same eerie feeling that I had just before I left Panzer Kaserne. Panzer Kaserne or New Utrecht, it was all the same thing. All of my friends were gone. Then, as now, in their places were ghosts and memories. Where are all of you guys, I thought? The sound of the laughter and the memories of former years were replaced by the sound of my footsteps. Their hollow sound echoed back as I walked through the now silent corridors. It was all gone.

I gave the lady behind the desk my name and she handed me an envelope containing my transcript. To avoid what I knew would be a public embarrassment I took the transcript outside. I sat in my car and I opened the envelope. It was as I expected it to be. It was awful but all made worse because my failures were there in front of me in red ink. I put the transcript back into the envelope and shoved it into my glove compartment. It might have been out of sight but it was still burning in my mind as I drove back to New Jersey.

I submitted applications along with copies of my transcript and equivalency diploma to various state colleges. Most of them didn't take the time to respond, and the ones that did all offered polite rejections.

"Hey, Jerry, what's the difference between my high school transcript and a death certificate?"

"I don't know," Jerry said. "Why don't you tell me?"

"They don't use red ink on death certificates."

"Very funny, you should have been a comedian."

"I bet the people who looked my applications over already thought that I was a comedian. They probably had a good laugh, and I don't blame them."

"Stop feeling sorry for yourself," Jerry said. "It's not over."

"I have a feeling that it's over," I said. "It was a pretty good idea and it really had me going there for awhile."

"It's just the beginning," Jerry said. "I called New York University, because they have a late enrollment and they're local. We can go directly to the admissions office. They haven't had a chance to see your transcript yet. It's always better going for an interview in person than it is applying through the mail. You can make your case that way. So we have an eleven o'clock appointment for this Wednesday."

"Oh, New York University! What a good idea!" I said. "Now why didn't I think of that? When every college in a town with two traffic lights rejects you after looking at your pathetic record and application, apply to New York University. Yeah, that's a great idea, and do you know what, Jerry? If N.Y.U. is short sighted enough to reject me like all of the others, we can always apply to Yale or Harvard. They're kind of local too. Give me a break."

Jerry totally ignored my logic. "It's a whole different ballgame when you go in person, Nicky. Believe me. It's more difficult to throw an application into the garbage when a guy is looking at you than it is when it's received in the mail."

"Yeah, you're probably right, so he'll wait for me to leave, and then he'll throw it into the garbage," I said.

"The difference is that before you leave you can make your case. It's not impersonal the way an application submitted through the mail is. There's the human factor."

I stared at my cousin, overwhelmed by the faith he was showing in me but also surprised at how unrealistic he was being. I was so discouraged and humiliated that I wanted to drop the whole college thing and just go back to sand blasting elbows at Austinel. Perhaps applying for a job with the post office would be more realistic. Jerry knew what I was thinking and interrupted my thoughts.

"Just don't be discouraged," Jerry said.

"Just let it go, Jerry. We tried, now let's move on."

"We're too close to quit now, Nicky. We already have the appointment. Let's just see what happens on Wednesday. You'll be fine. If he asks you what you want to major in, since it's the School of Education, tell him or her that you want elementary education."

"Should I tell him that I want elementary education before he sees my transcript, or should I wait until after he sees it?"

"Stop with the funnies. You'll know when it's the right time. I'll meet you in the School of Education office at 10:30 on Wednesday morning."

My mother had been listening to the conversation and remained silent the whole time, but now she broke in. "Nicky, I know how much you want this, and you're going to get what you want. Just wait and see. I've been praying to Saint Jude ever since you began sending out college applications."

My mother wanted this as much as she ever did and she might have believed that I wanted it as much as she did. At that point, I wasn't sure how much I wanted it any longer. I was frustrated at all of the rejection letters. I was trying to avoid the final rejection and the embarrassment of not being admitted into any college. I didn't want to spend the rest of my life telling people that I had tried to get into college but that not one would accept me.

Jerry looked at my mother with a silly grin on his face. He knew all about Saint Jude, but asked my mother anyway, "Saint Jude? Why Saint Jude, Aunt Helen?"

My mother lifted her eyebrows and was about to answer, but then she caught herself and stopped, so I answered for her.

"You know as well as I do why she picked Saint Jude. He's the patron saint of lost causes. You pray to him when you need a miracle for a guy like me. Watch me mess up his successful string."

"That's not what I meant," my mother said.

"It's too late now, Mom, now we know." It was a laugh that we all needed.

My mother, Jerry, and I sat in the waiting area outside of the Dean of Admissions office in New York University's School of Education.

"Now don't forget," Jerry said, "you want elementary education, and don't be nervous."

"Don't tell me not to be nervous," I said. "It only makes me nervous. Wait until he gets a load of my transcript. You should never be nervous when you're facing a firing squad."

"Nicky. It's gonna be fine," my mother said. "I ...."

Before she could finish I said, "I know, you prayed to Saint Jude."

"That's right," she said.

The door opened. "Mr. Bilotti?" A tall man with an affable smile held the door open for me. I guessed him to be in his mid-forties. "Come in, please." He pointed at a chair. "Have a seat, please. I'm Dean Harris. How are you today?" He extended his hand.

"I'm fine, sir," I said.

He settled back into his chair and looked directly at me as a person would if he felt that first impressions were important.

"Are you local, Mr. Bilotti?"

I hesitated for a moment because it sounded as if he had asked me if I was loco. Then I realized that he still had not seen my transcript. The time for questioning my sanity would come later.

"Well, I've lived in Brooklyn all my life but recently my family relocated to New Jersey."

"So you drove in from New Jersey this morning?"

"Yes, sir."

"Were you able to avoid the traffic?"

"Yes, sir. The late morning appointment helped us to avoid the early rush."

We made small talk for a while and when it over, he said, "Well let's see if we can take advantage of late registration for you. What do we have here?"

Dean Harris reached for a folder, which was in front of him. I could see my name printed on it in large black letters. The first envelope was a large one and it contained a copy of my New York State Equivalency Diploma. He pursed his lips and looked it over. He looked up at me.

"We really don't see equivalency diplomas very often here although I'm certain that it happens."

He didn't seem to be overly concerned, and I didn't know what sort of a comment I should make. I smiled wanly and I thought to myself, "You ain't seen nothing yet."

"How old are you, Mr. Bilotti."

"I'm twenty-two, sir."

"Hmm. That means that you should have graduated from high school in 1954. This equivalency is dated July 1958." He looked at me over his glasses. "Where have you been for four years, Mr. Bilotti?"

"Well, sir, I've been to lots of places, I had lots of jobs, and I've also been in the army."

He placed the diploma back into the envelope and reached for the other envelope that contained my application for admittance along with my high school transcript.

"Let's see," he said, as he removed the application and my transcript from the envelope.

I studied his face because I wanted to remember it for the rest of my life. I wanted to be able to describe it whenever I would tell someone a funny story about the time that I tried to enroll in New York University. The only thing that I expected to come away with as a result of this meeting was having a funny story to tell. Dean Harris looked at my transcript. His expression alternated from disbelief to confused amusement. I was tempted to look over his shoulder to see which classes in particular he found more amusing than others.

At long last, Dean Harris folded my transcript and placed it along with my application back into the envelope. Then he placed all of my paperwork into my folder and turned to me. The humiliation and the embarrassment that I was feeling caused beads of perspiration to run down the small of my back. I was willing to give Saint Jude a pass on this one.

Dean Harris interlocked his fingers, placed his hands in front of him on his desk, and then shaking his head he began.

"Mr. Bilotti, you seem to be a nice young man, and the last thing that I want to do is to hurt your feelings." He was looking for a way to drop me gently. "I've looked at your transcript and your application and I have to tell you that not everyone is meant to go to college, or should go to college. People find satisfaction and success in their lives without going to college. There's nothing wrong with doing something else with your life other than college. Many have been successful, and perhaps even more successful, than they would have been if they had a college degree."

"Here it comes," I thought. "He'll put his hand on my shoulder as he escorts me toward the door."

"I see nothing in the papers that you've submitted that indicates to me that you would be suited for New York University, or for any other college for that matter. I have nothing to go on. I just believe that college is not meant for you based on what I have seen here." He waited for a response from me, and when there was none he said, "I'm going to deny your request for admittance. I do wish you the best of luck if you choose to apply elsewhere." He handed me my folder.

"Dean Harris," I said, as I took my folder from him. "I understand exactly what you're saying. I knew that being accepted here was more than a long shot. I know how badly I screwed up in high school, and now I'm paying for it. Bad decisions and bad choices made by a fourteen-year old or a seventeen-year old kid. I don't even know that kid any longer. Yet those decisions and bad choices now threaten to affect my life into adulthood and forever. I'm not the same person now who I was then. I wouldn't allow my teachers to teach me in those days. I can tell you that life has certainly taught me now and it has been a hard lesson.

"I've worked in sweat shops, in factories, in steel mills and on trucks. I've been in the army and in Europe, and I have seen life, and I have seen death too. You asked me where I have been for the last four years. Well, I've jammed all of that living into the last four years since I left high school. I like to think that since then I've done all that was asked of me to the very best of my ability. No short cuts like before."

He politely allowed me to speak and there was one more thing that I wanted to say before the inevitable.

"What I'm telling you here is not to excuse the bad things that are undeniably a part of my record. I've screwed up and now I'm paying for it. Worst of all, at least to me, is that for the most part, I've disappointed my parents and I've broken their hearts in so many ways. My mom is outside. She drove in with me. Please don't let me have to tell her that I've failed again. Maybe I don't deserve it, but I'm asking you to allow me to prove myself." There was nothing else for me to say without rambling on.

Dean Harris squinted his eyes and sat looking at me. Finally, he said, "You've got a hell of a nerve putting the onus on me. There are people above me to whom I'm accountable. They trust me to admit qualified students. In your case, if it were to be reviewed, they would be perfectly correct to question my judgment because nothing that I've seen here qualifies you."

I sensed some wavering on his part. I remembered what Jerry had told me to say. "Maybe you could admit me as an elementary education student."

That only seemed to annoy him. "First of all, don't denigrate elementary education. It isn't easy and you just can't breeze through it. Secondly, you'd be in a program comprised mostly of seventeen and eighteen-year old girls right out of high school. You can forget about that."

He stared at me and took a deep breath. "I think that I should have my head examined." There was another pause.

"Here's what I'm going to do and don't ask me why. If you make me think about it, I might change my mind." Again, he paused. "I don't even know if you can throw a ball, nor do I care. You'll enroll in our physical education program, not in elementary education. The science program in physical education is extensive, and it will be difficult and a challenge for you considering what I've seen on your high school transcript. Physical education, unlike elementary education, is largely comprised of men. That's my offer. There is no discussion. Yours is only to say yes or no. But there's more to it if you agree. If you agree, you'll be on probation for one year. During that time, you will have to maintain no less than a "C" average. Fall below and you're gone. No second chance. Take it or leave it with no further discussion."

"I'll take it."

"You'll receive further instructions through the mail. This is late registration. Return everything immediately. Good luck, Mr. Bilotti. Don't make me regret my decision."

"I'll do my best, sir." He stood up and the meeting was over. I walked out of his office.

My mother and Jerry were sitting where I had left them. My mother stood up as I approached and Jerry said, "Well?"

"I'm in."

"Great," Jerry said.

"Oh, Nicky," my mother said.

"I know. Saint Jude," and in my heart I was starting to believe that maybe there was something to this Saint Jude and his intercession for hopeless cases.

Wasn't what had just happened some sort of a miracle? In case it was just dumb luck, I said to Jerry, "Quick, let's get out of here before he changes his mind."

CHAPTER 32

THEY WEREN'T SEVENTEEN AND EIGHTEEN-YEAR old girls fresh out of high school. Instead, they were seventeen and eighteen year old boys fresh out of high school. They were all around me and they were motivated. They were football, basketball, and baseball players. They were swimmers, gymnasts, wrestlers, and track and field athletes. They were expected to show some measure of proficiency in all areas of sports, and not just in their comfort zones. They expected to receive a degree in physical education from New York University and I was one among them.

Up to that point, my experience with sports was limited to neighborhood games, with fair to middling success in organized baseball. I had a brief encounter with high school track as well. Dean Harris hadn't cared if physical education was my first choice or even if I could throw a baseball, when for some inexplicable reason he allowed me into N.Y.U. It appeared that he was equally unconcerned about my ability on the high bar, the pummel horse, or the rings.

As much as a challenge as some of the athletic activities was to me, I approached them head on with determination. It was similar to the determination that had seen me through the difficult days in basic training three years earlier. In some ways, this new experience was very similar to basic training minus the harassment. As it was in the army, everyone was pulling for the guy next to him and helping to get him through. It was some consolation that almost everyone was at some disadvantage. For instance, the guy with the football scholarship nearly drowned when he jumped into the pool. The guy with the baseball scholarship had as much trouble as I did pulling himself up on the rings. Except for the occasional all-around athlete, there was some parity. I managed in the athletic area to keep my average at a "C" and, hopefully, I would be able to do the same academically if I expected to remain at N.Y.U.

The academic side of the physical education program was entirely different. Dean Harris had suspected that it was in the area of science that I would probably meet my "Waterloo". He had shown compassion, and perhaps even bad judgment, in allowing me into N.Y.U. He had made it clear that the rest was up to me. I was to either sink or swim on my own. It wouldn't take too long before we would know which of the two it would be.

I saw my academic program for my freshman year. It included chemistry and biology. The panic alarm went off in my head. I had not gotten beyond general science as a high school freshman eight years earlier. I couldn't remember whether I had made a passing grade or not. A quick check of my high school transcript would reveal if I had passed the course, but I didn't want to be even more depressed by looking at it again. Even if I had passed, what I had learned in general science eight years ago would be of little use to me in college-level science courses.

There had been no chemistry or biology questions on the equivalency examination. If there had been, I probably would still have been sand blasting elbows at Austinel. As I saw it, my only hope if I wished to remain in college was to do well in my physical education skill courses. I also had to do well in my English and social studies courses. I could not fail either chemistry or biology. I had to receive passing grades in both of them, even if they were minimal passing grades. Everything had to average out to a "C".

I purchased the required books for English, social studies, biology, chemistry, and physical education, and took my seat in each of those classes. I was pleased with my early results. In fact, English and social studies were taking me into areas that I had never been to. I was enjoying the experience. I discovered that biology could be accomplished by rote and memory. No matter how much effort I put into my chemistry assignments or how attentive I might have been in lectures, the instructors might just as well have been lecturing in Greek. My object was merely to survive in chemistry and to excel in the areas in which I could.

Things went along for me much as I expected that they would in academia in my first semester. While I was challenged by my science classes, I was being introduced to classical literature, and learning how the past had brought us to the present in my history classes. My physical education classes were a relief and mostly enjoyable, and in the process I was making many new friends.

Jerry and Aunt Claire had made room for me in their modest apartment in Brooklyn. On the weekends, we would usually drive up to New Jersey to spend time with my family. My mother and my father would listen eagerly to my stories about college life and about the new friends that I had made. I enjoyed the feeling that I was finally doing something for them. I was the first of their children to go to college and that was a source of pride for them. For me there was a personal satisfaction. At long last, I was not doing something exclusively for myself. If I were successful I would reap the reward, but college would have never entered my mind except for my parents' suggestion and the persistence of Jerry and Aunt Claire.

My father was proud and relieved at the same time. He was relieved that I would do something else with my life other than working in shops and factories. Soon I'd be, "Going to work wearing a shirt and a tie," as he put it. Although I thought of it often, I purposely never asked my father how things were going for him personally in the shop. He never brought it up, as well, but I imagined that not much had changed.

I was in school for about a month and Jerry, his mother and I drove to my parents' home.

"Nicky, I have a little surprise for you," my dad said. "It's not a big deal but it'll be okay for now. Come outside with me."

I had seen an old Volkswagen parked on the road along the side of our house. Now as we walked toward it, my father said, "I bought this car for you from one of the guys who works for me."

I looked at a brown Volkswagen Beetle. "Gee, thanks Dad, but you didn't have to do that."

"Look," he said, "you can't depend on Jerry and Aunt Claire to drive you home all the time. Now you can come home whenever you want to. It's not new but it's in good shape. I checked it out, and after you graduate I promise...."

I didn't allow him to finish, "Thanks, Dad." I opened the door and he handed me the keys. I started the car up. "It's fine," I said.

"Just do me one favor, Nicky. Buy one of those N.Y.U. stickers for your car window. You know the kind that I mean. I see people driving around all the time with the names of the colleges that their kids attend."

"Yeah, I know what you mean. They're called decals. I saw them in the bookstore."

"That's right," he said. "And, Nicky, when you buy the sticker, will you buy one for me too?"

"You've got it, Dad."

In November of 1958, six months after I had left Accurate, and two months into my college career, I drove home to spend Thanksgiving with my family. I was also there to celebrate my parents' twenty-sixth wedding anniversary. Both of those events happened to fall on the same day that year. It was Thursday, November 27, 1958. It was significant too, in another way, because it was the first time that my father died.

"It's one o'clock. Daddy should be home any minute," my mother said. She was putting the final touches on the Thanksgiving dinner of antipasto, ravioli, turkey, ham, fruit and nuts, pies and desserts. It was typical of the legendary dinners that most Italian families shared in thanksgiving for the opportunity that their adopted nation had given them. They had been assimilated as Americans and a special occasion also because it was my parents' wedding anniversary. Now all that was left was the arrival of my sister and her family, my brother, and my father.

"Why did Daddy go in today?" I asked. "Wasn't the place closed on Thanksgiving?"

"Yes, it's closed, but they scheduled an eleven o'clock meeting. Daddy said that it would be brief. He should be home pretty soon."

No sooner were the words spoken by my mother when we heard the sound of the crunching gravel under my father's car as he pulled into the driveway. It was followed by the slam of the car door. My mother peered out of the window. "Here's Daddy now," she said.

I got up from my chair and walked to the door to let my father in.

"Hi Dad. Happy anniversary." I kissed him on the cheek, but when I stepped back to look at him it was instantly obvious that something was very wrong. My dad's expression had always been an open book. The family had always teased him about knowing his moods by looking at his eyes. They seemed to smile even when he was trying to suppress a grin or when he was up to some mischief. The look in his eyes was always a giveaway. As I looked at him now, the smile in his eyes was replaced by dark circles, and his complexion was gray.

"Hi, Boy," he said. "Thank you." He removed his jacket and hung it in the closet and then he took a seat by the kitchen table, which had been set for the Thanksgiving and anniversary celebration. He reached into his inside jacket pocket and drew out an envelope. I watched as he stared at the envelope in his hand as if the envelope had a spirit of its own. Then he turned to look at my mother. His eyes were vacant.

"What's wrong, Sam?" my mother asked.

He didn't answer, but instead he continued to hold the envelope. He didn't offer the envelope to my mother but she walked to where he was sitting and took the envelope from him.

"What's this?" she asked, taking the envelope from his hand. My mother opened it, removed the contents, and began to read. Her expression turned into a squint as she read. I looked at my father. He sat quietly, his shoulders hunched and his head drooping forward. Finally, my mother brought the paper from which she was reading down to her side and she looked up.

"They're not gonna get away with this," she said.

Unable to remain silent any longer, I asked, "What is it? What's going on?"

"Read this," she said, as she handed me the paper. Then she walked over to my father, lifted his head and hugged him. I began reading.

"Dear Mr. Bilotti, This letter is to inform you that at a meeting held on November 26, 1958, which included the Board of Directors of the Accurate Forming Corporation, Everlast Metal Finishing Company, and the Janileen Realty Company of Franklin Borough and Ogdensburg, New Jersey, a unanimous vote was taken by the majority of the partners of the above-named corporations to remove you as one of the shareholders of the corporations as provided for by the by-laws of the corporations, effective immediately.

"At the same meeting of November 26, 1958, the partners and Board of Directors also voted to pay you a one-time severance payment of $25,000.

"We wish you every success in your future endeavors." It was signed by each of the four remaining partners.

I put the letter down and looked at my father. He was a totally broken man. There was no fight; no will left in him. The wonderful dream, which my father alone had stumbled upon while reading the newspaper in our kitchen in Brooklyn three years earlier, was gone. The unimaginable dream that he hoped for all of his life, and which really had come true, had become an unimaginable nightmare.

My mother was furious. All of the despair in my father was countered by a fury in my mother. There was no sign of capitulation in her. She placed her hand on my father's shoulders.

"Listen to me," she said, "hold your head up. This is not over. We're gonna get back what they stole from us." He looked up, but the smiling eyes were vacant. "Was Mike at the meeting this morning?"

My father shook his head slowly. "There was no meeting this morning."

"What do you mean there was no meeting this morning? Wasn't there supposed to be a meeting?"

"When I got there," he said in a barely discernible whisper, "Marilyn, the secretary, was the only one there. I asked her where everyone was. She said that she didn't know, and handed me that envelope." He paused. "Then she left."

"They made the whole damned thing up," my mother said. "There never was gonna be a meeting, and not one of them had the guts to face you, the damned cowards. They made Marilyn do it. Wait. I'll fix them good, but first I want to call my sister, Alice. I want to know how much she knows about this. Whatever they have, they have because of you." She looked at me. "Your father was the one who found the opportunity and shared it with them when he saw it in the paper that day. None of them would ever have had this opportunity, and this is what they do," and she lifted my father's head against her.

I had no idea what to say or do. In my heart, and from what I had seen during the short amount of time that I had worked in Accurate, I had the feeling that things could go bad in a hurry. No son, from the time that he was a little boy, wanted to think of his dad as, "low man on the totem pole," especially when you had so much love and admiration for that person. In order to deal with the reality, I totally blocked what I had seen from my mind.

"I could never have imagined this. I can't believe it. It's all gone. All gone," my father said. He was trying to make sense of it all. "We had our disagreements, but not this. I guess that they must have been planning this all the while. I just didn't see it. I was always too busy in the shop and I always thought that Mike would watch out for my interest up front, and now…." He didn't finish but shook his head slowly. He looked up at me again. "Then the other day, Andy was yelling and screaming loud enough for everyone to hear that for the salary that Eddie and I got they could hire four guys to do the same job."

There was the warning, I thought, and it would have been the perfect opportunity for my father to point out to Andy that they could hire six shipping clerks for what he alone was being paid. What he was after all was an overpaid shipping clerk. I wish my father had told Andy that he should keep his mouth shut. Everyone was expendable. But that was my style, and it was not in my father's nature, and now it was too late.

"So Andy specifically mentioned your name and Eddie's name. Did Eddie get a letter too?" my mother asked.

"No just me. Eddie was one of the four who voted me out."

"Oh, I see," my mother said. "Then how long will it be before Eddie gets his own letter? Then after him Andy or Bob, until Mike is the only one left. I know that none of this could have happened without Mike's approval.

"Remember, Sammy, when we argued because you agreed to take one hundred and fifty dollars a week for your salary, while Mike was taking a three hundred dollar a week salary? We disagreed about that but you said that eventually everyone would make the same salary, when the business 'got off the ground,' as you put it. Everyone would take the salary that he was earning when the business was started. You begged me not to rock the boat. I knew it was wrong. All of you put the same twenty-five thousand dollars into the business. Everyone should have made the same salary. That should have been made clear from the start, regardless of what they were making before. That's what a partnership is."

"You were right, Mom, but it's too late for that now. Let's figure out what to do next," I said. The truth was I did not know what we would do in the near future. I didn't even know what to do at that moment. Uncle Mike, I thought. How could it be? And then, my mind raced back to an event that happened in 1954.

It was a Saturday morning and I was surprised to see my father reading a newspaper rather than working at some sort of project around the house as he usually did.

"Good morning, Dad, what's going on?"

"Oh, I'm just killing some time before I go donate some blood for Uncle Mike's father."

"Uncle Mike's father? What's wrong with him," I asked.

"He's having an operation and he's going to need several blood transfusions. They're really expensive so a few of us are going over to Kings County Hospital. We're going to replace the blood that they give him so that the poor man won't have to pay for it." He paused a second. "Do you think that you'd like to do that for Uncle Mike? Donate some blood?"

I had never donated blood before. My father was in the "gallon club" having donated blood for the troops over and over again during World War ll.

"Sure, Dad," I said, and so off the two of us went to Kings County Hospital. Each of us donated a pint of blood for Uncle Mike's father. Now, four years later, Uncle Mike was extracting my father's last drop of blood.

"The first thing that I want to do is to call my sister, and the next thing to do is to find a good lawyer. I wish I knew one," she said. She went to the phone to call her youngest sister, Alice, who was married to Mike.

My father turned toward me. "Nicky, don't let any of this affect you. You concentrate on your college work, and

Mommy and I will find a way. We always have. Please don't make me worry about that."

"I know, Dad. We'll be fine," I said, but I knew that the world had just changed for all of us. Things would be very different from now on. I couldn't imagine how he had managed to drive home after he had read that letter.

"Hello, Alice? Yes, thank you, but that's not what I called you about. Do you know what your husband did to us today? What did he do? Well, let me read this letter to you."

My mother read the letter to her sister, and they spoke briefly and then they hung up. My mother came back to the kitchen.

"She said that she had no idea about any of this, and that Mike never speaks to her about business. She said she was shocked, but that when he got home from playing golf there would be a war. She said that she would get back to me after she confronted him."

My mother could not have known that it would be more than twenty years before she would speak with her sister again.

CHAPTER 33

WORD ABOUT WHAT HAD HAPPENED TO MY FATHER spread quickly around the family as you would expect that it would. Until the events of November 27th, my mother's family, aunts, uncles and cousins, had been a closely-knit group for the most part. The actions of the partners of Accurate Forming, and particularly my Uncle Mike's role in that action tore the family apart. My mother had four sisters and four brothers. Most of them chose to remain neutral since the situation pitted two of the sisters and their husbands against one another. It would be a no-win situation if they were to take sides.

It was Aunt Claire, her husband, Stan, and Jerry, who remained steadfast and loyal to my parents during those dark days. They believed that Mike's actions were shameful. They seemed unconcerned about who knew how they felt about the part that he had played in what had been done to my father.

Another one of my mother's sisters, Jean, and her husband, Paul, were less than neutral. The gods, it's been said, often toy and play strange games with us. My Aunt Jean and Uncle Paul, by some strange coincidence had lost their business under similar circumstances to my father's. Paul, too, had been voted out by a majority of partners in an automotive business. My Uncle Paul's heartbreak had occurred a year before my father's, but except for the fact that no family members were involved, the similarity was eerie.

"Now they know how it feels," Uncle Paul was quoted as saying. It was difficult to understand because my father had been sympathetic to his brother-in-law's loss and grief. It seemed as if now my father's pain made Paul's pain easier for him to bear. It's never easy to understand human nature. Be that as it may, the family had lost a little more of its innocence, and tragically, would never be the same again.

My mother was as determined to fight the actions of my father's former partners as she was at the time that she learned of the partners voting my father out. She immediately began a search for a lawyer without realizing that lawyers specialized in the same way that doctors do. In their naiveté, they didn't know that for specific types of legal claims you went to specific kinds of lawyers. It is the same as you would do with specific medical conditions.

We never had need for legal assistance prior to going into business. Even while forming the new corporation, everyone agreed to a single lawyer, if only to show how completely they all trusted one another. That was a mistake because we had no legal sophistication. In our innocence we would learn the hard way how misguided our decision was from the beginning. Each partner should have been represented by his own lawyer. Now with our present situation, choosing a lawyer who did not specialize in corporate litigation would be another costly mistake.

"I wish that I knew a really good lawyer," my mother said. "I wonder if Dr. Gino knows a good lawyer. Doctors use lawyers for their business and things. I'm gonna speak with Dr. Gino. I am gonna tell him what happened and see if he can recommend someone to us. That would be better than just going to a lawyer who we know nothing about."

It was the Saturday after Thanksgiving. My father was still in disbelief. He was struggling with the reality of what had happened to him and to his family with all of the ramifications that were inherent.

Dr. Gino was our family physician and we had become somewhat friendly with him over the years. Not knowing anyone else to turn to, my mother placed a call to Dr. Gino and explained our situation to him. Dr. Gino was totally sympathetic, and then he recommended that we speak with a lawyer friend of his, Frank Shapiro. Mr. Shapiro had been very successful as a criminal prosecutor. The fact that Mr. Shapiro was a personal friend of Dr. Gino was enough for us. We hired him to represent us in our suit against Accurate Forming. Mr. Shapiro never suggested that we see a lawyer who specialized in corporate litigation. Despite his good intentions, it would soon become apparent that Mr. Shapiro's expertise was in the field of criminal law. The partners from Accurate Forming had retained lawyers who dealt only in the area of corporate litigation.

There was an immediate change for me after my father was ousted from the company. Since I started college in September, I had been living in Aunt Claire's small apartment in Brooklyn, along with Jerry, and Uncle Stan. They were people of simple means. My aunt worked full time in a women's lingerie store. Jerry was in his fourth year as an elementary school teacher. Uncle Stan, had always made me feel welcome in his home. He was a shipping clerk in the warehouse of a large clothing chain in New York City. Even with their combined salaries, my aunt's family lived frugally out of necessity, and now I was another mouth to feed.

My mother and my father would give Aunt Claire fifteen or twenty dollars each week, which Aunt Claire was reluctant to take. In fact, my mother had to convince her sister to take the money. We had done that from September until November, but the amount of money that I now gave to my aunt, as well as the frequency in which I gave it, grew less as my father and my mother both searched for jobs. During that time my uncle, my aunt, and my cousin accepted this new burden as their own, and remained staunch supporters of my family.

The Christmas break followed rapidly on the heels of Thanksgiving. It was a time for relaxing and getting away from the classroom routine. It was also a time to start working on assignments that were due in January. Although I hadn't planned on it, just as important as writing term papers, was the opportunity presented to me by the Christmas vacation to work in Austinel. I needed to earn some money that my parents were no longer able to provide. The vacation also would give Aunt Claire and her family a breather from having me around all the time.

Several of us were gathered in the gym at N.Y.U. Christmas cheer had been replaced by impatience on the part of our instructor, Mr. Powell. He was not happy about being in a gym and not with his family two days before Christmas. As he saw it, we were too damned uncoordinated to accomplish various exercises on one or another of the apparatus in the gym. I was also annoyed but not for the same reason. I was annoyed because being in the gym had pulled me away from sand blasting elbows in Austinel. I had lost a day's pay, and I was forced to remain in the city as well.

I stared at the high bar wondering how the hell I was going to do this. We were expected to jump up and grab the bar. Then, once you had a firm grip on the bar, you had to pull yourself up high enough somehow so that you were able to hook one leg over the bar and onto the back of your knee, while your other leg dangled down. Then, while holding on with both hands, and keeping the back of your leg hooked over the bar, you were to thrust yourself forward and make at least two complete consecutive rotations for a passing grade on the high bar.

"Bilotti. You're up," Powell said, his grade book in his hand.

I looked left and right and then I walked over to the window ledge, and ran my fingers across the top of the ledge.

"Bilotti. What the hell are you doing?" Powell said impatiently.

"I'm looking for some rosin. My hands are clammy," I said.

"Bilotti, will you stop wasting my time? We would all like to get out of here. Now get on the bar."

"But."

"Get on the bar!"

I wiped my hands on my shirt, but that seemed to do little good. Rather than to plead my case for the rosin bag and risk further wrath from Mr. Powell, I jumped up and managed to grab hold of the bar. Then, with no regard for form, while using my elbows, my arms and my chest, I managed to get my leg over the bar and I locked the back of my knee on the bar. A few of my classmates were looking up, stifling grins behind their hands not daring to laugh out loud. It was obvious to them, and what I already knew, was that as a gymnast I was not quite ready for prime time. I really did not care. From my point of view, it was not really important how I got into the proper position for the next step. It was only necessary to get there and now I was there. I rubbed my clammy hands on my shorts one at a time, not daring to let go of the bar with both of my hands. I looked at Mr. Powell one last time. Before I could ask for the rosin bag he shouted, "Go!"

I lifted my body slightly off the bar and thrust my weight

forward to begin rotating. As I rotated, my classmates began to count out loud: one, two, three, and after the third rotation, some of them began applauding my success, but I wasn't done yet. My clammy hands had morphed into hundreds of ball bearings. No matter how hard I tried to squeeze my hands together to in effect put on the brakes, I only succeeded into picking up speed until number three became four, and four went into five and so on.

I was aware that some of my classmates were continuing the count and were shouting encouragement to me to keep going. They were cheering as if I had any control over what I was doing, or as if I was trying to break the freshman record for knee rotations on the high bar. I knew that if I were to lose my grip, which I felt might happen any second, all those cheering for me now would see me slamming downward into the floor or crashing upward through the ceiling. Neither option held much appeal to me. The one thing that I knew for sure was that however I would exit the high bar, I would probably not be leaving the gym the way that I had entered it under my own power and on my own two feet. And so I continued orbiting the bar, my teeth clenched, and my lips pulled back. When I dared to open my eyes, I saw various streaks of colors flashing by, as well as quick glimpses of the ceiling and of the floor and the grated windows. In the midst of my controlled terror, I heard Mr. Powell shout, "Bilotti, quit clowning and get off that bar now!"

"Mr. Powell. I don't think that he's clowning. He can't stop. I think that he's in trouble," someone shouted half in alarm, but half in amusement.

"Well then don't just stand there. Get him off!" Powell shouted.

Just before I was about to lose my grip and what seemed to be an eternity, two of my classmates, Neil Solomon and

Stan Workman, caught me in mid-rotation and held on. I finally released my grip on the bar.

"Man, that was awesome," Neil Solomon said. "Man, you were a blur. I never saw anything like that in my life."

"I lost friggin' count," Stan added as he laughed and pounded me on the back and shook his head in disbelief.

"Solomon, damn it. Will you stop laughing," Mr. Powell said angrily.

"You've got to admit, Mr. Powell, Nick must have set some kind of a record. That was really something else. Hey, Nick, can you do it again?" Neil whispered.

The room was still whirling around for me. I held onto Neil and Stan. "How many did I do?" I asked them.

"I don't know," Neil said. "I stopped counting at twenty-five, and I think that you were only halfway through. Let me tell you nobody is gonna come close to doing that many rotations in that short span of time."

"Nick, you've got the record. That was wild," Stan said.

And despite Mr. Powell, Neil broke into laughter again and walked over to the others waiting their turn.

Things were finally coming into focus again, and I walked toward Mr. Powell who was making notations in his book. He looked up at me. "What the hell was that all about?" he asked.

All I could think of to say was, "I told you that I needed the rosin sack."

"Okay. You passed. Get the hell out of here," he said.

I headed for the exit. It was a little after noon. As I hurried to my car, I thought that I'd better get that "C" average and get the hell out of physical education. I better do that before the science courses or the gymnastics killed me. Maybe if I hurried, I could get back to New Jersey and catch the four-to-twelve shift at Austinel. I could use the money.

CHAPTER 34

THE YEAR 1958 FADED INTO 1959. IT WAS THE FINAL year of an extraordinary decade, the events of which would have a profound influence on me for the rest of my life. In the brief time that I was an undergraduate at N.Y.U., I had come to know four or five of my classmates well enough to be invited to stay the night at one or another of their homes, rather than to make the weekend trip to New Jersey. It appeared that the type of friends that I gravitated to in college, had lots in common with others that I had befriended. Whether they were childhood friends, friends that I had made at various places of employment, or friends from the army, they seemed to have lots in common. They were without exception unassuming and unpretentious. None of them took life or themselves too seriously. For most of them, it was anything for a laugh.

There had always been hilarious times in my life. Sometimes the humor bordered on the immature and outrageous. It seemed that like a magnet, I attracted and I was attracted to, these free spirits. Some might even call us incorrigible. I would later discover that such Damon Runyon, *Guys and Dolls*-like "characters" would be my closest friends throughout my professional career. It certainly kept things interesting all my life. It was never boring.

We sat in the classroom listening to a lecture in health education given by a professor who had once been a Tuskegee

Airman, and was now an Associate Professor at New York University. The professor was as serious about health, diet, exercise, and caloric intake as he probably had been about approaching German fighter planes a few years earlier. Not so for me and my friends, one of whom was a master at double-talking. A few minutes earlier, my Greek friend, Kyro, had asked the professor a question, which started off coherently but lapsed into incomprehensible double talk. Without missing a beat, the professor responded to Kyro's gibberish. He went into great detail about why a high-protein diet although bad for human beings was harmless to a walrus.

I don't know what the others around me were doing to keep from guffawing. I didn't want to look in any of their directions, but I nearly bit my tongue off trying not to laugh out loud.

Just when I had gotten control of myself, I looked down the row of seats to my left and I saw a book being quietly passed down the row. Each person who received the book would read for a moment or two, and then put his hand over his mouth or duck down behind the seat in front of him. One of my friends hiding from the lecturer and turning beet red nearly choked in his attempt to hold back what should have been loud guffaws.

The book made its way to me. I took it from my friend, Stan, who had tears in his eyes as he tried to stifle his laughter. Stan slid the book onto my lap. I looked at the cover and it was a copy of *Lady Chatterley's Lover.* It was 1958 and the Supreme Court had decided that such books with strong sexual content that had once been banned could no longer be banned. Someone had obtained a copy and now these college freshmen were passing the book around like elementary school boys. They were fascinated by the pornographic descriptions, while reading and underlining some of the more outrageous passages. Keep in mind that such reading material had always been censored, or banned in Boston as we used to say, and was quite risqué for the time.

The passage that Stan wanted me to read was one in which Lady Chatterley was doing some strange things with the flowers that her lover, the gardener, had picked from the flower garden and brought to her.

"He'd better hope that those weeds that she's shoving up that guy's keester aren't poison ivy," Stan whispered to me.

That did it for me. I couldn't contain myself any longer. I ducked down and let all my pent up laughter out, which caused the whole row to break into laughter shattering the silence of the professor's lecture.

The professor was outraged by our sophomoric behavior. Not knowing why or who had instigated the disruption in his lecture, in his outrage, he indiscriminately threw two of the quietest members of our class out of the room. The two that he threw out were nowhere near those of us who were passing the book around. When they protested their innocence, he would have none of it. He shouted them out of the door and into the hallway. Their confused expressions made the whole thing funnier to those of us who had "dodged the bullet." Not one of us stood up to confess our guilt. We just cried laughing while listening to the professor shouting at the two in the hallway.

When order was restored, the professor spent the last half hour lecturing us about our immaturity and about how unworthy we were to be part of the student body of New York University. You could have heard a pin drop.

Over fifty years have come and gone since that event. We have all survived and we occasionally get together. Invariably that episode will be brought up by someone. Those of us who were there still chuckle and shake our heads about the events of that day. I don't know what became of the two guys who were thrown out of class. As funny as we still find it all these years later, I'm willing to bet that the two guys who were the victims of our behavior are still as outraged to this day by the injustice of the situation as they were on the day that it happened.

Several of my new college friends had recently been separated from the military like me. Unlike me, most of them were receiving the benefits of the G.I. Bill. Those who had the good fortune to be receiving the G.I. Bill were able to pay their tuition and they had some money left over for books and expenses as well.

None of them was aware of the recent misfortune of my father losing his business. How do you tell these recent friends about the financial crisis my family was in because of the Thanksgiving Day disaster? I didn't want to sound like I was whining or looking for sympathy. Rather than that, I guarded my secret carefully from them, but I changed my lifestyle. There were days when I would forego lunch or having a beer with my friends in a Greenwich Village hang out. I had enjoyed that before but things were no longer the same.

Purchasing books and other materials was a constant requirement. Those were more urgent and presented a greater problem than worrying about lunch or a beer. You could skip lunch and a beer after class, but you could not get around classroom expenses and requirements, which were weekly things.

We were also informed that in June, freshman physical education majors were required to go away to Lake Sebago in upstate New York for a week of boating and camping skills studies. There was a fee for room and board beyond the regular fee for tuition. These incidental fees added to my financial burden. I knew that I just couldn't afford to go to camp, even though you could not get a degree in physical education unless that requirement was fulfilled. Transferring out of physical education was becoming increasingly urgent because of all of the incidental expenses.

Stan was one of my closest friends in physical education and also an army veteran with whom I had lots in common. He had found a job in the West Side Y.M.C.A. as a counselor and a swimming instructor for young boys. Stan got several of us jobs along with him in the "Y". The money wasn't very much, but the hours were flexible, so that if I wasn't in class or in a library, I was in the West Side "Y", working with the seven or eight year olds. I might have been supervising a trip to a zoo, a museum, the planetarium, or working with kids in a pool. Every little bit helped so I continued my hectic schedule of either attending classes or running off to work at the "Y".

CHAPTER 35

MY AUNT JEAN, AND HER HUSBAND, PAUL, HAD A precocious daughter, Mary, now thirteen. They lived in the same apartment building as Aunt Claire and her family. In fact, the two sisters and their families lived on the same floor with their apartments opposite one another only separated by a small hallway. The families were so close that in effect it was as though the two apartments were one.

I pounded on the typewriter. I was nearly finished typing a couple of short papers for an English class. I had written the papers the day before. One was for me, and one or two were written as favors for a couple of my physical education friends. They were sometimes as challenged in their native language as I was in chemistry. The papers were due to be handed in that afternoon. As I concluded the papers, I thought to myself that all that was left to do would be to run across the hallway to borrow the stapler from Aunt Jean and to clip the papers together. Aunt Claire had the typewriter, but Aunt Jean had the stapler. I was the only one home. Everyone else was either at work or in school at 10 A.M. on a Tuesday morning in February.

I found the key to Aunt Jean's apartment in the drawer where Aunt Claire kept it, and I made my way across the hallway to Aunt Jean's apartment. I knew exactly where the stapler was kept. I turned the key and I heard the lock disengage. I began to open the door but the safety chain was in place and prevented me from opening the door completely.

Oh, I thought, someone must be home. "Hello. Aunt Jean? It's me," I said through the narrow opening that the chain allowed.

I heard someone scurrying toward the door, and then there was a voice that I recognized to be my cousin, Mary's, voice.

"Who is it?"

"It's me," I said. "I want to borrow the stapler."

"Okay. Wait a second. I'll get it for you," Mary responded.

"Well, open the door," I said. I could hear her scurrying away.

"Just a minute," she said.

She left and returned a few seconds later, and rather than opening the door she attempted to squeeze the stapler through the narrow space in the door that the chain allowed. Now my suspicions were aroused. This damned kid is probably smoking in there, I thought. Mary continued to angle the stapler through the narrow opening in the door without any success.

"Mary, this is ridiculous. Open this door right now." My suspicions had been aroused and my paper and the stapler were no longer the focus of my attention.

"I'm not dressed," she said.

"Well, go put something on and then open this door or I'm gonna rip the damned chain off the door," I responded.

"Nicky, if you don't go away I'm gonna tell my mother," she said.

"You're gonna tell your mother? I'm gonna tell your mother, so stop threatening me and open this door. I'm counting to three. If you don't take that chain off, I'm gonna rip it off. One...."

Before I could go further, I heard the chain sliding and she opened the door. I looked at her. She was wearing a robe, and she was visibly agitated.

"Are you smoking in here?" I asked, even though I could not smell smoke.

"No," she said.

"Why are you home? Does your mother know that you're not in school?" I made my way around the apartment, but I could see or smell nothing suspicious.

"No, she doesn't know that I'm home. I felt sick after she left for work, so I decided to stay home," she said as she followed close behind me.

"Have you called her to tell her that?" I asked, still looking around.

"After you leave I will," she said.

Mary was an excellent student who made high honors in all of her classes. Her parents both doted on her to an extreme. Her many academic achievements and awards were prominently displayed throughout the apartment. Some of them were framed and were hung on the walls for everyone to see in the interior hallway that led into the apartment. It all seemed tacky to me but they had Mary late in life and she was their only child. They were proud of her considerable academic achievements.

I walked past the bathroom and into the bedroom when I noticed that the bedroom door was a bit ajar. I pushed on the door forcing it back toward the wall, but the door wouldn't budge. I stepped into the room and looked behind the door. I saw someone in a fetal position scrunched down in a corner.

"What? What the hell?" I said, as I reached down and pulled a young boy to his feet. He was long and lean. I shoved him out of the bedroom and into the foyer.

"You better not put your hands on me," he said, looking

back at me as he sauntered toward the apartment doorway. "I'm only sixteen and you'll be in big trouble."

"Oh, you're a God damned lawyer," I said, the anger welling up in me from his arrogance. With that, I gave him a well-placed kick in his butt, which sent him hurtling toward the door. He opened the door and ran down the half landing as I stood at the top landing looking down at him. He pointed his finger at me.

"I'll be back here with my brother," he shouted.

"You son of a bitch," I said and started down the steps after him. He saw me coming and turned, and took the steps two at a time, down four flights of stairs and out of the building. I waited until I heard the main door slam and I went back into the apartment.

Mary sat at the kitchen table, her arms folded over her chest, her legs crossed, with one leg rocking forward and back. She stared defiantly back at me.

"Well?" I said.

"What?" she asked.

"Are you kidding me?" I asked. "What the hell was going on in here?" My mind was conjuring up all sorts of images. "Who was that and how long was that guy here?"

"He's a friend and he was only here a few minutes," she said.

"What were you doing?"

"I swear, we were just talking."

"Just talking? How did that guy know that you were home this morning? Did you call him and he rushed over here, or did you plan to be sick today? Why aren't you dressed?" She stared back at me without answering, but kept flicking her leg back and forth.

"Is this something that you do all the time? Is it something that you've done before?"

"No, Nicky. This was the first time. It was a dumb thing to do and I'll never do it again." There was a change in her tone now.

I looked at her and shook my head. "How am I supposed to believe anything that you're saying to me about what was going on here? What are you doing dressed in that bathrobe?" She did not answer. "You knew that this guy was coming over and you didn't bother to get dressed?" She had no answers for me. I was almost thinking and not really addressing her.

Now what do I do I thought? We stared at each other in an uncomfortable silence, her leg pumping back and forth. This was my thirteen-year old cousin. I knew that her parents would be shattered if I were to tell them about this. I knew that there would be lots of pain here for everyone involved no matter what I chose to do. I had my fill of family pain of late.

"Get dressed," I said. "I'm driving you to school. I can't trust you to be here alone."

She hurried out of the room and in a few minutes she was back and dressed and carrying her books looking like Betty co-ed.

Her eyes opened wide and she said, "Nicky, could you please not tell my parents? Please. I know that what I did was wrong and I swear that I'll never do it again. This taught me a lesson. Please?" She handed me the stapler and I had all to do not to knock her on the head with it.

Again, I shook my head and after a few seconds, I said, "Okay. I won't tell your parents." She breathed a sigh of relief and we went out the door.

I was late in handing in the papers, but the only thing on my mind the rest of the day was the episode in my aunt's apartment. I kept wondering if anything had happened before I got there, or how often Mary had done this. What would have happened if I hadn't stumbled onto the situation? I debated with myself about what the proper thing for me to do would be. I had given Mary my word not to tell her parents, and in my mind, your word was really your bond.

"Why so quiet tonight, Nicky?" Aunt Claire asked as I finished the last of my hamburger.

"Oh, I don't know. I just have a lot of things on my mind."

Jerry, was instantly alerted. "Is there something going on in school? How are you doing in chemistry?"

"I'm keeping my head above water in chemistry. That's about it, but I'm doing alright in everything else."

"Are you concerned about money?" my aunt asked.

"No, I'm not," I lied, even though money had become a problem that I had to deal with every day, it was not my biggest concern at that moment.

My aunt walked over to me and placed her hand on my forehead. "You don't have a fever," she said.

Uncle Stan lowered his newspaper, looked over his glasses at Aunt Claire, shook his head, and went back to his paper. Aunt Claire was forever feeling your head to see if you had a fever. If not that, she was dabbing an antibiotic on you face or neck if she spotted a pimple or a blemish.

"No fever, but something's wrong. Have you spoken with your mother?" she asked.

"Oh, I forgot to tell you. I spoke with my mother. My father found a job with Rowe Manufacturing, the company that makes vending machines. He's back to working on lathes."

"Well, that is good news," Aunt Claire said.

"My mother found a job in Netcong finishing women's coats. That will help them to get back on their feet. My mother also said that their lawyer, Frank Shapiro, has filed an action to get Accurate Forming to open their books. He wants to be sure that they are not hiding things, and he suspects that that is just what they've been doing."

"It's about time that that lawyer did something," Uncle Stan said. "There's not an honorable bone in any of the low-lifes in that group led by Mike. Tell your father to tell Shapiro to look under every stone where that group is concerned. That Mike wrote the book on dirty tricks. I know that guy a long time."

Aunt Claire left the kitchen. I assumed that she was making her way to her bedroom to prepare for going to work tomorrow. Jerry and I cleared off the table and cleaned up the dinner plates. As Jerry put things away, I drifted out of the kitchen to my aunt's bedroom. I had made up my mind, then and there, that I had to tell someone what had happened this morning. Perhaps if I told my aunt about those events and that I had given Mary my word to keep her secret, she would validate what I had done. If she did, she would relieve me of the tremendous burden that I was feeling.

"You gave your word?" Aunt Claire asked, a look of disbelief on her face, "and what about the unspoken word given by children who love their parents, which is to honor them and not disgrace them? You owe Aunt Jean more loyalty than you owe Mary. Are you kidding me? She's thirteen years old. I don't care how book smart she is. Even an average kid makes better decisions than that. If you had gone to a priest in confession and told him instead of me, he would tell you that you have an obligation to tell her parents. Once you tell them, it's no longer your responsibility. We've got to tell Aunt Jean and Uncle Paul, because, Nicky, if you don't tell them and something bad comes out of this, they'll never forgive you. If you don't want to tell them, I will. Let Mary hate me. I don't care and you shouldn't either. At least my sister won't hate either of us someday for not telling her what her daughter did."

We walked into the kitchen. "Stan, Jerry," my aunt said to her husband and to her son, "we have something to tell you and we want your opinions."

After I finished telling what I had told my aunt, Jerry said, "Nicky, my mother is right. We've got to go across the hall and tell her parents."

We looked at each other, waiting for someone to make the first move, and Aunt Claire said, "Okay, this is going to be painful, but let's go."

"I'll stay here," Uncle Stan said.

The door was not locked, as was the custom with the two sisters. When the three of us walked in past all of the academic awards that she had won, Mary stood up from where she had been sitting at the kitchen table to greet us. She looked quickly at me trying to read my expression. One look at my face told her to sit back down. Aunt Jean was putting the finishing touches on dinner, and Uncle Paul was looking at a copy of *Look* magazine.

"Hi. What's going on?" Aunt Jean said.

Aunt Claire got right to the point. "Jean, Paul, Nicky has something very disturbing to tell you," and she looked at me to begin.

I began to tell the story for the third time and as I did, Mary stared straight ahead, her eyes wide open like an animal staring into a bright light. There was total silence after I concluded. Uncle Paul, a veteran of the D-Day invasion, looked as I imagined he must have looked on the day of the invasion.

Aunt Jean dabbed a tissue to her eyes. "Mary. Have you anything to say about this?"

All eyes focused on Mary and I still felt some guilt about

having given my word and then broken it. Now I realized that I had been foolish for giving my word in the first place. If Mary felt any resentment toward me, I couldn't see it on her blank expression. After a moment or two, it became evident that their daughter was not going to respond to her mother's request for an explanation. Aunt Jean said, "Nicky, I'm sorry that you were put in this position. I hope that what you did will save the three of us from any more hurt, but can all of you leave now? The three of us have a lot to discuss as a family."

When we got back to our apartment, Aunt Claire could see the pained expression on my face. "Nicky," she said, "you did the right thing. There really was no other choice."

CHAPTER 36

I NEEDED A "C" AVERAGE AFTER MY FIRST YEAR TO BE removed from the probation list. It was equally as important to me to do well because I needed to prove to myself that I really belonged in New York University, or in any college at all for that matter. If not, then maybe I should follow Dean Harris' advice and try to find success outside of college. I thought perhaps I should look into taking the post office exam.

Most universities gave the option of waiting for grades to come through the mail on your transcripts. Those who preferred not to wait could leave self-addressed postcards for each professor. If you did that, you would receive your grades sooner.

My cards came in quick succession. I received a "D" in chemistry for which I was grateful. I did well enough in my other academic subjects and in my physical education classes as well, to achieve a "B" average. That meant that my name would be removed from the probationary status list.

The choice to either go to summer camp at Lake Sebago with my physical education classmates, or to go to work at Austinel was not a difficult one for me. If I intended to transfer out of physical education and into a different major, it seemed pointless to spend the time and the money required to go to Lake Sebago. Instead, I was back on the night shift in Austinel that summer where I continued to sand blast pipe elbows in front of the steel smelting furnaces. I later learned from my friends of the raucous good times that I missed at Lake Sebago. I had to forego the fun for the money that I would need for my sophomore year. There would be no falling back on army allotment checks to pay my tuition this time. They were all exhausted.

My family could never have imagined how different things would be for us almost one year later. A partnership in a thriving business full of potential with the promise of financial independence, no longer existed. Instead, both of my parents were forced to take jobs for which they were both overqualified, but nevertheless were grateful to have. All of this considered, I was on austerity and I was not about to ask my parents for a dime more than I would need to pay for absolute necessities. I worked forty hours a week and I accepted overtime when it was offered.

While I was in Germany, I had befriended a soldier from New Jersey. Probably because of my provincial upbringing, I seemed to find it difficult to form close relationships with anyone who was not from Brooklyn, or at least from one of the five boroughs. In the best of all possible worlds, he would be Italian. Maybe it was a cultural thing. I overlooked the fact that Al Orlando was a foreigner from New Jersey, because he knew what I was talking about when we spoke about things Italian, from food to family.

Al was the Catholic chaplain's assistant. He was about five years older than I was, and he rotated back to the United States three months before I did. One of the first things that he did when he got back home was to call my family and pay them a visit. Both of our families took an instant liking to each other. As strange as it seemed, Al never met a German girl that he was serious about even though he had dated several. When he got back to New Jersey, he met a German girl employed as a nanny, and within a year, they planned to be married.

"Nick, Annalisa and I are getting married." It was Al on the phone and it was May of 1958. "Would you do us the honor of being our best man? We're getting married in August."

"Hey, that's great, Al. I would love to do that. The honor is mine, and I'm so happy for the both of you."

It was August of 1959, almost a year to the day since their wedding. Annalisa and Al were visiting my parents and me at our home in New Jersey. We were reminiscing about their wedding reception and Annalisa said, "It was such a happy event for us and the year has gone by so quickly. Now we're going to have another happy event. We're going to have a baby."

"Hey, that's great." My parents and I were happy at the good news.

We all stood up to hug Annalisa and to congratulate her. While I was shaking Al's hand, he said, "Here I go again, Nick. It seems like I'm always asking something of you, but Annalisa and I would love it if you would be the baby's godfather."

"Are you kidding me?" I said. "I feel as honored now as I did last year when you asked me to be your best man. And you know, Al, it's not as if you haven't asked me to be a godfather before. I stopped counting at about twenty. I have lots of experience about being a godfather because of you but this one is special."

Al nodded his head, "You're right. That's true, you were always on call," he said, smiling at me.

My parents and Annalisa were looking at the two of us laughing at one another, confused expressions on their faces.

"What are you talking about?" my father asked.

"You know that I was Father Hickey's assistant in Germany," Al said. "Well, we had soldiers and family members often converting to Catholicism, and when we baptized them they needed a godparent to sponsor them. That's where Nick came in."

"Yeah, I can still hear Al or Father Hickey asking, 'Nick what are you doing tomorrow afternoon? We've got someone to baptize.' Father Hickey even came to get me out of the dispensary one time."

"So you have a lot of godchildren, Nicky?" my mother asked.

"Oh, oh," I said. I knew what was coming. "Bunches of them," I said, "and they were not all children. Most of them were older than I was at that time."

"Well, where are they now?" my mother asked.

"Where are they now? I don't know. They're all over the world." I could see that my mother was not satisfied with that response, so I said, "Would you like me to find out where they are and look them up?"

"Baptism is a very serious thing in our religion. It's a great honor and you shouldn't take it lightly. You know that, Nicky," my mother said.

All I could do was to secretly roll my eyes and look at Al, who was stifling a grin.

It was time to change the subject, "Hey guys, let's go outside and take a few more pictures. This is a day that we want to remember," I said. I picked up my Retina, a camera that I had purchased in Germany and which had cost me one hundred dollars, and we all went outside. Now one hundred dollars might not seem like a lot of money today, but in 1956, when the army was paying me eighty dollars a month more or less, one hundred dollars for a camera was a small fortune.

"Oh," Al teased, "you've got your fancy camera. I forgot

about that. Everybody else was sacrificing to buy fifty-dollar cameras and your son walks into the room with a camera costing one hundred dollars. We only paid fifty dollars for that beat up old Volkswagen that we had, and he marches into the room with that camera. We could have bought two Volkswagens."

"That's true," I said. "Maybe one of those cars would have burned more gas than oil than the Volkswagen that we had. You told me to bring the camera back. I'm glad that I didn't listen to you, because the technology in this camera makes homely people like you and me look like movie stars. Thank God for German engineering."

"Geez, you're right," Al said. "I'm glad that you didn't listen to me."

It was a beautiful early August day. I knew that Al and Annalisa intended to head for home after dinner to avoid the brutal summer traffic, so I busied myself lighting the barbecue.

"Nicky," my mother said, "take a few pictures. When the barbecue is almost ready, go down to the lake and pick your brother up. Will you do that please? Dinner will be ready when you get back."

My brother, Matthew, was fourteen years old now. He was still not old enough to drive, but old enough and responsible enough in my parents' opinions to be given more independence. He was at the lake with a few of his friends and I was on my way to get him.

The family car was a 1956 Oldsmobile, which my father had purchased shortly after he had gone into business. It was the first brand new car that he had ever owned. Up to that time, Dad had always purchased used klunkers that he would fix up. The Oldsmobile was an imposing vehicle built during the glory years of large American automobiles. The trunk of the car was nearly as long as the hood. I placed my camera on top of the abundant ledge of the car's trunk, and reached for the bag of charcoal. I filled the barbecue and started the fire.

"I'm off to get Matthew," I shouted to my parents. "Just give the coals a few minutes and it will be ready." My parents were engaged in conversation with Annalisa and Al as I walked around to the driver's side of the car. "I'll be right back."

"Be careful," my father said, as I backed out of our driveway and down the bumpy country road to the lake where my brother was waiting.

It was a great summer barbecue of burgers, Italian sausage, chicken, corn on the cob, potato salad, and garden salad, made even better with the company of family and friends.

"It's been a wonderful day and I hate to see it end," Al said as he sipped on a cup of coffee, "but we have a long road back. If we get an early start we should get home at a reasonable hour, even if we do hit traffic."

"It's so hard to predict the traffic," my father said. "Maybe you'll be lucky. Sometimes you're preparing for the worst and you fly right through. Other times, when you thought it would be clear sailing, you're bumper to bumper."

We said our goodbyes and waved at Annalisa and Al as they drove down the road.

"They're such a nice couple," my mother said. "I pray that you meet someone nice like Annalisa."

"Are you in touch with Saint Jude again?" I teased.

"That's how much you know. You pray to Saint Rita when you want your children to meet nice people. And what an honor it is that they asked you to be their baby's godfather. I can't wait to find out if it's a girl or a boy. If it's a boy, you'll buy a miraculous medal as a baptism gift. If it's a girl, you'll buy her a cross."

"Maybe the godmother will have other ideas," I said.

"Oh no, that's what you do when you baptize a baby. It's a cross for a girl and a miraculous medal if it's a boy." There was no further discussion on that subject. "Did you have to buy anything for all your godchildren in Germany?" my mother asked.

"Mom, I just shook their hands and congratulated them. This was a nice day, it's one of those days that you'll remember for a long time," I said. "I'm glad that I got so many good shots. I can't wait to get the film developed." Then, looking around, I said, "Where did I put my camera?"

At first, I was the only one looking for my camera. As I came up empty in my hunt for it, my brother and my parents could see the anxiety on my face. Soon we were all searching for it.

We had exhausted every possible place where I might have placed my camera and, in fact, we were now going back to places where we had already looked. My father and I sat on the patio. I looked at him.

"Dad, I'm embarrassed to tell you what I'm thinking, but how could I have been so dumb?"

"What's that?" he asked.

"I've been retracing my actions since the last time that the camera was in my hands. I get to the part when Mom asked me to light the barbecue and then to go and get Matthew at the lake. It was just after we took pictures of all of us with Annalisa and Al. Remember? I put the camera on the trunk of the Oldsmobile while I started the barbecue, and then I drove off to get Matthew at the lake," and then I was quiet.

A light of comprehension lit up my father's face. "Are you

saying that you think that you drove off with the camera on the trunk of the car?"

"I don't think that. That's what I did," I said.

"Oh, well that's great," my father said as he sat back in his chair.

"I'm certain that that's exactly what I did. I drove off with the camera on the trunk of the car. Dumb. Dumb. Dumb."

"Okay, no panic," my father said. "Let's start by searching down the road. Maybe it rolled off to the side and we can spot it. Or maybe one of the people in those summer bungalows down there picked it up. It's possible."

I knew that was a long shot. Five or six hours had elapsed from the time that I had picked up my brother. If the camera had been visible from the road, someone else would certainly have seen it earlier and picked it up. Perhaps someone would have rolled over it. The other possibility was that after falling off the trunk, the camera had rolled off the side of the road into the underbrush, which was thick on those country roads. If that had happened, it would take a miracle or a bloodhound to find it. Hopefully, the leather case that the camera was in might have kept it from being smashed on impact with the road. Whatever had happened to the camera, there was no doubt in my mind that the camera was gone forever.

"Matthew, get a few of your friends and ask them if they'll help us to look for the camera," my father said.

"Good idea," I said with a modicum of renewed hope. "And tell them there's ten dollars in it for the one who finds the camera."

"Ten dollars?" my brother said. "Does that include me?"

"You'll get five dollars and three free meals tomorrow," my father said. "Now go and round up your friends."

We scoured the road and beat the brush back for about an hour, but all to no avail.

"Look guys," I said to my search party, "we'll go to the end of this road and then we'll turn back. The camera would have slid off the trunk long before I got this far down this bumpy road."

"Hey, Sam, what's going on?"

I looked up and I saw a middle-aged man, cigarette in hand, wearing a black pair of pants, and a white dress shirt opened at the collar.

"Hello, Joe," my father said. "We're looking for a camera."

"A camera?" the man asked.

"Yes, it's a long story. My son forgot that he put his camera on the trunk of my car and he drove away with the camera still on the trunk. We think it fell off the car somewhere along the road here, and we're hoping that we can find it," my father explained.

"That sounds like something that I would do if I knew how to drive," he broke into a belly laugh.

"Oh, I'm sorry, do you know my son?" my father asked.

"No, I don't."

"Nicky, this is Joe Nicolosi. Joe is a good friend of Al Corio. They live in Brooklyn."

Al Corio was a neighbor of ours whose family spent the summers in New Jersey. It seemed as if most of our summer neighbors were from Brooklyn.

"Joe, this is my son, Nicky."

Joe extended his hand to me and as I grasped it, he said, "This is my wife, Agnes." He motioned toward a woman who was standing on a walk at the bottom of a wooden stairway, which led up to the bungalow entrance. She appeared packed and ready to return to the city, as she smiled and nodded in my direction, a shy but pleasant smile on her face.

"What part of Brooklyn are you from?" I asked Joe.

"We're from Williamsburg. That's God's country. We've

been here since Friday and now we're heading back to civilization. We're gonna wave goodbye to the birds and the squirrels and the trees until the next time." Again, there was the easygoing chuckle.

I looked away from the walk where Joe and Agnes were standing. To my right, I saw a girl standing at the top of a rock retaining wall that bordered the house. She apparently had walked out from the side of the house, and now she stood looking down at me and at the other searchers. I guessed that she was perhaps seventeen or eighteen. She was slender and attractive, and neatly dressed for traveling. I looked up at her. As depressing as the last hour or two had been for me, it was as if someone had opened a door and let in a fresh breeze. Without turning my eyes away from her, I whispered to my father, "Who's the girl on the wall?"

"I have no idea," he answered. But then Joe said, "Do you know my daughter, Sammy? No? This is my daughter, Camille. This is Sam and his son, Nicky. They live up the road."

"Oh, hello, Camille," my father said.

Camille looked at my father and me, smiled and nodded.

"Hi," I said.

Camille. I had heard my brother's friends talking about a girl named Camille who lived down the road. Adolescent boys constantly giggled about girls, so I paid no attention to their silly banter, but now I was looking at the Camille of their fantasies.

I walked toward the wall and looked up at her. Even in the brief minute since we were introduced, I searched her eyes for the subtle signs that I had learned to look for in the boy-girl game. I looked for curiosity, perhaps some subtle sign of interest, but hopefully not disinterest. If this was the beginning of a new and exciting game for me, it was advantage Camille. She had my interest, but I could detect very little interest on her part. There was something about her demeanor as she stood looking down at me. It was an aloof, guarded expression that really held my interest. The challenges and excitement of the chase had begun for me even if she did not realize it yet.

"Hi. I'm Nick."

"I'm Camille."

"I didn't know that you lived here," I said.

"How could you know? We have the bungalow about five years but we only come up occasionally," she said. "You wouldn't have noticed me. I was only thirteen when we bought it."

I did some quick calculations. That would make her eighteen now. I didn't know if she had made the point because I looked older to her or merely as conversation. I could understand why at twenty-three I'd be kind of old to a girl of eighteen.

"So you don't come up every weekend," I said.

"Well, we try to but we can't always make it up here. Both my parents and I work, and none of us drive. We have to take the bus back and forth from the city, unless one of my relatives drives us up. My mother really loves it up here, but it isn't easy. We do stay here when my parents have their vacations. So we come up when we can."

"And you're leaving right now?" I asked.

"Yes, we're waiting for the cab right now to take us to the bus in Landing."

"Oh, that's too bad," I said. "Isn't there a later bus that you could take?"

"A later bus? No. Why?"

"Well, if you take a later bus, maybe we could go to a

movie, and after the movie I could drive you and your family to Landing."

She had a strange look on her face as if to say, "I don't believe this guy. I know him five minutes and he's asking me to delay going home so he can take me to a movie. Oh my God."

That's what she was probably thinking, but she didn't say so. Instead, she said, "No, we can't do that. We've got to get home. Tomorrow is a work day for the three of us."

As she said that, the cab that would take them to the bus at Landing pulled up.

"Okay," I said. "Maybe we can do something next week."

She gave me a half smile and said, "Maybe. We have to go now."

We all said goodbye, and Joe, Agnes, and Camille got into the cab and drove away.

"What was that all about?" my father asked.

I looked at him and grinned. "I learned a new word in college, Dad. Serendipity. Do you know what it means?"

"Oh, of course I do. I use it all the time in the shop. What does it mean?"

"It means to find something of value when you least expected to find it."

"What are you talking about? You lost your camera."

"Well, I lost my camera today and I'll probably never see it again, but it's possible that I found something more valuable that I wasn't looking for. We'll see. Maybe Saint Rita is just as effective as Saint Jude."

"Saint Rita, Saint Jude, what are you talking about?" my father asked.

"Let's go home and ask Mom if there's a patron saint of lost cameras. I'm starting to think that this stuff really works. Maybe I can have it all."

My father gave me a confused look and shook his head as we walked back up the road.

On the bus heading for New York City, Agnes said to her daughter, Camille, "He seems like a nice boy, doesn't he?"

"I don't know much about him," Camille answered, "but there's one thing that I have no doubt about."

"What's that?" her mother asked.

"He's not shy."

The following weekend it rained hard from Friday through Sunday. I made several trips down to Camille's bungalow anyway, but no one was there. I was disappointed and I hoped that it was the weather that kept them away, and it wasn't because Camille was not in a hurry to see me again. I preferred to think that the bad weather had kept the family away.

CHAPTER 37

AFTER THAT RAINY WEEKEND WHEN I HAD BEEN SO disappointed that Camille and her family had not come up to their bungalow, things had brightened up. Two weeks after our first meeting, Camille and her family came up to the lake. I had driven by several times to see if they were there, and finally success. Although there was no car to indicate that anyone was at the bungalow, I was happy to see a light on in the house. I walked up the steps and knocked at the door. Camille answered the door and she was as pretty as I remembered the first time that I saw her. Almost as important, at least to me, was the warm way that her parents, especially Camille's mother, greeted me. I was unaccustomed by that immediate warmth and by the way that they received me. It was all so refreshing and new to me.

Months later, after they got to know me, I could tell that they approved of their daughter's choice. And I felt good about it. For the first time I had met a girl whose family did not look at me as a poor choice by their daughter and as a person really going nowhere. This time I believed that they wanted me to come back again, rather than just hope that I would walk away and not return. I loved not feeling defensive and on edge as Camille and I got to know one another.

Camille made it easy because she was pretty, but I soon learned that in addition to her being pretty, she was smart as well. She had been an honor society student in high school.

That was reason enough for me to keep my own high school academic record to myself. I had it all. I had found a pretty and intelligent girl from a welcoming family. In those dark days, so soon after my father's loss, Camille was my oasis and my only bright light.

It was my sophomore year and I was still in physical education. I had received my freshman grades too late to apply for a change in my major. I had every intention to make application to transfer into history or English before my junior year. That would allow me to keep all of the science credits that I had earned so far in physical education. I preferred history to English but I was in no position to be choosy. If I were fortunate enough to be allowed the change, I would accept the first one to approve of the transfer rather than to say no to one and risk not be offered a place by the other.

I attended my classes and continued to work at the West Side Y.M.C.A. during the day and between classes when my schedule allowed it. I also worked at the "Y" on weekends for what amounted to pocket money. When there were prolonged days off from school, I went back to New Jersey to work at Austinel.

Besides the usual fees for books that were common regardless of what your major was, there seemed to be no end to incidental fees required in physical education. I had avoided paying the camping fee for Lake Sebago. I couldn't avoid paying what seemed to me to be unending fees for athletic shoes, shorts or tee shirts, and athletic equipment as required by the department.

You were not always on campus, but you were always traveling from an athletic field, or to a court, or to a pool, and with that came the carfare involved. I looked forward to the time, perhaps in the next few months, when I could pay my tuition, buy my books, sit in my class, and be done with it.

"Nicky, did you see my sneakers?" Jerry asked. He was fishing around in the bottom of his closet looking for them, while I was sitting at the kitchen table working on an English assignment. It was a Saturday afternoon. I had intended to go up to the lake to see my parents, but I had decided to stay in Brooklyn instead to write my paper. That would save me the money that I would have had to spend on gasoline and tolls, and later I would be able to spend some time with Camille.

I looked up from my paper and I hesitated. "Yes, they're in my bag." It was my fault. I knew that I should have bought sneakers of my own. The pair that I had been using was a pair that I had before I had gone into the army. They were not in the best of shape to begin with, but after the rugged physical education regimen, they had broken down completely. I dropped them into a wire trash basket as I left the field one day in Red Hook intending to buy a new pair. At least I told myself that that was my intention.

The previous Thursday we were supposed to report to the field in Red Hook, Brooklyn, and I had not bought new sneakers. I was hoping to get by for another week or two before I was forced to buy my own. I knew that Jerry's sneakers were readily available. Jerry rarely used them and they were staring back at me at the bottom of his closet. The temptation to use them just this once had gotten the best of me. I would buy myself a pair after I received my next paycheck. In the meantime, I could use the sneaker money to buy lunch Thursday and Friday. Jerry wouldn't care, I thought. He probably wouldn't have even noticed that I had used them if not for the fact that during the football scrimmage the sky opened up. The rain came down in droves changing the fields into a muddy quagmire.

"Okay, ladies. There's no lightening so let's keep playing," the instructor said as he blew his whistle and handed the ball to the other team. "A little rain won't kill anybody unless you're afraid to get your sneakers dirty. Now let's run that play again."

He had hit the nail right on the head. I was afraid to get Jerry's sneakers dirty. When the scrimmage was finally over, I walked off the field. Jerry's sneakers were unrecognizable after that football war. They were covered in mud and slimy grass. I saw that same wire basket on the outside of the stadium. I was tempted to deposit Jerry's sneakers into the basket and just replace them. That would mean that I would now have to buy two pairs of sneakers, one for Jerry and one for me. To avoid having to do that, I decided to try to clean Jerry's sneakers with a good stiff brush and some bleach.

The brush and the bleach were no match for the mud and the grass stains. Although they were still damp, I had put the sneakers in my bag hoping that they would dry out before Jerry noticed that they were missing. My intention was to replace them for Jerry with new ones and to use his old ones for myself after they dried out. Jerry never used his sneakers so I knew it would work out.

"Nicky, where did you put your bag?" Jerry asked. "I've got a tennis date with some friends."

What's the old saying? "Timing is everything." Those sneakers had stood in Jerry's closet for weeks on end untouched. Just at that time when I was hoping that they would dry out and that I would get to my next payday to replace them, Jerry was searching for them.

I walked down the hall to where I kept my bag and I took the still damp sneakers out. Then I walked back to the kitchen and handed them to him.

Please, Lord, I thought, let him laugh it off. You know, big joke. I held my breath and I handed the sneakers to Jerry. He took them from me and turned them over in his hand.

When he looked up, he wasn't smiling. Without saying a word, he turned and walked down the hall. There was a dumbwaiter closet down the hall next to the front entrance. Without looking to see if the dumbwaiter was there or without bothering to pull it up, Jerry flung the sneakers into the shaft. He slammed the dumbwaiter door and then he turned to the door leading out of the apartment.

"Jerry," I said, "I'll buy you another pair. I get paid this week."

"Don't bother," he answered, and he left the apartment.

It was the first time that my cousin and I had ever experienced tension in our relationship.

CHAPTER 38

I STOOD IN THE NARROW AISLE OF THE BOOKSTORE pretending to be searching for a title.

"Excuse me, sir. Would you please open your jacket?"

I looked up. It was an N.Y.U. bookstore clerk.

"What did you say?" I asked.

"I want you to open your jacket," he insisted.

"Open my jacket? What for?"

"I have reason to believe that you're hiding something under your jacket."

I felt my face flushing and my ears growing warm. In a second, my throat seemed to dry up and I could feel my heart thumping. Several people had heard the clerk ask me to open my jacket. They stopped what they were doing to watch the scene play out before them. Their eyes riveted first on the clerk and then back to me.

I tried to gather myself and regain my self-control in front of the clerk and the onlookers. I feigned indignation because I knew that I was safe. I wasn't concealing anything under my jacket. Not that time, that is, but there had been other times recently when I had been hiding books under my jacket and left the store without paying for them.

I had rationalized my thievery by telling myself that I was not really a thief but a kind of self-righteous Robin Hood. All of my stealing was out of necessity. I had tried to convince myself of that, but I knew that what I was doing was wrong.

I told myself that it wasn't as if I was having lunch every day and going for beers with the guys. I'm going to school with a jacket more suited for April than January I thought. Someday, somehow, I'd make it up. Deep down, I knew that all common thieves rationalized their actions in a similar way. Instead, I tried not to give too much thought to what I was doing, but in the process, I lost self-respect.

If the clerk had waited five more minutes, I would have been discovered and expelled. All of my college dreams and aspirations would have ended in disgrace in that bookstore. Present troubles would have ended, where new ones, even worse, would have begun. Timing is everything. That recurring theme seemed more real than ever.

"Do you usually go around asking people to open up their jackets," I asked the clerk, "and why did you pick me?" I had collected myself and I had decided to play out my facade of indignation.

"I picked you because in keeping my eye out for shoplifters, you were behaving exactly the way a person does before he takes what is not his. We see it all the time and we know what to look for as suspicious behavior. Now please open your jacket. If you won't, I'll have to call security."

I unzipped and removed my jacket and placed it on a book cart. Then I lifted my arms and looked at the clerk. "Are you satisfied?"

The crowd began to disperse. A few of them seemed disappointed that the clerk had not made a collar, while others laughed at his expense. The clerk looked chagrined.

"I'm sorry," he said, "but if you knew the loss we take in stolen books you might understand. It's like an epidemic."

"Well, you picked the wrong guy this time," I said self-righteously.

"I'm sorry," he repeated. "Find your book and we'll give you ten percent off for you inconvenience."

"Ten percent off," I said with feigned indignation. "I'd rather pay full price someplace else," I said as I put my jacket back on. "How embarrassing," I mumbled. In truth, I had about fifty cents in my pocket, just enough for subway fare home, so I had to turn down the bargain of the ten percent discount. I left the bookstore, the cold wind turned my warm perspiration into ice after my close call.

CHAPTER 39

THE REALIZATION OF THE INCIDENT IN THE BOOKstore and of my continuing to live the spartan life that I had been living while doing desperate things the way that I had been doing them, caused me to reevaluate my future. I was as discouraged as I had ever been since I started college. I had hoped that I would remain in N.Y.U. with a new major, but now leaving college altogether seemed far more likely of all my options. I just couldn't keep doing this.

I was on my way to Red Hook in Brooklyn with my classmate, Stan. Stan and I had lots in common. Both of us had started college later than most, because we both had been in the army, both of us having served in Germany. Although the time of our tours had crossed, we were in different parts of Germany and we hadn't known one another until we enrolled in N.Y.U. In a short period of time, we had become good friends, but Stan had two distinct advantages over me. The first was that he was a better athlete than I was, which was a good thing to be if you were in physical education. The second was that he was receiving the G.I. Bill. He had entered the army a few months before the bill had expired. For both of those reasons, Stan was content being in physical education.

I had confided many things to Stan and other friends in the physical education department. The only thing that I was too ashamed to tell him, or any of my other friends for that matter, was how I had almost been exposed in the bookstore as a thief. I still shuddered when I thought about how close I had come to being expelled. It was late autumn of 1959.

Stan asked, "Nick, are you still thinking about switching out of physical education?"

"Yes, I am," I said. "The science classes are killing me in physical education. In fact, I'm not certain, but I'm pretty sure that my request for transfer into English for the fall semester will be approved."

"Hey, Nick, that's great. How do you know?"

"I've done well in all of my English courses. The last class that I took was with Dr. Pappas. I got an "A" in his class and the two of us hit it off pretty good. When I told him that I wanted to switch majors, he encouraged me to apply to the English department. He also told me that if I were serious about switching, he would put in a good word for me. He said that he couldn't see why the switch couldn't be made."

I wondered if I should tell Stan about the seriousness of my situation. Lately I had spent more time thinking about the likelihood of having to leave college, while giving less thought to changing majors.

"Hey, I'm gonna miss you, Nick, but if that's what you really want you've got to go for it. We'll still be on the same campus, so you'll get to see us all the time anyway." We sat quietly as the train rocked us back and forth, as it carried us to Red Hook.

"Are you ready for all of the reading and writing that you'll get as an English major? That's a lot of books. You'll be up to your ears in that stuff. Are you ready for that?"

"I don't know what the hell I'm ready for Stan. One thing that I'm pretty certain of, and I might as well tell you, is that barring some sort of a miracle I probably won't be back here in September. That is the reality regardless of what department accepts me."

"What's going on?" Stan asked.

"Well, you know how much time I spend working. I work at the "Y" during the school year. On holidays or on summer vacation, I work in Austinel in New Jersey. I just can't keep up with the money that I need to stay here."

"Are you really thinking about leaving school?" Stan asked.

"I don't know what else to do," I said.

Stan looked at me with an expression that I understood to mean that he wished that he had some answers for me.

"It'll take a miracle for me to stay," I said. I looked out of the train window. "Have you heard about many miracles lately, or are they just in the Bible?"

"Hey, Nick, I don't read the Bible very much, but the fact that the two of us are here is pretty much of a miracle. Don't sell miracles short. They probably do exist. A year ago, we were both marching around Germany, and today we're both enrolled in N.Y.U. That in itself is miraculous. Who would have thought it?"

"I guess you're right," I said. "I don't know about you but it's without a doubt a miracle that I'm here, that's for sure." I sat silently thinking about Dean Harris, and my close call in the bookstore. Maybe those were miracles but you're never satisfied. I prayed silently for another miracle hoping that I had not reached my quota of miracles.

Stan broke the silence. "What will you do if you really can't come back?"

"I'll try to find a job. Maybe I'll take the test for the post office. Or maybe I'll go to Delahanty's and see if they can stretch me so that I can meet the minimum height requirement so I can take the N.Y.P.D. test."

"Nick, come on, man. They'd have to stretch you a foot for you to make the height requirement. We agreed that there are still miracles, but now you're pushing the limit. If Delahanty's could do that for you, you'd have your own chapter in the Bible," and we both laughed out loud.

"How about taking out a loan?" Stan suggested.

"I could try to do that. In fact, I've been thinking about it, but the idea of borrowing four thousand dollars over the next two years scares me to death. I mean starting teachers' salaries are about four thousand dollars a year. What an anchor around your neck that must be, and then you'd have to pay it back with interest. I'd be working for the banks for ten years before I got to keep some of what I earned. No. I don't think so." We sat silently, and then I said, "Maybe there's one other thing that I could try."

"What's that?" Stan asked.

"My cousin, Jerry, graduated from Oswego."

"Where's Oswego?" Stan asked.

"It's all the way up by Canada someplace," I said. "It's a state school and the tuition there is a quarter of what it is in N.Y.U. My cousin suggested that I apply for admittance up there. Even if I had to apply for a loan to stay there, the room and board would be a fraction of the amount of money that I would need to stay in N.Y.U. If I could get accepted into that school and find some sort of a job up there like the ones I have here, I think that I could handle that."

"Isn't that the cousin that you live with?" Stan asked.

"Yes it is."

"He's probably got this all figured out. He kills two birds with one stone," Stan smiled. "You get to save money and to continue with your education, and he gets rid of you by shipping your butt to Oswego, or whatever the name of that place is."

I laughed out loud with Stan. After the situation with the sneakers, which was another thing that I hadn't told Stan about, I thought that he might have hit upon something.

"My cousin gave me the name of the Dean of Admissions at Oswego. Her name is Dorothy Scott. I think that I'll write a letter to see if they'll accept me up there." After a few minutes, I said, "Hey, Stan. Why don't you come with me? We could go up there together. I know that you're getting the Bill, so money is not the problem, but you could bank money with what it would cost you to go there. That includes room and board in the dorms. What do you think?"

"Aw, I don't know," Stan said. "That whole relocation scene...." He didn't finish. He didn't have to. I understood. Why would he change when there really was no urgency for him to do so? He looked at me and probably didn't want me to be let down by the finality of his decision. He said, "I'll tell you what. If you're gonna write a letter to that woman, Dorothy whatever her name is, and if you feel like it, write one for me too. What the heck. Make mine a carbon. She'll probably never know the difference. Most of these applications are dumped anyway in these small schools."

I went home that night and I wrote two letters. I chose the better of the two for myself because I knew that Stan was not really keen about going to Oswego. He had only consented to my writing a letter for him not to disappoint me. I signed my name on "the good one" and then I forged Stan's name, with his permission, on the other.

Two weeks later, Stan called. "Nick, I got a response from Dorothy Scott. She's in favor of my request for admission to Oswego, and she wants me to come up to the college with my transcripts for an interview. I don't believe it. Man that must have been some letter that you wrote. How about you? Have you heard from her? Maybe we can go up there together."

"Hey Stan, we're on our way. What were you saying about miracles? I haven't checked the mailbox. Let me run down and see."

"Okay, call me right back and let me know if you heard," and he hung up.

I took the steps two at a time on the way down. If Stan was accepted with the lesser letter, I had no doubt that I would be going to Oswego for an interview with my college transcript in hand. I opened the mailbox and I immediately saw the envelope with the Oswego return address on it. I tore the envelope open and the words glared at me. The first sentence was all that I needed to know. It read: "I regret to inform you that your request for admission to the State College at Oswego has been denied at this time." The bottom of the letter was signed in neat handwriting by Dorothy Scott. I walked back up the stairs, but this time I took them one at a time.

Even though my rejection for admission to Oswego left no doubt about its finality, Jerry encouraged me to drive up with Stan, who was going up to Oswego for his interview anyway. I agreed to ride up with him. Perhaps the personal appearance would work for me in the same way that it had worked when I was admitted into N.Y.U., and I could change Dorothy Scott's mind. So, along with Stan and a few other college friends, we made the trip.

No matter how I tried to arrange the interview with Dorothy Scott, she would not grant one. Even the Catholic chaplain on campus, who Jerry told me to see, was unable to arrange an interview. Miss Scott remained resolute in her decision to deny my application. A day or two after we arrived in Oswego, we started for home completing a journey of eight or nine hundred miles. The next time that Stan would make the trip to Oswego, he would be going alone.

CHAPTER 40

I WAS HEADING TOWARD THE DOOR AT THE CONCLUSION of my English class.

"Nick, can you hold on a minute?" It was Professor Pappas. "Can you spare about twenty minutes? I'm heading for my office and I'd like to meet you there if you're not busy." He was standing at his desk speaking with several students.

"Sure, Dr. Pappas," I said.

"Make your way over to my office. I'll be there in a few minutes."

I sat in Dr. Pappas' office looking at the pictures on the table behind his desk. He had been married recently, and two or three wedding pictures of the new couple and of their families, were prominently displayed.

"Sorry that I took so long, Nick. It happens after every class. You know, I don't mind staying after class. I just wish that these people would make a salient point about something that we were discussing. He shook his head in frustration. It's usually because they want to squeeze a "C plus" into a "B", or a "B" into an "A". By the way, it's always the same ones who wait for me after each class. They make me crazy, but that's the nature of English." He chatted on in the friendly way that he had of relaxing people, which had made him very popular with his students.

"You know, Nick, as we have discussed, there are various levels of meaning. What is the author saying? What does the author mean? Show it to me in the piece. What is the relevance of his message or his experience in our own lives? Everyone has his own opinion. That's fine, but I have to make it clear to them. When people can't produce a shred of evidence to substantiate their interpretations those opinions are invalid. So we go around in circles until I just have to tell them that their opinions are off the wall. I shouldn't be saying off the wall. A professor of English at N.Y.U. shouldn't be using clichés like that but it seemed to be the only thing that the last guy understood. He surely didn't understand the poem. Well, it ended our discussion pretty effectively, thank God." He settled into his chair.

"I've been looking at your wedding pictures," I said. "You, your wife, and your families all look so happy, and the bride is beautiful."

He turned to look at the pictures behind him.

"Thank you," he said. "What a great night that was. It was a blur. It went by so fast and I was sorry to see it end. And yes, Varcia is beautiful. She's a keeper." He laughed. "When I first I introduced Varcia to my family, do you know what my father asked? He asked me if she thought we were rich. I couldn't imagine why my father would ask a question like that. So I asked him what he meant."

"Look at her?" my father said.

"Oh, I get it. So you're saying that the only thing that a pretty girl like Varcia might find attractive in me is my money? My own father," and he laughed again.

"Yeah, it was a wonderful traditional Greek wedding. We had a lot of fun with Greek food and Greek dancing. Lots of tradition."

"All of that Greek culture and background and you wind up as an English professor in N.Y.U.," I said.

"That's what's wonderful about America, Nick," he said.

"And guess what. I have Greek roots and you have Italian roots and the both of us are privileged to be Americans now, and to teach our adopted language, English." He extended his hand and as I grasped it, he said, "Welcome to the English department, Nick. Your transfer from the physical education department has been approved."

I sat there speechless for a few seconds. It was what I wanted and I knew I should have been happy. I knew Professor Pappas expected me to be happy too. My recent Oswego experience and the whole absurd road that I had travelled for the past five or six years, as well as the misery of the past few weeks, flashed through my mind. I was filled with contradictory emotions. How was it possible to be so happy but so sad at the same time?

I realized that Dr. Pappas saw me shaking my head even though I thought the motion was imperceptible, but he had noticed.

"What's wrong?" he asked. "Isn't this what you wanted?"

"Oh, yes it is, Dr. Pappas. Please don't think that I'm ungrateful or that I'm some kind of a nut. It is what I wanted." I was searching for the right words. I was so afraid of sounding ungrateful or crazy after Dr. Pappas had extended himself on my behalf, so I began. "The expense of college life is a huge factor for me and what I do from here on. The simple fact is that I believe that I can no longer afford to stay in N.Y.U., or any other college for that matter. I probably should have thought about all of that before I put you through all of this trouble. At least I should have spoken with you about it." I shrugged my shoulder. "It's useless. I need a miracle but more than that, I really need a job. I can't stay here any longer," I said.

"Nick, you're here now. Do you think that you'd like to tell me about it?"

I took a deep breath. I really didn't know where to start but I began. He listened to me intently as I told him my whole story, from my misleading everyone about my high school graduation, about my taking refuge in the army, to the reasons why I was accepted only on probation into N.Y.U. I told him about my father losing his business and how that had drastically changed things financially for me and for my family. I spoke of the various jobs that I had worked at, and was still working at. I told him about my recent rejection from Oswego. The one thing that I couldn't bring myself to tell him about was my nearly disastrous confrontation in the bookstore.

When I concluded, I thanked him for the special interest that he had taken in me, and for all he had done on my behalf. "I'm sorry, Dr. Pappas, for having wasted your time. I appreciate all that you've done for me, and the thought of leaving here and of you having a diminished opinion of me is just one more nail in my coffin." I looked up at him. "How's that for a cliché to end on?"

He sat silently for a moment and then he said, "Nick, you're a miracle. What a story. You really should write it down someday. You can't make that stuff up." He cupped his hands to his mouth and his chin, and looked thoughtfully at me. When he removed his hands from his face, he had a faint smile.

"Hey, Nick. Do you want to match clichés with me? Well I've got one for you. 'It ain't over till the fat lady sings.' Oh, my God. If anyone should hear me, I'll be fired. Don't tell them what I said before I get tenure. Excuse me a minute."

He got up, walked out of his office and returned a minute later.

"This was posted in the office a few days ago. Read it." He handed me the paper.

The paper, along with an application, outlined a government program for a federal loan of two thousand dollars a year for students in the school of education. The borrower would have five years after graduation to pay it back. If the borrower remained in the field of education for five years after graduation, half of the amount of the loan would be forgiven. If he did not remain in the field of education for five years after graduation, the full amount of the loan would have to be repaid with interest.

"Do you understand what that program is offering?" Dr. Pappas asked.

Too much was happening too fast. "If I'm granted this loan," I said, "it'll change my whole life forever." I read the terms of the loan over again. "I can't even begin to think of the effect that this will have on me." I sat there and read once again the terms of the loan, and then I looked up.

"No more excuses," Dr. Pappas said as he handed me some papers. You don't have to look for miracles. They fall into your lap when you least expect it. Hold on to your job, fill out these forms, and submit them right away."

"Dr. Pappas, there is so much that I owe you and so many others. How can I ever repay…." I felt my eyes welling up.

"Why are you Italians so emotional? Nick, forget Oswego, and the fat lady ain't singing."

CHAPTER 41

IT WAS AUGUST OF 1960, AND IT WAS TWO YEARS AFter I had been accepted as a probationary student in physical education. It was one month before I would begin my junior year as an English major at New York University.

I had met Camille in August of 1959, almost exactly one year earlier. At first, she was cautious and unsure of how serious I was about our relationship, and with good reason. She was eighteen years old, a recent high school graduate, living at home with her parents. I was twenty-three years old, an ex-G.I., full of stories and experiences from my time in the army. I would have been worried if she had not been cautious and guarded about my intentions while she was getting to know me.

I didn't pay much attention to our age difference. I realized soon after meeting Camille that she was steady and mature beyond her years. Soon after graduating, Camille secured a position working as a secretary in Manhattan. She had progressed quickly from a secretary in a secretarial pool, to a secretary for a single individual. Her employers recognized the efficient manner in which she went about her job, and so she assumed more and more responsibility. With a year of experience on her first job, Camille decided to move on. She took a new position as a legal secretary at the law firm of Sherman, Sterling and Wright in Manhattan.

Camille and I had been dating for about a month when

my sister, who never held back an opinion, and after learning about our age difference, looked at me disapprovingly.

"What are you doing, robbing the cradle, Nick? Don't you think that girl is a little too young for you?"

"I really don't think about our age difference," I said. "That's probably because she seems to be so mature that I don't give it a thought, but maybe you're right. The next time I see her I'll ask her if she realizes how old I am and I'll let you know what she says."

We were walking by the lake. Camille listened intently as I told her about my meeting with Professor Pappas, and of my acceptance into English from physical education.

"Why do you want to switch?" she asked.

"There are many reasons," I said, "but I guess the main reason is that while I'm okay with the physical education part, physical education is heavily loaded with science classes. Science is not my strong suit. I would have preferred switching to social studies rather than English but I wasn't sure if either of them would accept me. I took English because they accepted me first and I didn't want to wait to find out if the social studies department would accept me. That's not a very scientific way to choose a major, but I didn't choose physical education scientifically either."

"How did that happen?" Camille asked.

"More about that later," I said. I wasn't prepared to tell her about the circumstances that got me into N.Y.U. and into the physical education department.

I casually took hold of Camille's hand. "If I were to stay in physical education, I might graduate when I'm thirty trying to pass all of the science classes that I would need to graduate. Can you imagine? Thirty? A little while ago, my sister said that at twenty-three I was already too old for you." Camille looked at me without responding. "I don't think you would be willing to wait for me until I'm thirty. I can't expect you to wait that long. That alone made it crucial for me to change majors." I looked over to see if she was smiling.

She looked at me from the corner of her eye, "What makes you think that I was waiting for you at all?"

"Well even if you'd wait for me, you would still be too young when I was thirty. At least according to my sister," I said.

We walked along silently listening to the katydids rattling in the trees heralding the end of summer. An occasional car moved us closer to the side of the road as it passed us.

"You know what?" I asked. "Things could be a lot different for me in a month."

"What do you mean?" Camille asked.

"Well, I'm getting a little ahead of myself. I'm talking about going into English in September. That would be wonderful. I applied for a federal loan. If I'm not granted the loan or if I don't hear from them real soon, I might be looking for a job."

I had told Camille about my father losing his business. She was aware of the struggle that my parents were facing trying to pay off loans that they had taken to go into a business that no longer existed for them.

"There are loans and mortgages and all of that for them to handle as well as lawyers' fees for a case that is still pending. Add to that my tuition and school fees. I can't put that kind of a burden on my parents. I would never tell them any of this. It would kill them. They wanted this whole college thing for me long before I did, and the part time jobs that I have won't get it done."

"Aren't there less expensive schools?" she asked.

"Do you want to hear something funny?" I answered. "I've been rejected by all of these rinky dink schools that didn't think that I was college material. The latest was Oswego. The only school that seems to have a place for me is New York University, the cream of the crop. Go figure."

"So if you don't get the federal loan you'll have to get a job instead of going to school?"

"That's what I am thinking right now," I said smiling at her. "Hey, if that loan doesn't come through, it might make your choice about hanging on with me an easier one to make."

Camille looked at me. "I never know when you're serious."

"I'm serious about what I'll have to do if that loan doesn't come through."

"Maybe you can go to night school," Camille suggested.

"Let's see," I said. "It'll take me four years to finish up what should be my final two years. That means spending six years as an undergraduate. I'd also have to find a decent day job while I'm going to school at night. I guess that means full time at Austinel. I could go back to reading gas meters. That was what made me make up my mind to go into the army four years ago. I'd be living at home trying to help my parents as much as I could. If everything went right, I'd be twenty-eight when I received my undergraduate degree. I don't think that I would have the intestinal fortitude required to do that. I just wouldn't have the stomach for it. Do you understand what I'm saying?"

I could see that she wanted to change the subject.

"It'll work out," she said. "There's every reason for you to get that loan. You meet all the requirements that you told me about for the loan. There's no risk on the part of the government. You said that if you remain in teaching you have five years after you graduate to pay them half of their money back as it was agreed. If not, you pay it all back with interest. I think that they'll give you the money because there's really no risk for them. Let's wait and see and be positive."

There was an example of the grounded maturity of a nineteen-year old.

In the next breath, she asked, "What do you want to do today?"

"I don't know," I said. "We are at the lake. We could go fishing. Have you ever gone fishing?"

"Yuck, worms. They're disgusting. Then you have to put the worms on hooks." she said. "When I think about fish eating worms, I don't want to eat fish."

"Yeah, you're right. So much for that idea," I said. "I don't know what I was thinking about."

"I can't imagine either," Camille said. We walked along and it was the quiet peace that I had not had very much of lately. Camille broke the silence.

"I have a friend who lives a few trails over from our bungalow. Her name is Sally. We met at the lake a couple of summers ago and I really like her. Her parents have a bungalow. She got married last year to someone she met up here. His name is Ron. Would you like to drive over and see if they're there? Maybe we can do something together."

"Sounds good," I said, "just as long as they don't want to go fishing." She looked at me.

"I thought you said that you wanted to go fishing."

"Yeah, but you know worms. Disgusting," I said as I shook my head with a feigned look of revulsion on my face. Camille gave me a playful poke with her elbow.

We went back to my house and got into my Volkswagen. Camille pointed the way to Sally and Ron's bungalow. When we got there, we were glad to see that Sally and her new husband were home.

The girls gave each other warm greetings and Ron and I were introduced to one another. The four of us chatted away while the girls did lots of catching up. I was comfortable with

Ron, perhaps because he had been in the Air Force and we had that as a starting point.

After a while, one of the girls suggested that we go to play miniature golf. The four of us piled into my Volkswagen. We made our way to the miniature golf course, which was located just down the road from the River Styx Bridge off Lake Hopatcong.

The four of us were good-natured participants in our golf game. We laughed at our lucky shots as well as at our blunders, which made the afternoon more enjoyable. I was glad that Ron and Sally were not overly competitive knuckleheads. I had my fill of that, especially in physical education. I had learned to avoid sore losers, but not before they had spoiled what had started out as being a fun time. That was never a pleasant experience.

After completing the game, the four of us found a small luncheonette. We finished our burgers and we sipped at our drinks when the talk turned to how Ron had met Sally and how I had met Camille. Sally told how she and Ron had first met at the lake and had their first date soon after. Ron remembered their first date a little differently from the way that Sally remembered it.

"My God," Sally said, "it wasn't that long ago. Why don't you remember?"

"Well, I do," Ron said, "but I don't remember acting goofy. You make it sound like I was goofy." And after a pause he added, "But now that I think of it, if I did act that way it was probably because I was giddy about being with you. I realized my good fortune in having found the love of my life." He winked at me, nodded his head up and down, and smiled.

"That's the way to turn a negative into a positive," I said.

"When you're married as long as we are, you'll learn too. There's a knack to it."

"How long did you say you are married?" I asked.

"One year," Ron answered.

"Hey, you're a quick learner," I said.

Sally looked at Camille. "How about you and Nick? Tell us about how you met and about your first date."

Camille and I looked at each other. "Well, it really wasn't the usual kind of first date. You know, the kind of thing you think of as a date, where you go to a movie or you go to dinner," I said.

"It was even better to me," Camille said. "It's such a nice memory."

"Well, it wasn't really a date," I said.

"Careful, Nick," Ron warned. "I already used that giddy thing."

Camille was talking only to me at that moment. Not to Sally or Ron, but just to me. "It was the first time that we were alone with each other after we met. You walked from your house down the road to my house. It was a Saturday night."

"I remember," I said. "We were sitting on the steps that led up to your bungalow door. It was a moonless night and so dark that you couldn't see your hand in front of your face. You guys know that there are no street lights up here. When you look up on a moonless night like that, you see so many stars that the sky is like a planetarium. The Milky Way looks like a cloud."

"That's right. It was a beautiful night," Camille said. "You see. You do remember."

"Every so often people would walk down the road with flashlights. The lights looked like giant fireflies in their hands. I remember, but would you really call that a date?" I asked.

"I liked it better than the usual kind of date when you go to a movie with someone that you're just getting to know,"

Camille said. "When you do that you don't even talk to one another. You just sit there in the dark. That's the usual thing, but we were sitting in the dark, and we were talking to each other. That was better. And then we walked up to your house."

"I remember," I said. "Once we started walking up that dark road I was hoping that you weren't getting the wrong idea. I didn't want to make a bad first impression. I would never have suggested that we walk to my house, but I really thought that my parents were home. I wanted you to get to know them. I had already met your parents, but I just didn't want you to get the wrong idea."

"Do you believe him?" Ron asked, grinning at Camille.

"Ron, quiet, let them finish," Sally said.

"Nothing like that was in my mind," Camille said. "It was a beautiful night and you were a perfect gentleman. I wondered if you would take my hand, but you didn't."

"I wanted to but I thought the better of it, so I didn't. Wouldn't you know it, when we got to my house my parents weren't home?"

"And you didn't know right? Nick, you rascal," Ron said.

"Ron!" Sally said, looking at her husband, disapproving of his interruption.

"I really didn't know where the heck my parents were, and I wanted you to get to know them. I almost turned around to start back to your bungalow."

"But we didn't. You asked me if I wanted to come in," Camille said.

"And you did. Now I'm thinking that I didn't want you to think that I planned this all along so I kept my distance. It really looked suspicious, and now when we went into the house, you sat down. I purposely sat on the other side of the room, even though it was a small room."

I looked over at Ron, who had his hand over his mouth, stifling a grin in order to avoid an elbow in the ribs from Sally.

Camille laughed. "You did sit on the other side of the room, and it was a small room. And then you asked me if I liked Vic Damone. I had heard of Vic Damone, but my friends and I were dancing and listening to Doo Wop. I wasn't about to tell you that," Camille teased. "That was the first example of our age difference. Maybe your sister was right," she laughed.

"Oh, Nick's sister was on to him," Ron said.

"Ron, will you please," Sally begged.

Camille looked at me. "The first song that played was perfect. I even thought that you might ask me to dance, but you stayed on the other side of the room."

I loved that album and all of the songs on it but I had to think back briefly because we had listened and talked while the music played, but in recalling it, the title of the first song had special meaning to me, and had the most memories for us. I didn't want to spoil a moment that was so lovely and vivid in her mind and was in mine too. Before I could answer, Sally asked, "What was the song?"

Camille and I had largely been talking to one another as we relived that night from a year ago, but we were not alone. Sally asked again, "What was the song?"

"It was, *You Stepped Out of a Dream,*" I said.

Shelly didn't seem to recognize the song.

"It's a beautiful song," I said. "I really wanted to ask you to dance to it but I was just getting to know you. I thought that that might be too much too soon. I was afraid that you'd go screaming out the door."

"That would have been a nice part of the memory," Camille said.

"What? You going screaming out the door?" Ron asked.

"No, having their first dance," Sally said, rolling her eyes. "Well, the title speaks volumes. It sounds so romantic," Sally said. "We don't have a particular song do we, Ron? There were so many popular songs when we met. We never really picked just one."

Ron looked at me wide eyed. "With her description of our first date, I'm surprised that she didn't pick *Hound Dog*, or *Up on the Roof*."

Sally gave him a playful jab to the ribs and we all laughed.

"Well, I agree with you, Camille. That sounds like it was a lovely first date, but how did you meet? You know that Ron and I met up here at the lake, but how did the two of you meet?"

"Well, we met up here too. It's a crazy story." Camille looked at me. "Do you want to go through the whole thing again?"

"I don't want to bore the two of you to death with another story," I said.

"No, now I'm curious because you said that it was crazy. Now you have me wondering what could be crazy about it. Tell us. You can give us the abbreviated version," Sally said.

"Okay," I said, and I began to tell about the day, almost exactly a year ago, when I lost my camera and found Camille. "The girl on the wall".

When I was done, Camille and I sat back, smiling at Ron and Sally. We expected the reaction that we usually got from people who had never heard our story before. They usually said things like, "Gee, see that. You lost your camera but you found each other." They would say, "The find was greater than the loss. It was just meant to be."

They would make remarks similar to that. Instead, Ron

and Sally looked at one another, and then they turned to Camille and me and stared at us. Neither of them was smiling.

I looked at each of them, and said to Camille, "I guess the story isn't as funny as we thought it was."

"Nick. You said you lost your camera on Knox Way about a year ago?" Ron asked.

"Yes, that's what happened just about a year ago."

"Nick, you're not gonna believe this but I think that we have your camera."

"You think that you have my camera," I repeated, waiting for a punch line. "Okay?"

"No, Nick. I'm serious. Sally and I were driving down Knox Way and it was just about a year ago. We saw something in the middle of the road. I stopped the car and picked it up. It was a camera in a leather case. From what you're saying it sure sounds like it's the one that you lost."

I looked from Sally to Ron. "How can that be? You're joking. It can't possibly be." I was in disbelief. "It has to be some other camera," I said, not wanting to get my hopes up.

"Well, I still have it. Let's go back to the bungalow and see if that is it. I put it up on the closet shelf on the day that we found it. It's still there."

We got back into the Volkswagen and drove up to the bungalow. Camille, Sally and I sat outside and Ron went into the bungalow. He came out a few minutes later and handed me the camera that he had found.

"Is this it?"

I recognized the camera even before I had it in my hands. I turned it over and looked at the case. "Oh my God, this is it. These things just don't happen. This is unreal." I shook my head.

"What are the odds that something like this could ever happen?" I looked at Camille. "I always thought that if I hadn't lost my camera, Camille and I would probably have never met, so it was worth the loss of the camera. Now, by some miracle, and on the exact day that I lost the camera, I get it back. I have Camille too. Is there a plan?"

"It was just meant to be," Sally said.

There it was. Sally had said what people usually said after hearing our story. This time the strange events of August 2, 1959 had come to an unbelievable conclusion on August 2, 1960. It was the craziest of Hollywood-type endings.

"Camille, Sally, and I set the whole thing up, Nick," Ron said.

"That almost makes more sense than what actually happened." Then, turning the camera over in my hand, I said, "It's amazing that the camera survived the fall from the car. It could have been run over, rolled off into the woods, or picked up by a stranger. Instead it's picked up by people who know us, and they returned it to me a year later to the day. What are the odds of that happening? What I am trying to say is if that was a plot in a movie or a book, it would just be bad writing."

I paused and I looked at Ron and Sally. "Do you know what? Life is full of miracles, and now I get to keep Camille and the camera. What more can I ask for?" Camille squeezed my hand.

I was still in disbelief as Camille and I drove back to my parents' home. Camille held my camera in her lap.

"We'll never let this camera go," I said. "That camera is God's plan for us."

"You didn't sound so sure of things when the day started," Camille said.

"You're right. It's amazing how quickly things can change. But there is one thing. I wish that Ron hadn't opened the back of the camera. I had all of the shots that I took of Annalisa, Al, and my family. That was the day that they came up to the lake and they asked me to be their baby's godfather. I would like to have had the pictures, but now the film is exposed."

"Oh, my God," Camille said. "You have your camera back after a year, when you never thought that you would see it again, and you're complaining that the film inside of it is exposed. You can't have everything."

"I don't want everything. I just want all of what I do want. Do you understand what I mean? This might sound selfish, but I want it all."

"What is it that you want exactly? I am not sure that even you know."

"Maybe you are right," I said. "I'll figure that out as I go along." I looked over at her. "I'm still working on it, but what I want starts with you."

We went into the house. Neither of my parents was home. On the kitchen counter, where my mother had left them for me to see, was some mail. I tore open the envelope with the New York University return address and I read the letter inside twice. I rested my forehead on my arms on the kitchen table and held the letter up to Camille.

"What is it?" she asked. She took the letter from my hand and began to read. "Nicky, Nicky, you got the loan!"

CHAPTER 42

WILLIAM SHAKESPEARE, THOMAS WOLFE, LEO Tolstoy, Charles Dickens, Herman Melville, Fyodor Dostoevski, and other masters of world literature were now the focus of my attention in September of 1960. One novel, play or poem came quickly on the heels of the other. The only pause was the mandatory analysis paper required upon the completion of each work.

Fortunately, I had completed my science requirements because of the many and varied science courses that I had taken while I was in the physical education department. I was able to focus all of my attention on my English requirements and, to a lesser extent, on history classes. However, history classes like English classes, required lengthy written papers. It seemed as though the education that I had not considered possible for myself at anytime, was now consuming most of my time. Camille was at my side all of the time.

On many occasions, and usually on weekends, I would write a paper that was due at the beginning of the following week. I would write a page, tear it out of my spiral notebook, and then I would hand it to Camille. She would proofread it and type it as I continued to write the next page. I was the envy of many of my friends who had to pay others to type their papers, and that did not include proofreading. They had to do for themselves.

Sometimes Camille and I would drive up to my parents'

home in Lake Hopatcong, and Camille would sit nearby patiently while I tried to make sense out of a particular work that I was assigned.

Although I stayed in close contact with my physical education friends, except for Stan, I had made new friends in the English department. Stan was now in Oswego, a place that he knew nothing about a few months before. It was just another of life's ironies. I had wanted to go to Oswego, and Stan was perfectly content in staying at New York University. The new term found Stan in Oswego, and it was I who was still in N.Y.U. Go figure.

One of the new friends that I had met in the English department worked in Memorial Sloan-Kettering Hospital in Manhattan. Al Brodie worked in the medical records and statistics department at Memorial, and he was able to get me, as well as a couple of other English department friends, jobs in the hospital. Although the federal loan that I had been given had relieved me of the tremendous burden of tuition and books, there were other living expenses for which I needed to have money. The job at Memorial paid more than the job that I had at the West Side Y.M.C.A., so I gladly changed jobs. The job at the hospital had the same flexibility in hours that I had at the "Y".

People from all over the nation and the world sought medical assistance at Memorial Sloan-Kettering. I filed and made available the records of the hundreds of patients who were seen each day.

While at Memorial, I saw examples of human suffering and misery that I never knew existed to the degree that it did. Seeing people ravaged by cancer on a daily basis was a very difficult thing to do. The compassion and the despair that I felt for the patients and the families who had been victimized by the disease were overwhelming. A walk through the hospital complex made me feel ashamed about situations that had appeared to be major obstacles in my life. Now each of my perceived obstacles appeared to be trivial in light of the misery that I was seeing on a daily basis. I have heard it said that people can become inured to misery if they deal with it on a daily basis. I never did acclimate to what I saw each day. Whenever I could, I avoided particular wards or floors and left the victims to their doctors, their families, and to God.

In the background, Frank Sinatra sang his upbeat version of *Witchcraft* as Pete and I ate our cheeseburgers and fries and sipped on our sodas. We sat in a recently opened burger place on Coney Island Avenue. It was just a few blocks away from where I was living with Aunt Claire, Uncle Stan, and Jerry. Pete and I had not gone to the same school. When we were twelve years old and in the seventh grade, we played baseball together. We were in the same parish and on the same team at Saint Bernadette. The church was the focal point of our lives. Pete and I were not very much alike. We even got into a fistfight once, but we learned to accept each other's differences, and we became good friends.

I'm not sure if all of my friends were typical of teenagers of that time. As I think about it all these years later, I can't explain why with just a few exceptions, the majority of my friends, and myself included, had made such a mess of our high school years. Our only recourse seemed to be for each of us to leave school and join the military. Pete was no exception. In 1953, as a seventeen-year old, he had left Brooklyn Tech and enlisted for a four-year stint in the Air Force. In 1960, he had gotten married, and he asked me to be his best man.

We made small talk before I asked Pete, "How are things for the newlyweds?" Pete was always brutally honest and never tactful. It was a trait that often caused him to be at odds with members of the group with which we had grown up. I had long since learned to deal with his frankness and that's why we were still friends.

"It's a big adjustment," he said. "First you have to learn to accept different ways of doing things in your life. That's like changing your whole way of thinking." He looked at me. "So you accept something new that your wife imposes on your life, or you reject it. It depends on how strongly you feel about whatever it is or if it's worth arguing about." Pete sat silently as if he was still trying to figure it all out, and he probably was.

"Yeah, it's a big adjustment," he said considering it. "More than that, for the first time in my life, it's all on me."

"What's all on you?" I asked.

"What I mean is growing up, you don't think about where your next meal is coming from. You just go home and the food is on the table. You use the phone, or you turn on the lights. You don't worry about electric bills, phone bills or paying the rent. Your parents worried about that. When I was in the Air Force, it was the same thing. The Air Force feeds you, gives you clothing to wear, takes care of you and then they point you in the direction that they want you to go." He stopped and pondered it all. "Well let me tell you, it's not that way anymore. Now here come the bills. I go around turning lights off in the apartment. Nick, I'm on a budget. Are you kidding me?" he asked rhetorically. He jabbed a French fry into a small cup of ketchup and took a bite.

"It's the next part of the process," I said. Pete looked up at me. He wasn't sure what I meant. "You know? The process," I said.

"Process? What process?"

"What I mean by the process is that you grow up. You get married. You have a family. The process continues, and life goes on. There are a lot of good things ahead. You and I are just getting started."

"Where are you getting this philosophy crap from? College?"

"Not really," I laughed. "I always thought that that's the way that life was. I knew that someday I would have to do all the things that you are doing now. Our parents did. I just avoided thinking about it too much because I didn't have any idea how I would ever be able to assume that kind of adult responsibility. What I did was not to think about it and hoped that things would work out. I had no idea how that was gonna happen. Thank God, I am not wondering about that anymore. Now I'm able to control my own destiny and not sit around hoping and waiting for things to just work out by themselves. That just doesn't happen. I'm kind of looking forward to being able to pay my own bills in my own house."

"So that's the process, huh? Well, in the process, it's really helpful if you're lucky enough to meet a girl from a wealthy family. That makes the process a lot easier."

"Were you that lucky?" I asked.

"Well, I didn't hit the lottery but I did okay. Thank God, Carol is an only child. No siblings, no sharing," he said laughing.

"Man, you are mercenary," I said.

"Go ahead. Call me names. You'll see soon enough how quick the rent rolls around." He finished the last of his fries. "How about you? How are you doing?"

"I'm good. I'm working hard but the finish line is about a year and a half away. Then maybe I can find a job, get a decent car, and my own place to live in. I love Camille and neither of our families have very much money, so whatever we do, we'll have to do it together. If we want a nice wedding or a house somewhere down the road, we will pretty much have to do it ourselves. Camille is smart, and we want to be together. Do you know what, you'll probably think that I'm crazy, but it's great to be young, and we'll build it together. I'm looking forward to paying those bills that you told me about. That'll mean that I'll have just one job for a change, and hopefully a decent income. Pete, I'm looking forward to it. Right now, I'm living in Aunt Claire's apartment and it's cramped. It's fine for my uncle, my cousin, and my aunt. One more adult pushes the limit and I've been living with them for almost two and a half years."

"What do you mean by pushing the limit? Are you getting on each other's nerves? I know that when you live close with people you can get on each other's nerves."

"Well, not really. You know how close I have always been with Jerry, my aunt and my uncle. Jerry is more like a brother than a cousin. Aunt Claire is about as close to me as my own mother, but there can be some tension in any family. In half the families that I know, somebody is not talking to somebody else. That's just the way it is."

"Something happened, didn't it?" he asked with a knowing smile on his face.

I told Pete briefly about the episode where I had destroyed Jerry's sneakers. It seemed to me that from that point on something had changed in our relationship. There wasn't that relaxed relationship when we had always enjoyed each other's company.

"I miss all of that. I don't know, maybe I'm reading too much into this. I'm beginning to wonder if Jerry is having second thoughts about the wisdom of asking me to live with his family for such an extended period of time."

"It could be," Pete said, "and I can understand it."

"So with that in mind, I try to make myself scarce by going home to New Jersey every weekend, and to spend more time at Camille's house."

"Where do you sleep in your aunt's house?" Pete asked.

"I sleep on a little fold-out bed in Jerry's room. Do you want to hear something funny?" I asked Pete. "We were reading Benjamin Franklin's *Poor Richard's Almanac*. You know what that is. Franklin published words of wisdom in his newspaper that usually hit the nail right on the head. So I came across one that seemed particularly appropriate. I was feeling a little uncomfortable about living in my aunt's house after the sneaker incident. I was sitting at the kitchen table and Jerry was opposite me. I was interested in what Jerry's reaction would be. I said to Jerry, this is funny. Listen to this. Franklin says, 'Fish and house guests stink after three days'."

"Oh, that was a good test. What did he say? I hope he laughed."

"No, he didn't laugh. He said Franklin was brilliant."

"Oh, that's it. You're outta there. That's what happens. Look at me. I haven't been around much in the past five years. It didn't take long after I got back home that my brother and I were on each other's nerves. There's a big age gap between us and we were never really that close. Toward the end of it, we were hardly talking to each other. I don't know why we were on one another's nerves, but we were. At least you know about the sneakers but my brother doesn't even own a pair of sneakers."

"It probably didn't help your relationship when you picked me to be your best man," I said.

"I don't know if it bothered him or not. He might even have said no if I had asked him. Besides, I get along better with you."

"Yeah, but we don't live in the same house."

"Thank God," he said, as he bit into his burger. "I might be looking at a different best man. I gotta get home," he said abruptly. "That's the way it is when you're married." We finished our burgers and we left.

CHAPTER 43

IT HAPPENED IN MARCH OF 1961, AND NOW ALthough many years have gone by, time has not been the great healer. It has always been someplace in my mind over all of the intervening years. I still have difficulty understanding and coming to grips with what happened that night. The events of that evening changed my life from that day to the present. It started out as an ordinary night, no different from a thousand others.

Aunt Claire, Uncle Stan, Jerry, and I sat in the small family room. It was the end of the day and the chance for all of us to relax before rising for work the next day. My aunt, uncle, and cousin were watching the television, while I sat on the sofa reading. I pushed as close as I could toward the end table attempting to get as close as possible to the lamp that was on the table. It was difficult trying to block out the noise from the television and from the conversation in the room, while trying to concentrate on the book that I was reading. In that small apartment, it wasn't possible to find a quiet place to study. I knew that soon everyone would be going to sleep. Then I would be able to focus all of my attention on what I was reading.

My uncle was in his favorite chair directly opposite the television. My aunt sat on the other end of the sofa from where I was. Jerry was stretched out on the sofa with his legs across his mother's lap. His head was propped up on my thigh as he watched the television. Those were the only chairs in the living room.

The program ended and Uncle Stan folded his glasses in disgust. "Do you mean to tell me that I've been watching that show for an hour and that's the way that it ends? Boy, I'm never gonna learn," he said. "It's always the same. These writers get you all involved for fifty-five minutes. Then they don't know how to get out of the hole that they've dug for themselves. Rather than to work out a reasonable conclusion, they just end it. Just like that and we're all left sitting here staring at one another wondering if we missed something. It's as if you were reading a good book and then you discover that the last chapter is missing." He looked at me for affirmation.

"I really wasn't watching, Uncle Stan."

"Well, that's good. You're smarter than I am. I was watching. I'm going to bed."

"I'm right behind you," my aunt said. "Goodnight boys, and don't stay up too late, Nicky."

"I just have a couple of chapters to read," I said.

"I'm just gonna see what's coming on next, and then I'm going to sleep too," Jerry said.

Jerry turned the volume down so as not to disturb his parents who were trying to sleep in their bedroom. The bedroom was separated from the family room by a light door that my aunt had installed to partition the family room off from her bedroom.

At first, I dismissed it as if there were nothing to it. It was just an attempt to find a more comfortable position. It was probably just movement to prevent the sensation of pins and needles that we have all experienced when we cut off the circulation to an arm or a leg. It continued. I didn't want to make more of it than it actually was. It was only in my mind, I thought. It had happened on one or more occasions when riding to or from New York University, packed into a crowded subway car during the rush hour. I wasn't sure if the person crushed against me, always a man, never a woman, was doing his best to avoid body contact. I have heard women complaining that lechers often took advantage of crowded situations in trains or in elevators to get closer to them than necessary. I had witnessed a woman throwing an elbow into a man standing closely behind her, as she warned him to back off, while he protested his innocence. I always wondered how much of it was really a perversion, and how much of it was unavoidable contact. That was exactly what I was thinking at that moment as I sat looking down at my cousin.

I wasn't sure, so I continued looking down at Jerry, who seemed to be staring intently at the television. Now there was no mistaking that the fingers on Jerry's right hand were rubbing the inside of my thigh and working their way up my leg, as he rested his head on his arm. Even at that, there was still major disbelief on my part. Maybe it was that unavoidable contact that I had experienced on other occasions. Maybe Jerry was joking, in either case I didn't move when perhaps I should have. If I said anything and I had misunderstood, I would insult my cousin. I waited and wondered about what was really happening.

I have thought about it repeatedly over the years. I believe that Jerry must have taken the fact that I didn't remove myself instantly from that situation as a sign of acceptance on my part. It was he who stood up.

"Let's go inside," he said in a hoarse voice.

"Go inside?" I repeated dumbly.

"Yes, let's go inside. Come on."

"No," I said. "I can't right now, I have some more reading to do." I was acting as if nothing had happened. I wanted so desperately to be wrong. I wanted Jerry to tell me that it was all a joke. I would have believed him if he had said something like, "I bet I had you going there for a while, stupid." Even if I could never really understand such a joke, I would have played along with the charade for the sake of cousins, for the sake of family, and for the preservation of a relationship, which would never ever be the same.

But it wasn't to be. Jerry stood in front of me for a moment and I looked at him hoping to see a smile on his face at the joke. Maybe he'd call me an idiot at having been taken in by it all. It wasn't to be. Instead, he dropped his chin to his chest and I diverted my eyes to the pages of my book as he turned and walked to his bedroom.

I sat for about an hour staring straight ahead and never gazing at the book on my lap. I was too embarrassed to go into Jerry's room. My mind was a blank. It was stuck in nowhere. How could this be happening? I avoided thinking about whatever would come next.

I could hear my uncle snoring on the other side of the partitioned doorway. I picked myself up and I walked to the bedroom that I had shared all this time with Jerry. In the darkness, I opened the small convertible bed that I slept on. I did not bother to take my clothes off. I lay quietly, trying to hear if Jerry was sleeping. I suspected that he was awake. I lay there wanting to say something to him. I was struggling to find the right words. I repeated the same words over and over again in my mind. Oh, my God, oh, my God, oh, my God.

CHAPTER 44

I ALTERNATED FROM RESTLESS SLEEP TO WIDE-EYED reality all night long. I went over again all that had transpired. It was an event that had taken a few brief minutes in the totality of my life. No matter how brief it had been, I knew that it would change my relationship with my cousin forever. It took years to establish that relationship and just a few minutes to destroy it.

I was trying to anticipate every possible scenario that I could think of for the next time that I came face to face with Jerry. Each of us could pretend that the episode hadn't happened. We could just not talk about it and to leave it at that. Jerry might offer some sort of explanation, which I would be quick to accept. In my heart, I knew that the next time that we met the meeting would be torturous.

As I have said, my mother had four brothers and four sisters. They, in turn, had sixteen children. My sister, my brother, and I made a total of nineteen cousins. We were a typical Italian family that looked forward to celebrating holidays together such as Christmas, New Year's, and Easter, as well as other important events. There were always birthdays and anniversaries to look forward to.

As I thought back to my childhood, I couldn't recall a harsh word uttered by any of my aunts or uncles, to any of their nieces or nephews and never to one another. There was always a sharing and a caring among the families. It might have been food or hand-me-down clothing that was being shared. That was especially so during the difficult years of the Great Depression, and later during the even more difficult years of World War II. At that time, many of my uncles and cousins went off to war. The foundation and the emphasis on family were established by my grandparents. They arrived in a strange land and struggled to learn a strange language and to adapt to new customs in 1900. Family ties had grown stronger in the next fifty-two years.

That's the way it was, but it all crumbled and fell apart in 1952, never to be regained. It could be traced to an incident that happened soon after one of my cousins was married. Strange how unaware we are about how really fragile relationships are which appear to be as strong as granite. It's reminiscent of how a hurricane or a tornado can take away all that you have built and achieved over a lifetime, in just a few minutes. The hurricane that destroyed the foundation of our family and took away the gold that we had all cherished came in the form of an interloper.

We were all gathered in my mother's sister's apartment. Unlike the festive gatherings that we had always looked forward to, this one was somber. My mother's sister, Alice, placed the cups and saucers into the cabinet above her head. Her husband, Mike, dried and handed them to her. My father paced back and forth from one room to the other while my mother shifted her eyes from one of her siblings to the next. No one seemed to be willing to maintain eye contact for long.

My cousin, Vera, sat close to Willi, her husband of one year. Aunt Adele was Vera's mother and Willi's mother-in-law. Adele along with her husband, Bill, was seated and looking in Willi's direction. The tension in the apartment was palpable. Willi seemed not to notice it at all, as he smiled in his usual jovial manner and attempted to joke and to make conversation. He seemed oblivious to the tension that was thick all around him.

It was Willi's father-in-law, Uncle Bill, who was usually the quietest and most reserved of all my uncles, who broke the ice.

"Okay. Let's stop all the shuffling and all the stalling." He stood up and positioned himself directly in front of Willi. "Willi, do you know why we're here?"

Willi looked up, the smile on his face disappeared as he saw the uncharacteristic gravity in his father-in-law's demeanor. Except for a slight shaking of his head, he made no attempt to respond. His eyes were wide open and he looked quickly from one of us to the other. I looked at him and I couldn't help being reminded of a cornered animal that upon sensing imminent danger looked quickly from left to right as it sought for a way to escape. Willi realized that something bad and unavoidable was about to happen. There was no way out for him. His eyes narrowed and focused straight ahead on the wall in front of him. His complexion turned gray. Willi was completely devoid of any expression or emotion. His mind had gone somewhere else, even if his body could not.

"Let's get right to the point," Uncle Bill, continued. "Matthew has told us that you took advantage of him by molesting him." He paused and waited for a possible explanation. When there was none, he continued.

"Matthew said that you molested him in your apartment. He told his mother that he got that cut on his forehead when he fell and hit his head while he was trying to get away from you." My uncle stopped and once again looked at his son-in-law hoping for an explanation. There was none. Willi seemed to not even blink as he stared straight ahead. After a pause, my uncle continued, "Matthew also said that you touched him inappropriately in your car. Is that true?"

Matthew was my seven-year old brother and he was not present.

"Well, speak up and say something," Uncle Bill demanded. Willi did not respond. He continued to focus his eyes into some oblivion. His wife, Vera, appealed to him in her desperation.

"Oh please, Willi. Say something. Tell them that this is all a misunderstanding and that none of this is true. Tell them that you have an explanation. Please, Willi," his wife sobbed. She tried to pull him in her direction to get him to look at her. Willi appeared to be unmovable and he continued to look away. He made no attempt to answer her. Willi had apparently blocked out everything and everyone around him.

Aunt Adele, Vera's mother, dabbed a tissue to her eyes. She placed herself between her daughter and her son-in-law. Ignoring Willi, she pulled her sobbing daughter up from the couch and away from him.

"Oh, Mom, oh, Mom, it's not true," was all my cousin could say. Her mother tried to absorb some of the pain that her daughter was feeling.

The rest of us had remained silent the whole time. Everyone realized that by not attempting to defend himself, Willi was admitting that he was guilty of the things that Matthew had accused him of doing. Uncle Bill looked down at Willi.

"Now Willi, if there's any honor in you at all, and if you were a man, you would go get a gun and blow your brains out and spare us all."

Uncle Bill's words rang out, but an awkward silence followed. After a polite delay, each of us quietly said our goodbyes. We left the apartment, but more than that, we left our innocence behind.

The case was brought to the police. We soon learned that other boys had come forward accusing Willi of molesting them. Willi had formed a boys' club and he had taken advantage of the boys while they were on outings.

Aunt Adele begged my parents not be the ones to press charges against Willi, but to allow others who were not relatives to do so.

Aunt Adele and Uncle Bill wanted the law to take its course and for the families and the boys involved to receive justice. If Willi was to be found guilty so be it, but they thought our family would be spared further pain and humiliation if my mother allowed others to seek justice. But the police had already taken a deposition from my brother, because he was the youngest of the boys who complained about Willi. My brother had received a cut on his face while resisting Willi. The detectives convinced my parents that because of my brother's age, and because of the fact that he had been cut, that my brother gave them the best chance for a conviction. So despite my aunt's pleas, my parents proceeded.

Willi did not take his father-in-law's advice to blow his brains out. He reasoned that spending five years in prison was by far the better option. So off to prison Willi went. His wife, Vera, inexplicably counted the days off and waited for her husband to return. There was an irreparable alienation between my mother and her sister, Adele. It was the first incident that marked the beginning of the end for what my family had been, and for what we had all meant to one another. It was all tragic for us but should have been expected. All good things come to an end. Robert Frost, the American poet, reaffirmed it in his poem *Nothing Gold Can Stay.*

It was nine years since the event when a stranger had

taken the soul out of our family. I lay in bed unsure of what to do next. The only thing that I was absolutely certain of was that I would never tell anyone about that brief moment of the night before. I would die before I would breathe a word to Aunt Claire. If she were to find out, it would kill her. I could never allow that to happen especially after all that she had done for me from my earliest memories. Even now, she was treating me like a son. Nothing would ever make me change my mind.

I did not believe that my family could survive another knockout blow coming so soon on the heels of the blow inflicted by Willi and the loss of my father's business. It would be worse this time because it involved two of their nephews.

In the morning, I heard the door lock as Jerry left the apartment. I could only imagine the torment that was going on in his mind. My uncle and my aunt followed Jerry shortly, as they left for the humdrum routine of their daily lives.

I couldn't clear my mind. I could think of nothing beyond what had happened the night before. Not school, not books or assignments as I readied myself to leave the apartment. How much of it was my fault? I had not reacted immediately by not leaving the couch while there was still some doubt. What was the state of Jerry's mind? What would our next meeting be like? That meeting was inevitable and the prospect of it happening soon was something that I wished that I could avoid. How strange it all seemed especially since we were such close cousins and we had always looked forward to each other's company.

I needed to release all that I was feeling. I needed to speak to someone, but I was unwilling to tell anyone what had happened. I thought of Camille, but I didn't want to burden her with my situation. Jerry and Camille did not have the kind of relationship that I would have liked for them. I didn't want Camille to have an even more diminished opinion of Jerry than she already had. There were personal differences between them. Because of that, I decided to keep the truth from Camille. I would say that nothing happened beyond a heated argument between Jerry and me. Camille had become my closest confidant but I would never have been able to tell her the truth. I was lost. I was devastated.

I had become friendly with a graduate student at N.Y.U. His name was Tom, and he was a psychology major. I never saw him on campus, but always in the student center where we became friendly. We often passed time in conversation between classes. Tom had a self-deprecating manner and a sense of humor, so I enjoyed his company during brief breaks. In my desperation to speak with someone who didn't know me or my family, I thought of Tom. I would not feel embarrassed or that I was tattling on Jerry, as I would have felt telling what had happened to someone who knew the both of us. I was desperate to speak with Tom, the psychology major. I needed to spill my soul to someone. I needed advice. I prepared to leave the train at the West 4th Street station. As fate would have it, as I was getting off the train, Tom was getting on.

"Tom, I need to talk to you," I said as I stepped off the train and he stepped on.

"Hi, Nick. Okay. I'm running uptown but I'll see you tomorrow." He looked at my face and asked me, "Are you alright?" The door closed between us before I could answer. I never saw him again even though I went back to the student center to look for him. It was as if he had been a figment of my imagination. I was on my own.

I purposely worked as long as I could at the hospital that night. Before that night, it had always been about the money.

Now it was about prolonging the inevitable first meeting between Jerry and me.

It was after ten when I entered the apartment. My aunt and my uncle were already asleep and Jerry was in bed. I showered and went into the bedroom that we shared. I opened the folding bed in the darkness and I lay down. In the silence of the room, I listened for the familiar breathing of Jerry as he dozed off. I knew that he was awake. Suddenly in a clear, steady voice Jerry said, "Nicky, I want you to leave."

I jumped at the sudden finality in his voice and in the starkness of his statement. There was no attempt to soften the inevitable dissolution of our relationship. Not even an attempt to explain in some way the events of the night before. I wasn't really surprised about what Jerry was saying to me. It was one of the possibilities that I had given thought to as I wracked my brain about every possible scenario all day long. Jerry had asked me to leave. I understood that. I expected it. What I didn't expect was the coldness in his voice. That was totally shocking to me. It wasn't just what he had said to me. It was his tone. It was so unlike anything that had ever been before.

I lay there thinking about a response. I even felt a sense of relief in some strange way. I had wondered how we would face one another in the future. How would we begin our conversation the next time we met? Now the ice was broken. In those few words, I instantly understood many things. With those six words, I knew that my relationship with my closest cousin was over. Jerry would not just let go and move on as I was willing to do and that I even hoped to do. Until then I hadn't known what my next step would be. Now I saw some direction. It was direction that I had sought all night and all day. That direction led to an exit and the loss my cousin.

Jerry remained quiet after that but I knew that I had to respond.

"What reason will I give for leaving?" I asked. I was no longer worried about Jerry and me. There was nothing that I could do about that. That had already been decided. At that moment, my concern was giving Aunt Claire a reasonable explanation without hurting her feelings or revealing the truth. How do you explain an abrupt departure? It was one that none of us had seen coming.

Very soon, my parents would need an explanation too. Whatever the explanation turned out to be, no one must ever know the truth, at least not from me. I believed that Jerry felt that way also. I was already trying to prepare myself to resist in a gentle way, my aunt's attempts to get me to change my mind about leaving. I had no doubt she would try to do that. All of these things flashed through my mind.

Jerry broke the silence. "I don't know what reason you should give," Jerry answered, "but you know why I want you to leave." After a pause he said, "Say whatever you want to say. Say whatever you think is necessary but I want you to go as soon as you can."

He hadn't asked me to lie about what had happened, but I believed that he knew that I would never tell the truth. We were both quiet for a while and then I said, "Jerry, I want you to know that regardless of what happened last night, I will always be thankful and indebted to you for all that you have been to me. I will never forget about what you and your mother have done for me, including encouraging me to go to college. I won't forget the cousins that we were growing up. What happened last night can never change the past. All of my life, you have been so much more than a cousin to me. You've been a brother. You have been a role model and an advisor who never gave up on me even when I had given up on myself." Jerry didn't respond.

"I hoped that you could look past what happened. I know that I can." Still there was still no response. I took his silence as a farewell such as you would give to someone who had died. That person was no longer a part of your future but only a part of your past.

CHAPTER 45

THE NEXT MORNING, AFTER I WAS SURE THAT JERRY and my uncle had left the apartment, I got up to speak to Aunt Claire before she could leave. I didn't think that this was the best time to tell her that I was leaving because I didn't want her to be troubled with it all day at work. Really, there wouldn't be a good time to tell her that I was leaving. I wanted to be out of the apartment before everyone came home from work, so this would be my only chance.

She was surprised to see me up.

"Oh, Nicky, why are you up so early? I was just about to leave."

How to begin I thought? "Aunt Claire, I have to talk to you."

She looked at me and she knew something wasn't right because this wasn't the routine. "What's the matter? Don't you feel well?"

"Aunt Claire, I'm gonna leave the apartment." All night long, I had thought about how I would start the conversation to make it easier for both of us. Now I had forgotten everything that I had planned to say through the sleepless night, and I just blurted out what I intended to do.

She looked at me as if I had lost my senses. "You're what?"

"I'm leaving."

"Nicky, I don't know what this is about all of a sudden or what's going on your head, but whatever it is, it's stupid.

It's too early in the morning for this craziness. Please, I'm late for work. Can it wait until we get home tonight? Uncle Stan, Jerry, and I will sit down with you and we'll talk about whatever is bothering you."

When I didn't respond, she said, "Nicky, why do you want to change things now? Hasn't everything been going well? You're so close to graduation. What is it? Is it so bad here?"

I really didn't know where I was going with this conservation or how to respond to her questions. When she asked me if it was so bad there, I knew that I couldn't allow her to think that it was. I didn't want her to think that I was ungrateful for her opening up her home to me. I appreciated all the generosity and love that she, Jerry, and Uncle Stan had shown to me all my life and especially over the last two and a half years. I knew that the blame for me leaving had to go to Jerry and me, and not because she had failed me in anyway.

"Oh, no, Aunt Claire, I have felt as comfortable here as I would feel if I were at my own home. It's not that. It was fine in the beginning but after two and a half years, Jerry and I have been getting on each other's nerves. It's not about a single thing. Lately it's over lots of things. That happens, I know that, but yesterday we had a bad argument. It got really heated and I said that I was leaving. Jerry thought that might be the best thing to do for the both of us. It was I who suggested it."

"Arguing over what? When did the two of you ever argue? What could possibly be so bad that it would cause you to leave, and for Jerry to allow you to go? You're cousins. You're almost brothers."

"We argued over so many little things," I lied. "We were at the point where we hardly spoke to one another unless you and Uncle Stan were around. It all came to a breaking point. We had a big argument yesterday over I don't even know what, but we said things to each other that will be hard for either of us to forget."

"What kind of crazy talk is this?" she said. "I never noticed this dissension. I never noticed." Her eyes welled up with tears. "Nicky, I'm brokenhearted. Maybe it's not too late. So you were both angry. By tonight, you'll both be cooled off and you'll both see how silly the whole argument was. We can all sit down and work it out. A few harsh words can't eliminate what the both of you are to each other. Wait until Jerry and Uncle Stan get home." She shook her head and tears rolled down her cheeks.

"No, it's too late for that Aunt Claire. We said too many things to one another to be able to smooth it over in five minutes. It's not that easy. We need time away from each other."

She was already late for work, but she was not emotionally ready to leave, and she walked into her room.

When she left the room, I went to the bedroom that I slept in, stripped the sheets from the bed and folded it. I didn't have many possessions there. Just some underwear and socks, a couple of casual shirts, an extra pair of pants, and bathroom items. I packed everything that I could into what we called in the army, an A.W.O.L. bag. Then I threw the rest of what I had, along with some books, into the back of my Volkswagen and I returned to the apartment.

I knocked on the door to my aunt's bedroom. "Aunt Claire, I'm ready to go."

"Come in, Nicky."

She was sitting on her bed. Her eyes were all puffy and red. "Nicky, I've been thinking. Do you think that Jerry is jealous of your relationship with me? Maybe he thinks that you've replaced him and that I love you more than I love him. Maybe he thinks that I show you more attention than I show him. It's not true. Nicky, I love you dearly but he's my son.

It's not the same thing. Maybe I need to explain that to him. Maybe that's it. I just don't know."

In her desperation to understand what might have contributed to this sudden conflict between Jerry and me that she had not seen coming, she was searching everywhere. She was even wondering if some of the responsibility was hers.

"I don't think that you or Uncle Stan had anything to do with it, in fact, I know that you didn't. Your names never came up. It was us. In the end, we just didn't get along. I'll speak to Uncle Stan. Until I do, tell him that I will never forget the generosity that the three of you have shown to me despite the differences between Jerry and me lately."

That only succeeded in bringing more tears to her eyes. "Where will you go? At least come back for dinner tonight. What will I tell your mother?"

"I have a room," I lied, "and I will tell my mother exactly what I told you. She'll understand that we were both to blame."

I hugged her and kissed her goodbye, and when I closed the bedroom door, I could hear her sobbing through the thin walls.

I drove my Volkswagen to the city, hoping to find a parking spot not too far from the school. My car would have to be my place of residence until I figured something out, and it had better be soon. It was mid-March and still cold at night, and it was only Wednesday. I was a couple of days away from Lake Hopatcong.

CHAPTER 46

I SAT IN MY CLASSROOM AND I COULD HEAR THE laughter and the voices of the lecturer and of the students as they exchanged ideas and opinions. It sounded as if their voices were coming from behind a wall that separated them from me. The only thing that I could focus my mind on was what happened between Jerry and me. I went over again and again in my mind the brief conversation that we had when Jerry asked me to leave. The last two days had been disastrous for me. The conversation that I had in the morning with Aunt Claire had made it worse. I thought about her reaction when I told her that I was leaving. I thought about the way that she had searched for an explanation for the sudden change of events in our lives. It hurt me that she had taken some responsibility for my leaving.

I also wondered about Jerry. I knew that his world would have to be as fractured and as shaken as mine. There was no way to undo what had happened. The future would be so different for the two of us. It was difficult for me to imagine. They were certain to ask him what had happened. I wondered what Jerry would say that evening to his parents. I had purposely been vague in my explanation to Aunt Claire, so anything that Jerry might say short of the truth, would not contradict what I had said to my aunt. If he were to tell the truth, which they would never get from me, it would have worse repercussions in our family than the Willi affair. That had happened nine years earlier, but it was still fresh in everyone's mind.

After my last class, I dropped my books into my car and I took the train uptown to Memorial Hospital. At about eight o'clock, I called Camille at her house from the hospital. Camille would be the first one that I would have to tell that I was leaving my aunt's apartment, but it had to begin somewhere.

"Hello."

"Hi, Camille, how are you?"

"I'm fine. Where are you?"

"I'm working in the hospital," I said.

"Oh, I was wondering if you were calling from your aunt's house." Camille knew that I hardly ever called from there to avoid tying the phone up and running up the bill.

"No, they asked me to work late tonight so I did."

"When are you going to leave?" she asked. "It's after eight."

"I'll leave in a few minutes." I hesitated a few seconds longer than I should have, wondering how to begin to tell her.

"Nick?" she said, responding to the dead air.

"Yeah, I'm still here."

"What's wrong?"

"Aw, nothing," I said, and then I began. "I had a real big argument with Jerry." I paused again.

"Really? What happened?"

I avoided answering her right away, and I said, "It was bad enough that I'm leaving."

"What?" she asked. "You're leaving? Was it that bad? What was it about?"

I was purposely vague. "You know, Camille, it was about so many things. I just don't want to go through the whole thing again. In the end, it was probably about each of us getting on the other's nerves after more than two and a half years."

I hoped that by keeping it vague, Camille would accept the fact that I really didn't want to go into detail.

"It happens, Camille. You live with a person long enough and it's possible to get on each other's nerves. There are lots of unhappy relationships out there. It's not always easy to live with someone."

"It's so sudden. It's hard to believe. Did your aunt and your uncle get involved too?"

"No, no. They weren't there when it happened. It was just between Jerry and me. We just had too many differences."

"I believe it," Camille said. "I know how close you are, and I never wanted to hurt your feelings, but Nick, he's not always easy to get along with. I've had my differences with him too right from the start, but I would never have thought this."

I knew that was the truth. Camille and Jerry had not gotten along. I tried to overlook the bad feelings between them because of the strong ties that I had with Jerry. I would often ask Camille to overlook some of the slights she felt that she had received from him. Even now, I changed the subject.

"You know, Camille, Pete and I were talking about this very same subject a couple of weeks ago. Pete and his brother had a tense relationship. I told Pete that I sensed the same thing was happening to Jerry and me. We agreed that it was probably because we couldn't get away from one another in that small apartment."

"So your Aunt Claire must know. What did she say?"

"She was heartbroken. She wanted to try to smooth it over and for us to talk over our differences. I told her that it was too late. Both of us need time away from one another after the argument."

"It's still hard to believe. What will you tell your parents?" Camille asked.

"I'll tell them the same thing that I told you."

"Well when are you leaving and where will you go?"

"Friday will be my last day in the apartment," I lied. "After that, I'll call Pete and I'll ask him if I can use his room for a while." I surprised myself with that statement because I really had no such plan. I hadn't thought of it but in trying to find a satisfactory answer for Camille, it had popped into my head. It even sounded plausible.

"Pete's room?" she asked. "Will you feel comfortable there? Do you know his family that well?"

"I know them pretty well, but I won't have to live with them. Their apartment has a different set up. Pete enters his room from an outside hallway. You go up the stairs to a main hallway, and each room has its own outside door that opens up into the main foyer. Pete was able to access his room without going through the rest of the house. You can come and go as you please without anyone knowing whether you are there or not." The more I spoke about it, the better an option it appeared to be.

"Do you think Pete will agree to let you use his room?" Camille asked.

"I don't know, but I'll ask him," and at that moment, it was the only thing that I could think of.

"Meanwhile, you'll have to go back to your aunt's apartment tonight. That's gonna be uncomfortable, isn't it?"

"I can put up with it for three more days," I said.

"Do you want to stay here with us for three days until you speak with Pete?"

"No, no thanks, it'll be alright."

"I feel so bad," Camille said. "It's bad enough that you

have to call Pete, but it's worse that you have to go back to your aunt's house after all that happened."

"Well, don't feel bad. It'll work out. Look, I've got to go now, but I'll call you tomorrow."

"Okay, but let me know what's happening, and don't wait too long before you call Pete. Three days will go by quickly."

"I'll be in touch. Camille?"

"Yes?"

"Love you."

"Me too," and she hung up.

I took the train downtown, and I moved my car. I found a spot in Greenwich Village where parking was allowed all day on Thursdays, and it was a reasonable walking distance to the school. I turned the motor off and I sat behind the wheel. This would be it for a while. I thought about crawling into the back seat for the night and wrapping myself up in my jacket, but on second thought, I decided against it. I was afraid that a cop walking his beat would see me there and not knowing whether I were dead or alive, he would start tapping on the window. Once he saw that I was alive, he would probably explain to me why I wasn't allowed to establish permanent residency in the back seat of my car and make me move. It just seemed like less trouble to remain behind the wheel. If a cop did happen by, it would be easier for him to believe that I had pulled over because I was falling asleep at the wheel. He would buy my story that I didn't want to have an accident. I leaned my head against the window and began to doze off, hoping that what Camille had said was true. "Three days go by quickly."

There were no policemen to wake me during the night. I couldn't keep my ears, my nose, and my feet warm no matter what I did. They kept me up a good deal of the time. I had enough at about six that morning. I grabbed my A.W.O.L.

bag and the books that I would need and I decided to walk over to the Loeb Student Center. I couldn't shower there but I could use the bathroom. I changed my socks and my underwear in one of the stalls. Best of all was that I could warm up and have a cup of coffee and a muffin before my nine o'clock class.

After the second night, and after the same routine as the night before, a sense of urgency took over. It was Friday morning and I had a late class from four to six. I was due to work at the hospital and it was also pay day. I couldn't put it off any longer. I would have to swallow my pride and go to Pete with my hat in my hand and risk rejection. I had to ask Pete if I could use his room until June, and I had to do it now.

To this day, I am uncomfortable about asking people for favors, even people with whom I have close relationships. I am much more comfortable helping friends and relatives. Lending a hand to friends when I can is something that I enjoy doing.

I thought of the old cliché, "A friend in need is a friend indeed," but sometimes a friend in need is a pain in the neck. That might be the case with me asking Pete for the use of his room. Perhaps this went beyond asking for a favor and bordered on being an imposition. The longer I thought about asking Pete for the use of his room in his parents' house, the more harebrained and presumptuous the whole idea appeared. I had sort of stumbled on the idea. It was the only one that I could come up with. I knew that over consideration often led to inaction, so without giving it any further thought, I dialed Pete's number.

"Hello."

"Hi, Pete, it's Nicky."

"Hi, Nick. What's up?"

"Aw, Pete, I have a problem."

"What's going on?"

I sighed into the phone, searching for the right words. "Do you remember when we had that conversation in the hamburger joint about me wearing out the welcome mat in Jerry's house?"

"Yeah, I remember. Oh no," he had guessed at what I was going to say. "What happened? Don't tell me."

"Yeah, well, you were right. It happened." I paused. "We had a big blowout a couple of nights ago. The welcome mat isn't there anymore. I can't stay there anymore."

"Geez, I'm sorry to hear that, Nick, but from what you told me, I'm not surprised. You must've seen it coming. Did Jerry ask you to leave?"

"No. It was a mutual agreement, and yeah, I did see it coming. I just didn't think it would come so quickly." I paused expecting Pete to ask me what had caused the argument. I hoped that he would accept the explanation that I had given to Camille, but he didn't ask for any details. It was apparently enough for him that we had a major argument after a period of tension.

"How about Aunt Claire, did she want you out too?"

"No. This is killing her. She wanted to try to smooth it over, but that's not happening."

"So now what are you gonna do? Are you leaving? Silly question. You said that you were."

"Yeah, I am, Pete, and that's why I'm calling you." How to do this, I thought? "Pete, I will understand perfectly well if you're unable to do what I am about to ask you. If you want to think about it awhile before giving me an answer, I'll understand."

"What is it?"

"Pete, do you think that I could use your room in your parents' house until June?"

"Sure. Of course." There was absolutely no hesitation on his part, which blew me away. Maybe I hadn't made myself clear.

"Then it's okay for me to use your room?"

"No problem."

I was instantly relieved of all of that anxiety that I had built up over all the hours of the last few days. Pete's response of a few words, which had only taken a few seconds for him to deliver, had changed it all.

"Pete, maybe you should ask your parents if it's alright first. They might not like the idea."

"No, no. I'll tell them, but they won't care. It's no big deal. You know how their apartment is set up. All the rooms empty into the outside hallway. You'll probably never even see my parents unless you want to. They never knew where the hell I was or when I came or went unless I went into their apartment. They'll never even know that you're there."

I was overcome by gratitude. "Pete, I don't know how to thank you. I can tell you that I didn't know what I would have done if you had said that it wasn't possible. I would have understood completely if you had said no."

"Listen, I'm telling you that it's not a problem. In fact, I'm going to my parents' house tonight to pick up a few things, so my room will be empty for you. You can move in whenever you're ready. When do you want to move in?"

"I'd like to be out of my aunt's house by tonight," I said, choosing not to tell him that I had spent the last few nights in my car. "Camille and I are going up to the lake to see my parents and to pick up a few things. Would Sunday be all right?"

"Sure, that's fine. I'll leave the key to the front door and to my room under the mat by the outside front door in case you get home late. That way you won't have to ring the bell, in case my parents are sleeping."

"Pete, you'll never know how much I appreciate this."

"Yeah, right. Just relax. Let me know how things work out. I've gotta go, but I'll talk to you," and he hung up.

Years later, while I was talking with Pete, I brought up the event from that time when he and his parents had welcomed me into their home. If I allowed my mind to take me back to those days, the events were nearly as sharp and as painful as they had been for me when they actually occurred. I felt the need on this particular occasion and in our twilight years, to tell Pete that I hadn't forgotten the generosity that he and his family had shown to me. Yet, as vivid as the memory was to me, it wasn't to Pete. As hard as it was for me to believe it, he didn't remember it. It was only with some retelling on my part that Pete remembered.

"It was something that I will never forget at a time when I didn't know where to go or whom to turn to. And the thing about it, Pete, was how quickly and unquestioning you were when you agreed to do it. I was prepared to understand all the reasons that you might give for not being able to do it. After all, I was your friend, not your parents' friend. It was wonderful."

"Nicky, don't you remember the hospitality that you and your family showed to me. Not just to me, but all of us as we were growing up. We were all so at home and comfortable in your house. How about all the time that we spent at the lake in New Jersey? And later on, your parents were just as cordial to our wives and children. So you remember what I did for you, and I remember how your family treated all of us. Mine was a small payback and that's what we did for each other."

CHAPTER 47

THE KEYS WERE UNDER THE MAT EXACTLY WHERE Pete said that he would leave them. It took a couple of trips to my car to bring all of the things that I had stored in my Volkswagen up to my new quarters. The room had a bed, a chest of drawers, a small closet and a ceiling light. There was a front window that looked over a small overhanging porch roof. Across the street, I could look into Leif Erikson Park, which was a part of Bay Ridge.

My mother had given me a set of sheets and a blanket, but Pete's mother had left a blanket, sheets and a pillow at the foot of the bed. I put my belongings away, and I made up the bed. I walked over to the window and looked into the park. I leaned my legs against the cast iron radiator, which was under the window, and I felt its warmth. It was a far throw from the uncomfortable cold of the three nights last week when I was sitting behind the steering wheel in my Volkswagen.

It was nice not having to share the room with anyone, but there was no bathroom. In order to use the bathroom, I would have to walk through the house, and I wasn't about to do that. The bathroom was located next to Pete's parents' bedroom. I would survive it as I had survived cold days in the field when I had avoided using dugout latrines as long as I was able to. I also had survived without showering or brushing my teeth. The only difference was that in the field everyone around me was as rank as I was. Well, I'd work it out and this was no time to look a gift horse in the mouth, as they say.

I lay in bed thinking about my parents' reaction when I had told them that I had left my aunt's house, and about the argument that Jerry and I had.

"Well, at least you landed on your feet. Pete really came through for you," my father said. "What would you have done if Pete hadn't given you his room? There's no way that you could have driven back and forth from N.Y.U. to the lake every day."

"You know, Dad, I don't think about what I would have done. It didn't happen. I have enough things to pay attention to without dealing with what I would do about bad things that didn't happen."

"You're right about that, Nicky," my mother, ever the fighter, said, "and I'm not bringing up what Jerry did, but only for my sister's sake. I'm also not forgetting about it very soon."

"Mom, Aunt Claire was heartbroken about this. She doesn't need any more grief. When you speak with her, don't make an issue over it. Besides, it was just as much my fault as it was Jerry's fault. At this point, I just want to let it all go and move on. Don't bring it up."

"I won't bring it up," my mother said, "but only out of consideration for Aunt Claire and Uncle Stan, not for Jerry's sake."

I mulled all of the events over in my mind, when I heard tapping at my door. I must have fallen asleep because daylight filled the room. I looked at my wristwatch, it was six o'clock in the morning. The tapping came again.

"Nicky, it's Mrs. Abrami." It was Pete's mother.

I reached for my pants, pulled them on and opened the door.

"Good morning, Mrs. Abrami."

"Good morning. I'm going to my daughter's house to babysit for my granddaughter. I don't know when you have to go to school, but you're welcome to come in and have some breakfast before my daughter picks me up."

"Oh thank you and I appreciate it, but no, Mrs. Abrami. I don't want to be a bother. I have a 9:15 class, and I'll have something to eat when I get to the city." I had made up my mind that I would be so scarce and so unintrusive that Pete's parents would wonder if I were even using the room, but on the first day I had already changed their routine.

"It's only toast and coffee that I made for myself too, and it's on the table. If you don't want it, why don't you at least use the bathroom?" She looked at me. "It's okay."

I knew Pete's parents over the years, but I had always considered them old school. I had never felt as relaxed with them in the same way that all of my friends had been at ease and casual with my parents. Pete's father was a very dignified and reserved man. I had never seen him not wearing a shirt, a tie, and a suit. He was a no nonsense guy whose patience Pete had often pushed to the limit. Like me, and for that matter like most of my friends, Pete had made a mess of his high school career, and yet his father allowed me into his home.

I looked into Mrs. Abrami's eyes. She had offered me hospitality and I knew that there was a fine line between being polite and being rude. In my attempt to be polite, I might be misunderstood and mistaken as being rude. It was the Old Italian thing that I understood so well. Be careful not to insult when you were shown generosity. I knew instinctively that this was not the time to refuse her every offer and risk hurting her feelings in my attempt not to intrude in their lives.

"Okay," I said with a smile. "Thanks for letting me have

Pete's room and for being so nice. Just give me a minute and I'll be right there."

She was satisfied. "You don't have to thank me. You're welcome to use the room for as long as you need it. It's just sitting here unused anyway. Just come in whenever you're ready."

When I got to the kitchen, Mrs. Abrami had coffee, toast, and orange juice set for me. As thankful as I was, I knew that I didn't want her to do this for me on a regular basis. She was making it very difficult for me to be a ghost around here, I thought.

"Nicky, I'm usually out of here by seven with my babysitting, and Mr. Abrami is already in his office by then. I don't know your schedule, but I don't expect you to stay in your room, especially if you have late classes. If I'm home and I'm having breakfast and if you feel like it, it's absolutely no problem if you'd like toast and coffee and you'd like to join me. Even if you don't want to eat, you can always use the bathroom. And don't tell me that you don't have to do that," she added.

"Oh, thank you for everything, Mrs. Abrami, for the room and for the breakfast." I knew that it would have to be a real emergency for me to use the bathroom, and to take her up on her breakfast offer, especially since there was a diner on the corner.

CHAPTER 48

MY NEW LIVING ARRANGEMENT WAS FINE. I CAME and went to my little room unnoticed. Occasionally I had breakfast with Pete's mother where we talked about family, and although I appreciated her hospitality, I did my best not to alter the routine of their lives.

It was the very first time that I had lived by myself. Actually, I was only alone briefly at night but it didn't take me very long to feel lonely enough to know that I didn't like living alone. I would often think aloud as if there were someone else in the room who could hear me. I delayed going back to my room by working late at the hospital or by going to Camille's parents' house. I would return to my room only to do school work, take my clothes to the laundromat or to sleep. On the weekends, I went up to my house on the lake and to Camille's parents' bungalow.

Although I hadn't seen Jerry at all since I left the apartment, I called Aunt Claire regularly. Our conversations never touched on my leaving the apartment or about my reasons for my leaving. Instead, we usually spoke about my progress in school, my work in the hospital, or my plans for the future.

"Nicky, can you imagine? In another year, you'll be a teacher. You won't have to work so hard the way that Uncle Stan and your father do. You'll go to work like a gentleman, in a shirt and a tie. Your parents will be so proud. And me too."

"You're right," I said. "I would never have believed this ending for so many reasons. Most of all because of the mess

I had created for myself throughout high school. Remember how discouraged I was all those weeks when I was either not hearing from colleges, or when I did hear it was always a letter of rejection from one college after the other?"

"Oh yes, I do," she said.

"Then, when I was about to give up, I was finally accepted by New York University of all places. Who would have believed it? I still wonder about all of those crazy events, and why things happened the way that they did."

"I can tell you why it happened the way it did. It's because prayers do get answered. Nicky, all you asked for was a second chance, and they gave you a chance," she said.

"I guess so," I said, "but if it hadn't been for the Dean of Admissions that day, and for you, my parents and Jerry refusing to allow me to give up, things would have been a lot different for me."

She didn't pick up on the mention of Jerry's name, and after a pause she said, "How about you and Camille? You've been going together for a couple of years. Next year, when you graduate, you'll be twenty-six. You must be thinking about getting married."

"Aunt Claire, we'll get married, but it won't be before June of 1963. That'll be a year after I graduate. By that time, I'll be working for a year and I'll have some money set aside to pay for a wedding. We'll have to do it ourselves. Both of our parents are not in a position to help us very much."

She had a way of talking to me and drawing things out of me that even my mother was unable to do, and here it came again.

"June of 1963, that's fine. In the meantime, you'll give Camille a ring and you'll get engaged."

"Give her a ring? What ring and with what? Didn't you just hear what I said? How can I afford a ring?"

"Nicky, stop talking silly, you'll get engaged. Of course you'll give her a ring. You'll surprise her. You'll go to Uncle Joe. I'll call him and tell him that you're coming and you'll pay him out."

She was talking to me in her no further discussion mode. It was the same one she had used when she told me that I would be going to college in 1958.

The Uncle Joe who Aunt Claire was referring to, was her older brother who had been a jeweler his whole life. For many years, he had a shop in the Wall Street section of Manhattan. Sometimes when I had a break in classes, I would pass the time in his shop watching him make rings and set diamonds. Occasionally, he would ask me to run an errand for him.

"Nicky," he'd say, "that's a five thousand dollar stone in that envelope. I want you to run it over to this address. If anybody holds you up, just give him the damned thing. Who wants to hear your mother?" He was a big tease, so I never knew if he was serious, but I would try to look inconspicuous while I clutched the stone in my pocket as I walked the crowded streets of Manhattan.

"So I'll call Uncle Joe when I hang up from you," my aunt continued, "and next week you'll go up there and he'll have some rings to show you."

"I don't know. Let me think about it. We'll see," I said.

"What will you see? You'll go. I never heard of such a thing to get married and not have some sort of an engagement ring. Don't worry. Uncle Joe will have something nice for you to see. Make sure you call me so that I can tell you when he'll expect you."

That was it. There was no further discussion. The next week I went up to my Uncle Joe's shop, and I walked out with an engagement ring. Done!

CHAPTER 49

BECAUSE OF MY FINANCIAL SITUATION, CAMILLE never asked for and didn't expect an engagement ring, even though we had spoken about getting married after my graduation. I had purchased a college senior ring, and this time not under false pretenses as when I had purchased my high school senior ring seven years earlier. I had given the college ring to Camille to wear, but the ring was much too large for her finger. I intended to purchase a gold chain so that she could wear the ring around her neck. Given the weight and size of college rings, it would have to be a substantial gold chain, so it would have to wait. Thanks to Uncle Joe, I had purchased a one-karat marquis cut diamond engagement ring for Camille. Now I had to think of a way to surprise her with it.

I knew that Camille kept my senior ring on her dresser in the box that it came in. I sat at the kitchen table in Camille's house, her engagement ring seeming to burn a hole in my pocket. I was so anxious to give it to her and to watch her reaction. I wanted to make her happy.

"Camille, it's silly to keep my senior ring in the box, and I don't know when I'll be able to get a chain for it."

"Do you want to wear it in the meantime?" she asked.

"No, I want you to wear it. Maybe I can put some adhesive tape on the back of the ring and then you'll be able to wear it. It's silly to leave it in the box. Let's try it out."

"I don't want to do that," she said. "Then I'm gonna have that big lump of tape in my hand all day. I'll wait for the chain, but why don't you wear it in the meantime?"

"Well, at least let's try. If it's uncomfortable, we can always take the tape off."

"Okay," she said reluctantly, and she walked into her room to get the ring.

Camille's mother busied herself preparing dinner. "Are you hungry, Nicky?" she asked.

"I'm famished," I said. I took the engagement ring, still in the box, out of my pocket and hid it in my hand.

The aroma of pork chops prepared in the way that only Camille's mother, my future mother-in-law, knew how to cook them, permeated the apartment.

Camille returned to the kitchen with my senior ring in her hand. "Here's your ring," she said, and she handed the ring to me.

"Thank you," I said. "And here's your ring." I held out the newly purchased engagement ring in the jeweler's box.

Camille took the box from me. She smiled at me, thinking that I was playing some sort of a practical joke. She opened the box and looked inside as if she expected something to pop out at her. Instead, she stared at the ring as if there were some mistake. Then she looked at me in disbelief. She took the ring out of the box.

"Oh, oh, Nick, I don't believe it. I never expected this." She continued to look at it. "It's beautiful." Her eyes welled up as she fought back her tears. She was completely taken by surprise. "How did you do it?" She stood in front of me and then with the ring in one hand, she put her other hand on the back of my head and pressed her forehead against mine.

"Do you like it?" I asked.

"Oh, my God, I love it. It's beautiful."

"What is it?" Camille's mother asked.

Without answering, Camille handed the ring in the box to her mother.

"Oh, my God," her mother said. "How beautiful it is. What a surprise." I could see the happiness for her daughter welling up in her mother's eyes as well. I knew that Camille's mother appreciated the ring that I had given to her daughter as much as she would have appreciated it if had been given to her. She handed the box back to Camille.

Camille kept staring at the ring. "Do you like it?" I asked again.

"I love it," Camille said, finally able to collect herself. She took the ring out of the box and turned it back and forth, watching how the prism of light caused the stone to sparkle back the rays of the sunlight reflected in the room.

"Aren't you going to try it on?" I asked.

"Can we afford this?" she asked.

"I bought it from, Uncle Joe. I'll pay him out. Try it on," I said, still wondering how I would do that. Then I lapsed into my I'll worry about it later mode.

Camille hesitated before putting the ring on. "It's yours," I said. I took the ring from her and put the ring on her finger. Camille turned her hand from side to side, as her mother looked over her daughter's shoulder. "I love it. It's beautiful," Camille said. "Look at how it reflects the light. A beautiful rainbow."

"It's a beautiful ring," her mother said.

"And now, the big spender that I am, I have another idea," I said.

Camille walked back to the table, and still staring at her ring, she said, "Another idea. I'll bet that it can't top this one."

"Do you have any money?" I asked Camille. "If you do,

we can go to Lundy's in Sheepshead Bay and have lobster to celebrate."

"Okay big spender," Camille said, "dinner is on me." Then looking toward her mother, she asked, "Do you mind if we go, Mom? You've been preparing supper."

"No, no, you go. I'll put the pork chops in the refrigerator. I want to make a few calls anyway."

Camille smiled at her mom. She knew that the news of our engagement would be the focus of her mom's phone conversations as well as her conversation at work for the next few days. Camille kissed her mother on the cheek. "We'll see you later, Mom," and we headed for the door.

"Have a good time," her mother said, and we left the apartment.

CHAPTER 50

THE MONTHS FLEW BY AND IN MY SENIOR YEAR I left Pete's parents' house and I lived with Camille's parents in what I hoped would soon be the end of my vagabond existence. My future mother-in-law, Agnes, and father-in-law, Joe, were as gracious in their tolerance of me as the Abrami family had been. They made it easy for me to swallow my pride by having to accept the largess of others for my existence. It was a lesson that I have never forgotten. I have attempted to give back what was given to me by never turning my back on family or friends whenever I knew that one of them was in need and I could help.

I was in the final few months of my undergraduate studies at New York University, and I had begun the mandatory student teaching phase. I was assigned to Sands Junior High School, P.S. 265K, in Brooklyn's Bedford Stuyvesant section. The K in the school's designation indicated that the school serviced students with special needs, mostly disciplinary. I knew that my training in Tolstoy, Chaucer, Shakespeare, and other literary geniuses would be of little use to me in my new assignment.

The first indication that I had that this was going to be an adventure far different from what I was learning in my education courses was on the first morning that I reported to 265K. I saw a police officer in the school's main office. My suspicions were aroused because of his relaxed manner and familiarity with the secretaries and staff. He was on a first name basis with all of them and he seemed almost to be a part of the faculty. Why should that be, I wondered?

As I was signing in, the principal's secretary must have seen the expression on my face as I sat watching the interaction between the officer and the staff.

"You're wondering what a police officer is doing in the main office," she said, as she smiled pleasantly.

"Is something going on?" I asked.

"No. It's routine," she said. Kevin reports here every morning. His job is to collect kids for their court appearances and bring them to court. His uniformed presence discourages troublemakers from acting out. We are lucky to have him."

In my twelve years in public schools in Brooklyn, I had never seen or heard of a policeman virtually stationed in the school almost as if he were a faculty member. We did have students who served on the service squad as hall monitors but not real policemen. It was, however, a foreshadowing on things to come. Later on, when I had been teaching for a few years, retired police and fire department members were routinely hired by the district as hall guards. We all accepted them as part of the faculty as Sands Junior High School had accepted Kevin years earlier. None of us thought of it as being unusual as I had done at 265K. It's a sad commentary on the deterioration of discipline in our school system.

I arrived one morning during the first week to see the same policeman ducking to avoid being struck while attempting to break up a fight. One of the kids in the fight was swinging wildly at his antagonist, using an antenna that he had snapped off a parked car as a whip. The principal was doing what he could to separate the two combatants. The policeman was finally able to take the antenna from the boy, who was whipping it back and forth, while pinning the boy's other arm up and behind his back. Then the officer crooked his other arm around the boy's throat, and he and the principal hauled both boys into the building.

I had learned how to be a medic in the army with on-the-job training. Now I realized that none of us had received any training in the education courses offered at N.Y.U. for what I had just witnessed. None of us was prepared to deal with what appeared to be everyday situations such as the encounter that I had just seen at Sands Junior High. It would be on-the-job training for me once again. The major difference in the training in the army was that we were all fit and on top of our game and ready for anything. We were soldiers who respected authority. The faculty at Sands had gone through college, not basic training, and the students were almost unanimous in their disdain for all authority. In that building, many of the students had contempt for their teachers who were symbols of authority, and now I was a teacher and no longer a soldier.

When I worked in the medical group in Germany, I had never seen cases of battle fatigue, since World War II had ended eleven years earlier. While I was at Sands, several teachers exhibited classic signs of battle fatigue as it had been described to me. Many of the teachers were in constant states of depression and were reluctant to return to their classrooms after breaks. Teachers considered themselves or other faculty members successful teachers, even if they hadn't taught a thing, but because they had survived the day without a major incident.

Their goal was to hang on as long as they could until they could transfer to a different school, or until they were able to find a different way to earn a living. All of the faculty members were male. No one on the faculty was much older than their mid-thirties, which meant that on average they were close to me in age. None of them remained at Sands very long.

I was assigned to a cooperating teacher, Keith Johnson, who also was not much older than I was. I sat in the back of his classroom day after day, observing him as he attempted to teach his classes. Keith's method was to allow most of the students to chat by themselves in small groups, while he spoke to four or five students who might have had some interest that day in hearing what he had to say.

Every thirty or forty seconds he would turn away from the group that he was instructing and he would look up and say, "Shhhh," to the small groups scattered around the room. That was an attempt to get them to lower their voices and to hold down their laughter and their conversations so that the few who were actually trying to pay attention to the lesson could hear what he was saying. From my vantage point in the back of the room, I was not able to hear much of the lesson, even though I knew what Keith's plan was for the day.

"Well, Nick, are you ready for your baptism of fire?" my cooperating teacher asked during his free period. "You've seen how adroit I am at handling the inmates. Are you ready to put the techniques that you've garnered by watching me over the past couple of weeks to use, and to launch your professional career?"

We were sitting in the teachers' cafeteria between classes. In the hall outside of the cafeteria, you could hear the usual din that accompanied the changing of classes. It was held down to some degree as student monitors, or trustees, as Keith described them, stood posted fifty feet apart while they held up signs that said, "SILENT PASSING!"

Usually the monitors holding up the silent passing signs were the most incorrigible kids in the building. The principal's theory in giving them that job was that it would make them more responsible if they were rewarded by his trust. The other students might, in fact, pass silently rather than to antagonize the toughest kids in the building.

Keith continued, "Perhaps you'd like to forego what you've picked up from me, and instead use the methods taught to you in your education courses at N.Y.U. You know, you can put into use all of the helpful hints that they have in those educational text books about how to stimulate classroom discussions with insightful questions, thereby whetting your students' curiosity and desire to acquire knowledge. Or how about the chapters that tell you how to reason with out of control students as demonstrated to you by that education professor who last taught third grade in that lily-white Wisconsin suburb thirty years ago. You know the professor that I'm talking about, the one with all the answers." He stirred his coffee. "I had the same professor when I was an undergraduate at Marist. That guy really gets around. I hope that someday I'll run into him again so that I can tell him how indispensible his course was to my teaching career."

"I would, however, like to ask him to add a chapter or two to help teachers deal with childhood pregnancy. You know that's an issue here, Nick."

"That would probably be helpful," I said.

"Hey Nick," Keith said. "You will never find this in an education book either, so let me give you another valuable piece of information. Never ever accept food from kids."

"How do you get food from kids?" I asked.

"Sometimes they bake a cake in home economics and they bring you some. Don't eat it."

"Why not?" I asked.

"Because you don't know what's in it. Play it safe. Pretend that you will take it home for dessert tonight and when you leave the building, chuck it into the dumpster. Play it safe," he repeated.

"Maybe they had good intentions. They are supervised in home economics. It is not as if they baked the cake outside of the building," I said.

"Nick, they don't have to leave the building for you to be the brunt of their jokes. You know Larry Klaskin. He teaches math. He appointed a kid to be his own personal Gunga Din. He would send the kid out to get him a glass of water from the water cooler every day, and the kid did. One day Larry thanked the ladies in the office for allowing the kid to get water from the cooler. It turned out that the ladies never saw the kid come into the office for water. So where was the ice cold water coming from?"

"Oh no," I said. "Don't tell me."

"You guessed it. From the toilet bowl. The little rascals would wait with baited breath watching for Larry to drink it every day."

"Are you kidding?" I asked.

"I am dead serious." He nodded his head. "I hope that even if you haven't picked up any points while observing me that you have learned something useful while at 265K."

I looked at Keith. It was hard not to feel revulsion at his story. "No, no," I said, "I've learned far more than that from watching you these past few weeks. I know now to never accept anything edible but I also learned a lot in the area of crowd control."

"What crowd control?" he asked.

"You know the way that you control the crowd that isn't listening to you by saying, 'Shhhh,' every thirty seconds. That really works. I've never seen that in an education textbook, but I'll use that one."

"Do I really do that? Do I really say that every thirty seconds?"

I grinned back at him without answering.

"Nick, I'm not even aware of it. I've got to get out of here before they hold up a silent passing sign for me, only it will be in memoriam. You know if I just didn't show up here, I don't think that the rest of the zombies on this faculty would even know that I'm gone."

"You're assuming that they're aware that you were ever here in the first place."

"You're right," he said. "Have you ever noticed how half of this faculty walks around in a daze?" I watched him as he shook his head and stared into his coffee. "Do you know who the luckiest guy in this building is, Nick?"

"How many guesses do I get?"

"None, I'll spare you. The luckiest guy in this building is the cop in the main office."

"What makes him so lucky? He's here too."

"Yeah, but at least he's got a gun," he said, smiling and nodding his head slowly up and down. He wouldn't last a week here if they took away his gun and handed him some chalk and an eraser."

We sat quietly for a while. "What would you do if you left teaching?" I asked.

"Oh, I'm already working on it," Keith said. "I have an agent working on it."

"An agent? Are you writing a book?"

"No, it's nothing like that. I'm a singer."

"A singer?"

"Yeah, that's my way out of here. Last summer, my agent got me a job in Las Vegas singing between shows. It was only for two weeks, but I loved it. My stage name is Buddy Ziegfeld. My agent told me to take that name because it's a name people will always remember. You know the Great Ziegfeld, and I'm Buddy Ziegfeld. You can't forget it."

"Yeah, well your agent was right. I'll never forget it. Catchy," I said. "How did your Las Vegas gig go?"

"Not bad, in fact pretty good except that people are eating when you're singing with the house band between shows. They're really not all listening to you, but I think that the ones who listened liked it."

"So you're saying that it was pretty much like what goes on here."

"Are you kidding me? No way. Not even close," he said.

"Well, what I mean is that in some ways it's pretty similar to the situation here in the way that you're describing it."

Keith looked at me. "What the hell are you talking about?"

"Well, it's like with the kids here. Some sit in front of you paying attention, but others are chatting away not listening at all. That's what you said happened in Las Vegas. A few people listened to you but most were eating and socializing." Keith looked at me and nodded his head as he realized the truth of what I was saying.

"You've got to get their attention, Keith. Maybe in between choruses you should say 'Shhh' nice and loud to the ones who aren't listening."

"Okay, wise guy. No free ringside seat for you when I make it big and light up the marquee on the strip. You can sit in the back of the room and critique my performances the same way that you do now."

"It all sounds so familiar," I said.

"Now you know my plan to get out of here, Nick, but we're running out of time. What about you? What do you want to teach to break your novice?"

"I'd like to try some poetry or a short story," I said.

"Are you kidding me?" Keith asked. "First of all, we don't

have a complete set of intact textbooks in the class. Even when we did, the stories and the poems were incomprehensible to these kids, so they took out their frustrations on the books. You'd have to find stories and poems that are suitable and that they might be able to relate to on some level. And then you'd have to run off copies on the ditto machine. By the way, they can't keep the ditto machine operational. The damned thing is exhausted. You're better off throwing stuff up on the blackboard." He thought about it a second. "Even if we did have a complete set of textbooks with a decent selection of poems and stories, I would discourage you from attempting to teach them."

"Why is that?" I asked.

"I want you to understand something, Nick. Please don't think that I was always this way. I came here right out of college, all fresh and raring to go just like you. It took a year or two for me to become so cynical. Here's a bit of advice to keep with you forever, along with the water story. Always consider your audience. With certain audiences, you should never teach anything that you love. They'll destroy it and they'll tear your heart out in the process. Stick with the business letter as a starter. While you put it up on the board, I'll watch your back. They'll find a way to destroy the business letter too, but at least you won't give a shit."

"The business letter?"

"Take my advice."

"Ugh."

I completed my student teaching at Sands Junior High, and after I left, I don't know what became of Keith Johnson. I never heard from him again. I doubt that he ever had a successful singing career because I also had never heard of a singer called Buddy Ziegfeld, and as Keith said, "That's a name that you can't forget." But I learned a valuable lesson from what Keith had said. I realized that the hardest thing for any teacher to do is to find a way to gain the interest of even the most reluctant students. If you can do that, you will always maintain class control.

Successful teachers have their own methods of keeping their students interested, and what works for one, might not work for another. If you can figure out what works for you, you will be mostly successful regardless of the subject that you teach.

I held my student's attention by submerging myself into the characters and into the stories that we read. I became those characters and I tried to relate what we were reading to their own lives. I added humor to warm my students up. I ignored the advice that Keith gave me, and I taught what I loved. I included only what they needed to know about the business letter when it was necessary, and then I moved on to my first love, which was always literature. It was exhausting to do it every day with students who had very little motivation to want to attend an English class, but it worked for me for thirty-five years, and it ended too soon. If I ever accepted food or drink, it was usually with the dumpster in mind. Some things just stay with you.

CHAPTER 51

"HELLO, AUNT CLAIRE?"

"Oh, hello Nicky. How are you? I thought that it might be the doctor."

"The doctor? Is someone sick?"

"Oh, Nicky, we're all so heartbroken."

"What's going on?"

"It's Uncle Stan. He has had a persistent cough and sore throat, but we thought that it was a cold or allergies and that it would soon go away. Well, it didn't and I have been begging him to go to the doctor. You know how he is; he refused to go. Finally, last week he gave in and we went to the doctor. The doctor didn't like what he was seeing, so he ran some tests and we got the results back this morning. They're saying that he has throat cancer."

Uncle Stan had been a heavy smoker all of his adult life, but he was a big burly man and we all thought of him as being indestructible.

"Oh, Aunt Claire, I'm so sorry."

"I know. I know you are, Nicky. Uncle Stan is walking around in a fog. They told him if the cancer is localized, as they believe it is, they'll just remove the cancerous tissue and they're optimistic about a full recovery."

"Well, that sounds hopeful," I said.

"That's what I keep telling Uncle Stan, but they also told him that they're pretty sure that in the process of removing the cancerous tissue, they'll also have to remove his larynx. Then he won't be able to speak again. I'm expecting a call from the doctor's office to tell us when he will be admitted for the surgery."

"They said that he won't be able to speak again?" I asked.

Her response was barely audible, "If they have to remove his larynx, he won't speak again."

"Oh, I'm so sorry, Aunt Claire. This is all so sudden. How is he handling all of this?"

"Oh, I don't know. Not very well. It was all so unexpected. We thought that he had a cold or an allergy. He doesn't talk much. His throat is so sore and his voice is hoarse. He picks up a newspaper and looks at it for a few seconds and then he puts it down. He walks from one room into the other. He'll watch television for a minute or two or he just stares at the wall. I can't imagine what's going on in his head. He said to me that everybody has to die. The thought of the surgery and the whole hospital thing is part of his concern. Then there's the likelihood of his never being able to speak again. He can't imagine a life where all he can do is listen to the conversation of others. Maybe death is preferable. That's what he told me."

"I can only imagine the extent of his depression right now. Maybe when it's over and he feels better, he'll accept it and make the adjustment. I know that's easy for me to say." She didn't respond. "You know Aunt Claire, he can have family, friends, and doctors all around him consoling him at a time like this, but when you get right down to it he'll have to face it alone, even with all of those people around him."

"You're right. There's a lot of misery in front of him. There's nothing that we can do except to do what the doctors tell us to do and be supportive. What else?" she said.

"Have you told anyone else in the family?" I asked.

"No, not yet, but I will when I hear from the doctor's office about when the surgery is scheduled. The surgery will be in St. Vincent's Hospital in the Village."

"That's walking distance from N.Y.U. I'll be there whenever I'm not in class, Aunt Claire."

"I know you will, Nicky. I have to hang up now so that I can hear from the doctor's office."

"Okay, I'll be in touch. And Aunt Claire, I'm so sorry."

"I know, Nicky. Stay in touch."

She hung up. I thought about our conversation. I realized that this was the beginning and that Uncle Stan was the first one in the family to face a major health crisis. Although my aunts and uncles, and my parents as well, could not be considered old, they were approaching the times in their lives when the vigor of youth begins to fade. As it faded, it took with it all of the defenses that youth had once provided. It was the natural order and would happen to us all. It was also exacerbated by the way we used or abused what was only lent to us. Uncle Stan was paying the price now for that abuse and for his heavy smoking.

Two weeks later, I walked into St. Vincent's Hospital. The surgery had been performed on my uncle earlier that day. I made my way to the visitor's desk. As I did, the elevator doors opened and Jerry walked out. I hadn't seen Jerry since I left the apartment the previous spring, but we spotted one another immediately. Jerry walked toward me and I thought that I discerned a self-conscious expression on his face. Before he could say anything, I asked, "How's your father?"

"Well, he's still in recovery, but Dr. Connelly said that he's sure that they got all of the malignancy out. They did have to remove his larynx."

"So does that mean that he won't be able to speak again?" I asked.

"His natural voice is gone, but there is a mechanical

device that he can learn to use to simulate speech. You speak through a kind of machine. It doesn't sound natural and it will take a little time for him to get used to it, and for us too," he added. "Another option is that there is a way of speaking by using your breath to form words. All of that is down the road. The most important thing right now is for him to recover. When he does, he'll have to decide which system he wants so use."

"Where is Aunt Claire?" I asked.

"My mother is up there now waiting to see when they'll put him in a room. I was just going to get her something to eat."

"Do you mind if I go along with you?" I asked. "I know a nice little deli not far from here."

"No, come on. Let's go."

We walked out of the hospital toward the deli. For the moment, the ice had been broken between Jerry and me. It had taken a crisis for it to happen. In my naiveté, I thought that this sad reunion might be a start to make things better for both of us. I had a deep desire to have things as they were when we were like brothers. I thought that we could allow time to heal the recent miserable events that had occurred between us. I wanted to put those events out of our minds. I hoped that we could forget about them as if they had never happened. That would work for me.

I would soon discover that it would never work for Jerry. It wasn't as simple for him. Even with the tragic event of his father's health, Jerry was unwavering. Similar heartbreaking events that were to occur in the future would have no effect on him either. Jerry could never look beyond what had happened that night in his parents' apartment.

CHAPTER 52

CAMILLE CONTINUED TO LOVE HER RING AND TO wear it proudly. I was so happy that I had not allowed money concerns to prevent me from buying it. If I had, it would have been an empty spot in our lives. You can't go back in time to make up for what you should have done earlier. Even if I had given Camille a ring twenty years later when she was in her forties, it would not have been the same.

Everything was in place I thought for a June 1963 wedding. Men usually think practically and unemotionally about such things as weddings. We just expect that it will happen someday and we just want to get it done. It's not something that we think of or plan about all of our lives in the same way that women and young girls do. Young girls play bride. Young boys never play groom. Instead, girls think of weddings, especially their own weddings, emotionally and in a fairy tale way. I was soon to learn that emotions trump practicality.

It was my final spring before graduation. We were in Camille's parents' apartment and I was reveling in the fact that I was almost finished. I had prevailed. College graduation was a few short weeks away.

"Nick, if we're going to get married next June, we should be looking around for a wedding hall right now," Camille said.

She caught me by surprise. "Why should we look for a

hall right now?" I said. "June 1963 is more than a year away. This is only April 1962. We have plenty of time."

"No, we don't. Weddings are booked a year or more in advance. If you wait too long, you might not be able to get the hall that you want. You'll get the dates that are left and that no one else wants."

"There are catering halls all over the place. We'll find a place we like with the right date," I said.

"Yes, but do you want any old catering hall?" she asked.

"Well, I guess I don't want any OLD catering hall. We'll find one that's not so old."

Camille persisted. "Well, why don't we just look around at different places? Come on. We have nothing to do and that might be fun."

"Oh yeah, fun," I said. "The people who run those places don't just want to have fun showing you around. They want to book you. They want you to sign on the dotted line. June 1963 is fourteen months away. Let's start looking in December." I looked at Camille's expression of disappointment. She really never asked for anything, and her disappointed expression was painful to me. I tried again. Here came the practicality.

"Camille, look. I'll graduate in a couple of months. In September, I'll have a real full-time job. Then, the two of us will be able to save some money from September until June. That's almost a whole year. Then, we'll have money for a wedding and for a honeymoon."

I looked at her. She didn't say anything but she had the same expression of disappointment on her face. I had discovered early on that Camille was one of the most logical and reasonable people that I had ever known, but this was not an ordinary situation. All of the logic that I thought that I had just laid out had not impressed her or convinced her in the slightest. She looked at me and forced a smile.

"No?" I asked.

"No, that's fine. I only wanted to look," she said.

She was killing me. I nodded my head, took a deep breath and said, "Okay. Let's go look. It'll be fun." I only wanted to make her happy.

She jumped to her feet and came over to me. "Oh, Nicky." She called me Nicky in rare moments so I knew that she was happy.

"My father has a friend who used to have a grocery store and a butcher shop in the neighborhood. His name is John. He and some of his partners just built a catering hall in Ridgewood. I haven't seen it but I heard that it's beautiful. It's about ten minutes from here. It's called the Ridgewood Gardens. Can we go to see it?"

"Aha," I said. So John went from a grocery/butcher shop in Williamsburg to the Ridgewood Gardens Catering Hall in Ridgewood. How did that happen?"

Camille shrugged and didn't answer. Her father, Joe, was watching television in the next room. He must have heard our conversation. He called out, "Don't ask questions." I didn't.

"Only in America can people achieve such success so quickly," I said. Camille ignored the both of us. She couldn't contain her excitement.

"Can we go?"

"Okay, let's go," I said.

"Is it okay if we take my parents? They'd love to see John's place."

"Sure. Let's go."

We arrived at the Ridgewood Gardens Catering Hall, and my future father-in-law, Joe, and the owner, John, greeted each other like old friends. John brought us drinks and began to show us around his new establishment. I must admit that the place was very impressive. After speaking with John for a while, I had a pretty good suspicion about how he was able to parlay the small grocery/butcher shop in the neighborhood, into such an upscale catering hall. I took my father-in-law aside and asked him again if he knew how John had achieved this amount of success in such a brief period of time. He looked to his left and to his right and then he looked up at the ceiling before he looked at me. From behind his hand, he said once again, "Don't ask any questions," which answered most of my questions.

The concrete still smelled fresh and I wondered if John had used any of his catering competitors to reinforce it. The more John showed us about his new establishment, the more Camille and her mother loved the place. I was somewhat disappointed that they were so pleased. That could mean that we might not have continued having fun looking at other places. I was looking forward to that.

Next, John produced a typical Ridgewood Gardens menu. He broke down how much it would cost us per person minus, of course, how much John would take off for old friends for a catered affair. I had been thinking about the traditional weddings of my youth, which we affectionately had called "football weddings". There were pitchers of beer and pyramids of sandwiches. People would search the piles for a sandwich that they preferred, and they would sit wherever they chose to sit. I was glad that I didn't have the chance to ask because before I could suggest a football wedding, John dismissed the idea as gauche. Football weddings were a thing of the past.

Who was I to argue with John? "You're right," I said, "so old fashioned."

"Yeah, now we have catered affairs and the way we do it at the Ridgewood Gardens is special," John said.

Camille was beaming because she would be the first in her family to have a catered wedding. We were trendsetters.

"Joe, Agnes, I am going to make sure that this is a special wedding," John said to my future mother-in-law and father-in-law. "If you really want to make an impression," John said, "you're gonna want to have a wedding that people will remember fifty years from now, if God spares." He made the sign of the cross over his chest. "You should think about a cocktail hour the way we do it here at the Ridgewood Gardens. We'll have ice carvings and champagne fountains. We'll have carving stations with ham, turkey, and roast beef, and we'll have various types of food like Italian and Chinese. We can do whatever you want. You select the offerings. You know, the works. Most of your guests will have never seen anything like it before. I'll work with you."

"Well, I appreciate it, but I...," before I could finish Camille's father said, "Oh, I would love that cocktail hour. What a great idea. Wait till my family and friends see that."

"That's not a problem," John said. "We'll do it. We have a house band that every bride loves. Not only do they play the best and latest music, but they go to the guest tables and play requests. They entertain your guests individually. They're special."

I had never seen Camille's mother, Agnes, so happy and animated at John's description of the band.

"Oh, I can't wait to hear them and to see the expressions on everyone's faces. I can't wait," she said.

I wanted to call a timeout to perhaps discuss this whole thing, but I must admit that even I was getting caught up in the rapture of the moment. John brought me back to my senses.

"This will truly be an affair to remember," John said.

I had seen the movie *An Affair to Remember* while I was in Germany. It had only cost me twenty-five cents to get into the movie theater on the post at that time. Now, five years later, this was a new "affair to remember," but not starring Cary Grant and Deborah Kerr. It was starring Nick and Camille. The best part was that it would only cost me two thousand dollars but only if we booked it today for December 1962, and only as a favor for Camille's dad. Ordinarily it would cost twice that amount in peak season, John told us, but December was the catering off-season. I did some quick mental calculations. Let's see. The average starting salary for a teacher in 1962 was between four and five thousand dollars a year. The wedding would cost two thousand dollars. Yeah, I can do that.

I was anxious to sign on the dotted line for our December 1962 wedding. Waiting for June 1963 would only have increased the cost of the wedding. I had just saved two thousand dollars, and I didn't want to allow this opportunity to save money to escape. Before John could make any more suggestions about how to further knock the socks off our wedding guests, I abandoned all of my former reluctance and I rushed to sign the contract. Then we hugged and shook hands all around, said goodbye to John, and we all got into my Volkswagen.

There was happy banter as I drove home. I thought to myself, let's see, two thousand dollars for the wedding, and I'm still gonna have to pay for the engagement ring. Next, I am going to have to buy a wedding band worthy of the engagement ring, and I'm hoping to find a job that pays me at least five thousand dollars a year. What was there for me to worry about? No big deal.

Not thinking about situations that seemed to be beyond my control had been a strategy that I had employed all through my life. It had always worked out in the past. Instead of worrying about it, I decided to join in the merriment by singing a song that had just popped into my head.

With a little luck, the band that I just hired might be familiar with the tune and I might be able to sing it for my guests at the wedding.

"Hey guys," I said, "listen up. I just composed a song in my head. Quiet down a minute and I'll sing it to you." They all turned to look at me. "Are you ready? You sing this song to the tune of Frank Sinatra's, *Pocket Full of Miracles*. Here goes," and I began to sing,

"Camille wants the wedding catered,
Dad wants the cocktail hour,
Mom wants the band to play,
And Nick just saw two thousand dollars fly away!"

Camille looked at me and shook her head. "You do know that you're nuts, don't you?" she said.

I crossed my eyes and twirled my finger around my ear doing my best impression of Daffy Duck until we all were laughing.

CHAPTER 53

I SAT BATHED IN THE HOT JUNE SUN SURROUNDED BY a sea of strangers in New York University's uptown campus. There were hundreds of graduates in their caps and gowns, grateful for the shade provided for us by the mortarboards that we wore on our heads. In some ways, the scene was reminiscent of my high school graduation on that June day eight years earlier, only this time it was not a charade. I was not a self-conscious imposter, out of place among my peers. I had done everything that I could think of to avoid being at my high school graduation, even though in the end all my schemes were foiled and I was made to be there. This time I had earned it. Nothing could keep me away. I actually belonged there with the others. I was a graduate, and I was fulfilled and content that I had made it. Unlike my high school graduation, now I was an equal among equals.

It was true that I had not done it alone. If not for the help and encouragement of so many others, I would never have been where I was at that moment. Now what I had accomplished was largely for my own benefit, and for the benefits that my family would reap, if I were to eventually have a family. I had also done it to a large degree for my parents as well. I realized how proud they were. I heard in my mind the often repeated words of my father, "Don't work the way that I've had to work my whole life. Do it for yourself. Do it for me." This was an honor that they had never experienced before. It was real this time. For once in my life, I knew that I hadn't disappointed them. They had never expressed any disappointment in me although there were so many times that they had reason to do so.

Even though I understood the importance of the moment, it wasn't until many years later, when I had children of my own that I fully comprehended that nothing that I had ever accomplished had ever given me as much satisfaction as the accomplishments of my children. It was probably that feeling that my parents were experiencing that day. You needed to be a parent yourself to truly understand it. I could not have given my parents a greater gift. They were communicating the joy and the pride that they felt at that moment by their expressions as well as their words. They were out there with Camille somewhere, sitting in the bleachers with the proud families of other graduates. Later on, I would locate them with some difficulty on this unfamiliar campus with its maze of people.

In the midst of all of the humanity around me, I searched for the faces of particular people, not people in the seats on all sides of me, but the faces of the people in my mind. I wanted to shout in the most primitive way to people who were out of my life and about whose whereabouts I no longer knew. Nevertheless, those people were there with me. They had changed my life's direction. I wished that they knew that I had heard them and that now they were with me. I thought of people like Mrs. Travis, my guidance counselor at New Utrecht High School. She had been right in telling me that I was squandering my life and whatever ability it was that she had seen in me. I did it, Mrs. Travis. I wish you knew.

I thought of Sergeant Russo, who had to virtually order me into that D.C.3 at Fort Drum to graduate with my high school class. He knew how important that day was and that my parents were waiting to see me graduate.

I thought of my two roommates in Panzer Kaserne in Germany, and my good fortune that our paths had crossed. By some miracle, I had been placed in the same room with them. There was Rich Avery, who thought that he was wasting his time and accomplishing nothing while admonishing me for my lack of ambition. Not true, Rich. Your time was not wasted. You touched my life. Bob Duncan, as well, who along with Rich through their long nightly discussions, educated me and stoked my curiosity in a way that no other teachers ever had before. How fortunate was it that a man like Dean Harris was interviewing that day. He risked taking a chance on me by accepting an ill-prepared candidate for admission to New York University. That he did so was and still is a mystery to me. Perhaps Saint Jude really did have an influence at a time when he was my last hope. There were others, and chief among them were Jerry, Aunt Claire, and my parents. Hey, guys and ghosts, look where I am!

My mind went back to 1953 in Camp Smith and my futile pursuit of the fictitious Cannon Report. The futility of that chase seemed to define my life at that point. It was an aimless pursuit with a ridiculous payoff that would have satisfied me and changed things for one weekend for me. And now, nine years later, I would only be satisfied with a degree from New York University, which would change my life and all of my weekends to come.

My thoughts were of all of the lunacy and experiences that I had packed into a nine-year period of time and of all of the people who had been players in those experiences. I hesitated to even think about how different things would have been for me if my life and theirs had never intertwined. They had interest enough to take time from their own lives to encourage me and even to scold me, if only not to allow the spark of hope to go out in me. Some had looked at me with despair, some with frustration, but I found in all of them honesty and encouragement. I needed every one of them in order to get to where I was at that moment. It all ran through my mind as I sat there in the sun. I didn't omit any of my memories. I was a happy and contented man waiting for the guest speakers to finally finish their speeches, so that I could take my "pocket full of miracles", look for Camille and my parents and start my new life.

THERE'S MORE!